MW00643383

CLASSIC MONSTERS
UNLEASHED

EDITED BY

JAMES AQUILONE

CLASSIC MONSTERS UNLEASHED

Editor: James Aquilone
Cover Illustration: Colton Worley
Cover Design and Interior Layout: STK·Kreations
Interior Illustrations: Colton Worley, Mister Sam Shearon, Jeremiah Lambert, Zac Atkinson

Trade hardcover ISBN: 978-1-64548-122-5
Trade paperback ISBN: 978-1-64548-121-8

Worldwide Rights
1st Edition

Published by Black Spot Books
www.ClassicMonstersUnleashed.com

DEADICATION

To those who created our gods and monsters,

Mary Wollstonecraft Shelley, Bram Stoker, Robert Louis Stevenson,
H.G. Wells, Edgar Allan Poe, Gaston Leroux, Oscar Wilde, Curt Siodmak,
Bela Lugosi, Boris Karloff, Elsa Lanchester, Lon Chaney Sr.,
Lon Chaney Jr., Claude Rains, Ricou Browning, Peter Lorre,
Charles Laughton, Christopher Lee, Basil Rathbone, Peter Cushing,
Vincent Price, Margaret Hamilton, Glenn Strange, John Carradine,
Colin Clive, Dwight Frye, Maria Ouspenskaya, James Whale,
Tod Browning…

Lindy Ryan

KELSEA Yu Linda D. Addison Lucy-S

Rena Mason Ramsey

Mercedes M. Yardley

JG. Faherty

Owl Goingback

Tim Waggoner

Dacre C Stoker

James Aquilone

"WELCOME TO MY HOUSE. COME FREELY. GO SAFELY;
AND LEAVE SOMETHING OF THE HAPPINESS YOU BRING."

–BRAM STOKER
Dracula

"IT IS TRUE, WE SHALL BE MONSTERS, CUT OFF FROM
ALL THE WORLD; BUT ON THAT ACCOUNT WE SHALL BE
MORE ATTACHED TO ONE ANOTHER."

–MARY SHELLEY
Frankenstein

"I AM NOT REALLY WICKED. LOVE ME AND
YOU SHALL SEE!"

–GASTON LEROUX
The Phantom of the Opera

"ALONE—IT IS WONDERFUL HOW LITTLE A MAN
CAN DO ALONE! TO ROB A LITTLE, TO HURT A
LITTLE, AND THERE IS THE END."

–H. G. WELLS
The Invisible Man

"I WANT TO BE A VAMPIRE. THEY'RE THE
COOLEST MONSTERS."

–GERARD WAY

"YOU MUST SUFFER ME TO GO MY OWN DARK WAY."

–ROBERT LOUIS STEVENSON

The Strange Case of Dr. Jekyll and Mr. Hyde

"LISTEN TO THEM—THE CHILDREN OF THE NIGHT.
WHAT MUSIC THEY MAKE!"

–BRAM STOKER

Dracula

"BEWARE; FOR I AM FEARLESS, AND THEREFORE POWERFUL."

–MARY SHELLEY

Frankenstein

"MONSTERS ARE THE PATRON SAINTS OF IMPERFECTION."

–GUILLERMO DEL TORO

CONTENTS

PREFACE
James Aquilone..*xiii*

INTRO
Kim Newman ....*xv*

INFERNO
Alessandro Manzetti *1*

HÖLLENLEGION
Jonathan Maberry.. *3*

THEY CALL ME MOTHER
Geneve Flynn... 23

OLD MONSTERS NEVER DIE
Tim Waggoner 43

SHE-CREATURE FROM THE GOLDEN COVE
John Palisano 57

DREAMS
F. Paul Wilson... 75

BLOOD HUNT
Owl Goingback 89

MUMMY CALLS
Simon Bestwick 107

THE VISCOUNT AND THE PHANTOM
Lucy A. Snyder 117

MODERN MONSTERS
Monique Snyman.. 135

BEAUTIFUL MONSTERS
JG Faherty 153

THE NIGHTBIRD
Michael Knost 171

GIVE ME YOUR HAND
David Surface 189

A TALE OF WICKEDNESS
Kelsea Yu.. 197

SOMETHING BORROWED
Lindy Ryan 205

MOONLIGHT SERENADE
Gaby Triana 211

DEAD LIONS
Richard Christian Matheson 227

MAI DOON IZAHN
Gary A. Braunbeck 233

HACKING THE HORSEMAN'S CODE
Lisa Morton 251

THE INVISIBLE MAN: THE FIRE THIS TIME
Maurice Broaddus 271

DIMINISHED SEVENTH
Sean Eads & Joshua Viola 283

YOU CAN HAVE THE GROUND, MY LOVE
Carlie St. George 297

THE PICTURE OF DORIANA GRAY
Mercedes M. Yardley 305

MAKE THE BLOOD GO WHERE IT WANTS
Alessandro Manzetti 317

DA NOISE, DA FUNK, DA BLOB
Linda D. Addison 325

RAPT
Rena Mason 333

"CAN" DOESN'T MEAN "SHOULD"
Seanan McGuire 353

ENTER, THE DRAGON
Leverett Butts & Dacre Stoker 359

SOMEONE TO BLAME
Ramsey Campbell 387

GOD OF THE RAZOR
Joe R. Lansdale 399

PREFACE

SET OUT TO create a monster book and I ended up creating (with the help of a small village) a *monster of a book*.

An anthology editor has much in common with a mad scientist. You get a crazy idea (what if I put together a collection of new stories featuring famous monsters, written by the best horror writers in the business?). You plot and plan and obsess alone in your lair (Staten Island basement). You plunder a graveyard (enlist said horror writers)…assemble the varied parts (stories, poems, and art from dozens of creators)… throw it on the slab (launch it on Kickstarter)…wait for lightning to strike (or nearly 1,000 backers, who came together to make *Classic Monsters Unleashed* the most successful prose horror anthology in Kickstarter history)…and—much to your shock and horror—your creation rises from the table and breaks free from the castle (gets published) to wreak havoc on the world (or bestseller list?).

You, dear reader, hold that monster in your hands. Our creation—assembled from 29 stories, one poem, 14 interior illustrations, the editors' and publishers' blood, sweat, and tears.

Inside these pages, you'll find stories that

reanimate, reimagine, subvert, and pay homage to your favorite monsters...Dracula, Frankenstein's Monster, The Bride of Frankenstein, The Phantom of the Opera, The Headless Horseman, etc....as well as eerie and creepy illustrations sure to send a chill down their spine.

Unlike Victor Frankenstein, I love my creation. And I hope you love our monster of a book, too. If you don't—well, you've seen the movies. It wouldn't end well for either of us. You end up with a broken neck at the bottom of a ravine. I run off in a ball of flames. And no one wants that. Now, turn off the lights, sit down, and—

Welcome to a new world of classic monsters...

James Aquilone
Staten Island, New York
October 1, 2021

INTRODUCTION

"**W**E HAD *FACES* then," says silent movie star Norma Desmond (Gloria Swanson) in Billy Wilder's *Sunset Boulevard* (1950), striking a note of menacing nostalgia as she gestures like Bela Lugosi. More than once, Norma is called a monster or gargoyle or living dead woman—though she's also a *femme fatale*, a diva, a tragic figure, and a transcendent cinematic presence. Like all great monsters.

One critic* has pointed out that *Sunset Boulevard* is almost a remake of *Dracula's Daughter* (1935), down to the casting of a bogeyman actor who's also a director as the female monster's devoted minion (Erich von Stroheim replacing Irving Pichel). Another critic# wrote a book called *Hollywood, the Haunted House* (1969), suggesting that the whole history of American movies is a gothic tale—albeit a California gothic, in the style of the old Bates House up on the hill above the sleekly anonymous motel where the horror happens.

Norma could equally have declared, "We had *monsters* then."

We know exactly who has earned their spots in that pantheon, their niches in that haunted soundstage (essentially, Universal Pictures' *Phantom of the Opera* set from 1926), their recurring spots on the cover of *Famous Monsters of Filmland*, their plastic incarnations as Aurora glow-in-the-dark hobby kits ("frightening lightning strikes!")…

Let us name the dark saints…

Dracula. Count Dracula. Count deVille. Count Alucard. Baron Latos. Dr. Lejos.

Frankenstein. No, the Frankenstein *Monster*. The Monster. Flattop. Mr. Boots. Herman Munster.

The Mummy. Imhotep. Ardeth Bey. Kharis. Klaris.

The Invisible Man. Griffin. Jack Griffin. Geoffrey Radcliffe. Frank Griffin. Robert Griffin. Adrian Griffin.

The Wolf Man. Lawrence Talbot. Larry.

Dr. Jekyll. Mr. Hyde.

The Phantom of the Opera. Erik.

The Hunchback of Notre Dame. Quasimodo.

King Kong. Kong. The Eighth Wonder of the World.

There are a cluster of others—one-shots, has-beens, pretenders, hangers-on, happy-to-be-invited, welcome guests whenever the top-line monster stars are sulking or temporarily dead. Hunchbacked or otherwise undersized, deformed and depraved assistants who might be called Fritz, Ygor, or Igor. The *Bride of Frankenstein*, a screen immortal on under five minutes of screen time. Paula Dupree, the Ape Woman. Irena Dubrovna, the Cat Person. Dorian Gray. M and the Lodger. The WereWolf and the She-Wolf of London. Dr X. The mystery man of the Wax Museum. The Creeper and the Spider Woman. The Mad Doctor of Market Street and the Mad Ghoul. Assorted zombies, some white. The Beast With Five Fingers and the Hands of Orlac. Count Zaroff and Dr. Fu Manchu. Dr. Orloff and Dr. Moreau. Tod Browning's *Freaks*. Karloff and Lugosi, teamed in *The Black Cat* and *The Raven*—their screen personae eclipsing mere character names, like Britain's Tod Slaughter, who was the same dastard whether he was

Sweeney Todd, Squire Corder, the Hooded Terror or Spring-Heel'd Jack. The Cat, the Bat, the Gorilla, the Vampire Bat, the Devil Bat, and *Sh! The Octopus*. Latecomers, the Creature From the Black Lagoon and—from across the Pacific—Godzilla.

A few outliers—mostly played by Lon Chaney, but don't ignore the silent fiends of Germany, Nosferatu, and Caligari and Mabuse and the Golem—stalked in the 1920s…when hands clutched and panels slid soundlessly open, but the true era of Classic Monsters began with *Dracula* in 1931, when monsters could talk, doors creak, winds rustle, and the children of the night put up a fearful row. When Universal Pictures, who almost had a monopoly, picked up the rights to Bram Stoker's novel and (crucially) two different hit stage adaptations, they hoped to lure Lon Chaney—a fright-fanged fake vampire in *London After Midnight* (1927)—back to their soundstage. But Chaney died and the studio reluctantly cast eager Hungarian Lugosi. On stage *Dracula* was billed as "the vampire play"—though, just a few years earlier, that would have suggested a gold-digging, heartless female lead wrecking men's lives rather than a cloaked count drinking women's blood. When Lugosi was interviewed at the time, he called *Dracula* a "mystery play," suggesting lineage from such Old Dark House efforts as *The Cat and the Canary*—and, later, of course, *The Old Dark House*. No one would have known what a horror film was, much less a monster movie.

A year on, after *Dracula* had been eclipsed by *Frankenstein* and Lugosi was supplanted by Karloff the Uncanny, horror films were all over the place. Every studio had one or two in production. Universal had a whole slate. Eventually, they ran to sequels, team-ups, monster rallies—the template for cinematic shared universes as yet undreamed of. In the future, there would be Abbott and Costello and a falling from favor—with the Bomb and the Reds and after the Nazis, were these monsters really *scary* anymore? Aliens, mutants, and big bugs and dinosaurs rampaged instead. Pods and blobs and experiments gone wrong. Then, in England, Hammer Films took another look and discovered that, yes, the Famous Monsters Pack could still be scary...and, on the whole, sexier, too. In color. With Peter Cushing and Christopher Lee and, in America, Vincent Price. Monsters were back back back and even *The Munsters* couldn't stop them.

Most of the key monsters came from 19th and early 20th century literature—though the German E.T.A. Hoffman, the American Edgar Allan Poe and the French Gaston Leroux made major contributions. Between *Frankenstein* (1818) and *The Lost World* (1912), we met a host of monsters—all of whom remain active presences in pop culture. Mary Shelley, J. Sheridan LeFanu (whose Carmilla had to bide her time till a loosening of censorship let her onscreen in the 1960s and beyond), Bram Stoker, H.G. Wells, Robert Louis Stevenson, Arthur Conan Doyle, H. Rider Haggard, Oscar Wilde, M.R. James, Henry James ("The Turn of the Screw" had to wait its turn, too), Arthur Machen, and Algernon Blackwood created characters or explored themes that have remained central to horror/monster/weird fiction. A few names were big for a while, but somehow didn't make the transition to the 20th century—where are the films based on Marie Corelli (*The Mighty Atom*), Guy Boothby (*Doctor Nikola*), Richard Marsh (*The Beetle*), or F. Marion Crawford (*The Witch of Prague*)?

The 19th century was, of course, a period of great social, intellectual, scientific, and political change...and just a curtain-warmer for what came next. Goya said that the sleep of reason produces monsters, but actually it was the age of reason that birthed the most lasting, versatile specimens of the form. The great monsters all sprang from issues we were worried about, which happened to nag at the creative minds who dipped pen into ink and brought them to life. Is *Frankenstein* about bad science or bad parenting—or both, and a lot more besides? Of course. And, in 1931, *Frankenstein* was informed by War and Depression and Freud, too. Mary Godwin (as she then was) wrote about a creature uncontrolled by its creator, loose in the world and wreaking havoc, so she shouldn't have been surprised when the whole thing got away from her. The writers who followed all went through the same thing—as their monsters escaped the page. Each generation finds new meaning—unimaginable to their creators—in Roderick Usher, Dracula, Jekyll and Hyde, or Dorian Gray. Somehow, these monsters have lasted...and will continue to last.

As what follows demonstrates, the story ideas don't dry up. There's always one more tale to tell before the candle goes out.

Even Abbott and Costello couldn't stop the Classic Monsters. The shackles break. The tombstone cracks. The Gods of Egypt or the rays of the moon or a bolt of lightning or a gush of blood on ashes brings back life, of a sort. Always, they'll return. Always, they'll have something to say—or scream, or sign, or shine, or snarl, or roar, or howl.

"I am Dracula, I bid you welcome..."

"In a solitary chamber, or rather cell, at the top of the house, and separated from all the other apartments by a gallery and staircase, I kept my workshop of filthy creation."

"Late one night, I compounded the elements."

"'Death eternal...punishment for anyone who opens this casket. In the name of Ra, the King of the Gods.' Good heavens, what a terrible curse!"

"Even a man who is pure at heart..."

"...for my monster from the slab began to rise, and suddenly, to my surprise...he did the mash...he did the Monster Mash."

"Science fiction—double feature... Doctor X will build a creature..."

"We belong dead."

Kim Newman, 2021

*Danny Peary, *Cult Movies* (1981)
#Paul Mayersberg

INFERNO

ALESSANDRO MANZETTI

THE HORN OF Hell plays, furious
and Francis Macomber is hiding underneath the bed;
A thousand thin devils belched from their black hole
like geysers of madness, screaming cold.
They are souls for monstrous bodies,
they are strings for giant puppets,
they are horror writers with fire tails
woken up from a white nightmare
of happy throats and still-full veins.

The horn of Hell plays, malicious
and Dolores Haze looks back;
Dracula is admiring her white swan neck,
he's hungry, still under the form of a wolf
with his green eyes, green like the lagoon
there, in the belly of the Amazon
homeland of the alien-blooded Gill-Man
who, like Moby Dick,
is not afraid of men and harpoons.

The horn of Hell plays, endless
and Whitechapel answers with its seven bells
alarming cops, pimps, the East End streets
always on parade of life, death, and misery
with their sharp patron, Jack the Ripper
who's cradling a heart just stolen,
the wrong one, the coward one, of Dr. Jekyll,
before putting it in his Frigidaire.

The horn of Hell plays, bleak
and Tom Joad brakes the truck on Route 66.
He feels the monster chasing him, not the toothed Oklahoma,
but the Mummy wrapped in banknotes
which, mouth wide open and with Theban flies in its pharynx,
weeps tears of nitrate and silver
while California-Eldorado is nearby, less than 3,000 years
and a lightning bolt lights up a living brain and a dead one,
there, in Ingolstadt, on the other side of the ocean.

The horn of Hell sounds, mournful
and Claude Monet hurries into his garden at Giverny
to paint flesh lilies for Griffin
the too invisible man, without muscles and lines,
escaped from the English countryside,
haunted by circus hunters
armed with rainbow's bullets and bloodhounds
who have already captured Erik, the trap lord,
during Andrea Chénier at the Opera — *Io son l'oblio.*

HÖLLENLEGION

JONATHAN MABERRY

-1-

"**G**OD IN HEAVEN," said the bearded Englishman, "what have I done?"

The woman, tall, slender as a filleting knife, measured out the thinnest slice of a smile.

"You've done something wonderful, Herr Prendick," she said, her Austrian accent refined and cool. "Quite wonderful."

They sat in the prow of a motor launch—Pendrick huddled into a pea jacket, his unkempt beard and long hair blowing in the sea breeze; she wore a canvas rain slicker and a man's cloth cap set at a rakish angle. They were as unalike as two people could be. Pendrick was in his sixties, and the years had not been kind to him, nor he kind to himself. His face was scarred and pitted with badly healed insect bites. Each of his fingernails was gnawed to the quick, and—despite the required washing aboard the ship—his skin was gray with decades of indifferent hygiene. The woman was in her thirties, lovely, fastidiously clean, and manicured.

"Baronin Hausser," said the officer in charge of the landing party, "there is the dock. Just as he said."

The woman smiled. "Excellent. Let me take a look."

"Please," begged Pendrick, "there's still time to turn around. It isn't too late."

The baroness smiled her icy smile. "Too late for whom, Herr Pendrick? Too late for what?"

Her tone was cutting and invited no reply. A sailor nudged the side of the Englishman's thigh with the barrel of a machine gun. He spoke no word, but his meaning was eloquent. They needed him alive, but there was no requirement that he be whole or healthy. The bruises on Pendrick's face was proof enough of that. Pendrick bowed his head and sobbed quietly.

The officer, Oberleutnant Weber, handed the baroness a pair of binoculars and waited patiently while she adjusted them. Although the woman was not herself an officer in the *Kriegsmarine*, she carried with her both the hereditary power of her family and the personal support of her friend and patron, Heinrich Himmler. That meant officers—even those far superior to an *oberleutnant*—jumped when she spoke. It was Baronin Hausser who was the de facto commander of this expedition.

Baronin Hausser studied the island. It was larger than she thought. They had entered a large bay enclosed by long arms of forested land fringed with dull-gray sand. Within the arms of the bay was a long, curving beach with coconut palms leaning out over the water. A dock with several slips, though no boats. Beyond that were the remnants of buildings the hungry jungle had long since consumed. The rest of the island was built like so many in that part of the South Pacific—humped mountains which were all that remained of some ancient volcano, and an incredibly lush forest rising from the rich ashy soil. Seabirds and jungle parrots flapped through the air, and all manner of animal cries echoed from deep within the dense green trees.

"The island looks quite pristine," observed the baroness. "Did you know that it appears on few maps, and among the sailors in this part of the ocean it is regarded as ill-omened? Since the catastrophe you described in your report, Herr Pendrick, no ship will come within a hundred miles of here. I have heard it called *cursed*."

Pendrick said nothing to that and merely looked at the green hills.

"The dock is useless," said Weber, pointing to a mass of charred timbers sagging into the incoming tide. "We will need to make a beach landing."

"Yes," she agreed.

"Once we have established our presence on the island," said the officer, "then we can erect the shelters and begin offloading the lab equipment. My men can have everything set up before nightfall."

"Excellent," said Hausser as she lowered the glasses. Then she paused and raised them again. "What is that?"

Weber snapped his fingers for a sailor to hand over a second pair of binoculars. He adjusted the focus and trained them on the part of the bay she indicated. Weber grunted.

"It looks like an animal of some kind," he said. "It's big—though I can't quite make it out. Too much sun glare."

"What is it doing there?" asked the baroness.

Weber paused. "It does not appear to be doing much," he said, "except…swimming. See? It's heading around to the far side of the headland. And, it's gone." He lowered the glasses. "Nothing at all to worry about. Some island creature curious about our ship. Or maybe one of Moreau's strange animals."

"No," said Pendrick sharply. "There are none of them left."

Weber glanced at him, then shrugged. "Whatever the case, it thought better of approaching and has buggered off."

Baronin Hausser studied that part of the bay with her glasses for a long moment. Then she lowered the glasses.

"Take us in," she ordered.

As the sailors noisily and efficiently checked their weapons, Pendrick buried his face in his palms.

- 2 -

OBERLEUTNANT WEBER WAS first out of the boat, jumping shin deep in the surf and running up onto the sand with his pistol up and out. Sailors swarmed over the gunnels and pulled the boat onto the beach. Two of the biggest men reached up and—very carefully and respectfully—lifted the baroness out and set her above the waterline.

Pendrick was pushed over the side into waiting hands and dragged through the salty water. His knees buckled and he dropped down.

"What do you see?" asked the baroness.

"Nothing, *verehrte Baronin*," said the officer.

"Come with me," she said, gesturing for Weber alone to follow. They went over to look at the dock, and the *oberleutnant* frowned as he jabbed at the timbers with the tip of his knife. He bent close and sniffed. "That's odd."

"What is?" asked the lady.

"This does not look or smell like something that burned more than forty years ago," he said.

"How long ago did it burn?" she asked so quietly only the officer could hear. "Your best guess."

Weber cut a sidelong look at Pendrick. "Two, three years," he said softly. "You see, *verehrte* Baronin, there's very little plant growth here. The core of the timbers are not even rotted all the way through."

The baroness looked away into the jungle for a moment.

"Let's go see what else there is to see."

They walked up the sand to a gravel path that led from the ruins of the dock through the woods to the cluster of buildings. There were many of them, made from weathered gray stone and wreathed in creeper vines with enormous leaves that glistened with oil.

"Please," begged a thin voice. The baroness glanced over her shoulder and scowled at the Englishman who was still on his hands and knees.

"Pick him up," she ordered, then softened a bit. "There is no need to be unnecessarily rough."

The sailors caught Pendrick under the armpits and hauled him to his feet. They were less rough but far from gentle as they frog-marched him after the lady and the officer. Other sailors spread out, their weapons at the ready as the party headed along the gravel path toward the buildings.

With each step Pendrick mumbled the same word over and over again.

"No, no, no, no, no…"

The path had once been wide enough for wheeled carts—evidenced by an overturned one that lay off to the side—but the jungle had taken it back. Only a narrow path remained.

"A game path," suggested Weber, but his left eyebrow was raised. Hauser said nothing.

The first buildings they passed were merely functional, with various tools rusting on their hooks, sacks of gravel, and other useless things. A few other small outhouses were similarly uninteresting.

Up ahead, largely hidden by palms that had grown wild every-where, was a heavy wooden gate, framed in iron and sturdy, but one of the doors hung drunkenly from a single twisted hinge. The other lay flat on the ground and wild shrubs had long since burst through the rotten wood.

Weber sent three seamen inside and waited until they gave the all-clear. Then the officer escorted the baroness and the prisoner into the compound.

To one side of the gate, hard against the remaining wall, was a large blockhouse. They went inside and saw that it was lined with many shelves but otherwise empty. Nothing of whatever had been stored there remained. The floor was littered with discarded cans and boxes.

The baroness studied Pendrick as he looked around at the empty shelves.

"This is where the food was stored, yes?" she asked.

He nodded weakly.

Hausser bent and picked up a tin can and turned it over in her hands.

"You said there were no people left on the island."

"None alive."

She showed him the can. "Look at this," she said. "These are tool marks. This was opened with a screwdriver or something like it."

Pendrick said nothing.

Hausser looked him in the eyes. "You told us that Dr. Moreau and Dr. Montgomery were dead. That all of the servants were dead. And that the *Tiermenschen* all reverted to…to what they had been."

"Yes," said Pendrick.

"*All* of them?"

His eyes slid away. "Yes. Of course."

"You are telling me the truth, Herr Pendrick…" she said, letting it hang without needing to make it a question. Without needing to speak the threat. Pendrick knew the risks of deception. The beating that left his face and body covered in purple bruises was not the first, nor the worst. It was, however, a reminder. The baroness had a pretty face and a charming smile, and they both knew that it was only as real as the red lipstick she wore on her cold lips.

"I'm telling you the truth," mumbled Pendrick.

"Look at me," she said, and there was steel in her tone. Weber heard it and shifted to stand at Pendrick's shoulder. Not touching, but close enough for the Englishman to hear him breathing slowly in and out through his nose. It was like having a hungry tiger behind him.

The baroness spent a long and silent moment just looking into Pendrick's eyes. "You came back here how many times? Three?"

"Yes."

"With no objection from your friends and family?"

"I…have no family."

"Oh really? Our research indicated you had an older sister, a mother who, though advanced in years, was still alive. And several cousins."

Pendrick winced. "I have been estranged from my family for some time."

"Is that why you went into isolation when you escaped the island the first time?" asked Hausser.

"Yes," said Pendrick quickly.

"I see," said the baroness. "So, no one tried to talk you out of returning here?"

"No one."

"And you searched the entire island?"

"Y-yes…"

"Finding nothing? Not one trace of the creatures Moreau created?"

Pendrick swallowed. Sweat ran down the sides of his face. "No. Nothing."

"Isn't that unusual? From your original account it was clear there were many of these animal men."

"They…reverted."

"Ah, yes," said Baronin Hausser. "Reverted. That was in your first report. What an extraordinary occurrence, though, considering that Moreau's amalgams of human and animal were accomplished largely through vivisection. Tell me, Herr Pendrick, how does one revert from vivisection? How does the animal that each had been slough off the effects of so many surgeries? You described so much of what you had experienced here on this island in great—even exhaustive—detail, and yet the reversal of Moreau's process was given but a few lines. There was no description, or even speculation, as to how the *Tiermenschen* became true animals again."

Pendrick did not answer but instead swallowed hard and licked his lips. He blinked as if fighting back tears.

She took a small step forward so that it was as if she and Pendrick stood together in an intimate little bubble. He felt her breath on his lips. She smelled of cigarettes and French brandy.

"You told us that none of the animal men were left when you first left the island, that they had all reverted, yes?"

"Y-yes..."

"And which animals were they?" asked Hausser. "The ones he transformed in his—what was it called?—the House of Pain? Which animals had Moreau experimented on that you know of?"

Pendrick glanced around as if the answer might be written on the humid air.

"Well," he said slowly, "there were people made from bears, dogs, oxen, apes of various kinds, sloths, hyenas, leopards, goats, swine, rhinoceroses, horses, foxes, pumas, wolves, and ocelots."

"And, as I understand it, many had been created as hybrids," said Hausser. "Were there already animals on the islands?"

"Of course. Many."

"Not the transformed ones, but others."

"I...well...birds and primates, of course," said Pendrick. "There were no large predators on the island, at least that's what Montgomery told me."

"What about the cargoes of animals brought here? I believe you said that many of these were either let loose or escaped during the rebellion against Moreau."

"Rebellion…" murmured Pendrick, tasting the word. Then he blinked and nodded. "Yes."

"What kinds of animals *were* they?" asked Hausser.

When Pendrick hesitated, Weber poked him in the back with something hard and round. Pendrick did not need to turn and look to know that it was a pistol barrel. It was pressed against his waist. A spot where—Weber had already told him—a bullet could pass through the body and do little harm but which would cause considerable agony.

"I…well…" stammered Pendrick, "there was a huge puma, as well as cages of rabbits, a llama, a group of staghounds."

"And it was your belief that other such shipments had arrived with some regularity to this island?" ·

"That's what I gathered from Montgomery and from the crew of the cargo ship. The *Ipecacuanha*. Very many species of animals."

The baroness studied him a moment longer and then dropped the can. It struck the floor with an unnaturally loud sound that made Pendrick flinch.

- 3 -

T HEY LEFT THE storeroom, and the group made its way to a cluster of small bungalows that lined one side of a much larger building.

"These are the apartments you described in your account?" asked Hausser.

"Yes," said the Englishman. "That one was Montgomery's. Mine was over there."

Each of the rooms was filthy, the floor covered with droppings, the walls smeared with offensive muck. Hausser looked at those walls. Some of the swirls and smears looked like a child's attempt to form words. Ugly words, to be sure, but words.

A hammock was slung across one corner of the room by a barred window that looked out toward the sea. She had a Luger holstered on her hip and reached down surreptitiously to unclip the flap. Only Weber seemed to notice it, and they exchanged a tiny nod.

They checked several other bungalows. Each looked as if animals had been nesting in them, and each smelled awful. Despite the windows being unglazed, the rooms held their oleos of rancid meat, waste, wet fur, and sickness.

Weber and Hausser studied the floors, where a jumble of footprints were pressed into the dust and debris. They were animal prints, but many lacked distinct outlines and were hard to identify. The officer and the baroness exchanged glances but did not comment.

The group moved around to the front of the main building and stopped there. Baronin Hausser and Weber flanked Pendrick, and the sailors fanned out around them. The gray walls were cracked and, in some places, collapsed, but overall, the building remained largely intact.

Hausser turned her head with mantis slowness toward Pendrick. "In your report, you indicated this building had burned down. A fire that was the result of you inadvertently knocking over a lantern. And yet…it looks remarkably intact for all that. Were you perhaps exaggerating in your writings? Adding some drama to it? Casting yourself more in the role of intrepid survivor? A latter-day Robinson Crusoe, but one trapped on an island of lost souls?"

Pendrick shook his head. "It burned," he said, then repeated it again in a softer, more inwardly directed echo. "It burned."

Oberleutnant Weber reached for the ornate handle and turned it, and it yielded without protest. Sailors on either side of him raised their machine guns, but the doors swung open to reveal an empty entrance hall. As with the bungalows, the floor inside was littered with filth and debris, and the air was rank.

They moved inside, the sailors surging forward to create a wide perimeter around the officer and the baroness. But there was nothing to shoot.

It was gloomy inside, and Weber sent a man to locate and assess the generator.

Hausser looked around. There were blackened spots on the walls and ceiling, but little sign of structural damage. The sections of damaged wall seemed confined to side rooms—offices, the pantry, a storeroom—but nothing of obvious importance.

Weber detailed men to search the entire complex, but they came back to report that the place was empty. The sailor sent to find the generator returned and gave a quick report.

"Fetch whatever tools you require from the ship," the officer said. "Be quick about it."

The man saluted and hurried outside.

Before the door closed, there was a sound that echoed from the jungle. A growl mingled with a roar. They all listened as it floated on the air, rich and strong and unnerving, and then faded into silence.

"What in hell was that?" murmured Weber, his hand resting on his pistol butt.

Hausser cut a sharp look at Pendrick. "You must know," she said. "Tell us what made that sound."

The Englishman shook his head. "I don't know. I...never heard anything like that before. Perhaps it is a bird."

"A *bird?*"

"Yes," he said. "Moreau brought many species here. Budgerigar from Australia, macaws from South America, cockatoos from various places in Oceania, and African greys. All of them are quite good mimics. Perhaps they picked up those noises from the animal men who were here."

"Birds," said Hausser flatly. "Really?"

"Some of them live a long time, and most can pass down learned calls generationally."

"Birds," said the baroness again. She smiled and turned away. "*Oberleutnant* Weber, what about that generator?"

The officer stared at the door, which was now closed, then shook his head and turned to the baroness. "*Verehrte* Baronin," he said, "my man tells me the generator is in good shape. It needs petrol and some adjustments, but he believes he can get it working."

"It wasn't ruined in the *fire?*" she asked, raising a single pencil-thin eyebrow.

"He said no."

"And the machinery has not been corroded by sea salt or tropical humidity?"

"He says it is in pretty good condition," said the officer. Both had this conversation while looking directly at Pendrick.

"Very well," said Baronin Hausser. "Let's get the lights on, shall we? And have the dock repaired as well. I want to get the equipment here as quickly as possible. I want our laboratory set up by midnight so we can begin work first thing in the morning."

"Yes, *verehrte* Baronin," said the officer. He turned to leave but paused as one of the sailors came jogging back into the room.

"*Oberleutnant*," he said, "we spotted something outside."

"What is it?"

"Animals, sir," said the sailor.

"What kind?"

"I...don't know, sir. They were hiding in the undergrowth where there are dense shadows. Big ones, whatever they are. Dogs or something bigger. I tried to chase them, but they outran me, and then one of the other men said he saw them in the surf."

Weber turned to the baroness. "What are your orders?"

She considered for a moment, her eyes cold and narrow. "Post sentries," she said. "Tell them to shoot any large animals on sight. Then bring the carcasses to me."

He gave a sharp bow and hurried outside with most of the men.

That left Hausser with Pendrick and two sailors as guards. The baroness strolled through the rooms, saying little, with the Englishman trailing behind under the watchful eyes of the sailors. When they reached the main laboratory, Hausser once more turned to her prisoner.

"Destroyed in a fire," she said slowly. "And yet…"

Pendrick had remained silent since the sailor made his report. His face was florid and sweaty and his hands trembled as if with palsy.

Hausser went over to examine a stainless-steel surgical table, bending close to study a cluster of small smears of brownish gunk. She scratched at it and then sniffed.

"Blood," she murmured.

While Pendrick stood in silence, the baroness spent quite a while prowling the room, looking at various tables filled with all manner of scientific and medical equipment. There were shelves filled with bottles of all shapes and sizes, some with handwritten labels and others bearing printed labels of the kind used in chemist shops throughout England, France, Austria, and Italy. Hausser spent a lot of time examining each. Finally, she came to stand with Pendrick and showed him two of the bottles. Although the bottles and contents were different, the manufacturer's labels were the same—*Die Pharmaceuthische Kompanie Vienna.*

"Herr Pendrick," she said in a voice that seemed to be filled with sunshine and flowers, "I found something very interesting. See these chemicals? Take a close look at the labels. Tell me what you see."

Pendrick did not look. His eyes were on hers and did not waver.

"I insist you look," said Hausser.

When he still hesitated, she held them up in front of his eyes. After a moment she lowered them.

"I know this company," she said. "I grew up in Vienna and went to school there. I use many of their products in my own work. A well-respected manufacturer of chemicals used in various aspects of science. Medical science. But…what is most interesting is that the company is a relatively new one, founded by Josef Herzig. He was a very close friend of my mentor, Dr. Reintzer. Herr Herzig founded *Die Pharmaceuthische Kompanie Vienna* with his two sons after the Great War. It opened its doors in 1922." She paused. "Now, how on earth could bottles of his chemicals have come to be on the shelves of Dr. Moreau, when Moreau died in 1896? Died before your very eyes."

She took a step closer.

"Tell me, Herr Pendrick, how can you explain so inexplicable a thing as that?"

The Englishman merely shook his head.

"Well, we may have to discuss that more at length later," said Hausser with another cold smile. She began to turn, but Pendrick shifted to block her. The sailors reached to grab him, but the baroness waved them off. "You have a question…?"

"What you are planning is madness," he said.

"Madness? No. It is pure science," said Hausser. "Dr. Moreau broke through many important boundaries with his work. The fact that he created these *Tiermenschen* is, by all common limits of science, miraculous. To elevate animals into thinking, speaking creatures approximating humanity is…is…well, words escape me. Also, in your so-wonderful account, there are references to hybrids of all kinds. A hyena-swine, I believe? A *faux* satyr made from a goat and an ape. That combination of horse and rhinoceros must have been magnificent, as well as the bear-bull man. Others, too. Fascinating amalgams of creatures. Created, according to you, through vivisection."

"Yes," said Pendrick weakly.

"But now…reverted…? How interesting."

Pendrick said nothing.

"Out of curiosity, Herr Pendrick, when the satyr reverted…did it go back to being a goat or an ape?"

"I…"

"Which aspect of the creature was dominant? And what happened to the other aspects? How did reversion eliminate those qualities?"

Pendrick licked his lips.

"And how did the vivisection undo itself?"

"I don't have those answers," he said.

"Don't you? How strange," said Hausser. "You claim ignorance and yet you returned here again and again. You have never really said why."

"No, I told you—I wanted to make sure that Moreau's work was never used by anyone."

"Ah, yes," said the baroness, then she turned and looked around. "Glass bottles, delicate instruments, finely crafted machinery… Surely, it would have been the work of a single day to destroy it all. The sea would be your ally in eliminating it. Saltwater and thrashing current. A better ally, perhaps, than fire…which did not seem to do much harm at all."

Before Pendrick could answer, there was another roar, and this time it was close enough to be heard through the closed doors. It rose high and tore at the air, then faded out.

Faded, but not entirely. Some aspect of it—more a quality than actual sound—lingered on the air. It was not the same roar as before, Hausser was sure of it.

"What lives on this island?" she demanded.

Instead of answering, Pendrick said, "You came here to continue Moreau's work. You've said as much, but tell me, Baroness—*why?* What can you hope to gain? I heard you and Weber talking one night during the voyage here. He said a word, a name. *Höllenlegion.* I know enough German to translate that. Hell's Legion. And I'm no fool. I think I know what your intentions are. It's why you brought me here."

She smiled again. "Clever boy. What is it you think you know?"

Pendrick straightened. "I know more than you think, my lady. I know that you are part of Himmler's cabal of metaphysicians. The Thule Society. Corrupt madmen hoping to discover some kind of supernatural—or *unnatural*—weapon in a last-ditch effort to save your beloved Third Reich from its inevitable demise." He waved an arm in the general direction of the ship. "You're losing the war. The Allies are going to invade France. That's obvious. You're being beaten in Africa and Italy and elsewhere. Do you really think you can build an army of animal men—your *Tiermenschen*—and use them as shock troops? Horrific in aspect and in nature?"

Her smile brightened, but there was a slightly fragile quality to it. "Yes, Herr Pendrick, that is exactly what we intend. What *I* intend. The *Tiermenschen* has the full support of Herr Himmler and of the Führer. And you, despite your lies and obfuscations, have left this lab curiously intact. Operational, even. So you tell me, are you part of some Allied plot to do exactly the same thing? If not against us, then against the Russians, because you know that if Berlin falls, the Russians will turn on you."

"No," said Pendrick, "that is not our plan."

The moment froze as his words sank in.

"*Our* plan…?" she asked.

Before Pendrick could answer, another roar slashed the air. The sailors brought their weapons up, aiming them at the door.

"Yes," said the Englishman. "*Our* plan."

As he said that, Pendrick straightened, and he seemed to change. The weak and quivering man he'd been seemed to melt away, leaving in its place a figure of more obvious strength and self-possession. Even his voice changed in its quality, losing the fearful tremolo. Baronin Hausser took an involuntary step back.

"What…?"

Pendrick chuckled. It was an unpleasant sound. "You haven't figured it out yet, have you? I enjoyed watching you tug at the edges of it, but you lack the insight to put it all together. God above, you even *told* me some of it, teasing me as if you were the clever one."

There were more roars, and now they came from multiple places outside.

"What are you saying?" she demanded.

"Moreau's vivisection? Of course that wasn't his method. Did you think I would be so foolish as to tell the world of his true motivation? His true methods?" He shook his head. "For Moreau, vivisection was a hobby, but his genius was biochemistry. He was perhaps the greatest chemist this world has yet seen. I'm good, but I stood in his shadow and now stand on his shoulders."

"What? You were never Moreau's colleague," said Hausser. "That was Montgomery's role."

The Englishman smiled very broadly. A rather lupine grin. "Yes. It was."

Her eyes went wide. "You...you're Montgomery? *Gott in Himmel!* Then...what happened to Pendrick?"

Montgomery shrugged. "You read the account of my death, but as I wrote that story I took the license of changing a few things. It was Pendrick who got drunk with the beast-men, and it was Pendrick who was throttled by them. I was a friend to those poor, tortured, magnificent creatures. I took care of them, tending to their wounds after the battle. I left the island and spun that pack of lies to frighten people away from here—and it worked. And I came back time and again, bringing food, supplies, and more equipment to continue Moreau's work. Or, rather, to correct his mistakes. Moreau fancied himself a god overseeing a forced evolution. I am not so arrogant. I worked *with* the beast-men, helping them become more fully what *they* wanted to be. Not men, not beasts, but something else. A new and complex species, as beautiful in their nature as they were hideous in aspect. I felt I owed it to give them—especially the hybrids—the chance to explore their new natures and choose their destinies."

"No..."

"Oh yes. And this island—forbidden to all—was to be their kingdom. Their sovereign nation. A place where they could live out their lives with dignity and grace." Montgomery stepped toward her, and the sailors pointed their barrels at him. He ignored them. "Until your lot plunged the entire world into war. Had you kept your fight in civilized lands, then the beast-men here would have been content to stay out of it. But, no…you read my account and began looking for this island. Tell me, Baroness, did you think your search would go unnoticed? Such arrogance. I heard about it more than a year ago. I came here on one of my trips to warn the people here."

"*People…?*"

"Yes, people. They think and feel; they are sentient and introspective. I daresay they have souls, which you, in my estimation, do not."

There were more roars, and suddenly the air was torn by the rattle of gunfire.

"*Verehrte* Baronin," cried one of the sailors. "We should return to the ship."

Montgomery laughed. "No, I don't think that is a very good idea at all."

Gunfire tore the night, but the roars were louder, and they seemed to come now from everywhere.

"You saw that the beast-men can swim," he said. "They can climb, too. Human intelligences in bodies crafted by Moreau's science to have the agility and strength of apes, of bulls, of tigers. You have brought your war to their sanctuary. You have invaded *their* home. Do you think they—*we*— would not defend it? Do you think that we would not prepare for you?"

"I will have you killed," hissed the baroness. "You and all of these animals."

"Oh, you may kill me, and if so, the science dies with me. I was Moreau's *only* apprentice. Sure, you may have the chemicals and instruments, but not the science. And it would take you decades to reconstruct what Moreau did and longer to figure out how I have built on his work. Kill me, and your *Höllenlegion* dies with me."

Gunfire was constant now, and some was distant. Out to sea.

The screams, though, were everywhere, and there were so many of them.

So many.

"Moreau would have done what I have done," said Montgomery. "A French-born émigré to England. Two nations your people have inflicted unpardonable harm upon. I, too, am English, and I've seen what your *Luftwaffe* has done to London and elsewhere. I've heard rumors of the horrors in camps throughout Europe. How could I allow you to bring your horrors here?"

There was a heavy *thud* against the doors and the sailors swung their weapons that way. The sound repeated, and both sailors opened up with their machine guns, tearing the heavy oak doors to splinters. There was a shriek outside, but it was not one of pain. No, it was a twisted kind of laughter.

A hyena's laugh.

The shadows in the room seemed suddenly darker to Hausser and she looked around, flinching at sounds from the deep darkness. The scratch of claws on the stone floor. The heavy breathing of something large. And murmurs of strange voices.

Outside, the gunfire was diminishing and other sounds filled the air. More screams, but these were not animal challenges. They were the terrified and agonized shrieks of men in awful pain.

Those screams faded.

Faded.

And were gone.

The night fell silent.

Montgomery looked at the baroness.

"You are the most important biologist in the Thule Society. You are Heinrich Himmler's prize genius. He would be lost without you. He sent you here because he needed his best and brightest to manage this last great effort."

There were soft growls from every corner of the room. From behind closet doors, from the darkness beneath the rafters, from black hallways. Many, many growls. The sailors fired at the darkness.

Hitting nothing.

Wasting bullets.

From every patch of darkness there was laughter. None of it was even remotely human.

"You do remember what this place was called, don't you?" asked Montgomery. "This suite of laboratories? You said it earlier."

Hausser, her face drained of all color, breathed the words. "The… House of…Pain…."

"Yes," said Montgomery. "That is what we call it."

The room was filled with roars. With howls and shrieks and cries.

And with dreadful screams.

THEY CALL ME MOTHER

GENEVE FLYNN

Do not question the sisters.
Do not entertain male visitors.
Do not travel in darkness.

WILLA HURRIED ACROSS the bridge that led to Seward House, patting her bonnet, ensuring it was still in place. She was late, and the strange conditions of her contract did not help to ease her frayed disposition. Still, she and Nate had few other options; she would make the best of things.

As she stepped off the rough stone onto the other side, a rich, loamy breath rose up around her, like the scent of rain on parched earth. There was a hint of citrus. Oranges?

Willa stumbled. She had been here before, in this moment.

Her hearing grew muffled and she was heavy with a sudden weariness. She shook her head and blinked. Through the silver birches, she spied a road, and the roof of a building was visible as a dark peak above the treetops.

Willa straightened. That was it. She had been brought on to nurse the children at the orphanage. She squared her shoulders and took a deep breath. Nurse them she would.

IT SEEMED HER introduction to Sister Dorothy would not be favorable. The matron stood in the cavernous doorway of the manse, arms crossed and coldly elegant. Her black hair was pulled back and her uniform was crisp. Willa thought Sister Dorothy would have been a great beauty, if not for the dour twist of her lips.

Willa hurried up the steps and bobbed a curtsy.

"Tardiness will not be tolerated," Sister Dorothy said in lieu of a greeting.

"My apologies, Sister. Settling into a new town has left little time for orienting myself." Willa smiled, hoping to lighten the air. "And Seward House is quite a distance from Whitby!"

Sister Dorothy remained stony. "It suits our purposes. The children are not contagious, but their illness makes the villagers…uneasy." She turned on her heel and Willa had to double her steps to keep up as the matron marched across the foyer.

Seward House was large and ornate. Rich tapestries hung from the walls, and a chandelier glittered above the landing of twin staircases that soared left and right. They passed an empty ballroom. The polished parquetry floor gleamed in the late morning light.

"Was this a residence before?" Willa asked, daring to pause for a moment. She loved to dress up and dance. But that was before marriage. Nate said it wouldn't do to indulge in such vanity.

"Seward House was once owned by a doctor. He died suddenly. We are lucky to have had such a benefactor."

Sister Dorothy swerved right and arrived at a pair of carved wooden doors. She swung them open and Willa hurried through.

Two women, who could only be sisters or, at least, kissing cousins to Sister Dorothy, watched over some twenty children in a common area. The space was bright and airy, but the children played listlessly. An open door at the rear showed a sizeable kitchen.

The women had alabaster skin, the same aquiline noses and large, shapely eyes as Sister Dorothy. One had dark red hair, the other, ash-blond.

"Sister Geraldine cooks for us," Dorothy said, indicating the red-headed woman. "Sister Cornelia looks after the laundry."

The blond woman nodded to Willa, picked up a pile of sheets, and hobbled out of the room. Her shuffling steps could be heard traveling up one of the staircases.

"Hello!" A man's voice called from the kitchen. "Delivery!"

Dorothy's face brightened. "Edward is here. I must see to this."

Geraldine's face also lit up and she was swift on Dorothy's heels as she left the room.

Willa stood, uncertain, in the center of the room. The children seemed not to have noticed her and she wasn't sure how to approach them. She fidgeted for a moment before walking to the door that led to the kitchen. The murmur of voices carried a current of excitement and she peeked, curious.

The cart man carried a large sack over one shoulder. A broken seam trickled blood down his arm. He tossed the bag onto the counter with a moist thump. For a moment, Willa saw the shape of a child's body in the lumpen form. She pressed her fingers to her mouth. Then Geraldine yanked the ties loose and the gore-flecked head of a lamb lolled out.

Willa exhaled. *What a strange thing to imagine!*

"Can I call you Mother?"

A small boy, of about seven, tugged at her sleeve. His hair was mousy brown, like hers, and he clutched a ragged doll to his chest. He smiled, and it was as sweet as a spring morning.

"Just to pretend?" he asked.

Poor little thing.

She knelt. "What's your name?"

"Arthur."

"Well, Arthur, very soon, someone will come and adopt you. Then you'll have a proper mother, and a father." Willa smoothed his hair, marveling at the downy curve of his head. "Their house will have a lovely, warm fireplace. And they'll give you tea and cakes. And perhaps you'll have a brother or a sister."

"And a rabbit?"

Willa beamed. "And a rabbit. Two, or three! A whole hutch of rabbits."

Arthur flung his arms around her and kissed her cheek. Willa froze, startled as much by his sudden affection as the strong metallic smell of him. Then, as quickly as he had appeared, he skipped away to play.

Willa stood and turned, straight into Sister Dorothy's thunderous expression. "Come with me."

Dorothy didn't wait to see if she complied, but marched back into the kitchen. Willa followed, her heart fluttering in her throat.

The matron spun. "Do not give them hope when there is none," she hissed. "He will live and die on these grounds. In this house. Under this roof. Like all the others."

Geraldine appeared at the back door, carrying a handful of rosemary.

The lamb's carcass pooled blood on the counter, and Willa's stomach rolled. "How can you be so cruel? They're children, for God's sake!"

"God has nothing to do with this place," Geraldine muttered.

Dorothy gave her a warning shake of the head and turned back to Willa. "You will go and inventory the infirmary. You will tend to nursing. Nothing more."

Willa stared, open mouthed. "I—"

"Nothing. More. It is the second door on the left, after the ball-room."

Willa glanced at Geraldine, but the redheaded sister would not meet her eyes.

With a nod, Willa left to do as she was bid.

THE SUN WAS low in the sky by the time Willa had sorted all the various tinctures and ointments. Doctor Seward had been lapse in his management. The sound of many footsteps climbing the staircase brought her out of the infirmary. The children marched up the steps in exhausted silence. One by one, they entered the rooms that lined the upper level. Arthur gave her a small wave. The sisters stood ready, each with a ring of keys in hand, and they proceeded to lock the doors.

"I say, what are you doing?" Willa asked. "Why are you locking them away?"

Dorothy paused and stared down at her. "That is twice you have questioned our methods. Need I remind you of the terms of your contract?"

"They're not animals in a zoo!"

"Cornelia. Show her."

Cornelia flushed, but shuffled down the stairs. She lifted her skirt.

Willa stifled a gasp. An angry purple scar puckered the otherwise smooth skin of her calf. A fist-sized chunk had been bitten from it.

Cornelia smoothed her skirt. "The children are sometimes seized with a mania," she said quietly. "They are a danger to us, and to themselves. It is another reason why the orphanage is situated so far from the village. The children cry out. You would be surprised how the sound carries."

"Go home, Willa," Dorothy said. "That is enough for today. I'm sure you will need your rest for tomorrow."

AS WILLA STEPPED onto the bridge, the events of the day weighed heavily on her. She walked the rest of the way home with her chin tucked low, seeing only Arthur's weary wave before the door closed on him.

She arrived at the bedsit that she shared with Christof. Although he was well into his years, frail, and mute, the thought of him lifted her spirits. Nate had been lucky to find accommodation for her at such short notice and with such low rent. In exchange, Willa cooked and cleaned for Christof.

She had been in Whitby a week now, but the people here were insular and suspicious, not like her beloved London. With Nate traveling for work, Christof was her only friend.

"Let us sup out on the porch," Willa said as she wheeled him outside, a tray of sandwiches and soup balanced on his lap.

Christof beamed and patted her hand. She set him up, took a sandwich but only nibbled at it.

Christof tilted his head: his way of asking a question.

Willa sighed and everything that had troubled her came tumbling out. When it was all said, she stirred her soup, unseeing. "Isn't it cruel to show the poor things the harsh, unvarnished truth? What harm is there in allowing them to believe that things will end happily ever after?"

He raised a trembling hand to his face.

She looked up and was dismayed to see that tears glistened in his eyes. "Oh, Christof! Curse me for a fool. Here I am, bringing tales of misery and woe to you, when you've been cooped up, all alone."

She took a sip of her soup, now cold, and smiled brightly. "I will speak of only happy things with you. Soon, Nate will return from his business abroad, and all will be well. Let us enjoy the last rays of the sun. Then I shall fetch us a slice each of taffety tart."

DESPITE HER EFFORTS, there was no rescuing the evening. Willa helped Christof to bed and retired herself. As she drifted off, the dream visited her again.

Her love lay his hand low upon her belly, and it stirred something inside of her. Her sleeping self yearned toward him. He kissed her, soft and gentle at first, then rougher, more insistent. It was her husband, but this forwardness was not him. A deeper part of her mind whimpered and drew back. His hand slid down, between her thighs. She arched up to it, shocked by her own wanton response. He positioned himself above her and they coupled—a savage, delirious act.

Willa cried out in pleasure and woke.

She clapped her hands over her mouth, still throbbing and giddy. Had she woken Christof?

She curled up on her side, flooded with shame.

At the last moment, the light of the moon had revealed that the man in her dream was not her husband.

AN AGUE PENETRATED Willa's bones and she shivered. She cracked open her eyes, then sat up swiftly with a curse. It was at least after noon. She changed as quickly as her aching body would allow and attended to her toilette. As she passed Christof's door, she paused. It would be the right thing to face her mortification head on and apologize. She knocked tentatively.

"Christof?"

There was no answer, but she thought she heard the smallest creak of a wheel behind the door. Her cheeks bloomed with heat. He must have heard her in the night. Willa pressed her lips together and quietly left, closing the door behind her.

SOUR SALIVA FLOODED her mouth as Willa once again stepped off the bridge onto the dark, rich soil. She swallowed and clutched her stomach. She really should have paused to eat something, but she could ill-afford to lose this posting.

Seward House came into view, and Willa was relieved to see that Sister Dorothy was not at the door, waiting. Instead, she spied Edward, the cart man, at the side door to the kitchen.

She slowed in her approach. He carried a small, limp form wrapped in a sheet. Once again, Willa had the impression that what he carried was not the carcass of an animal (for why would he be collecting such a thing from the orphanage?) but of a child. She quickened her pace and stopped him before he reached his cart.

"Edward, forgive me, I'm Willa, the nurse. What has happened?"

Edward kept his gaze lowered and said nothing.

Willa lifted the sheet.

"Oh no."

A small, pale face lay against Edward's broad chest, terribly still, and tinged with blue. It was a boy, but not Arthur.

Edward stepped around her and gently laid the body on the back of his cart.

Willa rushed inside the side door and found Geraldine washing her hands at the porcelain sink. "What happened to the boy?"

Geraldine continued to lather her hands. They seemed to be clean, but she reached for more soap. "One of the children passed in the night."

"Of what? Why was I not called?"

Geraldine turned on the tap and steam billowed around her face, wilting her red hair. "It would have done no good. They all suffer from the same affliction."

Willa winced as the sister plunged her hands into the scalding water. Geraldine's expression remained distant.

"Should we not at least call for the coroner?"

Dorothy appeared at the door that led into the common room. "The risk of contagion is too great."

Willa bristled. "But you said the illness wasn't a risk to the villagers."

The sisters exchanged troubled looks and Willa noticed, for the first time, the silence from behind Dorothy. She pushed past and expected to see the common room empty. Instead, the children moved around the room wordlessly. Some lay lethargic as snails on the floor, some drifted aimlessly, toys forgotten in loose hands. Several curled up into themselves, clutching their stomachs, grimacing in pain. Arthur stared at Willa but did not seem to recognize her.

One of the children had pulled the fire shovel over and was chewing on it. Her teeth made dreadful grinding, cracking noises. Dorothy calmly walked over and plucked it from her hands. The child made no protest. Her mouth opened and closed, like she was a baby bird, hoping for a worm.

Something swam up from Willa's memory, of something else performing the same insensate motion of mindless hunger. What was it? She tried to reach for the recollection but it drifted away.

"What is wrong with the children?"

Dorothy rolled the child onto her back, where she lay, mouthing. "We don't know. They are all like this, sooner or later."

Willa bent to examine a boy closest to her. "Then we must call for a doctor."

"We need no outside help."

"Perhaps it is some disease that we do not yet know of. Perhaps it is a form of malnutrition."

Dorothy arched an eyebrow. "You saw what Edward delivered yesterday. That lamb was eaten down to the bone. The children have everything they need."

Willa stood. "Then there is some other neglect happening here. I don't know what it is, but I will report to the Royal College of Physicians that you and the other sisters have refused to get these children medical help."

"No one will believe you."

A knot wound through Willa's stomach. "What do you mean?"

"We know that you and your husband have been touched by scandal." Dorothy adjusted her sleeves primly. "More than that, you've *drowned* in it. That's why you've had to settle here. Why you've had to leave your precious London. Why your husband must travel, taking whatever work he can."

Roaring filled Willa's ears. What scandal had she and Nate been tainted with? What had they done? What had *she* done? She thought hard, but there was nothing but a vague echo of her life before Whitby. Like a poorly made daguerreotype.

Then memory of her dream rushed in, followed by shame, setting her neck and face aflame.

Do not entertain male visitors.

The corners of Dorothy's lips rose.

"Leave her be, Dorothy." Cornelia shuffled in, carrying a basket of dirty linen.

Willa straightened and lifted her chin. She walked from the room with as much dignity as she could summon. But by the time she was at the bridge, she was running.

———

CHRISTOF'S DOOR WAS still firmly closed when Willa reached home. She didn't blame him, but loneliness cored her. In any case, what could she say?

If only Nate were here, there would be at least one person on her side. Willa rested her head on her door, and tears threatened. Perhaps he traveled so much because he, too, couldn't bear to look at her. She dragged herself to her bed, aching and sickened. She curled up into a ball and closed her eyes.

WILLA SURGED UP out of bed and groped for the small sink in her room. Her insides were caught in a vice as she lurched, over and over again, strings of bile dripping from her lips.

With a soft groan, she rinsed her mouth and splashed water on her face. Desperate to clear the tang of iron from her mouth, she scraped her tongue against her top teeth.

She had tasted this before.

Not tasted, smelled.

Arthur.

When he had embraced her, there had been a distinct metallic scent. Had she been infected by the same disease? Yet the sisters showed no symptoms. Surely, they had been exposed for far longer.

Willa dragged her suitcase from under her bed. She pulled out her medical books, a precious gift from Nate, and flipped through them, her mind stumbling ahead. The stomach pains, the paleness, the mania and disorientation. The metallic taste. The child, trying to eat the iron shovel.

Her fingers raced down one page, then another.

Porphyria.

Yet it was a disease of the genes. How could all the children have it? There were twenty or more. Surely, they were not born from one single family. If so, why had they all been placed at the orphanage?

She traced along the entry and found what her consciousness had alerted her to.

Possible cause: lead poisoning.

Willa smiled grimly. The sisters were poisoning the children. But what reason did they have? She thought back to the opulence of Seward House. The rich tapestries and polished floors. The sisters with their cold beauty, so out of place in an orphanage. They seemed much more suited to a life being served, than in service.

She would put a stop to it.

SEWARD HOUSE STOOD in darkness. Willa slowed her pace as she neared, her skin prickling.

Do not travel in darkness.

The sense of disorientation at the bridge trailed her like a miasma, but she forged on. She climbed the front steps and tested the door. It opened without sound and she entered. The lamps were all doused, and only the light of the moon and her own lantern lit the gloom.

Willa climbed the stairs, wincing at each creak, then froze at the top. All the children's doors were ajar. Silent shadows waited beyond each threshold.

A rustle from three doors ahead.

Arthur's room.

"Arthur?" she called quietly. She crept along until she reached his door. There was a strange susurration from within, like a fast ebb and flow of the tide. Like a single, huge organism making swift exhalations.

"Arthur?" Her voice was barely a whisper.

The respiration caught, then became a long, hungry inhalation. Trembling, weak as a lamb, Willa raised her lantern. Where were the children? Were the sisters feeding them to some infernal beast?

At the touch of her light, several small heads turned. An icy chill doused Willa. The children's chests hitched in eldritch unison. Their eyes reflected, black as volcanic glass. Once again, the respiration caught, and they lifted their noses, scenting her.

"Mother?" Arthur murmured.

"Mother. Mother. Mother." The others took up the call.

With a cry, Willa fled, scurrying back down the stairs. She skidded to a halt. The light of a lantern shone beyond the open front door. Willa shuttered her light, hissing as the hot metal seared her fingers. She stood, still as a deer, praying they had not seen.

"What should we do about her?" Geraldine's voice sounded from the front porch.

"I tire of this. It's getting harder and harder to control her." Dorothy, hard-edged and petulant. "Why does he favor her? Let's kill her, once and for all. And her brats."

Who were they speaking of? Who favored whom? Willa's head swam and another cramp ripped through her. *Please, not now.*

The side door.

Doubled over, she stumbled through the common room, tripping over strewn toys. She burst into the kitchen and uttered a terrified squeak. A body was laid out on the cutting board. A human body. Willa unshuttered her lantern an inch. Even though a rich, coppery smell crawled up her nostrils, the man's carcass had been bled white. She scrambled for the side door and bounced off Edward's cart, landing hard on her rump.

Edward was nowhere to be seen. Light from another lantern wavered from the front of the house. Willa extinguished her lamp and scrambled up into the bed of the cart. She flattened herself against the wooden boards and pressed a hand over her mouth, taking tiny sips of air.

The lantern drew closer, heavy footsteps accompanying its approach. The light lifted and shone down on her. Willa stared up at Edward, unable to move. Over his shoulder was another body, white as bone. He paused. He lowered the lantern to the ground and reappeared. His face was lit from below. A ghastly mask.

Then he touched a finger to his lips. He lowered the body on top of her, covering her as best he could, then left.

Willa lay, shivering. The body was a cold, dreadful weight. The smell of death was all around her. Tears trickled into her ears, but she dared not wipe them away.

"Someone's been here." Dorothy's voice rang out, laced with panic. "The front door was open."

"Begging your pardon, Sister," Edward's voice rumbled. "'Twas me. I forgot to close it after myself."

A sharp tsk. "Take the bodies away. Return tomorrow with another lamb for the children."

"And the other…deliveries…for you and the sisters?"

"We've had our fill." Dorothy's voice was a luxuriant purr. "No need until Friday."

Silence fell, broken only by indistinct murmurs. Willa listened hard for several long moments. She would make for the bridge. She inched the body off her, gagging at the stiff, gelid flesh. The lantern light returned. She froze. She was no longer hidden. Edward reappeared, the body from the kitchen over his shoulder. He gave her an almost imperceptible shake of the head, then lowered the second body over her. The dead man's face pressed against her cheek. A damp sigh escaped the body, ripe with putrefaction. She bit the inside of her mouth to contain her cry.

The cart shifted as Edward climbed up onto his seat and flicked the reins. With a jolt, they began to move away from Seward House.

———

IT WAS ONLY when Willa heard the merry rill of the river and felt the grind of the cart's wheels on stone that she dared to throw off the bodies. She scrambled back, scrubbing at her face and hands.

Edward cast a glance back at her and pressed his finger to his lips again. She nodded and hunkered in a corner, as far from the corpses as possible.

They finally reached Whitby. Willa scrambled upright and clutched Edward's arm. "Please, you must go to the constabulary."

He looked down at his large hands. "'Twon't do any good. No one dares the night, missus."

Willa looked around and saw that he was right. The moonlight illuminated only deserted streets. All windows were firmly shuttered and doors barred.

"Then we must hie away from here. To the next village. I'll tell them you saved me."

Christof. She couldn't leave him behind.

"Please, Edward—" She gasped as a cramp doubled her over.

He placed a hand on her arm. "Wait here. I'll fetch your friend. He'll be a comfort to you, I think."

Willa could only nod, cradling her stomach, which now felt swollen and gravid. Her pelvis throbbed with a deep ache and she moaned. Something *rolled* inside her and she cried out.

Edward returned, carrying Christof as easily as a sack of flour. He clambered onto the back of the cart and lowered him beside Willa. Christof took her hand. The cramps came one after the other and Willa's vision narrowed to a tunnel.

The cart creaked again. Someone else had climbed aboard. Edward grunted and the cart bounced as he stepped down.

"It is almost time." The voice was dark silk, a cool breath against her flushed brow.

Willa looked up. A tall, pale man knelt before her. His face was angular and beautiful. He laid his hand low on her belly, and despite her pain, desire jolted through her. The man from her dream.

"Don't touch me," she croaked.

"Hush, Mina," Christof murmured, rubbing her back. His hands were sure and strong, no longer infirm. "It will be over soon."

Mina?

Willa turned and saw that it was not Christof who held her, but Nate.

No.

Not Nate.

"Jonathan?" She panted as another series of contractions rippled through her. She forced away the narrowing of her vision. "What is this?"

The pale man smiled. "Family. Raised upon the soil of my ancestors."

Soil. So dark and loamy, smelling like oranges. Willa grunted and fought the urge to push.

Jonathan glared at the man. "Why must you terrify her? Why must Mina remember, each time?"

The pale man chuckled. "For unto woman, He said, 'I will greatly multiply thy sorrow and thy conception. In sorrow thou shalt bring forth children; and thy desire shall be to thy husband, and he shall rule over thee.' Nature allows a woman to begin forgetting soon after birth. It is your god, Mr. Harker, who insists on punishment."

Jonathan shook his head. "You're a monster."

Willa shuddered. *Monster.* "No, we killed you. We escaped."

The pale man smiled, languid. He ran a long finger over her stomach. Willa shrank from his touch. "Did you? Or did it serve my purposes to allow you to believe that things ended. Happily. Ever. After."

Willa shook her head. "No. *No.*"

"Yes, Wilhelmina, but only one of you fought the harsh, unvarnished truth."

She snarled, hating that he threw her words back at her.

"One of you," the pale man continued, "agreed quite readily."

Jonathan cradled her cheek. "Be calm, please. I only did what was best for us."

The pale man raised his palms like a preacher. "This is the price of your husband's salvation. Your womb for his soul. What better way to rule your wife, than to bargain her body, which was consecrated with my blood, and survived?"

Willa felt the remnants of the pale man's blood, still lying dormant in her veins. The same blood that allowed him to get her with child, over and over again. How many times had she lived this horror? She snapped her head away from Jonathan's touch.

"Mina, my love," Jonathan begged. "I knew you could survive this. You, who have such grace."

The urge to push surged through her and Willa squeezed her eyes shut.

Jonathan's hand was on her back once again, but she had no ability to cast him off. "Yes, that's it," he murmured. "Close your eyes and forget. It will all be better soon. It will be as if it never happened."

The child inside her twisted, blindly driven to erupt from her body. She shut out Jonathan's mewling. She turned inside, drawing hard into herself. She found her faith, a glowing ember in the center of her heart. With a snarl, she extinguished it. She grunted and bore down, crushing her obedience, her geniality. The pale man's blood roared to life in her body and she screamed, forcing his spawn clear.

Jonathan smoothed the hair from her dripping brow. "Good girl. You did it."

Willa snapped her eyes open. He scrambled back from her, hands raised in supplication. She grinned at the terror on his face.

"Please, Mina, there was no other way!"

She raised her gaze to the pale man. He bent over the bloodied infant. It already crawled, scenting the air. She reached for her babe. The pale man bared his teeth and hissed. Willa yowled, a wild, shrieking that rose and rose. The pale man drew back and she snatched up the child.

She hunched her back, drawing forth her wings. Willa grabbed

Jonathan by the scruff and shot into the sky, chased by the pale man's furious screech.

SHE DROPPED JONATHAN in front of the orphanage. He screamed and landed with a crunch. Earth puffed up beneath her feet, rich and loamy. Citrus. She stretched her throat long and called to her children. There came an eager, chittering sound, and they crawled from Seward House, some from the windows, some from the doors. They circled Jonathan, chests hitching in beautiful unison. The infant in her arms, a girl, struggled against her hold, and with a delighted laugh, Willa lowered her to the ground. The baby crawled, with her brothers and sisters, and as one, they fell on the shrieking man.

The ground juddered as the pale man landed between Willa and the children, his wings flared and trembling in a display of dominance. Dorothy, Geraldine, and Cornelia swooped down beside him, hands reaching out, not quite daring to touch him.

He grinned, sure of his triumph.

The children drew forth their own neophyte wings. They were no longer pale and weak, but replete and thrumming with dark life now that they had fed. Fed properly.

"Ask your brides how they have cared for your children," Willa called.

The sisters hissed at her. The pale man turned on them and they cowered. "What does she speak of?" he thundered.

Willa laughed. "Tell him, Sister Dorothy! Tell him how you fed them the lesser blood of the lamb, while you and your sisters gorged on the humans."

With a roar, the pale man struck Dorothy, sending her flying.

Willa charged him. He tumbled backward, his wings now a tangle. He leaped up, fangs bared.

Willa bared her own teeth, new and sharp and strong. The children scampered away from him and spread out to either side of her, growling low in their little throats. Cornelia covered her face and wept. Geraldine slunk away.

"What is this?" the pale man shrieked. "They are mine!"

Willa grinned.

"They call *me* Mother."

OLD MONSTERS NEVER DIE

TIM WAGGONER

YOU SIT CROSS-LEGGED on the ground in front of a small fire. It's late January, and the flames do little to warm you, but that's okay. You don't mind the cold, barely feel it, in fact. You're wearing a thick jacket, but you haven't bothered to zip it up, and the top three buttons on the flannel shirt you have on beneath are undone. The clothes are a bit large on you. This is partly due to how thin you've become over the last several months, but you've always preferred your clothes loose and comfortable. They're easier to tear off that way, in case the change comes on you sudden and unexpected, which it sometimes does, especially these days.

It's after midnight—you don't have a watch on you so you don't know the exact time—and the sky is free of clouds, the stars clear, crisp points of light, bright jewels set in a vast curtain of black satin. The closest town is over twenty miles away, so there's no light pollution to spoil the view. No moon tonight, which is a shame. Your people don't need it to change, but their blood sings loudest when the moon is full

and high. The scent of woodsmoke is thick in your nostrils, making it difficult to discern other smells, but not impossible. Your senses might be dulled by age, but they're still far sharper than an ordinary human's, and you can detect the scents of trees all around you, of animals that have passed through this clearing over the last several days—squirrel, racoon, groundhog, possum, deer... Winter has been relatively mild this year, and the forest animals have been more active than they normally would be in January. *An easy winter makes for good hunting,* you think. For a moment, you're tempted to shuck off your clothes, change, and lope off in search of a deer. You salivate at the thought of fresh meat in your mouth and hot blood on your tongue, but you haven't come here to hunt.

You've come here to die.

You continue sitting in the middle of the clearing, surrounded by leafless oak and elm trees, branches stirred by the wind, rustling and clacking. You listen to the sound of night birds singing, gaze into the dancing flames before you, and wait. You should be relaxed, at peace with what is going to happen this night, but you aren't. You're on edge, right foot bouncing, fingers digging furrows into the dirt on either side of you. You don't want to be here, would rather be back in your cabin, sitting next to your woodstove, reading a book, listening to music, watching some mindless show on television, doing *anything* instead of sitting here waiting. But this is your people's way, and as much as you resent being bound by their traditions, bound you are—to some of them, anyway.

Later—a few minutes, an hour, it doesn't matter—the night birds fall silent. Your fire has grown low, but you don't put more wood on it. It has fulfilled its traditional purpose, to act like a beacon for whomever has come in search of you, a signal that you are not attempting to conceal your presence, that you are unafraid of them. You rise to your feet, joints once smooth and supple complaining at being forced to work in the cold.

A figure emerges between the trees and starts walking toward you. Five years ago—okay, maybe ten—your vision was strong enough that the clearing would have seemed bright as day to you. Not now. You can't discern the features of the one approaching until she's almost in range of the fire's light. But you know her scent as well as your own, for it *is* partially yours, just as it is partially her mother's.

She has come to you in human form, which is an insult, for it means she sees you as no threat, and she's come alone, which is an even greater insult. Among your kind, respect is shown by the number of those who attend one's Final Challenge, whether to participate or observe. But no one else in the pack has come to honor you, and no doubt Elena is here to perform what she sees as a distasteful duty, nothing more. You should've expected this, and you suppose you did deep down, but you're surprised by how much it still hurts.

She stops when she reaches the fire.

"Father."

Long brown hair, hard features, tall, garbed in a black shirt and old jeans, feet bare. She looks so much like Natalie—her mother—that the sight of her makes your heart ache.

"Elena."

You smile at her. She doesn't smile back. You speak the required words.

"Have you come to challenge me this night?"

She looks at you a moment, face impassive, eyes gleaming.

The traditional response to your question is *Prepare to defend yourself, Honored One.*

Instead, she says, "I haven't come to kill you." She smiles, displaying a mouth filled with sharp teeth.

"I've come to do something much worse."

"I DON'T THINK I can do it, Daddy," Elena whispers.

You and your daughter, who is ten years old, crouch behind a large oak. It's dusk in mid-April, and while the sky above the western horizon is a dark blue, the rest of the world is draped in shadow, and it will be full night soon. The oak lies at the edge of a stand of trees that form a half circle around the back of a small playground—swings, climbing equipment, monkey bars, slides, merry-go-round—beyond which is a soccer field, and then a suburban street. Cedar chips are scattered around the play equipment to absorb the impact if any children should fall, but there is only one child here this night. A girl, scarcely older than Elena, wearing a windbreaker over a T-shirt, along with jeans and sneakers. She sits on the middle swing, hands gripping the chains, tips of her shoes on cedar chips. She twists right, left, right, left, slowly, barely moving. You hear her soft whimpers, smell the salt of her tears. The girl's upset about something. She's too young to have had a fight with a lover. Maybe she had some sort of conflict with her parents, or perhaps a falling out with a friend. The specifics don't matter. Whatever has upset her has driven her to come to this small park as night falls, so she can sit on a swing and be alone with her sorrow. It couldn't be more perfect for Elena's first time.

You put a reassuring hand on your daughter's shoulder and speak, your words so soft only those with your people's keen hearing can detect them.

"Of course you can do this. You're an excellent hunter."

You squeeze her shoulder tighter, and without consciously willing it, your fingernails grow longer and sharper.

"I can hunt *animals*," Elena whispers, "but I don't think I can hunt a...a..."

"Human?"

"Person."

"We've been over this, sweetheart. Why do we hunt them?"

Elena hesitates. Your claws extend farther, points becoming sharp as needles, the tips piercing Elena's shirt and dimpling the young flesh beneath. Not quite drawing blood, not yet.

Elena begins to speak, but the words are without emotion, little more than rote memory.

"The Moonborn came into being at the same moment humans did. All things in nature exist in balance, and we were created to balance them. We are their greatest predator, and it is our sacred duty to thin their numbers, to keep their kind strong and healthy. To help them not only survive, but thrive. Humans don't know it—and if they did, they wouldn't believe it—but Moonborn are the best friends they've ever had."

"It's not enough to say the words. You have to *believe* them, too. Do you?"

You chose a night of a full moon for Elena's first human hunt, as is tradition, but moonrise is still an hour away. If the moon was up, she would feel it calling to her, filling her with strength, confidence, and desire. But you know your daughter can't afford to wait until then. The girl on the swing might leave at any moment, Elena needs to strike while the girl is wrapped up in her emotions and her guard is down.

Elena doesn't answer. You remember your first time, almost thirty years ago now. You felt much the same as Elena, and you remember what your mother did to help you get through it. You say the same words to your daughter that your mother spoke to you on that long-ago night.

"If you do not kill her, *I* will, and the death I give her will not be swift. I will make it hurt, and I will make it last."

Elena has kept her gaze focused on the girl the entire time you've been talking, but now she whips her head around, a shocked expression on her face. You've always taught her that it's a kindness to deliver the gift of death swiftly. She's never heard you talk like this before.

Her nostrils flare as she inhales, drawing in your scent to determine if you're telling the truth. Her eyes widen as she realizes you are.

Images, sounds, and smells flash through your mind—a boy sitting on the edge of a creek holding a simple wooden fishing rod, your mother darting past you when you refused to kill him, the boy screaming as your mother began to slowly tear him apart… The next time she took you out, you killed the child she'd selected for you, and you did so without hesitation. A cruel lesson, perhaps, but a necessary one.

Moments pass as you and Elena look at each other silently. Finally, she breaks eye contact, turns away from you, starts to move toward the girl, her bare feet making no sound as she goes. The girl senses something, though, and she looks over her shoulder. Elena shifts form in less time than it takes a human to blink, and she rushes forward, wraps a fur-clad arm around the girl's chest, grabs her chin with her opposite hand—claws digging into soft flesh—and then with a single sharp motion, she breaks the girl's neck. The crack of snapping bone is loud as a gunshot to your ears, but you doubt if anyone else hears it. Elena pulls the dead girl off the swing before she can fall and quickly drags her back into the trees. She drops the girl onto the ground near you, and then she crouches over the body and begins to feed.

She starts slowly, gingerly tearing small pieces of flesh and chewing them with a grimace. She's eaten human meat since she was a toddler, but it's always been procured for her by her parents. She's never had to feed herself like this before, and she finds the process distasteful. But instinct takes over, and soon her head is buried in the girl's abdomen as she seeks out her most tender organs, making snuffling-growling sounds of satisfaction all the while. The rich smell of fresh blood makes your mouth water, but you do not join your daughter in this feast. This is her first kill, and no one may share it with her. You're so very proud of her, and you're about to tell her so when you see the dead girl's face for the first time. You rarely look upon the features of prey. Why would you? They're just meat. But something about this girl catches your attention, and you realize it's her hair—long, straight, and brown, just like Elena's. *Exactly* like. Their faces are different, though. The girl's is broader, and she has a small scattering of freckles on her cheeks. Her wide, staring eyes are blue, not green like Elena's, but the girls are the same basic height and weight, and nearly the same age, and for the first time in your life, you see not a prey animal but—as Elena said—a person. And not just any person. You see someone's daughter, and you think about how it would feel to you if some beast killed Elena and savaged her corpse like this, swallowing bloody gobbets of meat and making throaty *mmmmmm* sounds of pleasure.

You experience a sudden urge to backhand Elena and knock her off the girl, but you don't do it. You fight the revulsion you feel, tell yourself it's temporary, merely the result of seeing your sweet, innocent child become a blooded hunter for the first time. Elena is growing up, and it's only natural for a parent to have mixed emotions about this, right?

As enthusiastically as Elena eats, her small belly can hold only so much, and when she's full and draws away from the corpse, the body still has plenty of meat on it. It's the parent's duty to finish off whatever remains of a young one's first kill, but your gut roils with nausea, and you fear that if you get your face too close to the girl's body, you'll vomit. You don't want Elena to see this.

Elena is still in wolf form, and she looks at you with her green eyes, as if seeking your approval. You force a smile.

"Good job," you say.

But your tone is flat, your words without life, and Elena's eyes narrow. She knows you're lying, but she doesn't know why. Neither do you, really.

AFTER THAT NIGHT, you found it a struggle to eat human meat, and you were no longer able to kill any of them. Gender, age, race, social position, state of health, none of it mattered. You viewed them all as people now, and you could not raise your claws against them. At first your wife feared you might be sick, and she said nothing when you went out hunting for animal meat, although she would not allow you to bring that *filth* into her house. The two of you tried to hide your... problem from the rest of the pack, but word got out eventually, and the pack elders asked to speak with you. The meeting did not last long. They offered you a human liver to eat, you refused, and you were a member of the pack no longer.

Your excommunication didn't extend to Natalie and Elena, but it brought great shame on them both. You wished that could've been avoided, but you knew that was impossible. You moved out of your home—your wife wouldn't allow you to say goodbye to Elena—and moved into a cramped trailer on the edge of the woods, and you've lived there ever since, thirty-one years now, and in all that time, you haven't tasted human blood or meat. You haven't seen your wife or daughter, either, and you've come to believe you'll go to your grave without looking upon their faces again.

It turns out you were wrong.

———

YOU EXAMINE YOUR daughter's features. She's forty-one now, but you can still see the ten-year-old girl in her middle-aged face, especially in her eyes, which look as green and vibrant as they did when you last saw her.

"You look weak," Elena says, "and I can smell death on you."

Your arms and legs are thin, your cheeks sunken in. Beneath your shirt, your stomach is concave, ribs prominent. You tremble, but not from fear. Well, not *only* from fear.

Elena continues. "What's wrong? Your special diet not agree with you?"

It's true. Your kind needs human meat to survive, and you've been slowly starving yourself for three decades, becoming weaker with each passing year. This is why you've chosen the Final Challenge—better to die on your feet, fighting, than to continue wasting away.

"Have you come to taunt me?" you ask.

She smiles. "I've come to offer you a choice."

She looks over her shoulder, and as if this is a signal, another figure emerges from the trees on the far side of the clearing. The wind is coming from that direction, blowing stronger now, and you pick up the newcomer's scent sooner than you did Elena's. It's not one scent, though, but two: Elena's mother—Natalie—and another scent, this one human. You don't understand at first, see only Natalie walking toward you, but as she comes closer, you realize that she's carrying a human child, a boy from the smell of him.

Natalie joins Elena, and you see the years have been kind to your wife. Ex-wife, you suppose, although you've never been officially divorced. Then again, you were never legally married, not as humans understand the process. Her long hair is gray, but her face looks much the same as the last day you saw her. A few wrinkles here and there, but you have far more. Her lips are pressed together in a tight, disapproving line, and her eyes fix on yours, and you see contempt in them, along with a small measure of pity. She's wearing an unzipped hoodie, a T-shirt, and jeans. Like Elena's, her feet are bare. The boy she holds is around ten years old—the same age as the girl who was your daughter's first kill, a girl whose name you never learned—and he's awake. Duct tape covers his mouth to keep him silent, but his eyes are wide with terror. He wriggles, trying to squirm free, but Natalie, even in this form, is far stronger than a human, and when she squeezes him against her, he moans behind the tape and stops struggling. When he's still, she drops him to the ground. He lands on his belly, and before he can attempt to rise, she places a foot on his back to hold him down. His face is lit by the dim orange glow of the dying fire as he looks at you, eyes pleading. *Please don't do this,* they say. *Let me go, I won't say anything!*

You're surprised your wife and daughter have come. As required by tradition, you found one of the pack—a middle-aged man who works at a feedstore in town—drinking alone in a bar and told him you were ready for your Final Challenge. You told him where you would be and when, and the man simply nodded and went back to his drink. You left, knowing that he would spread the word to the rest of the pack, and then, if the pack had any love left for you at all, someone would come to challenge you this night. But Elena and Natalie surely must hate you for the shame you've brought upon them, and you cannot imagine either possessing the merest scrap of affection for you. But they *have* come, although to offer you a far more terrible challenge than combat.

Elena's smile broadens, displaying her sharp teeth.

"Kill this boy, eat his flesh and drink his blood. Prove to us that you are still worthy of being Moonborn, and I will give you your Final Challenge."

Hearing these words, the boy starts screaming behind the tape. He thrashes, arms and legs flailing, but Natalie's foot holds him firm to the ground. You look at the boy, and you wonder where Elena and Natalie found him. Is his family aware that he's missing? Are they frantically calling friends and neighbors, hoping that someone—any-one—knows where he is?

"I told you he wouldn't do it," Natalie says, mouth curled into a sneer. "He's nothing but a simpering dog, afraid to follow his instincts, too afraid to be what nature made him."

"I am what I choose to be," you say.

"You're a coward." Natalie practically spits this last word.

"If you *choose* not to kill the boy," Elena says, "I'll kill him here, in front of you, and leave his corpse to keep you company. Mother and I will go, and no one in the pack will ever offer to challenge you. You will continue to weaken until you die, alone, and no one will sing your death-song."

"Although if you want to hurry up the process, you could always kill yourself," Natalie says. "It would be a fitting end for you."

Your people can heal any wound—even those caused by silver, despite what the legends claim—but an injury caused by the teeth and claws of one of your kind will prove fatal if it's serious enough. This includes self-inflicted injuries. One swipe of your claws across your throat, and you'd bleed to death in moments. Suicide is considered the ultimate expression of weakness among the Moonborn, and if you take this route, you will be reviled by the pack for generations. You tell yourself you don't care what they think, but you know it's a lie.

Elena's face softens then. "We're giving you a chance to reclaim your honor and restore ours. Take it. *Please.*"

You understand then that Elena and Natalie haven't brought the boy to you as a taunt or punishment, at least that's not their only reason. Elena is doing for you what you once did for her. You wanted to usher her into the full life of the Moonborn, and now she wants to bring you back to it. She sees the boy as a gift, not as a person with his own life to live, his own destiny to fulfill.

You look at the boy once more. You've saved hundreds of lives by not killing humans these last three decades. It wasn't easy to abstain, for despite your desire to cause no harm to humans, the temptation—the *craving*—for their meat was always there. You learned to live with the hunger, but it was a struggle to keep it in check. You deserve a proper end to your life, just as any Moonborn does, and it's only *one* boy...

You feel the change come upon you, so swift there's barely any transition between your two forms. You gain height and mass, gray fur sprouts across your entire body, your hands become large and clawed, your face lengthens, teeth sharpen, ears become pointed. Your coat and shirt are too tight now, and you tear them off and drop them next to the fire. A corner of your shirt catches flame and the cloth begins to burn.

The boy absolutely loses his shit at the sight of your true form. His eyes grow so wide it looks as if they might pop out of his head, and a corner of the tape over his mouth has come loose, and when he screams, the sound is loud and shrill and echoes throughout the clearing. Natalie looks stunned, as if she thought you didn't have it in you, while Elena cries happy tears, believing her father is about to reclaim his place in the pack and redeem himself.

You snarl, leap over the fire, and attack.

WHEN IT'S OVER, you take human form again. You're covered in blood, some of it yours, most of it not. Elena and Natalie lie on the ground, bodies savaged beyond recognition. The wounds they inflicted upon you burn like hell, but during the battle you swallowed some of their meat and blood—more out of reflex than anything else—and you feel stronger than you have in years, alive and vital.

The boy is gone. Once Natalie's foot was off his back, he sprang to his feet and ran for the trees, screaming the whole way. You don't know where he is right now, but you'll find him. You'll do your best to calm him, and then you will lead him to town, where hopefully he will be able to find his way back to his family. You can't really show up on their doorstep to deliver him, shirtless and covered with blood. After this, you'll return to your trailer to clean yourself, get fresh clothes, and then you'll set out again. You've realized something this night. You may have saved some humans by refusing to eat their flesh, but that didn't stop the rest of the pack from continuing to prey on them. You could have—*should* have—done more these last thirty years, and while there's nothing you can do about that now, there is something you can do moving forward. You will hunt the Moonborn and make sure they never hurt anyone ever again. And when you're finished killing your pack, you'll move on to another, and another after that. You will become a greater monster than any of them could ever be—a monster's monster—and Moonborn parents will tell their cubs stories about you to frighten them into behaving. *Be good, or the Gray Hunter will get you.*

You smile at the thought.

You gaze upon the bodies of your wife and daughter one last time.

"Thanks," you say, breath misting on the cold night air, and then you begin walking.

SHE-CREATURE FROM THE GOLDEN COVE

JOHN PALISANO

IT'S ALMOST IMPOSSIBLE to capture so much beauty in one shot." Lou's father clamped a hand on his shoulder. "But if anyone can do it, my money's on you, kid."

Lining up the frame in his viewfinder, Louis panned right just enough to make sure he got the striking blue Grecian water behind his mother, too. "Do you have all of me, Louis?" she asked, tipping her head and hat back just a bit, her smile wide, her eyes shut just a bit as though she were laughing. "You always look like a star, mom," he said. "The brightest one in the sky. Even during the middle of the day." He clicked the shutter on his handheld stereo camera, knowing the moment could pass in a blink, especially when shooting on the water.

She laughed, deep. "You should be my agent." Pointing at his dad, she nodded. "You can learn a thing or two from the way he talks to a woman."

"Indeed, I should," he said, gliding toward her as smooth as Gene Kelly. "Did I tell you this was going to be as beautiful as you, or what?"

He turned on the charm physically, too, taking her hands and giving her a dip.

Louis snapped a shot, his small Realist camera quiet and unobtrusive. He couldn't wait to see how the pictures would turn out, especially in 3D.

Greece was the most beautiful place they'd been—so different from the endless fields and roads of their San Fernando valley home.

"You're probably never going to see a blue like this ever again in your lives," his father pronounced in his biggest, boomiest producer's voice. "So, get a good look now. We're talking once in a lifetime." Louis felt transfixed as the bright sparkles of the Grecian Sea led toward the cove. Seemingly glowing from within—its very walls and ceiling all radiating an ethereal blue—Louis was sure they were sailing right inside the world's largest gemstone.

Unimpressed, his mother—the one and only Luna Safira—forced a half-smile and cocked her wide-brimmed hat just a bit downward as if shielding herself from another parade of photo flashes at one of the endless premieres from Grauman's Chinese or Egyptian. The famous actress wife of Mathew Lockwood, producer of a string of Hollywood hits, arriving to celebrate the latest cinematic marvel. Only they weren't on Hollywood Boulevard—they were floating a world away. You can take the girl out of Kansas, as they say.

"Wow, would you look at that," Louis proclaimed, mimicking the high-pitched cadence of his favorite actors. "This doesn't even seem real. It's like something you'd see on the backlot from an H.G. Wells picture or something."

"Better than that," Louis's father said. "You can always see the seams on those. See the structures when you go round or just too far to either side. This is…real."

Louis took after his father in that he was much more versed in the practicalities and realities of making films. "Dad? You should think of something to film here. The production values are built in. You wouldn't even need to bring lights. The new high-speed Technicolor film stock would be able to capture it." He pulled out his light meter—a gift for his sixteenth birthday along with the stereographic camera—and took a reading. "Just as I suspected. It's 'F 5.6' everywhere. Perfect. It'll be clear as a bell."

"That's quite clever of you," Lockwood said, proud of his boy. He'd taken to photography, just as he had. Louis knew his father's story by heart. After the Great War ended, Lockwood grew to be an agent for cinematographers and then grew again, finding himself a producer on some low-budget pictures that did better than they should have. He found Luna during that time, too.

Taking photos had taken a backseat. He missed it. Terribly. The trip was a promise to his family to rekindle that part of him. He even promised Luna many sittings. "The light in Greece is among the most flattering in the world. We'll have pictures of you that will rival any of the best of 'em!" She'd liked that. Even smiled as he hadn't seen from her in ages.

They putted along toward the island's cave. "Look at how still the water is. Even the ripples from the *Athena* die out and flatten not so far from the hull," his father said. "We've come upon one of the most perfect tides I've ever experienced." Louis thought the sea felt so calm it was as though it wasn't even part of the same body of water as the churning, massive force they'd made it through only days earlier. He turned around a moment to the top of the yacht to spy Captain Hansen, hand on the wheel, eyes locked straight ahead.

"We've earned this," Lockwood said. "It's God's way of blessing us for all we've done and for working so hard the last ten years."

———

THE BRIGHT SUN turned to shadow as they entered the mouth of the island's cave. "The entire ship can fit inside here," Louis said. "Wow." He was so impressed he forgot about his camera for a moment. The cave smelled of minerals and salt even more so than the sea.

They rounded a small bend and could no longer see back out to the ocean. Louis looked up at the cave's roof, putting the average height at about eighty meters. He'd gotten good at estimating distances from his photography. The cave didn't feel claustrophobic at all, though, which surprised him. Once his eyes adjusted, he realized the illumination was lower, but it remained the same pleasant turquoise. It reflected off the water and seemed to paint the entire cave in its hue. The effect was remarkable and beyond beautiful. He'd never have believed water could look such a way had he not been experiencing it for himself.

"Old Mickey was right," his father proclaimed. "Something to see if you're ever over there. There's an inside like nothing else on Earth." He'd heard of the string of small islands with caves from Mickey Star, the lead in his World War II drama *The Shore*. They'd heard the story many times before embarking on the trip, enough that no one replied. Intrigued by the actor's tale, Mathew Lockwood insisted he'd have to see it at some point…believed it'd be something to bring the family together. His instinct had been right. The trip had been the right idea—the perfect solution to put the spark back into their family in order to recharge and reconnect them.

The stunning blue color changed to yellow…no…gold.

Brighter.

Impossibly so.

Louis craned his head upward, expecting to see a hole at the top of the cave, the sun visible above, shining down its full power. But there was no gap. No sunlight. Nothing to easily explain the phenomenon. The inner cove seemed illuminated from within by some invisible force. Lining up a shot, Louis was careful to frame a large outcropping in the foreground to show off the depth.

They all had to shield their eyes, though, as the brightness seemed to increase tenfold. The *Athena* slowed as it entered a large crescent-shaped cove. Painted in strong golden light, the cove reminded Louis of the elaborate churches they'd seen in Spain the week before, only with the walls being made of rock instead of plaster and wood. The gold light seemed warmer, reminding him of stepping into the throw of a line of Mole Richardson lights on set. He half expected to see a key grip or a gaffer somewhere just behind a rock ledge, barely sneaking an eye around the corner.

To the starboard side, Louis spotted a small sandy shore. Upon it, not very far from its crest, rested a vessel not unlike their own. He eyed a trail of debris near the small boat. *Doesn't look too old. Looks... fresh.* The paint on the wood hadn't yet faded, nor did the hardware seem dull and spotted as it would had it been sitting unattended for months or years. It glistened. "Look at that. A wreck," he said, as much to himself as to his family. "We should look for survivors."

The *Athena* stopped. "Shall we drop anchor?" cried Captain Hansen.

"Yes, good sir," his father hollered back over his shoulder. "Seems we have a shipwreck."

"Watch out," Hansen called from above them, the anchor's chains rattling as it descended. It splashed and clunked into the shallow sand. Better to be sure it was secured, even though the waters remained still. The seas could change in a matter of seconds, the difference could be losing the boat or not. The thought of losing the yacht and being stranded within the cove frightened Louis. None of them were terribly adept swimmers, after all. Once upon a time, his mother would have referred to herself as a water fiend, but it'd been years. Decades, even. His laps in their pool a few times a week would hardly qualify him to head an at-sea rescue. He felt chills just thinking about it.

The boat stopped rocking as it settled. Louis eyed the line connecting the boat to the anchor and, seeing it taut, knew they were safe.

The benches inside looked intact. A single oar stretched across one side. Other than a huge crack in its hull, the boat appeared in relatively good shape. The thing he was most looking for and expecting—signs of life or death—were absent his immediate glance.

As his gaze traversed the wreck, Louis spotted what looked like tracks in the sand close to the wreck. He eyed the path, following them upward to where they disappeared behind an outcropping.

Movement.

Something from behind the outcropping.

A flash of light reflected off something he couldn't identify.

He expected the worst.

A single hand walked around the edge of the outcropping, its thin, elegant fingers like those of a crab's legs.

Then a face as pure as the golden sunlight of the cove peered at him. Its eyes shone in a different but equally striking blue as the ocean water. Its skin was as reflective as the movie screens at all the film houses. His mind raced. Didn't they add aluminum or silver to the paint to make them more reflective? Little glass beads? It was as though her skin had been given the same treatment. And it was most definitely a woman, he could tell, as she stepped from behind the rocks, her feminine form and movement elegant and gentle in a way he'd only seen from women.

The woman, pale and thin, stood near the top of the small beach. Still and as regal as a statue, her flowing light hair didn't seem to move. For a moment, it was difficult to tell that she wore anything as the color of her dress was as light as her skin.

His parents waved. Louis winced. Somehow, the cove seemed even brighter. He checked his light meter to try and get a reading, but it was too bright to see the dial. *My arm for a pair of sunglasses,* he thought.

Onshore, the lost woman had stepped closer. Louis had been distracted by the goings-on aboard and had missed her walking.

"Miss?" his mother called out to the woman. "Are you alone? Are you all right?"

She didn't answer. She didn't even appear to blink or to register his mother's voice.

"Poor thing's probably in shock," his father said. "We can send over the raft."

"Yes," his mother said.

Louis observed his parents and thought they looked like movie stars, especially his mother. The gold light softened her skin. Her characteristic cheekbones kept their definition but were smoothed in a way even the best makeup artists couldn't have accomplished. Not even the best cinematography crews would have been able to light her quite as well, he was sure. Louis was nervous, though, for a reason he couldn't figure. Something was just off.

The lost woman stepped toward them. The bottoms of her feet were not visible as they were sunk into the sand. She wore a long flowing frock with a matching white fringe that started near her middle and fanned and moved in a way that made it look like she was walking underwater.

"We can send a boat over to you, dear," his mother said.

She moved faster as she approached the water. His father shook his head. "She's not stopping, is she?"

In a blink, the lost woman was in the blue water, then underneath and out of sight.

"Where did she go?" his mother asked.

"I don't know, Luna," his father said. He turned and put a hand to his mouth, shouting to Captain Hansen. "Eyes on the girl?"

"No, sir," Captain Hansen said.

It was then Louis noticed they were not the only spectators. Other men hung over the railings of the *Athena*, watching the scene unfold. It was like a crew monitoring a set, Louis thought.

"Anyone see her?" Captain Hansen called.

None had.

A man's scream pierced the air, echoing off the cave walls. The crewmen looked to each other for a moment, off guard. Where'd it come from?

They raced toward the other side of the yacht. Louis and his parents did the same.

An arm reached out from the water, its fingers splayed. Foam and bubbles. The hand pulled underwater in a blink. A moment later, a last large bubble surfaced and broke.

"She got 'im!" one of them yelled. Their voices became a chorus of hysteria.

Lockwood waved frantically toward the captain. "Get us out of here!" he commanded. "Now."

The anchor chains were so loud as they were retracted that Louis had to cover his ears; he stared down at his camera hanging from its wrist loop. The anchor was pulled up and hit the side of the yacht harder than he'd expected.

Meanwhile, several crewmen had taken up whatever arms they could. A spear. A large fishing hook. Pocket knives. They all stood at attention surrounding the deck.

"What is happening?" his mother asked.

"We need to go inside," his father said. "Now."

His father's hand on his back, nearly shoving him inside, Louis tried to look around to see the lost woman. He didn't. "Come on," his father urged. "Don't stall." Louis's heart felt hollow from fear. His legs were weak, and his temperature seemed to run hot and cold at the same time.

Someone had just died. One of the men from the boat. Their boat. The crew was small, numbering maybe eight total.

Could that woman from the shore have drowned him?

Inside the main cabin, his father kept them moving along. "Into the stateroom," he said as they passed the main lounge and entered the long hallway that ran the center of the yacht. The ship moved beneath them, and they all shook from it. "What's going on, Matt?" his mother asked.

"We can't be certain," he said. "I need you both safe."

There were no other men inside the hallway with them. Louis hoped he'd see one or two guarding either side, but they were alone.

Finally, they made it into their main room.

What had seemed luxurious earlier felt vulnerable. Rushing toward the windows, his father shut them. "Stay away from the outside," he demanded as he checked the locks. "Don't even peek." He pulled the curtains across, the view of the golden cove closing like at the end of a show at one of the big Hollywood movie houses. They were the same red and had the same type of gold rope and tiebacks, too.

The boat swayed and tilted. His mother had taken a seat at their round dining table. She held onto the table as she sat, steadying herself. "Come," she said to Louis. "Sit with me." He did as she asked, and happily so. "Mathew?" she said to his father, who paced the room. "Won't you sit, too?"

"This is not the time to relax," he said. "One of our men is missing."

Everything tilted hard and his father scrambled to keep his footing, but still ended up half-sprawled across the closest bed. Had the chairs and table not been built-in, Louis and his mother would have tumbled, too. "Jeez Louise!" his father cried. "What are they doing?"

They heard the hollers from the men, muffled and loud, even through the walls of the *Athena*. He recognized Captain Hansen's voice, barked out commands, even if he couldn't distinguish the actual words.

The *Athena* righted and they felt her move, the sound of her engine roaring. "Here we go," said Lockwood. He went to the windows and peeked behind the curtain. Louis glimpsed the golden walls of the cave rush past, blurry like an out-of-focus shot.

My camera, he thought, looked down, and raised his hand. It looked fine at first, but he noticed a piece broken loose as it dangled from its wrist loop. He was aghast to find it was one of the stereoscopic lenses. "Oh, no," he said. He tried to see if the lens would fit back on easily. It wouldn't. The retaining ring had cracked.

His mother saw his plight. "Don't worry, dear. We'll get you another camera once we're onshore."

"That'll do, but I sure hope the film is all right inside," he said. He examined it and saw the iris of the shutter behind the lens remained shut. "Should be, that is."

They weren't going more than a few minutes when they heard someone shout, "Hold," from the foredeck.

His father looked out the window again. "What's going on now?" he asked. "I can't see anything." The light had gone from gold to blue; they'd left the golden inner cove, at least.

The *Athena* slowed and stopped.

"Should we go and check?" Louis asked his father.

He waved him off. "We're not leaving this room until we know it's safe."

His mother covered his left hand with her right. "It's going to be fine, Louis," she said, her voice soothing. She always knew when he was upset, and always knew just what to say.

"Thanks, Mom," he replied. "You're right. It will."

A knock made him jump. "Mister Lockwood? Are you in there?" Louis didn't recognize the voice.

His father went to the door. "Yes," he said as he went to open it. "We're in here."

A young man stood in the doorway. "There's something blocking the entrance," he said. "Or rather several somethings. Seems some boulders must have fallen since we came inside the cave."

"How can that be?" his father asked. "That seems impossible."

ON THE FOREDECK, the Lockwoods peered out at the three large boulders. "It's like a huge beaver dam," Louis said. "How did it happen so fast?"

"Earthquake?" his father said as much as asked. "Who knows."

"Wouldn't we have felt it?" Louis prodded.

"Maybe not. The water could have absorbed the shock." His father didn't sound like he believed himself. His face was scrunched up with worry—the same way it did when he was reading *Variety* and *The Hollywood Reporter* to check the returns on his pictures.

Three of the crewmen had scaled the rock ledges near the entrance and seemed busy examining the boulders. Louis couldn't think what they'd be looking for. He did recognize the entrance, though. It'd been the same as from where they'd come less than an hour before. "Aren't they afraid that…lady…will come back?" he asked.

"I don't know if they are," his father said, "but I am. Stay close."

"Maybe we shouldn't be out here," his mother added. "Maybe she had something to do with this."

His father didn't say anything. That was usually a sign that someone had just delivered bad news. His mother was right, Louis thought. It'd make sense. "We're like fish in a barrel," he said. "They've got us trapped."

Hours passed. A plan was hatched to use a fishing net to move one of the boulders. The crewmen threw it over the smallest. Two ropes trailed from the net and connected to the huge winch on the port side of the *Athena*. She wasn't a fishing vessel per se but had the ability to provide fresh food for longer sojourns.

They watched as the winch turned, the ropes tightened, and blessedly, the boulder moved a little at first, then enough to send it toppling down into the water. "Cut the line!" someone yelled. Two ran toward the rope with knives and sawed. When it snapped, one nearly lost his head. The risk paid off.

"Do you think we're going to fit through that?" Louis asked.

"Barely," his mother replied. "Hopefully enough to get us out of here." She wrapped a large towel around him.

Light faded. The sun was setting. The crewmen hurried back to the decks, hurriedly jumping aboard via the rolling walkway. Once they were all accounted for, the *Athena* rolled forward, slowly.

Everyone held their breath when she passed through. A loud screeching sound kept them alert. The fit was tight, and she suffered a long scratch to her port side on account of a jutting bit of rock, but the damage was superficial.

As the last fingers of sunlight stretched across the sea in front of them, the *Athena* slipped from the mouth of the cave and sailed again on open water.

His mother retreated to their cabin while he stood with his father. Louis couldn't help but look back at the island that had almost taken them.

She stood above the mouth, on the fore of the upper cliff, her eyes staring right into him, he knew.

"Dad…"

He tugged his father's elbow.

"Yes?"

Louis pointed. "She's watching us."

His father turned in time to see the lost woman duck and seem to blend into the background.

"Did you see her? Dad? Did you?"

His father nodded. "Aye," he said. "And hope she's on that island to stay."

Louis looked around to see if anyone else on board had spotted her. They were alone on deck.

"There. Look." His father pointed then. Not one but several forms moved over the face of the cliff. "And now we know how those rocks got moved."

They cruised until the sky darkened and the stars flickered. Moonlight lit their path, its reflection on the water like a long distorted road, disappearing into a vanishing point somewhere over the horizon. Louis and his father kept to the foredeck. "Do you think we should check on mom?" he asked.

Without looking at his son, his father said, "I think we should let her be alone. She's been through enough."

They both watched the sea and the sky, silent for several minutes.

"What we saw today," Louis said. "That woman…"

His father turned; the line of his jaw clenched. "The sea has many secrets we don't yet understand. Best we don't mess with them if I'm to be asked." He put a hand to his son's shoulder. "I'm just grateful that you and your mother…and all of us…are now safe."

"Do you think we're safe now?" Louis didn't feel safe. Not one bit. Not even after sailing nonstop for a few hours. "Shouldn't we be getting close to land again soon?"

"Aye, son, we should be. I should go check in with Mr. Hansen," he said.

"I'll go to the room," Louis said.

His father shook his head. "Let your mother be," he demanded. "She needs her rest."

"Then…I'll go with you?"

"Stay here, kiddo," his father said. "You won't be out of my eye. I'll just go up to the captain's. We'll see you plain as day."

"All right." Louis watched his father strut away, his slight limp showing itself. He knew it was all code so his father could share a quick drink out of his mom's eye. Thinking his father needed it, he still felt nervous. The way the people…those things…moved. The way they were able to move those boulders in so short a time! Why, surely they could swim…

He stopped himself thinking. It'd do him no good. His father would curse him if he ran up and disturbed his moment just for spooking himself. He had strict orders not to disturb his mother, too. More than anything, he wished one of the crew would come out on their rounds. Maybe see him alone. Take pity on him. Talk to him. Stay with him. But no one came. He watched the captain's window until he saw his father enter. Shake hands. Share a laugh. Men's men, he thought. Wondered if he'd ever grow up to be like them.

Something cold touched his forearm. No. Grabbed. So sudden! He didn't yell or scream or make any noise at all. He pulled away, recoiling like a snake, but it was no use. He'd been caught. She'd found them. *It* had found them.

Slinking up and directly in front of him, the lost woman of the cove looked right into his eyes. As dark as night and as endless as the void, its gaze deep inside him was only broken when it blinked twice, its lids as big as tea plates, moving side to side instead of up and down.

Her head turned to the side just a little, eyeing him. She looked both human and of the sea, with moon-shaped flaps of flesh under her neck flexing. At the edges of her skin, moonlight shone through enough to make her seem translucent to a degree. Her mouth seemed shaped like a woman's when it was closed, but when she opened it, the hinge was far greater than that of any human's. Rows of small, sharp teeth rimmed her inner gums; saliva stretched in tethers between the top and bottom. Louis knew then what had befallen the man they'd taken back at the cove, ripped and pierced by its teeth.

Her hair appeared fine and light-colored, although it looked closer to seagrass in texture. She wore a thin dress—or was it truly a long, elegant fin as delicate as crepe paper, wrapped around to give the appearance of clothing?

At first glance, she looked like a beautiful woman. With scrutiny, and up close, it was obvious she was not.

She pulled his arm and he realized she had both his forearms. How'd he miss that? Was he so shocked and transfixed by her?

He lost his footing and fell forward against the rail. A surprised sound escaped his mouth—a noise he'd never made before.

He heard his name. Shouted. Screamed.

Felt hands upon him.

"Louis!"

His mother's voice. She'd come!

How could she? Wasn't she in the room?

There she was, though, pulling at her child with every motherly strength she could summon.

The lost woman let go, no match for his mother. Louis felt himself fly backward. For a moment, he felt weightless and very much the same as when he'd first dive into water. He landed on his rear and nearly cantilevered onto his side. "Mom!"

An image of her developed like a snapshot in his mind. She stood, arms tight to her side, her eyes on him, the outline of her striking profile against the moonlight. Things crawled up and over her body...moving, living things that bound her...appendages from the water woman wrapping his mother like a spider spinning something unlucky.

Her mouth opened. Did she say his name? Ask for help? He couldn't tell. Frozen with fear and shock.

"Luna!"

His father's voice filled the deck. His heavy steps as he ran. The creature looked at him and, in one swoop, lifted his mother up and away, over the railing and silently into the sea below.

Lockwood raced to the rail, grabbed it with both hands, leaned over, screamed his wife's name.

Louis got up. Joined his father. Searched the formless sea and saw nothing but waves and wake. "Mom!" he yelled over and over. "Luna! Luna!"

The crew came.

The *Athena* stopped.

His father jumped into the water, screaming for her, yelling and pleading, but she was not to be found. Even as several others jumped in with life preservers and lines, the night's efforts brought no trace of her.

As the sun came up, Louis watched as two men helped his water-logged father back aboard the deck. The strength of the godlike man Louis had known was gone; he stumbled like a drunk, collapsing onto a lounge, his eyes shut, his body limp.

Captain Hansen came for Louis and brought him to their cabin. "Stay in here, boy, until we come for you." Louis fell asleep that morning to the sound of the *Athena's* engine starting up.

———

THE REST REMAINS a blur. He can't recall how much longer they stayed in Greece. Knows there was a search party. Remembers them calling it off. His father had no emotion. Blank. Can't remember anything they said after. They flew back to Los Angeles.

His father never mentioned what happened again. Taking the cue, Louis kept it to himself, too. So, too, did he keep the prints he had made from the trip. He could look at them only once after he received them, tucking them into a folder behind his books.

———

IT'S DECADES LATER.

The screening room stays dark during the entire film. Louis wants to turn to look at his father—wants to see what he's thinking—but all he will risk is a glance out of the corner of his eye.

He'd cast the woman purposely, using the stereographic of his mother as a guide. The actress was uncanny. Louis had made sure to provide the cinematographer with extensive notes as to lighting and exposure.

Only when her hand grasps the railing of the ship does his father look away. He averts his gaze the entire rest of the scene and does not look back again until it passes. His jaw clenches. Louis is sure he'd lost his father.

The final reel unspools.

A rescue crew, led by the family, finds their missing mother deep within a golden cove, defeats her captor, and brings her back to safety.

As the lights come up, his father blots his eyes with a handkerchief. Louis helps him into the wheelchair parked at the end of the aisle.

He rolls his father out into the sunlight sparkling down on the Buena Aqua pictures backlot. So bright it is blinding.

"So, what'd you think, Dad?" he asks, finally.

His Dad looks up at his son, the slightest smile beaming. "I got to see your mother again in that picture. My Luna." He clamps a hand on his shoulder, his fingers as strong as they were when Louis was a kid. "And I got to see you up there, too, kiddo." He turns his face up toward the sky...the most striking blue...the shade of which he hasn't seen for so many years...somehow the same color they'd seen in Greece...and far away the sun is just about to set, golden lines of light stretch from behind the San Gabriel mountains, over the suburbs of the Valley until it touches and glistens off the metal handle of his wheelchair...and he turns his hand upward so that it looks as though he catches it for a moment. He clutches his fingers, holds them tight for a moment, then opens them and lets the golden light go.

DREAMS

F. PAUL WILSON

THE NIGHTMARE AGAIN.

I almost dread falling asleep. Always the same, and yet never quite the same. The events differ dream to dream, yet always I am in a stranger's body—a huge, monstrous, patchwork contraption that reels through the darkness in such ungainly fashion. It's always dark in the dream, for I seem to be a creature of the night, forever in hiding.

And I can't remember my name.

The recent dreams are well formed. My head has cleared in them. So unlike the early dreams, which I can barely remember. Those are no more than a montage of blurred images now—a lightning-drenched laboratory, a whip-wielding hunchback, *fear*, a stone-walled cell, chains, *loneliness*, a little girl drowning among floating blossoms, a woman in a wedding gown, townsfolk with torches, fire, a burning windmill, *pain, rage, PAIN!*

But I'm all right now. Scarred but healing. And my mind is clear. The pain from the fire burned away the mists. I remember things from dream to dream, and more and more bits and pieces from long ago.

Illustration by MISTER SAM SHEARON »

But what is my name?

I know I must stay out of sight. I don't want to be burned again. That's why I spend the daylight hours hiding here in the loft of this abandoned stable on the outskirts of Goldstadt. I sleep most of the day. But at night I wander. Always into town. Always to the area around the Goldstadt Medical College. I seem to be attracted to the medical college. The reason rests here in my brain, but it scampers beyond my grasp whenever I reach for it. One day I'll catch it and then I'll know.

So many unanswered questions in these dreams. But aren't dreams supposed to be that way? Don't they pose more questions than they answer?

My belly is full now. I broke into a pastry shop and gorged myself on the unsold sweets left over from yesterday, and now I'm wandering the back alleys, drinking from rain barrels, peering from the shadows into the lighted windows I pass. I feel a warm resonance within when I see a family together by a fire. Once I must have had a life like that. But the warmth warps into rage if I watch too long, because I know such a scene will never be mine again.

I know it's only a dream. But the rage is so real.

As I pass the rear of a tavern, the side door opens and two men step out. I stumble farther back into the shadows, wanting to run but knowing I'd make a terrible racket. No one must see me. No one must know I'm alive. So I stay perfectly still, waiting for them to leave.

That's when I hear the voice. The deep, delicious voice of a handsome young man with curly blond hair and fresh clear skin. I know this without seeing him. I even know his name.

Karl.

I lean to my right and peer down the alley. My heart leaps at the sight of him. It's not *my* heart; it's the huge, ponderous heart of a stranger, but it responds nonetheless, thudding madly in my chest.

I listen to his clear, rich laughter as he waves good-bye to his friend and strolls away toward the street.

Karl.

Why do I know him?

I follow. I know it's dangerous, but I must. But I don't go down the alley after him. Instead I lumber along in the back alleys, splattering through puddles, scattering rats, dodging stinking piles of trash as I keep pace with him, catching sight of his golden-haired form between buildings as he strides along.

He's not heading for home. Somewhere in my head I know where he lives, and he's headed in the wrong direction. I follow him to a cottage at the north end of Goldstadt, watch him knock, watch a raven-haired beauty open the door and leap into his arms, watch them disappear inside. I know her too.

Maria.

The rage spewing up in me is nearly as uncontainable as it is unexplainable. It's all I can do to keep myself from bursting through that door and tearing them both apart.

Why? What are these emotions? Who are these people? And why do I know their names and not my own?

I cool. I wait. But Karl doesn't reappear. The sky lightens and still no Karl. I must leave before I am seen. As I head back toward the stable that has become my nest, my rage is gone, replaced by a cold black despair. Before I climb to the loft, I pause to relieve myself. As I lower my heavy, crudely stitched pants I pray that it will be different this dream, but there it is—that long, thick, slack member hanging between my legs. It repulses me. I try to relieve myself without touching it.

I am a woman. Why do these dreams place me in the body of a man?

Awake again.

I've spent the day talking, laughing, discussing the wisdom of the ages. Such a relief to be back to reality, back in my own body—young, lithe, smaller, smoother, with slim legs, dainty fingers, and firm, compact breasts. So good to be a woman again.

But my waking hours aren't completely free from confusion. I'm not sure where I am. I do know that it's warm and beautiful. Grassy knolls flow green through the golden sunshine toward the majestic amethyst-hued mountains that tower in the distance. Sweet little hummingbirds dart about in the hazy spring air.

And at least when I'm awake I know my name: Eva. Eva Rucker.

I just wish I knew why I was here. Don't misunderstand. I love it here. It's everything I've ever wanted. Friendly people wandering the hills, wise men stopping by to discuss the great philosophies of the ages. It's like the Elysian Fields I read about in Greek mythology, except I'm alive and this is all real. I simply don't know what I've done to deserve this.

I have a sense that I was brought here as compensation for an unpleasantness in my past. I seem to remember some recent ugliness in which I was unwittingly involved, unjustly accused, something so darkly traumatic that my mind shies from the memory of it. But the wrong was righted and I've been sent here to recuperate.

I think of Karl and how he became part of my dream last night. Karl…so handsome, so brilliant, so dashing. I haven't thought of him since I arrived here. How could I forget the man I love?

A cloud passes across the sun as my thoughts darken with the memory of the dream-Karl in the dream-Maria's arms. Maria is Karl's sister! They would *never!*

How perverse these nightmares! I shouldn't let them upset me.

The sun reemerges as I push the memory away. It's wonderful here. I never want to leave. But I'm tired now. The golden wine I had with dinner has made me drowsy. I'll just lie back and rest my eyes for a moment…

Oh, no! The dream again!

I'm in that horrid body, stumbling through the night. Can't I close my eyes even for a few seconds without falling into this nightmare? I want to scream, to burst from this cocoon of dream and return to my golden fields. But the nightmare tightens its steely grip and I lurch on.

I stop at a schoolhouse. I'm hungry but there's something more important than food inside. I break down the door and enter the single classroom with its rows of tiny desks. I rip the top off one desk after the other and carry it to the shafts of moonlight pouring through the windows until I find the paper and pencil I seek. I bring them to the teacher's desk. I'm too large to seat myself, so I kneel beside the desk and force my huge, ungainly fingers to grasp the pencil and write.

I know this is a dream, but still I feel compelled to let the dream-Karl know that even though my body has metamorphosed into this monstrosity, his Eva still cares for him.

After many tries, I manage a legible note:

KARL

I LOVE YOU

YOUR EVA

I fold the sheet and take it with me. At Karl's uncle's house—where Karl lives—I slip it under the door. Then I stand back in the shadows and wait. And as I wait, I remember more and more about Karl.

We met near the University of Goldstadt where he was a student at the Medical College. That was in my real life. I assume he remains a student in my dreams. I so wanted to attend the University, but the Regents wouldn't hear of it. They were scandalized by my application.

No women in the College of Arts and Sciences, and especially in the Medical College. *Especially* not a poor farm girl.

So I'd hide in the rear of the lecture halls and listen to Dr. Waldman's lectures on anatomy and physiology. Karl found me there but kept my secret and let me stay. I fell in love with him immediately. I remember that. I remember all our secret meetings, in fields, in lofts. He'd teach me what he learned in class. And then he'd teach me other things. We became lovers. I'd never given myself to any man before. Karl was the first, and I swear he'll be the only one. I don't remember how we became separated. I—

Here he comes. Oh, look at him! I want to run to him, but I couldn't bear for him to see me like this. What torture this nightmare is!

I watch him enter his uncle's house, see him light the candles in the entryway. I move closer as he picks up my note and reads it. But no loving smile lights his features. Instead, his face blanches and he totters back against the wall. Then he's out the door and running, flying through the streets, my note clutched in his hand. I follow him as best I can, but he outdistances me. No matter. I know the route. I sense where he's going.

When I arrive at Maria's house he's already inside. I lurch to a lighted window and peer within. Karl stands in the center of the room, his eyes wild, the ruddy color still gone from his cheeks. Maria has her arms around his waist. She's smiling as she comforts him.

"—only a joke," she says. "Can't you see that, my love? Someone's trying to play a trick on you!"

"Then it's a damn good trick!" Karl holds my note before her eyes. "This is how she always signed her notes—'Your Eva.' No one else knew that. Not even you. And I burned all those letters."

Maria laughs. "So what are you telling me? That Eva wrote you this note? That's certainly not her handwriting."

"True, but—"

"Eva is dead, my love."

The words strike like hammer blows to my brain. I want to shout that I'm here, alive, transformed into this creature. But I keep silent. I have no workable voice. And after all, this is only a dream. I must keep telling myself that.

Only a dream.

Nothing here is true and therefore none of it matters.

Yet I find a horrid fascination in it.

"They hung her," Maria is saying. "I know because I went and watched. You couldn't stomach it, but I went to see for myself." Her smile fades as an ugly light grows in her eyes. "They *hung* her, Karl. Hung her till she stopped kicking and swung limp in the breeze. Then they cut her down and took her off to the Medical College just as she requested. The noble little thing: Wanted her body donated to science. Well, by now she's in a thousand little pieces."

"I know." Karl's color is returning, but his flush seems more a shade of guilt than good health. "I saw her brain, Maria. Eva's brain! Dr. Waldman kept it in a glass jar on one of the lab tables as an example of an abnormal brain. 'Dysfunctio Cerebri,' his label said, right next to a supposedly normal brain. I had to sit there during all his lectures and stare at it, knowing the whole time who it had belonged to, and that it was not abnormal in the least."

"It should have been labeled a 'stupid' brain." Maria laughs. "She believed you loved her. She thought I was your sister. She believed everything we told her, and so she wound up taking the blame for your uncle's murder. As a result, you're rich and you don't ever have to think about her again. She's gone."

"Her brain's gone, too. I was so glad when pranksters stole it and I no longer had to look at it."

"Now you can look at me."

Maria steps back and unbuttons her blouse, baring her breasts. As

Karl locks her in an embrace, I reel away from the window, sobbing, retching, running blindly for the stables I call home.

Awake again.

Back in my Elysian fields, but still I cannot shake off the effects of the nightmare. The dream-Maria's words have roused memories in my waking mind. They are partly true.

How could I have forgotten?

There was a murder. Karl's rich uncle. And I was accused. I remember now...remember that night. I was supposed to meet Karl at the house. He was going to introduce me to his uncle and bring our love out into the open at last. But when I got there, the door was open and a portly old man lay on the floor, bleeding, dying. I tried to help him, but he had lost too much blood. Then the Burgomeister's men arrived and found me with the slain man's blood on my hands and the knife that had killed him at my feet.

And Karl was nowhere to be found.

I never saw Karl again. He never came to visit me. Never answered my notes. In fact, his barrister came to the jail and told me to stop writing to Karl—that Karl didn't know who I was and wanted nothing to do with the murderer of his uncle.

No one believed that I knew Karl. No one but his sister Maria had ever seen us together, and Maria said I was a complete stranger. I remember the final shock when I was told that Maria wasn't his sister at all.

After that, the heart went out of me. I gave up. I lost the will to defend myself. I let them do with me as they wished. My only request was that my body be given to the Medical College. That was my private joke on the Regents—I would be attending the University after all.

I remember walking to the gallows. I remember the rope going around my neck. After that...

...I was here. So I must have been saved from execution. If only I could remember how. No matter. It will come. What does matter is that since arriving here my life has been a succession of one blissful day after another. Perfect...

Except for the dreams.

But now clouds gather over my Elysian fields as I remember Karl's betrayal. I'd thought he avoided me in order to protect his family name, but the dream-Maria's words have not only awakened my memory, they've shed new light on all the things that happened to me after that night I went to Karl's uncle's house.

The clouds darken and thunder rumbles through the distant mountain passes as my anger and suspicion grow. I don't know if Karl lied and betrayed me as the dream-Maria said, and I don't know if he was the one who killed his uncle, but I do know that he deserted me in my hour of most dire need. And for that I will never forgive him.

The clouds obscure the sun and darken the sky, the storm threatens but it doesn't rain. Not yet.

The nightmare again.

Only this time I don't fight it. I'm actually glad to be in this monstrous body. I'm a curious thing. Not a seamless creature, but a quilt of human parts. And powerful. So very powerful. My years of farm work left me strong for a girl, but I never had strength like this. Strength to lift a horse or knock down a tree. It feels *good* to be so strong.

I head for Maria's cottage.

She's home. She's alone. Karl is nowhere about. I don't bother knocking. I kick down the door and step inside. Maria starts to scream but I grab her by the throat with one of my long-fingered hands and choke off all sound. She laughed at me last night, called me stupid. I feel the anger surge and I squeeze tighter, watching her face purple. I straighten my arm and lift her feet off the floor, let them kick the empty air, just as she said mine did in the dream-death she watched. I squeeze and squeeze and *squeeze*, watching the blood vessels burst in her eyes and face, watching her tongue protrude and turn dusky until she hangs in my hand like a doll. I loosen my grip and shake her, but she remains limp.

What have I done?

I stand there, shocked at the rage within me, at the violence it makes me capable of. For a moment I grieve for Maria, for myself, then I shake it off.

This is a dream. A *dream!* It isn't real. I can do anything in this nightmare body and it doesn't matter. Because it's only happening in my sleeping mind.

The realization is a dazzling white light in my brain. I can do anything I wish in my dream-life. *Anything!* I can vent any emotion, give in to any whim, any desire or impulse, no matter how violent or outrageous.

And I will do just that. No restraint while I'm dreaming. Unlike my waking life, I will act without hesitation on whatever occurs to me. I'll lead a dream-life untempered by sympathy, empathy, or any other sane consideration.

Why not? It's only a dream.

I look down and see the note I wrote Karl. It lies crumpled on the floor. I look at Maria, hanging limp from my hand. I remember her derisive laughter at how I'd donated my body for the further-ance of science, her glee at the thought of my being dissected into a thousand pieces.

And suddenly I have an idea. If I could laugh, I would.

After I'm finished with her, I set the door back on its hinges and wait beside it. I do not have to wait long.

Karl arrives and knocks. When no one answers, he pushes on the door. It falls inward and he sees his lover, Maria…all over the room…

in a thousand pieces. He cries out and turns to flee. But I am there, blocking the way.

Karl staggers back when he sees me, his face working in horror. He tries to run but I grab him by the arm and hold him.

"You! Good Lord, they said you'd burned up in the mill fire! Please don't hurt me! I never harmed you!"

What a wonder it is to have physical power over a man. I never realized until this instant how fear has influenced my day-to-day dealings with men. True, they run the world, they have the power of influence—but they have *physical* power as well. Somewhere in the depths of my mind, running as a steady undercurrent, has been the realization that almost any man could physically overpower me at will. Although I never before recognized its existence, I see now how it has colored my waking life.

But in my dream I am no longer the weaker sex.

I do not hurt Karl. I merely want him to know who I am. I hold up the note from last night and press it against my heart.

"What?" he cries hoarsely. "What do you want of me?"

I show him the note again, and again I press it to my heart.

"What are you saying? That you're Eva? That's impossible. Eva's dead! You're Victor Frankenstein's creature."

Victor Frankenstein? The baron's son? I've heard of him—one of Dr. Waldman's former students, supposedly brilliant but highly unorthodox. What has he to do with any of this?

I growl and shake my head as I rattle the paper and tighten my grip on his arm.

He winces. "Look at you! How could you be Eva? You're fashioned out of different parts from different bodies! You're—" Karl's eyes widen, his face slackens. "The brain! Sweet lord, Eva's brain! It was stolen shortly before you appeared!"

I am amazed at the logical consistency of my nightmare. In real life

I donated my body to the Medical College, and here in my dream my brain has been placed in another body, a patchwork fashioned by Baron Frankenstein's son from discarded bits and pieces. How inventive I am!

I smile.

"Oh, my *God!*" Karl wails. His words begin to trip over each other in their hurry to escape. "It can't be! Oh, Eva, Eva, Eva, I'm so sorry! I didn't want to do it, but Maria put me up to it. I didn't want to kill my uncle, but she kept pushing me. It was her idea to have you blamed, not mine!"

As I stare at him in horror, I feel the rage burst in my heart like a rocket. So! He *did* conspire to hang me! A crimson haze blossoms about me as I take his head between my hands. I squeeze with all the strength I possess and don't stop until I hear a wet crunching noise, feel hot liquid running between my fingers.

And then I'm sobbing, huge alien sounds rumbling from my chest as I clutch Karl's limp form against me. It's only a dream, I know, but still I hurt inside. I stand there for a long time. Until I hear a voice behind me.

"Hello? What's happened here?"

I turn and see one of the townsfolk approaching. The sight of him makes my blood boil. He and his kind chased me to that mill on the hill and tried to burn me alive. I toss Karl's remains aside and charge after him. He is too fast for me and runs screaming down the street.

Afraid that he'll return with his neighbors, I flee. But not before setting fire to Maria's cottage. I watch it burn a moment, then head into the countryside, into the friendly darkness.

Awake once more.

I have spent the entire day thinking about last night's dream. I see no reason to skulk around in the darkness any longer when I'm dreaming. Why should I? The townsfolk realize by now that I'm still alive. Good. Let all those good citizens know that I am back and that they must deal with me again—not as poor Eva Rucker, but as the patchwork creature from Victor Frankenstein's crazed experiments. And I will *not* be mistreated any more. I will *not* be looked down on and have doors shut in my face simply because I am a farm girl. No one will say no to me ever again!

I will be back. Tomorrow night, and every night thereafter. But I shall no longer wander aimlessly. I will have a purpose in my dreams. I will start by taking my dream-revenge on the University Regents who denied me admission to the Medical College. I shall spend my waking hours devising elaborate ways for them to die, and in my dreams, I shall execute those plans.

It will be fun. Harmless fun to kill them off one by one in my dreams.

I'm beginning to truly enjoy the dreams. It's so wonderful to be powerful and not recognize any limits. It's such an invigorating release.

I can't wait to sleep again.

BLOOD HUNT

OWL GOINGBACK

October 1885, the Dakota Territory

THE OLD INDIAN sat on the hill alone, motionless, as one with the earth and sky, the tall grasses, the soaring eagles, and the autumn wind. He had sat that way for hours, nearly naked but unfazed by the cold, staring straight ahead, barely breathing.

A man of medicine, he perhaps saw more than the empty prairie stretching endlessly before him. Maybe he imagined the millions of buffalo once roaming the land, slaughtered and left to rot so the native people would starve. Possibly he saw the ghosts of Lakota men, women, and children hunted down and killed by Long Knives in blue coats. Could he hear their voices on the wind, their songs, or their screams?

Twice, William "Buffalo Bill" Cody started up the hill to check on his friend, worried he might have expired while sitting there. But twice he stopped himself, fearful of interrupting him. He heard Sitting Bull was a man of great visions, once even predicting soldiers would fall

like grasshoppers at the place his people called Greasy Grass, known to the ill-fated Seventh Cavalry as the Little Bighorn.

Cody sat on his horse quietly smoking a cigar, patiently watching Sitting Bull, imagining what he saw, what he felt. Like the Indian, he too mourned the loss of the Western frontier, hated the changes brought by too many white men and too much civilization, knowing it was the closing chapter for his way of life and for all the native people.

Most of the tribes had already been rounded up and forced onto government reservations, their children taken away to boarding schools to be indoctrinated into the ways of the conquering race. Kill the Indian, save the child was the rule of the day. Only a few tribal bands remained free, and their days were numbered.

Sitting Bull had given up his freedom, and laid down his guns, to save his people, leading the remaining members of the Hunkpapa band of the Lakota to Fort Yates and the Standing Rock Indian Reservation. He had sacrificed everything to save them from being hunted into extinction.

After Sitting Bull turned himself in, Cody used his political clout to get him hired as one of the Indian performers in Buffalo Bill's Wild West Show. Not just a performer but a star, billing him as the chief who fought General George Armstrong Custer.

The Hunkpapa leader eventually earned the respect of the once hostile crowds, turning their boos into cheers and applause. He had toured more than forty cities in the United States and Canada, not fully understanding why there could be so many poor people living in nations so powerful and rich.

The show was over for the season and Sitting Bull was on his way back to Standing Rock, accompanied by Cody. The two of them had gotten off the train near Bismarck to make one final ride together south to *Papa Sapa*, the Black Hills, sharing a few weeks in the great wide open of the frontier, savoring every moment.

Nearly five hours had elapsed when Sitting Bull suddenly stood and turned around. Seeing Cody sitting on his horse, patiently waiting for him to finish his ritual, made the Indian smile. Being a man of few words, he only said, "We ride now."

THE SUN WAS slowly setting to the west, shadowy fingers of darkness reaching out to caress a lonely train depot on the edge of the tiny town of Miller, at the eastern edge of the Dakota Territory.

Michael Schroeder stopped and looked at the locomotive waiting for him on the tracks in front of the depot. A thin trickle of smoke rose from the engine's smokestack, telling him that Karl, the fireman, had arrived earlier to heat the boilers and start preparations for their trip.

Michael pulled out his pocket watch, checking the time. Ten years working as an engineer for the Chicago and North Western Railroad, he had never once departed late. Not once. And he was anxious to get started on this trip, but the wealthy passenger paying expenses had sent specific instructions that all travel take place after sunset. An odd request, but Europeans were known for their unusual behavior, especially those of royal blood with enough money to pay for a two-week hunting expedition on the frontier.

In addition to hiring the train, and crew, the Count had rented an expensive private coach for himself and his guests. The luxury coach sat at the end of the train, decorated in rich shades of red and gold. Between the coach and engine was a boxcar for carrying all the necessary supplies for the trip.

Slipping his watch back into the pocket of his overalls, Michael pulled his engineer cap lower on his head and continued walking to the train. Reaching the engine, he climbed up into the cab to begin the necessary preparations.

"Karl, are you here?" he called out. But the fireman was not at the gauges. Nor was he in the adjoining coal tender. Michael opened the engine's furnace door, seeing that coal had recently been shoveled into the firebox. Closing the door, he looked around. "Karl?"

After climbing down out of the cab, Michael slowly walked to the rear of the train. When he reached the coach, he climbed up the iron steps to the small platform at the back of the car. He hesitated before knocking, listening, but there were no sounds coming from inside. No voices or laughter, just silence.

"No party? No drinking?" He knocked three times, waited, then knocked again. He tried the door, finding it unlocked.

He opened the door and stepped inside. The coach was beautiful, a rolling mini-mansion eighty feet long, divided into staterooms, a parlor, observation deck, dining area, pantry, and service area, all of it decorated with carved mahogany, brass fittings, and expensive furniture.

Several lamps burned brightly, but there was no sign of human activity. The ashtrays were empty, all the crystal glasses unfilled.

"Hello?"

Michael looked around, noticing all of the windows had been painted black, every single one of them, blocking the last rays of sunlight from entering. The car would have been pitch black were it not for the glow of the lamps.

Painting the windows made no sense. Why pay good money to see the frontier, then black out the windows so you could not view it? He wondered if it had something to do with the orders to travel at night. Perhaps someone in the hunting party had a medical condition and was sensitive to daylight.

At the front of the car, he stepped out onto a tiny metal platform facing the boxcar. The boxcar had been modified with a narrow door and platform at the rear, allowing access from the private coach while the train was in motion.

Thinking the hunting party might be checking supplies, he stepped to the boxcar's platform and opened the door. But there was no one inside. Nor were there any supplies, except for a few empty wooden crates at the opposite end and what looked like an ornate coffin.

"What the hell?"

Not only was the boxcar empty, but the floor was covered with a layer of dirt several feet thick. Wooden boards had been placed against the boxcar's large sliding side doors to keep the dirt from falling through the cracks.

The dirt stank of blood and rotten meat, and he wondered if it came from a slaughterhouse. Were they going to use it to attract predators, mountain lions or perhaps grizzly bears?

The smell was overpowering, forcing the engineer to retreat back out onto the tiny landing. As he stood there, breathing deeply, he felt a rush of air behind him and heard the flapping of leathery wings.

Michael turned, shocked to find himself facing a dark-haired man with a pale complexion and powerful gaze. The gentleman was dressed in an expensive black suit, the fabric rumpled and dirty.

"My apology. I did not mean to startle you," the man said in a thick European accent.

"It's okay. I thought I was alone." He looked past the gentleman at the interior of the boxcar and, for a moment, thought he saw shadows moving in the darkness.

"Allow me to introduce myself. I am Count Dracula. Are you a member of the crew?"

Michael nodded, taking a step back. The gentleman may be European royalty, but he was in dire need of a bath. His breath also stank, strong and coppery like raw meat. "I'm Michael Schroeder, the engineer."

"Excellent." The count smiled, nodding. "Then we are all ready to begin our journey."

"Ready?" The engineer was confused. "But what about supplies, and your guests?"

"I already have everything, and everyone, I need," Dracula answered.

Michael looked around. "Yes, sir. I just need to find Karl, my fireman."

"Ah, Karl. Yes. Yes. He was here, but I sent him on an errand. He will return momentarily."

"Errand?" Michael asked. "What…" He did not finish his question, suddenly distracted by the front of Dracula's shirt. Something moved beneath the fabric. As he watched, an ugly yellow spider-like insect, about a half-inch in diameter, crawled out from the opening between two buttons and skittered across the count's shirt, disappearing beneath his suit coat.

Michael watched, spellbound as several more of the wingless insects crawled across the count's chest, taking refuge beneath his suit. "Count Dracula, you have…"

One of the vermin appeared from under Dracula's collar, crawling up the right side of his face. It stopped on his cheek, biting into his flesh like a large tick. The count seemed not to notice.

The engineer was horrified by the sight of the hideous parasite feeding on the count. "Excuse me, sir. You have something on your face."

Count Dracula reached up and casually pulled the pest from his cheek, leaving behind a tiny speck of blood where it had bitten him. He held the insect between his thumb and forefinger, studying it for a moment, then bit into it, sucking the blood from its tiny body.

"Bat flies," Dracula said, flicking it away. "An acquired taste. But where are my manners? Would you like one?" Dracula grabbed his lapels and opened his coat, revealing hundreds of bat flies. They lay thick in the folds of his shirt, and under his arms, scurrying everywhere as they were exposed.

Michael stepped back, repulsed. He turned to run, but Dracula grabbed him by the collar and held him in a vise-like grip. "Bat flies are just an appetizer. A snack. Time now for the main course."

Count Dracula's jaws stretched impossibly wide, revealing canine fangs longer than a wolf's. He bit into the engineer's neck, slicing through flesh and muscle, severing his jugular vein.

Michael tried to scream, but his throat filled with blood and he only gurgled like a drowning swimmer. His body spasmed and then went limp, his vision slowly fading to black.

CODY AND SITTING Bull camped near a grove of cottonwood trees and then collected fallen branches to make a small fire. It was a pleasant evening, the prairie around them illuminated by the glow of a full moon.

They spoke in quiet whispers, talking about their experiences at the Wild West show. Sitting Bull worked hard to learn a little English, hoping to better communicate with other members of the troop. He was especially fond of sharpshooter Annie Oakley, adopting her as a daughter and giving her the Indian name of Little Sure Shot. He had hoped he might talk with the President of the United States, on behalf of the Indian people, but the Great White Father turned down his request.

Cody had just finished the last of his coffee when the prairie wolves started their evening chorus of howls. It sounded like hundreds of them on the hunt, but the frontiersman was not worried with his Winchester rifle and Colt Navy revolver close at hand.

He noticed Sitting Bull's rifle leaned against a tree near the horses, while his primitive bow and quiver of arrows were within easy reach. "Chief, you leave a good rifle far away, and keep an old bow and arrows beside you. Why?"

Sitting Bull touched the leather quiver, which held twenty flint-point arrows. "Old ways are better."

Cody thought about his words for a moment, then nodded. "Very true. But this world is changing. Maybe there is no more place for old ways, or for people like us."

Just then a loud howl sounded, different from the other wolves, a long mournful cry so haunting it brought chills to Cody's spine.

"Medicine wolf." Sitting Bull stood, grabbing his bow and arrows. He faced the direction of the eerie howls, listening carefully.

Buffalo Bill also stood. He had heard stories about the medicine wolf. Fellow frontiersman Jim Bridger claimed it was supernatural, a spirit or shapeshifter, something to be feared.

Both men stood listening when the sounds of distant gunshots split the nights, followed by a woman's scream. The shots and scream came from the same direction as the howls.

"Someone needs help." Cody turned toward his partner, but Sitting Bull already raced toward his horse. Slinging his quiver and bow, he then grabbed his rifle and mounted his white mare bareback. Cody grabbed his guns and also mounted bareback, Indian style, having learned to ride that way as a boy.

They raced across the open prairie at full gallop, grateful for the bright moonlight to light their way. Topping a narrow ridge, they spotted two unhitched wagons in the valley below. A large campfire burned between the wagons, illuminating a scene of chaos and carnage.

Several bloody bodies lay scattered on the ground, while a young man, armed with a lever-action rifle, stood facing an enormous gray wolf. He fired several times, but the bullets seemed to have no effect on the beast.

"Medicine wolf." Sitting Bull pointed.

Out of ammo, the young man clutched his rifle like a baseball bat. The wolf charged, striking the man in the chest and knocking him to the ground. Powerful jaws seized him by the throat, shaking him like a rag doll.

Cody and Sitting Bull rode full speed into the encampment, charging through a pack of smaller wolves circling beyond the glow of the campfire. Cody fired his rifle several times, and the smaller wolves scattered, frightened into the night. But the shots had no effect on the medicine wolf.

The giant wolf lunged at a young woman in a pale blue dress, no more than sixteen years old, dragging her to the ground and clamping its murderous jaws around her delicate throat.

"No!" Bill Cody quickly dismounted, working the lever of his rifle and firing repeatedly. A skilled buffalo hunter and military scout, and an excellent shot, he did not miss as he pumped three rounds into the savage beast.

The giant wolf released the girl and came toward him in an unhurried trot, head low and teeth bared. Buffalo Bill fired again, and again, emptying his rifle.

"What kind of demon are you?" Cody drew his Colt revolver and fired, but he had no better luck with the pistol then he did with the Winchester.

The wolf lunged at Cody. As it did, a wooden arrow shot through the air striking it in the back leg.

The beast twisted in midair, howling in pain, landing on the ground next to Cody. Sitting Bull, still on horseback, quickly notched another arrow to his bowstring. But before he could release the second arrow, the wolf turned and fled from the camp. He chased after it.

Cody raced to the woman's side but was unable to save her life. Her throat had been torn out, and she quickly bled to death. The other people in the camp were already dead. Getting back on his horse, he raced after Sitting Bull.

He found the Indian about a hundred yards out of camp. Sitting Bull had dismounted and was studying tracks in the dirt. Cody stopped his horse beside him, also dismounting.

"It got away?" Cody asked.

Sitting Bull nodded.

"What kind of wolf was that? I shot it point-blank and couldn't drop it."

"Maybe not wolf. Maybe man who walks like wolf." Sitting Bull pointed at the ground near his feet. In the bright moonlight, they could clearly see the footprints of a wolf. The tracks continued for a few feet before stopping. In their place were the footprints of a man.

The human prints continued for another sixty feet, then stopped completely. There were no other tracks around.

Cody removed his Stetson hat, looking around. "There has to be more tracks."

Sitting Bull looked up at the night sky, a frown tugging at the corners of his mouth. "Maybe he flew away."

"Flew?" Cody laughed. "That's impossible, chief."

Sitting Bull nodded. "So is wolf that becomes man."

THEY CONTINUED SEARCHING throughout the night, but found no trace of the medicine wolf. It really did seem to have vanished into thin air, and Cody was beginning to wonder if the legends were true.

It was nearly morning when they reached a level valley where the railroad ran. Sitting on a sidetrack was a Chicago and North Western locomotive, pulling a boxcar and ornate private coach.

"Hunters?" Sitting Bull studied the train.

"Maybe." Cody had served several times as a hunting guide for the wealthy, including Grand Duke Alexei Alexandrovich of Russia. "Let's pay a visit. "Maybe they have seen the beast we track."

They approached the train at a slow trot, not wanting to appear threatening. As they drew nearer, they realized no one was around. Everything was eerily quiet.

They tied their horses to the iron railing on the coach's back platform. Grabbing their weapons, they climbed the steps to the door. Cody knocked, the door opening at his touch. He started to call out, but Sitting Bull motioned him to silence.

"Bad smell," Sitting Bull whispered.

Cody nodded. He cocked his rifle and entered the car. The coach was beautifully decorated, but there was no sign of life. No food, drinks, or even cigars. Nor were there any guns or ammo boxes, nothing to indicate the coach had been rented by a sportsman.

Buffalo Bill picked up a lantern off a coffee table, lighting it with a wooden match. Reaching the other end of the car, they spotted a puddle of blood on the floor. Mixed in with the blood were bits of regurgitated flesh and a piece of lacy fabric—part of a collar from a woman's blue dress.

"I think we found our wolf," Cody said, looking around. "But does it walk on four legs or two?"

Sitting Bull cocked his rifle, keeping his bow and arrow slung over his shoulder.

They left the coach and entered the boxcar, Cody holding his rifle in his right hand and the lantern in his left. But the boxcar was empty. No horses, animal feed, or provisions; just a few wooden crates, and an ornate coffin, at the opposite end of the car. A thick layer of dirt covered the floor, reeking with the stink of death and decay.

Sitting Bull saw the movement first, a rippling under the dirt that started near the wooden crates, rolling like an ocean wave toward them. The wave stopped and something emerged from the dirt, rising up to face them, illuminated by the lamp Cody held.

It was a man, dressed in heavy work boots and the striped coveralls of a railroad engineer. The man was pale as a corpse, his clothes covered with dirt and grime, bugs crawling upon him. There were also two noticeable puncture wounds on his neck.

The engineer hissed and rushed toward them, arms outstretched and fingers hooked into deadly claws. Cody dropped the lamp to the soft dirt, raised his rifle and fired. The 44-40 bullets slammed into the man's chest, stopping him dead in his tracks. But the bullets did not kill him, or even cause him to fall. He stood there and laughed at them, a sound more animal than human.

Seeing that bullets had no effect, Sitting Bull pulled his hunting knife from the sheath on his belt and rushed forward. He slashed the man's neck, cutting so deeply he nearly severed his head. The engineer's head tilted backward, hanging by a thin sliver of tissue and muscle.

"What the hell?" Cody said, shocked that the man still stood.

The Indian swung again, slicing through the remaining flesh. The man's head rolled across the room, the body finally collapsing to the dirt.

"Thank God," Cody said aloud.

Sitting Bull looked at his friend, frowning. "No God here."

No sooner had the engineer fallen than the dirt covering the floor of the boxcar began to ripple and undulate as things moved beneath it. Cody and Sitting Bull backed up.

Suddenly, an Indian woman launched herself out of the soil. Dressed in the beaded buckskin dress of a northern Cheyenne, dirty and disheveled, she hissed at them, revealing long pointed fangs.

Cody rapid-fired his rifle, taking off most of her head in a spray of blood, bone, and brains. The woman took two steps toward them, and fell face-first to the dirt.

Cody turned to look at Sitting Bull, knowing the Lakota were blood brothers to the Cheyenne. "Sorry."

Sitting Bull nodded. "Woman already dead. Now she can make the journey."

They had almost reached the open door when the lid of the ornate wooden casket at the opposite end of the boxcar exploded into the air, launched with such force it bounced off the ceiling. Cody and Sitting Bull turned to face the new danger.

A grayish mist slowly flowed from the open casket, like early morning fog rolling across a lake. The mist floated toward them, growing thicker, heavier. Within the moving cloud, shapes formed and took on definition, silhouettes of a large bat, and then an enormous wolf, finally a man dressed all in black.

The mist faded into thin air, but the man did not. He stood before the frontiersman and Indian, dressed in a black suit, his hair dark as his clothing, his skin white as ivory. Unafraid and defiant, he radiated strength and an intense evil. Buffalo Bill tossed aside his empty rifle, pulling his pistol.

"Foolish man, your weapons cannot hurt me." The man laughed. "Surely you must know that by now. And they call you a great hunter."

Cody kept his pistol trained on the man. "Who are you?"

"My name is Count Dracula." He made a slight bow. "And you are the great Buffalo Bill Cody, king of the Wild West."

"You know me?"

"The books written about you inspired my voyage to the New World. I wanted to see the frontier before it was gone, wanted to hunt something new."

"There is little to hunt," Sitting Bull spoke up. "The buffalo are gone."

Dracula laughed. "Not buffalo. I came here to hunt Indians, the vanishing Americans. Their blood is quite delicious."

"Those were not Indians you killed last night," Cody challenged.

Dracula shrugged. "Like the buffalo, Indians are also getting scarce. Sometimes a hunter has to settle on lesser game."

Sitting Bull raised his rifle and fired, hitting Dracula dead center in the chest. The count looked down at the hole in his shirt. "Stupid savage, this is my favorite shirt. Do you know how hard it is to get quality merchandise in this god-forsaken country? I will kill you last for that, slowly and painfully."

Dracula launched himself at Cody, closing the distance between them in a single leap. Cody rapid-fired his pistol, but the bullets had no effect. The vampire crashed into him, grabbing Cody around the throat in a powerful grip, and taking him to the ground.

Sitting Bull tossed aside his rifle and unslung his bow and quiver of arrows. He quickly notched an arrow to the bowstring, as he had done in combat dozens of times before. He pulled the string back, held his breath, sighted, and released the arrow.

Dracula's deadly fangs were almost touching Cody's throat when the arrow hit him in the side. The count let out a cry of pain and jumped back from Buffalo Bill.

As Dracula jumped back, turning to face Sitting Bull, three more of his undead minions rose up from the soil and stood behind their master. An army of blood drinkers, two more Indian women and another man dressed in the clothing of a railroad worker.

Cody quickly got to his feet and reloaded his pistol. Dracula stood facing them, looking more demon than man, his mouth crowded with incredibly long fangs.

"I will make you my slaves!" he screamed, pulling the arrow from his side and tossing it away. His mouth stretched impossibly wide, his eyes blazing like burning brimstone.

"I am already the slave of the white man," Sitting Bull replied. He released his bowstring, shooting an arrow deep into the chest of the railroad worker, a wooden stake through the heart, sending his tortured soul on a one-way trip to the happy hunting ground. Dracula screamed in rage.

Cody watched in amazement as Sitting Bull rapidly notched and fired two more arrows, moving with a fluid motion that came from years of being a warrior and numerous life-and-death struggles on the battlefield.

The arrows struck the two Indian women in the chest, piercing their hearts and freeing their spirits from their undead imprisonment. As they sank lifeless to the floor, Sitting Bull said a quiet prayer in Lakota for them.

Dracula screamed again, a cry filled with centuries of unholy rage. His hands clenched in fists, fingernails cutting into the flesh of his palms and causing blood to flow.

Sitting Bull pulled back his bowstring and released another arrow. It flew straight, striking Dracula in the chest and piercing his heart.

The count shrieked in agony, clutching at the arrow's shaft. But his palms were slick with blood, and he was unable to pull the arrow from his chest.

Spirals of mist rose up from Dracula's body, like steam from a cooking pot. His flesh withered and pulled tight, aging before their very eyes.

The vampire sank slowly to his knees, his hands still clutching the arrow's shaft. Gray smoke billowed out from underneath his clothing, looking like his body was on fire. Hundreds of yellow spider-like insects fled from beneath his garments, like rats leaving a sinking ship.

The count let out a final groan and toppled forward, his body deflating, flesh flaking away from his bones. And then his bones turned into dust, leaving nothing behind but an empty suit.

The soil around the count rippled for a moment, then grew still. From somewhere in the distance, wolves began to howl.

Cody slowly holstered his pistol, not believing his eyes. He did not know exactly what Dracula was, but knew the count was dead.

He turned to look at Sitting Bull. The Indian stood there, looking at the dust that was Count Dracula and clutching his bow tightly in his fist.

Noticing Buffalo Bill looking at him, the medicine man smiled and raised his bow. "Old ways are best."

They left the train of Dracula behind and rode off into the night. Two men, once mortal enemies and now dear friends, maybe the last of a dying breed. Like the wild frontier, their time was quickly coming to an end. But for now, they had the open prairie and a million stars in the sky. And for them, that was enough.

MUMMY CALLS

SIMON BESTWICK

DEAR EDITOR,

I don't know if this will be suitable for your anthology, as it isn't a work of fiction. This is something that actually happened to me. Unfortunately. However, it involves a mummy, which is why I thought you might be interested. Not Egyptian, though, and not particularly old. Compared to Tutankhamun, she's a babe in arms.

You don't have to take my word for most of this, by the way: five minutes on Google will tell you all about my distant relative Hannah Beswick of Birchin Bower, aka the Manchester Mummy.

I grew up in Manchester, a city in North West England: a good-sized city by British standards, with plenty going on in terms of cuisine and culture, the arts and the LGBT scene. Worth a visit if you're ever in the UK. My surname, Bestwick, is an old one in this part of the country, going back to the eleventh or twelfth century. Like most English surnames, it's had a lot of alternative spellings over the years, one of them being "Beswick." Which brings me to Hannah.

She was born in 1688 and died in 1758. Her parents, John and
Patience, owned Cheetwood Old Hall in Manchester, and when John
died in 1706, Hannah inherited a substantial fortune. She had several
siblings, including a brother, also called John, who was the reason she
became a mummy.

It's not clear when this happened or how old Hannah was at the
time, but at some point John fell ill and was pronounced dead; they
were literally lowering his coffin lid when someone saw his eyelid
twitching. John recovered and lived a long and healthy life, but the
incident gave Hannah a lifelong terror of being buried alive.

Her will's contents are still disputed, but one provision was supposedly that she be kept above ground for a year and periodically
checked for signs of life. Whether she wanted to be mummified is
more debatable; that idea might have been her executor's. Dr. Charles
White had an impressive collection of "curiosities" and might have
been unable to resist adding Hannah to the collection. The exact
process of embalming isn't known, but probably went something
like this:

1) Pump turpentine and vermilion into the arteries.

2) Remove organs.

3) Wash body in alcohol.

4) Replace organs.

5) Inject more turpentine and vermilion.

6) Pack body cavities with camphor, nitre, and resin.

7) Sew up incisions.

8) Pack orifices (the mummy's, not yours) with yet more camphor.

9) Place body in box of plaster of Paris to absorb remaining
moisture.

10) Coat body with tar to preserve.

You'd think keeping Hannah above ground would've been unnecessary, given that if that didn't kill her, nothing would, but keep her they did: first at Ancoats Hall, which belonged to another of the Beswicks, then at Dr. White's house in Sale, South Manchester, where he displayed her in a clock case. She became a sort of posthumous celebrity, with distinguished visitors such as Thomas De Quincey calling on White to view her.

White bequeathed the mummy to a Dr. Ollier, who in turn bequeathed it to the Manchester Museum; Hannah took up residence there in the entrance hall between a Peruvian mummy and Egyptian one, as "The Manchester Mummy, or The Mummy of Birchin Bower," for the edification of the public.

I'm going to go out on a limb here and say I don't think that's what she would have wanted.

After the museum was transferred to Manchester University in 1867, it was decided that Hannah was "irrevocably and unmistakably dead," and in 1868, 110 years after her passing, Hannah Beswick was laid to rest in an unmarked grave in Harpurhey Cemetery.

At least, that's what it says on Wikipedia. The reality is rather different.

She lives with my Mum and Dad.

———

WELL, NOT EXACTLY *with.* I don't think *living's* quite the right term either, but I've no idea what is. It all started a couple of weeks ago, with a phone call from my Dad.

"Can you get down here, love?" he said.

"Is everything okay?" My parents are both in their seventies—Dad's eighty next year—and although they'd been fully vaccinated against COVID, any number of other things could go wrong with the human body.

"Oh yeah, everything's fine. Well—" He hesitated, which wasn't like him: Dad's never lost for words. "Something we need to talk to you about."

That was no less worrying. "What is it you need to—"

"Best if we just show you, love. Don't worry, we're both all right, but—well, we need to talk to you."

Cate and I live in Wallasey, about fifty miles from Manchester, and neither of us drive, but the lockdown was finally easing so getting there wasn't hard—a taxi to the station, a train to Manchester, and a Metrolink tram to Brooklands, South Manchester, where my parents live. I spent the entire journey trying to guess what shameful episode from my teens might be coming back to haunt me.

Dad picked us up outside the Metrolink station; I kissed his rough, stubbly cheek and climbed into the passenger seat; Cate got in the back, and he drove us home. He kept up a stream of questions about the journey, the weather back in Wallasey, and so on. Anything to avoid explaining why we were there. It was the first time I've ever seen him engaging in nervous chatter; normally I'm the one doing that, which usually annoys the pants off him. All this only made me more worried, and when I caught Cate's eye I could see she felt the same.

My parents live in a cul-de-sac, one of a row of semi-detached bungalows populated by fellow pensioners. Mum came to the front door as Dad parked the car and hugged me very tightly. There's nothing like a hug from your Mum, especially when you're at the age when there'll be only so many more. She hugged Cate next, then bustled us both inside. Dad locked the car and followed.

None of us apparently wanted to broach the subject, so we sat in the lounge drinking cups of tea, chattering determinedly and aimlessly as grey squirrels bolted back and forth across the back garden.

"So," said Dad, finally.

I put my cup down. "Okay, Dad. What did you need to see us about?"

"Just show him, Roger," said Mum. "Cate, do you want to see some pictures of Simon when he was little?"

Cate's seen my baby pictures before, but she said yes. If we didn't argue, we'd get this done faster.

"Right you are," said Dad. "Come on." I followed him outside to his "office," a small brick-walled extension attached to the house where he keeps his computers and does whatever else he does in his spare time. He shut the door behind us and locked it—another unusual action that left me a little uneasy. Not afraid—this was my *Dad*, after all—but uneasy, because he wasn't being his usual self. Neither of them was.

His laptop was on his desk, switched on. Dad clicked a key, tapped in a password, and unlocked the screensaver to display a Wikipedia page. "Have a read of that," he said, motioning me to his chair.

I did as he asked. The Wikipedia page was headed "Manchester Mummy" and basically told me everything you've just read: Hannah Beswick, her fear of being buried alive, the mummification, Dr. White, and so on.

I'd read about the case when I was younger, and remembered the basics, mainly because of the surname. Which was a good thing, as I was getting very nervous now—for Mum and Dad to be so reluctant to discuss it, it had to be serious. And when I'm nervous, I struggle to focus on things like Wikipedia pages. It's probably the same for you. I guessed from the context I might be about to learn I was related to the Mummy of Birchin Bower, but I didn't get why that made my coming out here so urgent.

"Finished?"

While I was reading, I'd heard Dad dragging something across the office floor; when I turned, I saw he'd rolled back the carpet to expose the floorboards. A square section had been cut out; Dad prised it up and lifted it away in one piece. Under it, a steel trapdoor was held in place with bolts and padlocks, which Dad began unfastening.

"What's this?" I said.

"Just have a look in the top drawer there, love," he said, laying the padlocks aside. I opened the drawer and found a pair of torches. "Hand me one and take one for yourself."

"Okay."

Dad pulled the bolts back and held out his hand for a torch, then prised open the trapdoor. Cold damp air wafted out, along with a host of odors too faint and too mixed to decipher.

"Put your torch on and go down the steps."

I was completely lost by now, but he was switching his torch on, too, so at least I knew he didn't expect me to go down into the cellar or crawlspace alone. I shone the torch down a flight of wooden steps and started down: they creaked under my weight, prompting one of Dad's trademark sighs at my general unwieldiness. That would normally have been pretty annoying, but just then it was oddly comforting, because it was familiar.

The torchlight gleamed on gray stone flags. Something hard and dry scratched and scuffled over the stones, and I started to raise the torch.

"No!" snapped Dad. "Keep your torch pointed at the ground, Simon. This is important."

I moved away from the steps as he descended them. He also kept his torch pointed at the floor; saw he was holding a plastic bag with something heavy in it in his other hand. The scuffling, scraping sound continued, moving away from us and around to the side. Circling, I thought.

"All right," said Dad. "Now when I say, bring your torch up, slowly. And—Simon, I need you to keep quiet and stay calm. Think you can do that?"

"I'll try."

"Don't *try*," he said irritably, "*do* it." He'd say that all the time when I was younger: used to drive me mad, but once again its familiarity was reassuring now. Now he spoke slowly and loudly, as you might to someone deaf, or slow-minded. "Simon, this is Hannah; Hannah, this is Simon." He poked my arm. "Now."

We raised our torches, and the thing in the cellar's corner opened its blind, blackened mouth, hissed at us and scrabbled forwards on all fours.

——————

THERE ARE NO photographs, or even sketches, of the Manchester Mummy. We've got only a brief description of the body, which was wrapped in thick, heavy sheets: it was well-preserved, but the face was shrivelled and black.

I can vouch for the last part: the skin of the face was like old leather that'd dried out and gone hard. A dirty, ragged swatch of cloth was wrapped around the body, leaving the arms, legs, and shoulders bare. The limbs were very thin, and blackened, shrivelled and hardened like the face.

I gasped "Jesus Christ," or something along those lines, which was pretty restrained under the circumstances. Dad frowned, but the thing stopped only for a second before continuing to approach us. I was surprised how small she was. But then she'd been— literally— a little old lady. Even so, the thin bony fingers, scratching at the concrete floor, were an unsettling sight. I didn't want them touching me.

"It's all right," said Dad. I realized he was talking to the mummy, not me. "It's all right."

The mummy crouched like a cat, back arched and snuffling, sniffing at the air. The light fell on the shrivelled face. Its eyes were holes. There might have been the remnants of eyeballs in the sockets somewhere, but whatever else had been preserved, its sight hadn't. That was why he'd told me to be quiet: she must navigate by sound. Although, from the snuffling, I guessed her sense of smell was intact, too.

Dad took out the contents of the plastic bag. Something wet dripped on the concrete floor: blood.

"Oh my God," I whispered. "What's that?"

What had been Hannah Beswick lifted her head, snuffled at the air again, then made a quick, shuffling move toward us. Dad gave me a look. "Leg of Welsh lamb. What'd you think it was? Here you go, Hannah."

He tossed the joint toward the mummy, who grabbed it and set about it with her shrivelled jaws. Dad had dragged up a couple of folding chairs that had been propped against the cellar wall. "Here. Take a seat."

"What for?"

"She needs to get used to you."

So we sat and watched the mummy feed, sucking the blood from the joint, bolting the meat, then gnawing at the bone, teeth clicking loudly on it in the stillness till it splintered and cracked.

Dad told me what he knew, which, like much of Hannah's story, was annoyingly patchy. He'd no idea exactly when anyone realized she wasn't, in fact, "irrevocably and unmistakably dead," much less why or how she wasn't. Maybe Dr. White had used some sort of secret ingredient when he was trying to preserve her. Maybe she hadn't been happy about being turned into one of his "curiosities" and it had taken over a century to be able to make her displeasure known. What was certain was that the whole "burial" at Harpurhey in that conveniently unmarked grave was a cover story to get the increasingly cantankerous mummy out of the public eye. "Basically," he said, "they went back to the nearest relatives they could find and said, 'Here she is, she's your great-granny or whatever, you deal with her.' And we've been stuck with her ever since."

By now Hannah had disposed of all traces of the lamb leg and crept over to us. Her eyeless face turned from Dad's direction to mine. A faint whispering, twittering sound came from her mouth, a bit like the sounds crickets make. "How much does she understand?"

"No one's really sure. She likes classical music, but who doesn't? Can't have a conversation with her, but that's not her fault."

I listened to that whispering, twittering voice for a while; once or twice I thought I was about to understand what she was saying, but I never did. I hoped there wasn't anything to understand: she'd be better off if she was incapable of thought. "Why didn't someone just…" I lowered my voice to the quietest possible whisper "…kill her?"

"They tried," said Dad. "Couldn't chop her up because the blades just broke off. Tried burning her, but she wouldn't. There was no getting rid of her, so in the end we were lumbered. Someone has to keep looking after her, keep her fed, and all the rest."

"What happens if they don't?"

"What do you mean?"

"If they don't feed her? Does she go on the rampage or something?"

"Not as such, no. Just gets more bad-tempered."

"Couldn't they just… I don't know, lock her away or something?"

Dad looked disgusted. "She's your family, Simon," he said. "Is that what you'd do to your mother and me?"

"No. Course not."

"Well, then. Same here. She's your family. So you're gonna have to take care of her."

Hannah whispered and twittered in the shadows for a minute or two before that last sentence sank in. "Me?"

My sister lives in New Zealand; I'm now wondering if I know why she really emigrated.

"Yes," said Dad sternly. "Your mother and I won't be around forever, you know."

SO, THAT'S WHERE things are right now. I still haven't told Cate what happened. I keep promising to. I know I'll have to eventually. Dad suggested I could introduce her to Hannah next time we come to visit.

The next time.

Normally, I'm the first one to fall asleep at night. Cate's always pretended to grumble about it, because it takes her ages. But lately, I've been awake long after her, just lying there. I keep thinking I can hear Hannah's voice in the darkness: whispering, twittering, calling to me. I keep thinking I'm about to understand whatever she's trying to say.

I've no idea what I'm going to do.

Best,
Simon

THE VISCOUNT AND THE PHANTOM

LUCY A. SNYDER

November 23, 1888

VISCOUNT RAOUL DE Chagny smoothed the front of his tuxedo and stepped down into the ornately gilded loge and settled on the red velvet seat beside his older brother, the Comte Philippe de Chagny. He surveyed the trite, gaudy Christmas wreaths and garlands hung throughout the auditorium, skeptical that he'd enjoy the evening. Music never excited him, and he knew little about it. He suspected others were lying when they claimed to be moved to tears or passions by it. Female opera singers' voices in particular grated on his nerves. As far as he was concerned, women should be mostly seen and seldom heard. He did enjoy hearing them scream in pain, but only when he was the cause of it.

But Philippe had promised that the Paris Opera was an endless source of carnal diversion, thanks to the ballerinas, many of whom were recklessly eager to please a bachelor of means.

Illustration by COLTON WORLEY »

"I trust your autumn in England was…productive?" Philippe's tone was cool and sly.

The Palais Garnier's orchestra was just warming up in the pit below, and the occasional scrape of scenery being moved into place behind the heavy maroon theatre curtains was audible above the strings and woodwinds racing up and down their scales.

"Quite." Raoul smiled to himself, remembering the heart-pounding thrill of fleeing from the police through dark cobblestone alleys.

"I suppose that business in Whitechapel was your work?"

Raoul laughed. "Well, I did tell our dearest aunt I was off to study anatomy. Wouldn't want to make a liar of myself, would I?"

"The Ripper's crimes were all over the newspapers," Philippe said, his tone a mix of disapproval and envy. "I never raised such alarum when I was off sowing my own red oats. I trust you'll be more discreet now that you're home? I can't have you spoiling this lovely buffet of quim."

"Simple fornication seems so dull to me now." Raoul sighed, feeling his loins stir as he remembered cutting into the prostitutes' flesh. Watching the light die in their terrified eyes. Tasting their blood on his dagger, which he kept strapped to his ankle under his trouser leg.

"Well, I'm not saying you must abstain from your indulgences entirely," Philippe said. "I *did* think of you before I invited you here. The Palais Garnier presents a unique opportunity for a young gentleman of your tastes."

Raoul stared at his brother, intrigued. "Indeed? How so?"

"There is a persistent rumor of an Opera Ghost haunting the backstage and cellars here. Allegedly, the managers have even reserved Box 5 for the spirit." Philippe pointed at an empty loge on the other side of the auditorium. "They're afraid to rent it to anyone else lest the Ghost inflict bad luck upon the productions here."

"They've reserved the box? It must be a humbug for publicity," Raoul replied.

"That's my suspicion. But, apparently, some stagehands and patrons have gone missing. Not many. But enough that there's always talk of the Ghost. I expect there are some in the audience who buy tickets partly in hopes of witnessing a supernatural intrusion or entertaining disaster. But the Ghost, real or fraud, is certainly a handy scapegoat."

Philippe paused, lowering his voice. "Even better, there's a lake beneath this building's cellars. When Charles Garnier's crew was building this place, they broke through to an underground reservoir and could not keep the water at bay, so they constructed a cistern to contain it. It's quite large, very dark, I'm told. No-one is certain how far those watery passages go. And Garnier could not have designed a more perfect place to dispose of a body. Say, the corpse of a girl who had no family to miss her, weighed down with chains."

"*Very* interesting," Raoul said. "I'm liking this place more and more."

"All I ask is that you avoid the kind of flagrant evidence you left in London. No blood, no bodies. *Certainly* no human hearts left boiling in a pot! The Opera is full of watchful gossips. None must suspect you."

"None ever have." Raoul couldn't keep the resentment out of his voice. Philippe acted as if he had not already eluded every detective at Scotland Yard and dozens of port cities besides! "I'm not the callow youth you take me to be, Brother. I've sailed around the world, remember?"

"I meant no offense. At my age, every man your age has the look of a boy." Philippe gazed at him appraisingly. "But I suspect many will take you to be younger than you are. And with that fair hair and those wide eyes of yours, if you behave as a gentleman should in public, everyone here will assume you're an innocent angel."

Raoul grinned at him. "And I'll be every inch the devil I wish to be in private."

THE OPERA WASN'T terrible, Raoul had to admit. The elaborate costumes and spectacle of the whole thing were diverting enough. And Méphistophélès' dramatic flourishes were quite amusing.

"What's the name of this, again?" he asked Philippe.

"Faust," his brother replied tersely.

Raoul focused on the very young soprano who'd taken center stage. She seemed to be singing with real joy and passion. Lovely and fresh as a newly budded carnation in her high-necked white satin dress. He imagined himself slicing her apart with his favorite blade, her blood staining the virginal fabric crimson. "Who's that little birdie?"

"Christine Daaé. La Carlotta was supposed to perform as Margarita, but she was unexpectedly ill this evening. Christine wore trousers and played the boy Siébel till now. Bit parts and the chorus in productions before. Who knew she was hiding such a lovely coloratura? She must have found an awfully good voice coach, but no one has spoken of him."

"Indeed." Raoul didn't give a single fig about opera details. "Introduce me afterward, would you?"

Philippe gave him a hard sidelong stare. "Oh no, little brother, you shan't go after that one. She would definitely be missed."

"I just want to meet her," Raoul replied smoothly. "Don't you want me to be on good terms with the important players here?"

"I suppose so." His brother sounded profoundly suspicious.

Raoul stared at Christine. Something about her stirred his memory. "And I feel as if I've seen this little birdie before."

Philippe shrugged. "I can't imagine where."

"Ah!" Raoul snapped his fingers as his childhood memories fell into place. "The seaside at Lannion! She and I both spent a summer there. Surely she will remember me. Don't worry about introducing me, Brother. I can accomplish that myself."

CHRISTINE DAAÉ'S DRESSING room was a crowded, excited bustle when Raoul arrived. Blasted nuisance. How was he going to get the girl alone?

But fortune soon smiled. Poligny, one of the Opera's managers, clapped his hands to get everyone's attention. "Mademoiselles and Messieurs, please, our brilliant Christine needs to change out of her costume. Let's all move along to the foyer to enjoy champagne!"

The crowd, clearly enthusiastic at the mention of champagne, oozed out of the door past Raoul and bumbled down the hallway to the stairs. As the last of them herded past, he stuck his foot in the closing door and slipped into the dressing room. The only people left were Christine and a maid, who was no doubt there to help her undress. Good. No men to challenge him here. He'd still have to watch himself, but could act more boldly

"Monsieur?" The maid looked confused. Concerned. "Don't you want to get champagne with everyone else?"

Christine turned as she spoke, and gazed at Raoul with suspicion and annoyance. "Who are you?"

Raoul swept to her and knelt to press a kiss on the back of her reluctant hand. "Mademoiselle. I rescued your scarf from the sea many years ago. I am the Viscount Raoul de Chagny."

To his surprise, she uttered a sharp laugh of surprise. How dare she laugh at him? He had to tamp down a hot swell of anger, lest he lose control and let the little quim taste the back of his hand.

Instead, he stood and straightened the white silk vest of his tuxedo. "Mademoiselle. We saw each other every day for weeks. I am surprised you are so pleased to not recognize me."

"It's an odd thing, memory." Her expression turned grim. "You recall retrieving my scarf. Whereas I more clearly recall how you were very cruel to my puppy when you thought no one could see you."

Raoul pursed his lips. He didn't remember her dog, or what he might have done to it. There had been so many animals before he followed Philippe's example and turned to amusing himself with women.

"I do not recall the incident you speak of, but if I caused harm, I regret it," he replied coolly. "I was but a boy. You must know that boys are heedless creatures who naturally have untamed impulses. It's simply the way of things. Surely you should not hold something I did as a child against me now that we are both adults?"

The diva sighed as if he'd just told her the most tedious thing she'd ever heard. "I should like to be alone. Please, go away."

She waved him off. As if he were some peasant from the streets! He hadn't encountered this level of insolence from a woman in years.

I will break you, he vowed to himself. *I will break your pride. I will break your talent. I'll cut up that lovely face of yours and reduce you to whoring in the filthiest alleys of Paris. I'll see you utterly destroyed before you die penniless, debased, and forgotten.*

Aloud, he said, "As you wish, Mademoiselle." Then gave her a little formal bow, turned on his heel, and left her dressing room.

But Raoul did not go far. The entire corridor was deserted now, so he found a shadowy doorway and waited, cloaked in darkness, for the maid to leave. Christine would be a real challenge. He needed to seduce her in order to get inside her mind and destroy her from within. And that seduction in the face of his childhood error would require every bit of charm he could muster.

Eventually, the maid left, carrying Christine's costume on a hanger. When she'd disappeared down the hallway, Raoul crept to the dressing room door and carefully tried the polished brass knob. The door was locked.

But through the thick wood…he heard voices! He was certain that the maid and Christine had been the only people left in the small room. Who could this other person be? He pressed his ear to the door, trying to hear what was being said. Words were still unintelligible.

One voice was clearly Christine's, but the other was a lower timbre. A man? A woman? He just couldn't tell.

Then, abruptly, the voices stopped. As if the room were now empty. Raoul pulled out the lockpicking kit he kept in a silver cigarette case in his inside breast pocket. He worked at the door briefly with a couple of iron skeleton keys, and heard the latch click open.

The room stood empty. How was this possible? Raoul pulled the door closed behind him and relocked it so he could investigate at his leisure. The tall silvered glass mirror on the wall to the left of the vanity was canted ever so slightly, reflecting the room at a different angle. A pull at the edge revealed a dark corridor. A secret passage! And beyond, he could just barely hear someone speaking in hushed whispers.

RAOUL HAD PLENTY of experience in moving silently in dark spaces to follow women. His cobbler cut the soles for his dress shoes from vulcanized rubber that made little noise on floors. His ears were sharpened, and although he could not see in the dark, he'd learned to pay attention to the changes of the air on his face and hands to avoid obstacles and sudden drops.

He followed the voices through corridors and down narrow, dark stone stairways to the underground lake. Christine and her companion were closer, now; they'd gotten into a flat-bottomed skiff and cast off from the stone embankment. He could barely see the silhouette of a tall figure poling the boat along a few dozen yards ahead. Critically, the flickering yellow light of the lantern hanging from the prow cast enough illumination for Raoul to see the narrow stone ledges on either side of the cavernous passageway.

Raoul stepped onto the ledge. Hugging the damp stone wall, he followed the skiff as it wound through the dark, watery maze until it reached another stone landing. A short flight of steps led to a set of heavy wooden doors banded with wrought iron. He hung back, watching as the tall figure nimbly jumped out of the boat and moored it to an iron post, then helped Christine out and up the steps.

He waited until they'd disappeared behind the heavy doors and worked his way toward the landing. Made a perilous leap across the water into the skiff, hoping the sudden slap of water against the stones wouldn't alert anyone. He waited, crouching low on the boards. But no one emerged from the heavy doors. So he carefully hopped out of the boat and crept up the steps. Eased the door open and peeked inside.

The foyer hall beyond was lined with mirrors alternating with dark wood panels lit with guttering gas lamps. Coat hooks studded the panels below the lamps, and upon them hung black satin cloaks and grinning, spectral death's-head masks.

Ah, so the Opera Ghost is indeed a clever humbug. He smiled to himself.

Some masks appeared to be carved from wood; others were plaster or fabric. The mirrored hallway took a sharp turn to the left, and he couldn't see much beyond the turn.

Raoul slowly eased the door open and slipped inside. He paused to examine one of the more grotesque masks. It was artfully made from rubber painted onto linen. If he wore the mask for adventures upstairs, then it would be much easier to blame the Ghost. He carefully folded the mask and slipped it into his inner breast pocket, then crept down the hall, being mindful of reflections.

"Won't you ever relent and spend a weekend above ground with me?" Christine sounded weary and frustrated.

"I'm sorry, my dear. I just can't bear it," said her companion.

Raoul got down on his hands and knees to spy around the corner, low enough that the mirrors wouldn't give him away. The room before him was luxurious, appointed in gilded furniture that surely came from before the first Revolution. Heavy velvet drapes adorned the stone walls. Christine and her companion sat at a small dining table, sharing red wine, a plate of cheese, and a sliced baguette. A huge iron candelabra dripped white wax from a dozen tapers on the silver tablecloth.

Christine's black-clad companion was tall and lean, with very pale skin and a short shock of white hair. Raoul at first thought it was an older man, but as his eyes focused on the unlined, pink-cheeked face, he realized it was neither old, nor male. Long white lashes graced eyes the pale blue of a cold winter sky. A keen intelligence gleamed within.

The companion was a female. Unnaturally tall, but probably not tall enough to earn a living as a sideshow giantess. Her features were too angular to be properly feminine, and her bust much too small. But there was something fierce and dignified about her countenance. If he were being honest, his first instinct was to imagine her as the queen of some fantastic snow-bound kingdom.

But Raoul was seldom honest, and that mind's-eye image of her ruling over a great frozen land disturbed him on such a profound level that he had to push it far away. He focused on small physical details he could claim were flaws, could believe were weaknesses, and he decided she was ugly. An ugly woman was worth nothing at all. And no woman could be a plausible threat to a man like him.

"Erika." The diva set down her glass of wine. "You are certainly not a monster. A bit of blush to put some color on you and a wig and no-one would think you out of place."

The companion squirmed in her seat, clearly distressed. "You say so, and I would never claim you a liar. But I just…I just don't think I can go out without a mask. Without the armor of a costume. I cannot bear their gazes, my dear. You are so lovely…their gazes are bound to fall upon me, too."

Christine shook her head sadly. "I hate what your mother did to you. Your voice is far too good to be hidden away down here."

"My mother, God rest her soul, taught me all that I know about costumes. Stage makeup. Music. She taught me the Opera inside and out. I won't condemn her. I was not what she hoped for in a daughter. If my voice is worth anything at all, it's thanks to her."

"She saw you as a thing that might bring her fame and fortune, and when she decided that you could not, she discarded you. She was no real mother to you. I hope that someday you will see that." Christine took a sip of her wine and sighed. "I *so* wish we could perform together on the stage. You are so much more talented than anyone else in the company."

"Is it not enough that I am your Angel of Music?" Erika implored her. "Is it not enough that I teach you all that I know? Is it not enough that I intercede as the Phantom on your behalf? You will be famous enough for both of us."

Grinning, Raoul retreated and crept back to the water. He had the mask, and he understood the game. The Opera Ghost was nothing more than a shy, ugly woman. Nobody in the whole palais could keep him from indulging his red pleasures now.

———

PROWLING THE CORRIDORS and catwalks in a black opera cloak and the rubber death's-head mask was deeply satisfying, Raoul had to admit. It was especially satisfying when he caught a very young corps de ballet dancer alone in a back storeroom. She was so frightened she could barely speak.

"Oh, please, Monsieur Phantom, have mercy," she whispered brokenly as he loomed over her with a length of rope. He planned to choke her unconscious, bind and gag her, and carry her down below where he could take his time with his dagger.

"Hey! What are you doing?" a man shouted.

Raoul turned, and saw a bearded, red-faced stagehand hurrying toward them. The dancer whimpered and scampered away.

"This is none of your concern," Raoul growled.

The stagehand stopped short, staring uncertainly at the viscount. "You're—you're not Erika. Who in the blazes are you?"

Raoul responded by throwing the rope around the man's neck to garrote him. The stagehand was quite strong, but Raoul had the advantage of height and experience. He shoved the stagehand down onto the dusty wooden floor and stood on his back as he heaved up on the rope, crushing his windpipe. In moments the man was dead, his face purple as a berry and his tongue and eyes bulging.

PHILIPPE GRABBED HIM by the arm as he stepped out onto the second-story balcony to smoke and yanked him aside.

"Careful, this is a new coat," Raoul complained, shaking his arm from his brother's grip.

"You killed Joseph Buquet!" Philippe hissed.

"Am I supposed to know who that is?" he replied coolly.

"He was a stagehand. A ballerina rushed into the lobby claiming she was accosted by the Opera Ghost. When the managers investigated, they found Buquet's corpse. Three of his brothers work behind the scenes here, and they're calling for blood!"

Raoul paused, feeling the slightest shiver as he imagined himself beaten half to death and dragged onto a gallows by an angry mob. Dying in terror just as his great-grandfathers had in the Revolution. But he wasn't about to admit his fears aloud, so pushed them aside and feigned annoyed innocence in his reply: "Why not take this up with the Ghost, then?"

Philippe scowled. "Because the Ghost has never left a body behind. That's a habit of yours! You need to leave right now, and never return!"

Raoul had no intention of being banished from the Opera, not when he was just getting his sea legs.

"Come, come, let's not argue out here," he whispered. "Let's go downstairs. I know a place where we won't be overheard. I *promise* you, I have a plan to remedy the situation. All I ask is that you hear me out."

MURDERING PHILIPPE WAS much easier than Raoul expected. He expected to feel some twinge of last-minute regret, some swelling of conscience that would stay his hand before his fratricide was completed. But it never came.

For Philippe's part, he looked absolutely shocked when Raoul whipped the garrote around his neck. In his surprise, he put up far less of a fight than Buquet had. He died nearly as meekly as a lamb at the slaughterhouse.

Raoul crouched beside the gaping, wide-eyed corpse. "Thought you were above it all, Brother? Alas, you were not."

Raoul dragged his brother down the stone stairs to the landing and took Philippe's calfskin wallet and silver pocket watch before he rolled the body into the dark water. He knew he probably should have taken the time to weigh the corpse down, but what did it really matter if anyone found Philippe? Everyone would simply blame the Ghost.

THAT NIGHT, RAOUL dreamed not of his brother but of Christine and Erika. He was walking through the snow in the Cimetière du Père Lachaise when he spied the diva, dressed in black mourning clothes, kneeling at her father's grave. Her face was shrouded by a dark lace veil. Erika, also dressed in somber black, stood nearby playing a funeral dirge on a violin.

He stepped on a twig, and both women looked up at him. Pale Erika dropped her violin and pointed the bow at him.

"You are not welcome here." Her bow had become a gleaming cavalry saber. "You should run."

Raoul turned on his heel and ran from her, weaving in and out of the gloomy stone crypts to try to escape. When he chanced a look behind him, Erika had become the Phantom. She rode atop a red-eyed white horse, thundering down upon him, her saber raised.

Shielding his face, he stumbled backward, and plummeted through darkness.

———

RAOUL WOKE FROM the dream with a start, and he never slept well again.

———

HE WORE HIS best tuxedo along with a white half-mask to the New Year's Eve masquerade ball at the Opera. The Bal Masque was being held in part to celebrate and welcome the arrival of the Opera's new managers, Armand Moncharmin and Firmin Richard. Raoul didn't know and didn't care whether his recent activities had led to Debienne and Poligny retiring. Apparently the new managers had pooh-poohed rumors of the Ghost, so he presumed that the outgoing managers had somehow managed to mollify the angry brothers and pass the stagehand's death off as an accident.

Christine was Raoul's primary concern that evening. After that strange sleep-ruining nightmare, he was more determined than ever to seduce and destroy the young diva. But Christine, who wore a gorgeous green ball gown and a lacy black half-mask that reminded him uncomfortably of her veil in his dream, was constantly surrounded by admirers competing for her attention. Getting her alone was going to be a significant challenge.

He'd managed to get within a few feet of Christine when the Phantom made a dramatic appearance atop the grand marble staircase. The Opera Ghost was dressed in crimson robes and a feathered Musketeer's hat, much like the Red Death from Edgar Allan Poe's celebrated tale. Costumed revelers scattered as the Phantom descended the stairs, regal as any Emperor.

Once on the mezzanine, the Phantom banged a skull-topped cane against the marble floor and spoke: "Beneath your feet are the bones of tortured souls! I rebuke your merriment, and I rebuke the villain amongst you who dares to leave new corpses in my name!"

The Phantom's voice was unexpectedly deep and didn't sound anything like Erika. This unnerved Raoul—was he entirely mistaken about the Phantom's identity? But what set his heart jumping in his chest was the chance that the Phantom knew *his* identity and might call him out in front of all these people.

Raoul turned and raced to the back stairwell, which led up to the attic and the roof.

THE ATTIC SEEMED dark as the inside of a whale. Raoul felt around himself and found a lantern hanging from a hook beside the door. A quick shake revealed it was still half-filled with kerosene. He pulled his tin of Lucifer matches from his pocket and lit the lantern.

The yellow flame illuminated the vaulted, spacious room. The floor was well-worn planks, and the walls were lined with brass ballet barres for dance practice. Trapdoors in the planks led to spaces for various cables and pulleys involved in supporting and counter-weighting the massive chandeliers in the palais. Deeply recessed round windows looked out over Paris.

I'll just stay up here a bit until the furor has died down, he thought.

"I know who you are," said a familiar deep voice.

Startled, Raoul looked toward the sound. The Phantom stood at the other side of the room brandishing the skull-topped staff, staring at him with those deep-set pits of eyes.

"You are the Viscount Raoul de Chagny," the Phantom said.

"Murderer of my friend Joseph Buquet. Murderer of your own brother. Attempted rapist of poor little Meg Giry. You are not welcome here. If you value your life, you should leave now and never return."

Raoul threw his lantern toward the specter. It made it only halfway across the room and shattered on the boards. Fiery kerosine splashed all over one of the trapdoors. The old, dry wood seemed eager to burn.

He fled from the flames and smoke back down the stairs, certain the whole Opera was going to become an inferno. As he reached the mezzanine, he heard people inside the auditorium start screaming a moment after the groan and snap of cables giving way and ripping through plaster.

Then the tremendous bone-jarring crash of seven tons of bronze and crystal plummeting into the theatre seats below.

The revelers stampeded for the exits. Some smaller women teetering on heels fell, only to be trampled by the people rushing close behind them. Their panicked shrieks annoyed Raoul. He swore to himself. If the fire spread as quickly as he feared, he'd die in the crowd before he could shoulder his way outside.

So, he hurried around the back corridor to one of the hidden entrances that led down to the cistern. He didn't relish going so close to the Phantom's lair, but rock and water would not burn. And perhaps there was some other way out from there.

RAOUL SPOTTED THE Phantom, still in the Red Death costume, standing in one of the submerged corridors with a lantern. The flat-bottomed skiff floated nearby. The water was much shallower than Raoul would have guessed and only went to the Phantom's knees. The figure seemed to be hunting in the water for something.

He hung back, steadying his nerves, studying the Phantom. It was still difficult for him to imagine Erika inside the costume. Difficult to believe that the dread specter was just a woman in disguise. But Erika was tall enough. And the imposing qualities of the figure could be a trick of the costume. Padding the shoulders and arms might be enough to create the illusion of masculinity.

But what of the voice? It certainly did not seem womanly. But Raoul reconsidered: as a youth he'd attended a séance with friends, and the female spiritualist made many strange groans and low growls during her performance. Perhaps Erika had learned a similar vocal trick? Christine had claimed she was talented, so surely such a thing was possible.

The Phantom was Erika, and Erika was just a woman. And therefore she could not possibly be a true threat to him. He knelt and drew his double-bladed dagger from its sheath at his ankle. It was time to erase Erika and take her secret domain for himself. He would become the new Phantom. The Opera and its women would be his to use as he pleased. If Christine had survived the fire and stampede, he'd destroy her body and soul, and then sleep peacefully in luxury far underground.

Erika set the lantern on the wall ledge and stripped off her feathered hat and death's-head mask. She casually tossed the costume pieces into the boat and resumed feeling around in the dark water, her white hair pointing every which way in sweaty spikes.

She'd turned her back to him. Raoul lowered himself down into the water as quietly as he could and began wading toward her, his dagger ready in his hand.

When he was very close to her, he shouted, "What are you looking for?"

She rose up from the water alarmingly fast, whirled, and skewered him in the belly with the sharp, polished saber she'd pulled from the water. He'd never been hurt like this before, and in his pain and shock, he dropped his dagger and grabbed at the sword blade, only succeeding in cutting his fingers.

Erika shoved the blade deeper. The agony was extraordinary. His vision briefly went all white. He flailed, trying to hit her, but the blade was long and she was beyond his reach. Groaning, he splashed backward in the water, trying to free himself, but soon she'd backed him against a rough, cold wall. His blood spilled freely around the fierce steel.

"Christine is fine, by the way." Her tone was calm and conversational. "The fire brigade is dealing with your vandalism. A few people were injured in the rush, and unfortunately you crushed one of our patrons beneath the chandelier. A few more had to go to the hospital. The Opera might have to close for a week or two, but the show *will* go on."

"G-go to h-hell." His whole body had gone cold, and his teeth were chattering.

"Did you really think I didn't know you were lurking back there?" Glaring at him with her frosty blue eyes, she twisted the blade. "Did you really think I didn't know you'd trespassed and stolen from me? Did you really think I didn't see right through you from the moment you set foot in my Opera house? You and your brother were two of the most transparent, venial, small-minded men I've ever had the displeasure of encountering."

His vision was darkening at the edges. His knees were shaking beneath him, threatening to collapse. He tried to curse her again, but pain had driven the air from his lungs.

She shook her head. "Do you think you're the first to try to harm the women here? But killing upsets Christine so very much…she has softened my heart. I gave you a chance. And for the sake of little Meg and Joseph and his family, I regret that very, very much. I should have disposed of you when you crept through my door, but I didn't want to spoil dinner."

Erika pulled the sword free. "I won't make that mistake again."

The last thing Raoul's dying eyes glimpsed was the blade gleaming crimson in the lamplight right before she slashed it deeply across his neck.

MODERN MONSTERS

MONIQUE SNYMAN

LOST IN A turbulent sea of raging ghosts and regretful memories, Iris Coventry stood outside a long-abandoned compound located in buttfuck nowhere, West Virginia. It had been decades since she'd last been anywhere near the squat cinderblock building, decades since she'd committed the most heinous of sins. Tendrils of mist coiled around the edges of the dilapidated building and reached toward the rusted fence with its faded red warning sign, beckoning Iris to enter once more.

Her heart, no longer what it used to be, beat faster as her fear took root. Decades may have passed, but her recollection of this doomed place and what hell she had unleashed on the world remained fresh. Inescapable guilt plagued her every hour of every day, and she carried an unimaginable dread with her wherever she went. Iris's only peace had been in hoping—*praying*—the general had enough sense to have destroyed every part of her research when the project was scrapped.

People like Iris, however, didn't deserve a modicum of peace.

"Iris, it's time," Alec Rowland said, the forced solemnity in his voice unmistakable.

She watched as he moved toward the cut wire fence, held open by one of the people who'd accompanied her on this grave journey into her past, and trespassed on government property. Joey, who carried a camera and tripod, followed. Maxine went next, the purple-haired rebel who Iris thought couldn't be older than twenty. While they set up the cameras, she stood outside the fence, terrified of what she would find inside.

"Professor Coventry?" said Elliot, the teenaged boy who looked like a younger Alec. "Are you going inside?"

"Are *you?*" she asked.

"Nah," he said. "My dad doesn't let me go into these creepy places. Says I'll just get in the way." The boy shrugged.

"So, you're just going to sit in the van and wait until we get back? Sounds dull."

He held up his cellphone and flashed her a genuine smile. "I keep an eye on the feed, usually, but I also know how to keep busy if things get boring."

"You'll be able to see everything the camera sees then?"

"Yup." He returned his cellphone to his pocket, leaned down, and pulled the fence back for her again. "Whenever you're ready, professor."

Unable to put off the inevitable any longer, Iris sighed as she stepped closer to the fence. She ducked beneath the opening and climbed through. A distinctive chill rolled down her spine, made the baby hairs on the back of her neck stand on end. Her gaze shifted to the compound again as she straightened, the past flickering to life in those too dark windows.

The tenuous reunion was short-lived as Maxine approached, a cautious, tight-lipped smile on display as she held out her hand to Iris.

"We're going to start," Maxine said, lowering her hand slowly when Iris ignored the gesture.

Iris nodded and made her way closer to where they had set up the filming equipment.

She watched as Alec—framed by the large entryway—squared his shoulders and looked into the camera. His expression neutral, black hair perfectly imperfect, icy-blue eyes penetrating.

"Today," he said, "we are at Riverside Compound, an abandoned military research facility with a tainted history and a peculiar present." Alec gestured to the building behind him, dark brows almost touching as he frowned. He grimaced, shook his head, and lowered his arm. "Sorry, can we start over?" Alec asked, repositioning himself in front of the entryway.

Iris raised an eyebrow.

"He's a bit of a perfectionist," Joey, the cameraman, whispered her way.

"Ah," Iris answered.

"We could be here a while." He snickered.

Iris looked up at the sky, where emerald canopies kept most of the gloomy afternoon light from reaching them. "I didn't sign up for a night tour of the place."

He responded with an apologetic smile but said nothing to quell her worries. The last thing Iris needed was to be stuck at Riverside Compound after dark, especially if the evidence Alec and his team had gathered about *something* stalking the good ol' folks from nearby towns was true.

Maxine walked closer, holding a camera set in what looked like a harness. "Professor," she said, holding the contraption out towards Iris. "It's so we can see everything you see."

Iris held out her arms and Maxine helped her to put on the camera, tightening the straps like a pro.

"Tonight," Alec began again, "our journey through the unknown— Ugh, my voice came out shit. Okay, okay, let me try something else."

Alec shook his hands and clicked his neck this way then the other way. He jumped up and down a few times, loosening up, before he stood on his nonexistent mark and stared into the camera.

"Tonight, on *Modern Monsters*," Alec said, "we embark on a journey into the Riverside Compound, a military research facility with a tainted history and a peculiar present." He shifted his body slightly, but his penetrating gaze was unwavering. "Joined by Professor Iris Coventry, the former head of the science department, we discover what long-forgotten secrets this place holds and how Riverside Compound remains at the heart of some of West Virginia's most infamous unexplained mysteries."

"And cut!" Maxine yelled. "Perfect."

"You sure?" Alec asked. "I can do it again?"

Iris, no longer amused by these childish games, wandered off toward the entryway. Metal doors, dented and scratched beyond recognition, hung on rusted hinges. She peered into the darkness beyond, cautious yet curious. Instead of the clinical white walls and floors she had expected, a layer of dust disappeared into the black interior, where only a silhouette of a creeping vine or growing weed could be spotted in the waning light.

Heart still racing, Iris took a step forward, grit crunching beneath her sneakers.

"Woah! Hold up there, Iris," Alec's voice intruded on her thoughts. "Let's just set up the handheld camera and—"

Iris shot a glare over her shoulder, which effectively shut him up. Without a word, she stepped back and waited for the crew of *Modern Monsters* to catch up with her. How Alec had persuaded her to humor him and be on his show, to become part of this farce, she didn't know. Iris didn't even like him—he was far too arrogant for someone who had only his looks going for him—but here she was, ready to blow the whistle on a top-secret government project because of him.

"Are you done?" Iris asked. She crossed her arms and tapped her foot against the cracked concrete.

"Almost," Alec called back.

She turned her gaze skyward again, looked past the intertwining branches and lush leaves, until she saw only the threatening gray and silver clouds. The weather certainly hadn't improved since she had last been to Riverside.

"Okay, we're ready for you," Alec said, out of breath, as he rushed up to her side. He held out a flashlight to Iris, which she accepted, and flashed her a used-car salesman smile. "Are you ready?"

"I just want to get this over with," Iris said.

Alec's smile faltered slightly as he nodded. He glanced back, gestured for the crew to get ready, and switched on his flashlight.

"Just act naturally," he whispered to Iris, before he spun on his heels and amped up the charm. "The Riverside Compound was built in the early 1990s by the US Government for the sole purpose of exploring and advancing fringe sciences. Many of these top-secret projects failed, which is why the compound was eventually abandoned." The flashlight's beam cut through the darkness as he took the lead and ventured into the building. "Professor Coventry, as the head of the science department, can you tell us what type of research was conducted here?"

Iris followed him into the dark, her gaze travelling the length and breadth of the neglected, overgrown entrance of the Riverside Compound. The reception desk was overturned, no doubt the work of vandals, and damaged beyond repair. A few errant papers fluttered across the floor, coming to a stop near an old beer can. Once upon a time, this had been a mecca for some of the greatest minds in science. They had roamed the halls of Riverside, on the cusp of new and exciting discoveries that could change the world as they knew it.

"Professor Coventry?" Alec repeated.

Iris inhaled through her nose and said, "Have you ever heard about the Philadelphia Experiment?"

"Yes. Maxine did a whole segment about it on our blog a few months ago."

"Well, one of the projects we were working on was similar in nature to the Philadelphia Experiment, and somewhat successful, thanks to—" Iris cut herself off before she could say too much. Being a whistleblower was one thing, but there were still lines she couldn't cross for the sake of humanity. "We experimented with teleportation, basically," she ended, wandering a few steps ahead. "Other stuff we worked on included gene-splicing and cloning."

Iris pursed her lips and turned her back on the camera.

"Surely, this place isn't big enough to have included all those labs, though?"

"The compound is larger than it appears," Iris said. "Most of the facility is underground."

"Why didn't you tell me earlier?" Alec whispered to her as he swiped a finger across his neck, indicating to Joey to stop rolling.

"You didn't ask." She shrugged.

Alec groaned in frustration, before he continued, "Look, Iris, we need to establish trust here if this is going to work. I know this is hard for you—"

"You have no idea what this is to me," she snapped back. "Do you even know what happens to whistleblowers? They get taken out by the government. Now, I'm lucky, because the general who ran this shitshow was untouchable and most of what happened here was destroyed by him personally. The *only* reason I agreed to be on *Modern Monsters* and open up to you is because of the images you showed me." A shudder crawled across her skin as she remembered the grainy trail camera pictures of something resembling her biggest mistake and greatest regret. "I need to make sure." Iris mumbled to herself as she stomped off to the hallway.

The darkness intensified around Iris, swallowing her whole as she made her way deeper into the compound. The flashlight beam barely cut through the inky black interior, which seemed to stretch an eternity. She heard the crew following, their shoes crunching on unseen debris, and could feel their eyes boring into her back. Some whispering accompanied the trek, but she couldn't care less about whatever they were talking about.

Iris halted in front of a metal door that had been bent out of shape, the bottom corner somehow lifted high enough for someone or something to crawl through. She shone the flashlight to the wall beside the door, where a biometric keypad remained untouched.

Her palms perspired as fear rushed through her system.

"It almost looks like something clawed its way out," Maxine said from somewhere behind Iris.

"Nah. It's probably kids who tried to get a glimpse of whatever was behind the door," Alec said. "Can we get in there, though?"

"I don't know, Alec, maybe it's not such a good idea," Joey said.

"C'mon, man! This is a once-in-a-lifetime opportunity for the show," Maxine argued. "We have someone from the inside who's giving us a freaking tour, and—"

Iris reached out and placed her sweaty palm against the keypad, hoping the electricity was well and truly—

The biometric scanner suddenly came to life, casting a faint bluish light beneath her palm. Something on the other side of the door hissed, and locks, rattling and screeching from disuse, slid out of place. The door, buckled and broken, popped open just enough for a glimpse of the abyss lying beyond.

Iris held her breath.

"There's your answer," Alec said, stepping forward. He slid his hands into the space between the door and the frame and tugged a few times. The metal scraped loudly against the floor, announcing their whereabouts to whatever may have been left behind in this godforsaken place. "A little help?" he grunted.

Joey set down his camera and reluctantly joined the host of *Modern Monsters*. Together, they pried open the door, while Maxine and Iris watched. Eventually, after some exertion, the gap was just large enough for an adult to squeeze through.

"There we go." Alec backed up, grinning triumphantly as he studied his handiwork.

A sinister stench wafted through the air, smelling like rot.

"Joey and I'll go in first to document what secrets we've just uncovered," Alec continued, before turning to Iris. "We'll give you and Maxine a shout when it's all clear."

Iris nodded, grateful for a few extra minutes to gather herself before wandering deeper into her past. As she watched Alec and Joey disappear into the void, Maxine walked closer. The purple-haired girl pushed her flashlight through the gap and peered inside, trying to sneak a peek at what awaited them.

"Are we rolling?" Alec asked from inside.

"Yeah."

"For years, surrounding towns have been seeing a rise in missing persons, but officials have been dragging their feet in giving answers as to why this has been happening." Alec's voice drifted out to where Iris stood. "Witnesses report seeing something strange in the area before each kidnapping, though. A humanoid creature of some kind. Some have claimed this as the work of aliens, but…" His voice grew too distant, the words indistinct.

Iris remembered the administration office lay directly beyond the door. Nothing interesting happened there, really. Some paperwork, admin, the boring parts of running any business. Beyond that sat the research offices, where headhunted graduates and seasoned scientists tended to the nitty-gritty parts of their duties. Theoretical stuff, mostly.

More interesting, yes, but not quite as hands-on as what happened in the laboratories and practicums.

Fact and fiction became indistinguishable *there*.

"So, like, what did you do with your experiments when they succeeded?" Maxine asked without turning around.

"We were usually tasked with trying to either monetize or weaponize them," Iris said.

The purple-haired girl spun around. Her eyes were wide, lips parted, and the blood slowly drained from her youthful cheeks. "Seriously?"

"Why else would the government care about science if they can't use it to make money or destroy their enemies?"

"That's crazy scary," Maxine said.

"You have no idea."

"Hey," Alec's voice interrupted as he popped his head out of the door.

"Motherfucker!" Maxine gasped. She placed her hand over her heart, stared at the obnoxious host. "You're *so* unnecessary sometimes."

"Sorry," he chuckled. "You can come in now." He disappeared again.

"Prick," Maxine hissed as she followed Alec into the darkness. "How many times do I have to tell you not to scare me?"

Iris rolled her eyes as she squeezed through the gap, following the foulmouthed purple-haired girl into the admin office. The smell of rot became more distinct, but whatever had died—whatever was *killed*—was farther off. Something could have crawled in through the damaged door, died somewhere in the dark. It's plausible.

"I'm just having some fun," Alec said.

"Yeah, well, I don't think it's funny."

While Alec and Maxine argued about him scaring her, Iris made her way through the administration office and headed toward the research offices, where she found Joey getting some footage. The doors leading in and out of these sections stood wide open, though, and were completely intact. She walked down another long hallway, her flashlight beam moving across the walls, ceiling, and floor.

"Wait up, Iris," Alec called behind her.

The stench grew stronger, the decay became more pronounced. Something big had died recently, she decided. Something the size of a bear, perhaps? Again, Iris knew this was only wishful thinking on her part.

"Where are you going?" Alec asked right beside her.

"The labs," Iris said.

"Why?"

She grimaced. "Don't you smell that?"

"What do you think it is?" he responded.

Iris shrugged.

Scritch-scritch-scritch.

The sound gave Iris pause. Her mind reeled with possibilities as she directed her flashlight down the hallway, searching for whatever may be waiting. It could, perhaps, be a critter that'd made its way into the building—a rat or a possum. Iris tried to remain positive, but some part of her knew they were being stalked. Hunted.

Scritch-scritch-scritch.

She spun on her heels, the strange noise now coming from behind them. Calculated, intelligent, testing the response of everyone who'd ventured into this doomed place. Flashlights searched the hallway, crisscrossing and illuminating the darkness and finding nothing overtly weird.

Iris's every instinct screamed at her to run, to leave Riverside behind and get as far away as possible. She couldn't leave them, though. These poor, naïve fools would meet their end if she left them now.

Scritch-scritch-scritch.

"What the fuck?" Joey swung the camera in a different direction.

"What is it?" Alec pushed forward to get to the cameraman, excitement rolling off him in waves. "Did you get something on film?"

"I don't know, man. There's something moving around us fast," Joey answered.

"This is great stuff! This could—"

Maxine's shrill scream cut Alec's excitement short and sent everyone into panic mode. Flashlight beams moved toward the girl, who was now down on her knees, yellowish-white goop running down her neck and shoulder, landing on her chest. Red bubbles started to form as the camera swiveled to capture the unadulterated horror on her face.

"What is happening to her?" Alec shouted as he moved to Maxine's side, not knowing where to touch or how to help. "Call an ambulance!"

Shock probably kept Joey from moving, whereas Iris knew nothing could be done to save the girl—*nothing* could save any of them anymore.

Maxine's screaming continued as her flesh bubbled and blood rained down her shirt. The yellowish-white slime oozed as the enzyme worked to liquify muscle, sinew, bone, which made it easier to digest. Chunks of her body broke off, fell onto the grimy floor. Bubbling, breaking down, until all that remained was a meat milkshake.

Those anguished cries ended as quickly as they began.

Iris watched as Maxine's eyes rolled back into her head, her expression turned neutral, and she fell forward, landing face-first in a pool of dissolving human tissue.

Alec bent down. He reached out to touch her, hesitant, just hovering over her prone form.

"Don't touch her," Joey bellowed without turning the camera away from the unfolding scene. "It looks like acid."

Alec recoiled and looked up to the camera with watery eyes. He opened his mouth to say something, but the *scritch-scritch-scritch* sound started anew. The camera moved away from *Modern Monsters'* host and scanned the area, while Alec stood and shone his flashlight around.

"We need to get out of here," Joey said in a quivering voice, already moving up the hallway, back to the administration office. "Now, Alec.

We need to get—"

"We can't leave without knowing what killed Maxine," Alec said. "We need answers. *She* deserves answers."

Joey shook his head as he carefully stepped around Maxine's corpse. "Nah, man, I didn't sign up for this shit." He finally pulled his face away from the camera and looked Alec straight in the eye. "Sorry, Alec. I— I can't. I'll call the—"

Before he could finish his sentence, something reached down and grabbed hold of Joey. He was lifted into the air by something with inhuman strength. Plastic pieces scattered across the floor as the camera fell from his hands, while the poor cameraman dangled in midair. A surprised shout was cut short with a resounding *crack*.

Alec backed up, gaping at the deformed creature against the ceiling. A few moments later, the heinously disfigured hybrid creature stepped into view. Bulging eyes glared between Alec and Iris. Coarse black hair, visible even from afar, covered parts of the poor soul's body. The humanoid form, genetically altered with the DNA of a common housefly, no longer resembled the person it used to be, yet there remained an intelligence behind the glassy compound eyes.

"Dear God," Alec gasped, stumbling back. He leaned against the wall, legs buckling. "W-w-what is that thing?"

"A mistake I never thought would have survived this long out here by itself." Iris swallowed the bile pushing up her esophagus.

Alec ducked down, grabbed hold of the shattered camera, and made a run for it back to where they'd come from.

"By itself?" A familiar, albeit aged voice said somewhere behind Iris. The chuckle that followed was as brittle as an autumn leaf.

Iris spun around, flashlight beam searching for the voice's owner. "Dutch?" she asked, unable to keep the surprise from entering her tone.

"Yes, dearest Iris, it is I." An older man with stooped shoulders, wearing a filthy lab coat, came into view. His hair had grayed considerably over the years, while liver spots dotted his otherwise pale skin. He looked nothing like the man she once knew. "I wondered if you'd ever return to us."

Iris felt her knees go weak at the sight of Dutch—a former colleague and sometimes lover. They'd embarked on this journey together, so very long ago, but their paths had not crossed since the dismantlement of the compound. Had he truly been here all this time?

She opened her mouth to speak, but there were no words.

"You seem surprised to see me, Iris darling," Dutch said, shambling closer.

Iris didn't trust the false smile he wore. Still, she'd come here to put things right and if it meant dealing with an apparent madman, then so be it. She flicked her gaze down the hallway, where she heard Alec's footsteps growing fainter, then turned her full attention on Dutch.

"You were able to weaponize and control our creation?" Iris asked.

"*Our* creation was merely the beginning, and it was subpar in comparison." He gestured to the monstrous half-fly half-man creature. "It died within a couple of months of your abandonment. My tweaks to the original formula created something far superior," Dutch said.

"Will you show me?" Iris took a step closer to Dutch, hoping to keep his attention from returning to the host of *Modern Monsters*, who was, hopefully, already in the administration office.

A twinkle of excitement gleamed in Dutch's eyes, the possibility of showing off his work too great of an opportunity to pass up. "Of course," he said.

She forced a smile.

"But first we should deal with your friend who's fleeing," Dutch said, peering past Iris.

"Oh, no. Alec is of no consequence." Iris waved her hand through the air, appearing unconcerned by his presence. Deep inside, however, she feared a horrible death on the horizon. "He was merely an escort."

Dutch laughed. "Be that as it may, we can't allow any classified information to fall into the wrong hands."

"Come now, Dutch, we have more important things to concern ourselves with than children running amok," Iris said in as humorous tone as she could muster. The last thing she wanted was to be the cause of someone else's death, especially one who has a child waiting outside. She walked up to him, tilted her head to the side, and touched his shoulder. "Show me what I've missed out on."

Dutch relented with a sigh, turned around, and—

Iris gasped as she spotted the crooked, limp translucent wings, tinged yellow at the base, protruding from tears in his lab coat. The hump on his back, pronounced even through the layers of fabric he wore, had a bulbous, almost tumorous quality to it.

"What did you do to yourself?" Iris asked, eyes wide with horror.

Dutch shrugged. "An experiment in partial gene-splicing."

"Y-you have wings, Dutch."

"They don't work," he said in a matter-of-fact tone. "They can't cope with the weight. Too small." He shrugged again, acting as if this horrendous body modification meant nothing. "Come along. I'll show you some of my more successful experiments." Dutch picked up the pace, shuffling across the grit and debris without stumbling.

Iris followed him deeper into the compound, heading toward the cloying smell. She cast a look over her shoulder every now and then to make sure the creature was within sight and not following Alec out of the facility.

The smell of death became more distinct the nearer they got to the laboratories. She tried to cover up her gagging with a disheartened chuckle, something Dutch could perceive as excitement. Whether he believed her horrendous acting, Iris couldn't be sure, but he made no comment on it. Instead, Dutch slowed his pace and reached out to touch the wall.

"I hope you're ready to see something spectacular," he said.

Click.

It took Iris a moment to accustom her eyes to the blinding white light, which illuminated old smears of blood covering the walls and floor. Fat, sluggish, common houseflies buzzed around the once-sterile laboratory, disturbed by the light. Some flew around in a daze, without a care in the world, while others went right back to sit on...organs and decaying tissue? Iris didn't know whether the organs were of the human or animal variety, or both. And there, in the back, she spotted the "telepods"—teleportation devices that'd initially been used to splice genes when the technique had still been in its infancy. Why had Dutch returned to such a crude technology?

"Mind the mess. I didn't expect visitors," Dutch said. He made his way inside and, undisturbed by the flies buzzing around him, walked toward the back of the laboratory.

She watched him go, the broken wings shifting slightly as he moved. Iris hesitated, wondered if she could escape before he realized she was gone, before the *scritch-scritch-scritch* of Dutch's creature reminded her they were not alone.

"Come, Iris. Come look," he said, pointing out of the large window serving as an observatory to one of the practicums on the floor below.

She stepped into the laboratory, her skin crawling in disgust. Alarm bells went off in her mind, growing louder and louder, the farther she went. Iris had come to rectify a mistake, but this problem was far more complex than anything she could fix by herself.

"Look!" Dutch grabbed her by the arm and whirled her to view his creations.

Deformed half-human creatures crawled across one another, bloody and broken. Mistakes, each and every one of them, yet they were doomed to suffer a terrible existence with only a mad scientist to tend to their needs.

Some had retained their human faces, their expressions pained, showing suffering in indescribable ways. Eyes stared up at the observatory, their silent pleas for mercy evident in the tears running down their cheeks. They had ugly, too-small wings, fly-like legs that couldn't support their weight, misshapen half-torso half-thoraxes. Others had no redeeming human qualities left in their faces, though. Labella sat in awkward places, which would make feeding difficult, antennae grew from backs or stomachs or necks, compound eyes were—in some cases—completely missing.

Were these the people who'd gone missing in the surrounding towns? Surely, she must be mistaken, because the Dutch she knew wouldn't kidnap people and transform them into these heinous monstrosities. Would he?

"Aren't they beautiful?" Dutch beamed.

"W-w-what have…y-you done?"

His triumphant expression faltered, and confusion took over. "What do you mean? This is the pinnacle of scientific exploration. This—"

"This is…" Iris shook her head and stumbled back a step, unable to rid herself of the image of Dutch's madness. "This is *wrong!*" she shrieked.

"You certainly didn't think it wrong to embark on this project all those years ago."

Iris couldn't argue with him there, but *this* had never been the purpose of their experiments. Besides, she'd realized the error of her ways the moment she'd seen what they'd created. A modern monster—no longer human, but not quite insect either.

"*You* put me on this path, Iris, and then you just abandoned me?" Dutch continued. His face reddened, eyes grew wider, fury made his stooped shoulders shake. "Abandoned *us?*"

Scritch-scritch-scritch.

Iris glanced up, saw Dutch's creature sitting right above her. Agitated, compound eyes focused on only her, ready to pounce at its master's command.

"But you won't leave us again," he said. "Never again."

EXECUTIVES DECIDED TO end Season 2, Episode 9 of *Modern Monsters* just before the creature attacked Professor Iris Coventry, which left the public speculating her fate for weeks. As a result, the show's ratings went through the roof, earning Alec—the sole survivor—newfound fame and fortune. The critics, of course, cried foul by pointing out how certain scenes had "*subpar CGI and SFX makeup.*" There were even those who said they'd seen both Maxine and Joey alive and well. Most positive reviews mentioned how the episode was reminiscent of a 1980s body horror film and how the abrupt ending was the perfect way to spark debate.

Alec knew better, though.

Both he and Elliot had watched helplessly as Iris was dragged to some contraption by Dutch's creature and forced into the tiny cubicle as she fought tooth and nail. She had screamed bloody murder all the while, but Dutch simply stood there smiling.

Alec didn't know what truly happened to Iris—her camera feed cut out during the experiment she'd been subjected to—but he couldn't imagine it being anything good after seeing those squirming humanoid monstrosities Dutch had created.

The police weren't helpful in getting to the bottom of things either. Apparently, the land was still owned by the military and, as such, did not fall within local law enforcement's jurisdiction. Any calls to the Pentagon for assistance in retrieving the bodies of Maxine, Joey, and, possibly, Iris had been ignored.

Eventually, Alec realized he had no other option than to go on the search for the next modern monster, smile for the camera, and pray the executives didn't give in to the public's requests for a follow-up on the mystery of Riverside Compound.

BEAUTIFUL MONSTER

JG FAHERTY

I'M A MONSTER.

Shari's lip quivered as she tried to hold back tears at the sight of her terrible face. A face she knew all too well, each twisting, wrinkled brick-red line burned into her memory from countless hours staring at it, praying for a sign that five years of her aunt Victoria's treatments had made a difference.

They hadn't.

Despite the agony of her weekly injections, she remained a hideous beast. The perfect blue of her eyes and elfin features only emphasized the utter horror of the rest of her.

"Don't give up hope." Victoria eased the mirror from Shari's hands, freeing her from the awful creature that mocked her. Still weak from the effects of the serum, her skin already beginning to burn as the sedatives wore off, Shari could only nod.

Victoria's equipment filled the basement with sounds as incomprehensible as the functions of the machines themselves. Pumps gurgled and hissed, motors clattered and whined. On a nearby table, opaque fluids swirled in beakers atop magnetic stirrers. Liquid pain harvested from the samples Victoria collected in secret at the clinic. Some of it flowed in her veins now; the rest waited to be discarded, containers of failure destined for the garbage, just like the bags Aunt Victoria hid in dumpsters throughout town.

"I'll fix you," Victoria whispered. "I promise."

Shari forced a weak smile, knowing her aunt needed it. She'd begun to think it was a promise Victoria would never be able to keep. But as long as her aunt believed, Shari would pretend to as well. She owed her that much. Owed her everything. Her life.

Even if it was a life of hell.

AS WAS OFTEN the case after a treatment, nightmares plagued Shari's sleep.

Running in the darkness. Bright lights appearing out of nowhere. Coming at her.

And then nothing until she woke in Victoria's laboratory, with no memory and a jigsaw puzzle for a body.

In the five years since, she'd survived on hopes and prayers and the agonizing treatments, barely making it from one month to the next without separating at her many seams.

In the hours before dawn, unwilling to risk slumber again, Shari found herself praying for a normal life, the kind Victoria insisted they'd had before the accident. Going out to movies and shows, dining at cafés and restaurants. Simply leaving Victoria's musty old house without fear of being seen. Because if the police ever found out what Dr. Victoria Frankstone did in her laboratory, or at the clinic, she'd be locked away forever.

And then what would happen to me? Alone, with no relatives, no friends, no money?

No treatments?

Shari knew the answer. She'd fall apart, scar tissue slowly weakening until she lay in bloody pieces on the floor.

Things could always be worse.

The world was a dangerous place. Murders, rapes, violent protests. Drugs everywhere. Terrible people who would like nothing better than to see Victoria in jail and Shari cut open like a lab rat.

"The sixties and seventies were much better," Victoria often said. "This new decade has brought out the worst in people."

That's why they spent most of their time listening to classical music or reading romance novels. When Victoria did turn on the television, they watched programs or movies from "the better days," before the accident that stole Shari's memories. *Laverne & Shirley* or *Happy Days* during the week, *Annie Hall* or *Saturday Night Fever* or *Close Encounters* on a Saturday night.

Sometimes Shari wished she could leave the house when her aunt went out. Just a drive in the car, even at night, so people wouldn't see her. Anything to break the endless monotony.

Warm tears tickled her cheeks, following the uneven paths of her scars.

You're trapped. Trapped inside the house, trapped inside your body, trapped inside a life that will never change until the day the treatments stop working and you die.

Down the hall, the shower began to run. Victoria was getting ready for work. Another night at the clinic. She wouldn't be home until late, especially if she had to steal more samples.

Shari's chest tightened as an idea came to her. Perhaps a bit of freedom was possible after all.

If she dared break Victoria's rules.

SHARI HAD NO idea she'd fall in love when she sat down.

All she'd wanted to do was rest her aching feet. She'd found an empty bench across the street from a busy hospital. Dark enough to hide her gruesome features from passersby, but it allowed her to people watch.

The world had been more overwhelming than she'd expected. Bright lights everywhere. Music blasting from stores and car windows. And the people! So different from what she saw on TV. Girls with skirts above their knees. Boys in black leather jackets with chains and spikes like medieval warriors, their heads shaved everywhere except down the center. Women wearing bras but no shirts, walking arm-in-arm with men in brightly colored suits.

The constant flow of people entranced her. What were their lives like? Where did they come from? What brought each of them there?

"Excuse me, but do you mind if I sit?"

Shari jumped at the unexpected voice and found a young woman standing there.

"Um, no." Shari automatically slid to the far side of the bench, her guts twisting in fear. She tilted her head so her hair and the darkness hid Victoria's patchwork repairs.

I shouldn't be here! What if she sees me? What if she tells someone? What if Aunt Victoria finds out?

"You waiting for the bus, too?" The woman lowered her thin frame with a sigh.

"Umm…"

"Like, I wish they'd put a bench across the street at the bus stop. Totally uncool having to stand and wait. Especially in my condition."

Shari risked a sideways glance. What condition? The woman seemed healthy enough. About her own age, late twenties, with black hair that hung down in bangs. She wore black leather pants and a black T-shirt with the words *The Cure* across the front.

A delivery truck turned the corner. Its headlights swept across the bench, briefly turning night into day. Shari gasped and raised her hand to hide herself, then froze as the lights revealed the other woman's face.

Blue eyes surrounded by dark makeup. Dainty eyebrows with a natural arch. Skin the color of milk. A petite nose.

Pale, pink lines that crossed her cheeks in irregular checkerboard patterns.

The truck finished its turn and shadows fell across the bench once more, returning both occupants to mystery.

"Your face," the woman said.

"Yes." Despite the exposure of her own ravaged features, Shari felt no fear or shame. Only curiosity. And an odd attraction.

The stranger raised both hands and pushed back her hair, exposing herself in a manner more fundamental than if she'd stripped off her clothes. Mesmerized, Shari copied the motion, the first time in five years she'd let someone other than her aunt see her in all her terrible glory.

The woman broke into a wide smile that bent and twisted her scars into new patterns.

"We're two of a kind."

Shari felt her own smile forming. A happiness unlike anything she'd ever known burst into life inside her.

"Twins," she said.

"Peas in a pod."

Shari nodded. Looking at the beautiful creature before her was like seeing a better version of herself in the mirror.

They both burst into laughter, which changed to gleeful shouts and then to tears. They fell into each other's arms, hugging and squeezing and crying, words blending together as they spoke at the same time.

"What happened?"

"Who are you?"

"An accident, I—"

"Rachel, my name—"

"Shari, I don't—"

"—hospital, seeing my OB—"

"—out for a walk."

"I was in a car accident a few years ago," Rachel said, when their emotional release ran its course and they were able to speak normally. "A bunch of us were out partying. I went through the windshield. The doctors did what they could. I guess I was lucky. My friends all died."

"I don't remember my accident, or anything before it." Shari didn't hide the sadness in her voice for a lifetime of memories lost. She didn't have to, not from Rachel, her mirror-twin. "My aunt Victoria—she's a doctor, Victoria Frankstone—says I went for a walk. She found me on the side of the road. Dead. I'd been hit by a car. She revived me. Sewed me back together."

"Is that who you're waiting for?"

"No." Shari shook her head. "I snuck out. I'm not supposed to leave the house, because of..." She touched her face, the scarlet trails rough against her fingers.

Rachel frowned, creating unearthly designs that made Shari's heart soar.

"Your scars? That's bogus. Why?"

"I'm a monster," Shari said. "If people found out about me, they'd take me away from Aunt Victoria forever."

"No way. Your face is rad." Rachel ran a finger across Shari's cheek, tracing one of the irregular seams.

Shari shook her head. "I'm nothing like you."

"Dude, we're twins, remember?" Rachel clasped Shari's hands, and for the first time Shari noticed her new friend had thin pink spiderwebs of lines on her arms. Nothing like her own ropes of twisted, wrinkled skin, but more evidence they were two of a kind. "If I'm beautiful, so are you."

Hot tears seeped into the crevices of Shari's scars, igniting tiny rivers of pain. She wanted to wipe them away, but that meant letting go of Rachel's hands. Looking into Rachel's eyes, she allowed herself a tiny smile.

"A beautiful monster."

"Yes!" Rachel jumped up, pulling Shari with her and swinging her around. "That's what we are. Beautiful monsters!"

In that moment, spinning in a dizzying circle, Shari understood one thing.

Fate had brought the two of them together for a reason.

She could never go back to her old life.

DESPITE HER FEARS of getting caught, Shari snuck out the next night. She couldn't stop herself. She had to see Rachel again. She'd spent the last five years a caged bird, but Rachel had set her free.

They met at an all-night diner, where they ordered blueberry pie and coffee. So simple, yet it sent Shari's heart a flutter.

Because she did it with her face exposed. In front of everyone, under neon lights and everything.

Reeling with exuberant abandon, she hardly heard Rachel talking about her job working in a company mail room.

"It's boring and lonely, but it's so easy a monkey could do it. I just put on my Walkman and rock out."

Shari kept stealing looks at the other patrons, amazed that besides a few lingering glances, no one paid them any attention.

Rachel fed quarters into the tiny jukebox against the wall of their booth, playing songs by bands Shari had never heard of. The Cure. Depeche Mode. The Police. And the one that ended up being her favorite, A-Ha's "Take on Me."

The words touched her soul, as if the writer knew exactly how she felt. Especially the part about it being another day to find you and coming for your love.

Rachel chatted on, unaware of how each smile or touch sent tingles of joy down Shari's back and into her belly.

Afterward, they walked hand-in-hand down the sidewalk, just like ordinary people, talking about everything from the weather to their favorite TV shows—*Cheers* and *Moonlighting* for Rachel, *Happy Days* and *The Odd Couple* for Shari.

"Those are, like, old peoples' shows," Rachel said.

"Victoria only lets us watch certain programs. She says most shows today have too much sex and violence."

"That's awful."

Shari shrugged. "I've never known anything different."

If it had been up to her, Shari would have walked all night with Rachel, until the city disappeared behind them and the rest of the world lay ahead. Instead, they ended up outside Rachel's apartment, eating ice cream cones and enjoying the warm night in comfortable silence.

Until Rachel looked down and whispered, "I still haven't decided if I'm keeping this baby or not. I don't know who the father is. Some guy I met at a club. We got high and did it in the bathroom. Never saw him again. Four months later, look at me now." She rubbed her belly, which was just beginning to bulge.

Rachel's confession made Shari want to share as well.

"Sometimes I think about running away. But then I feel guilty, because Aunt Victoria's given up her whole life for me."

"I'm scared to raise a baby all alone, but I'd hate myself if I gave it up." Rachel sniffed back tears and leaned her head on Shari's shoulder. "Look at us. A couple of total head cases. We really are twinsies."

Later that night, lying in bed waiting for her aunt to come home, Shari reflected on how brave Rachel was, faced with a life-changing decision and no relatives to help her.

But mostly she thought about how good Rachel's body had felt against hers.

AS WAS OFTEN the case, Shari woke before Victoria in the morning. She sat up and then cried out as sharp pains raced down both her legs. Even before she looked, she knew what she'd see: her flesh glued to the sheets by fluids that had leaked out while she slept. She'd overdone it the previous night and now she was paying the price.

For one brief second, Shari considered just ripping the sheet away, tearing open the crusty scabs so the puzzle pieces of her skin fell apart and she slowly bled to death on the bedroom floor.

Then her hands relaxed. Death was no longer an option. Not when she'd discovered the joys of living, of having a friend.

So instead, she sat back against her pillows and waited for Aunt Victoria to help her.

And cried because she had no way of contacting Rachel to tell her what happened.

"JUST A PINCH," Victoria said, in the cold, emotionless voice she took on in the lab.

After the sting of the needle, Shari lay back on the table and waited for the sedative to kick in. All around her, machines whirred and bubbled and thumped, mixing chemicals with things Shari preferred not to think about—things that would soon be part of her. The pungent odors of alcohol and bleach burned her nose.

Please, let it work. Just a little. I'm not asking for a miracle.

Of course, she *was* asking for a miracle. The same one she begged God for each time she put herself in her aunt's hands for another treatment.

Let this be the last time.

"DID IT WORK?"

As always, Aunt Victoria had been there when she woke, assuring her she'd come through just fine.

"It's too soon to say." Her aunt's clinical tone told Shari everything she needed to know. No miracle. No cure.

She climbed off the table, her body itching and stinging like she'd fallen into a nest of wasps, slipped into her robe, and headed upstairs. Only after a painkiller and a long soak in a cool bath did she dare approach the mirror.

When she saw herself, she burst into tears.

On the other side of the glass, the monster did the same.

FIVE DAYS AFTER meeting Rachel, Shari found herself wondering how life could be so wonderful and terrifying at the same time.

After missing their date, she'd worried Rachel might be upset, that maybe she wouldn't want to see her anymore. Instead, she'd gone to Rachel's apartment and found her just as anxious, thinking maybe Shari had grown tired of her.

"Never," Shari said, once they'd hugged each other so tightly Shari feared her seams might split open. "I…I had an accident and needed an extra treatment."

"You poor thing." Rachel stroked a finger down Shari's neck, making her shiver in a delicious way. "I know what will cheer you up, though. Let's go to a movie!"

Shari let out a squeal. "A movie? I've never been. Not that I remember, anyway."

"You're gonna love it."

Ten minutes later, they were pressed against each other in the back row, sharing a bucket of greasy popcorn while the opening credits of *Flashdance* rolled across the screen.

Shari turned to thank Rachel for buying the tickets and discovered her leaning forward. Instinctively, she did the same. When their lips met, it felt to Shari like they'd been lovers forever.

Mirror-twins.

The rest of the movie was a blur for Shari. All she could think about were Rachel's soft, warm lips on hers.

"What a feeling…"

Arms linked as they left the theater, Rachel asked what time Shari needed to be home.

"Not for a few hours yet."

Rachel smiled and raised her eyebrows. "Wanna go back to my place?"

"Sure," Shari said, hoping it would lead to more kissing.

It had, on the couch and then in the bedroom, where for the first time since being reborn, Shari took her clothes off in front of someone other than her aunt.

Sex with Rachel turned out to be more wonderful than anything she'd ever imagined. Their bodies meshed as perfectly as their lips, every movement choreographed in flawless synchronicity while in the background Robert Smith sang about going to bed.

It was only later, when Rachel asked her to stay the night, that the cold reality of what she'd done extinguished the warmth in Shari's heart.

"I think I made a mistake," she said, gathering her clothes from the floor.

"A mistake?" The hurt in Rachel's voice stabbed Shari with a pain worse than a hundred death-filled needles. "Being with me was a mistake?"

"Yes. I mean, no." Shari shook her head, unable to look at Rachel. "Being with anyone. Victoria doesn't know, and she'll be so hurt that I broke the rules…"

A soft hand touched her chin, the gentle pressure guiding Shari to lift her gaze. To her surprise, Rachel wore an amused smile.

"I get it. You feel like you owe her. And she's afraid of losing you again. That's why she's so crazy protective. But she's gotta realize this is the eighties. Girls wanna have fun."

Rachel's words made sense, but in her head, Shari heard Aunt Victoria's objection.

"You can't put our lives in jeopardy just for some fun."

Shari expressed her concerns to Rachel, who shrugged.

"She can't keep you a prisoner forever. I mean, she sounds like kind of a downer, you know? You're an adult. There's no reason you can't spend some nights with me and some at home. If you want, I can come over so she can meet me. We can convince her together."

"What if she still says no?"

"Then maybe it's time for you to fly the coop."

Yes. Shari smiled at Rachel, her heart aflutter at the sight of her mirror-twin smiling back.

"Come to my house tomorrow. We'll tell my aunt it's time to set me free."

SHARI LET THE hot water pour down on her, wishing her fears would wash away as easily as soap and shampoo. She'd barely slept, terrified by the things she'd agreed to, things that now seemed like very bad ideas.

Telling Rachel to come over? Confronting Victoria with the news that she'd met someone? How could she do that without hurting Victoria? *The person who took me in when my parents died? Who saved my life and not only rebuilt me, but has kept me alive all these years?*

Shari leaned against the cool tiles of the shower wall, wishing she could pound her fists against her thighs or dig her nails into her palms. But that would just rip open her seams. And she couldn't do that, not with Rachel coming over. Rachel, who was the greatest thing to happen to her in…well, for as long as she could remember.

My monster-twin.

Young and vibrant and beautiful and fun and daring. She let Shari be everything Aunt Victoria forbade.

Why was life so unfair? Why did it have to be one or the other?

Wait. Why did it?

Maybe there was another solution.

She could slip out before Rachel arrived. Meet her down the street. Tell her Aunt Victoria had agreed they could see each other. But not in public, because her medical treatments were illegal and if Victoria got caught, she'd go to jail. That part was true, after all; Rachel didn't need to know the gruesome details of why.

It might work.

She'd still have to sneak out during the days or nights when her aunt was at the clinic, but she'd gotten good at that. So what if she lost sleep? It was worth it. Once Victoria found a permanent cure, then she could think about leaving for real.

Her anxiety eased, Shari finished her shower. As she toweled her hair, she heard a sound downstairs and paused.

What was that?

Some kind of muffled thump, like books falling on carpet. Shari stood still, listening.

The uncomfortable tingling started up again in Shari's stomach. Had Rachel come over early? She imagined her aunt answering the door, Rachel introducing herself, and Aunt Victoria slamming the door shut in her face.

Unease exploded into full-blown fear and Shari hurried into the bedroom. Still half an hour before Rachel was due. Sure, it could have just been Aunt Victoria dropping something, but suddenly she was *sure* Rachel had arrived too soon.

Her hair still damp around her neck, she pulled on a blouse and a long skirt, stepped into sandals, and headed for the stairs.

Her body wanted to take the steps two at a time, but she forced herself to walk calmly. The last thing she needed was to come barreling down only to find Victoria sitting quietly in the living room sipping a cup of tea.

Except when she reached the bottom of the stairs, the living room was empty.

Shari looked around. Everything seemed normal. Door shut. Curtains drawn, creating an artificial dusk. Throw pillows arranged neatly on the couch. A book on Victoria's chair, waiting to be read later. The end table, where the reading lamp…

Lay on its side.

Pulse thumping in her ears, Shari moved from room to room, searching for other signs of disturbance. Nothing seemed out of place.

Shari stopped at the door leading down to the basement. The only place she hadn't looked.

The laboratory.

Shari opened the door and peered down the stairwell, her heart pounding harder than after a treatment. She hated the lab. It was the place of pain and failure, where promises shriveled and died like the aborted fetuses from Aunt Victoria's clinic, where hope fell apart and only torture thrived.

Her breathing quickened as she descended. At the bottom, the faint gurgling and humming of Victoria's equipment reached her.

One step. Another. Into the lab proper, its contents as familiar and disturbing as the scars on her body.

Machines lined an entire wall. Motors with coiled hoses and wires joined to metal boxes. A generator with long cables that ended in flat metal squares. Transistor tubes that glowed and hummed. As she passed them, her scars itched and the tiny hairs on her arms stood up.

A series of long tables ran the length of the room, their tops obscured by glass jars and containers of all sizes and shapes.

Except for the very last table.

A body lay on it, the identity hidden by a bloodstained sheet.

Shari's stomach twisted.

Oh, my God. Is that—

A sharp pain stabbed her shoulder and she cried out. Her body went numb and the floor came rushing up at her.

"I'm sorry." Victoria's voice echoed from deep within a dark, hazy tunnel.

Then the tunnel closed around her.

AN ALL-TOO-FAMILIAR AGONY greeted Shari when she woke. The acid fire burning her skin told her she'd been subjected to another treatment.

Despite the pain, she tried to lift her head.

There'd been something, something she'd seen...

"You're awake." Victoria's voice, somewhere behind her.

"Why did you...?" Shari mumbled. The first few minutes waking from a treatment were always a foggy nightmare.

"To save you," Victoria said. The clink of glass-on-glass alternated with the duller sounds of drawers closing. "I recognized her as soon as I opened the door, you know. You don't remember that night, but I do. I remember it like it was yesterday."

Shari struggled to make sense of Victoria's words. Her who? What night?

"I prayed she'd died. That bitch and her drunken friends. I wanted them all dead for what they did to you. That's why I left them there, except for the pieces I needed."

She...Rachel? Is she talking about Rachel?

A memory of lights racing toward her. A car. The pain...

"I was in a car accident a few years ago." Rachel's words.

Oh, god. Rachel was in the car that hit me.

"You were trying to leave me that night, too," Victoria continued. "You said I was too strict. But I had to be. I made a promise at your mother's grave that I'd keep you safe forever. Running away almost killed you once. I couldn't let it happen again. Especially not with her. Now we'll never have to worry about it."

Not with her... Shari remembered the body under the sheet.

"What did you do?"

"Of course, if you hadn't brought her here, I'd never have accomplished my miracle."

Miracle? Shari tried to lift her head again, but all she managed was a groan as the room spun around her.

Ignoring Shari's struggles, Victoria continued speaking.

"Live cells. That was the key."

Live cells? Shari fought the fog surrounding her thoughts. Her aunt didn't use live cells. She couldn't.

"All these years, working from the notes of my grandfather, and his father before him. None of us ever thought...but then tonight... well, sometimes the greatest discoveries happen because of good luck."

"No..."

"Before you get all weepy, I want you to see something."

A face, blurred and missing a body, appeared above Shari, blocking her view of the cracked, stained ceiling.

No, not a face. A mirror.

Shari blinked several times and the image cleared. Blue eyes, a smallish nose, lips with a natural upturn at their corners...almost familiar.

That's...me?

It couldn't be. The rippling scars, the scarlet tracks of her pain, were gone, replaced by faint pink lines sketched delicate web patterns on her pale skin. For a moment, Shari felt sure she was looking at Rachel. Then she blinked and it was just her reflection again.

No, not her. Not anymore. Someone different.

Someone beautiful.

"I wish I'd thought of it sooner," whispered Victoria. "All that time wasted with cold, aborted tissue when all I needed was a single living fetus. And now look at you. Pretty as the day we met. I've finally gotten you back."

We're twins, remember? If I'm beautiful, so are you.

Rachel's words, the night they'd met. She'd seen past Shari's mutilated flesh down to the beauty hiding beneath.

We really do look alike.

Not do. Did. Rachel is dead. Cut open and harvested for her baby's cells.

"I did it. What I always promised." The mirror slid away and then there were hands under her shoulders, helping her up.

I'm cured.

Rachel is dead.

A cold numbness settled over Shari, a deadening of flesh and soul that left her struggling to form coherent thoughts.

Rachel is gone. I am returned. Rachel is dead. I'm alive.

"Let's celebrate," Victoria said as if she hadn't just stolen everything in Shari's life worth living for.

Celebrate? Celebrate what?

Freedom. Rachel's voice appeared in her head. *You're not a monster anymore. I gave my life for you, twinsie. Don't waste it.*

Shari took a breath as everything became clear.

"Yes. Let's celebrate."

SHARI STOOD JUST inside the front door and stared at the living room. Victoria slept soundly upstairs, her slumber deepened by a bottle of champagne.

The darkness reminded her of the first night she'd snuck out, the night she'd met Rachel. She'd walked out with a heart chained by fear and returned unshackled and free.

And now she was doing it again.

Only this time Rachel was a part of her, and always would be. Her monster twin, joined by a thousand twisting, turning lines of fate.

Shari lit the pack of matches and dropped them to the floor. Yellow-orange flames burst to life, following the lines of the chemicals she had stolen from the lab.

Goodbye, Aunt Victoria. Goodbye, Shari.

She turned and walked out into the warm summer night, one hand holding Rachel's purse—hers, now, along with the keys and identification it contained.

At the bottom of the driveway, she turned left, toward the center of town. Toward Rachel's apartment.

She felt no sorrow at the thought of the house burning down. The atrocities her aunt had carried out in the lab would remain a secret. She owed Aunt Victoria that much. After all, the family name had been sullied enough over the centuries.

And from the ashes of Shari, Rachel would rise again.

My beautiful twin. Together forever.

THE NIGHTBIRD
MICHAEL KNOST

NUMBING COLDNESS FROM the stone bench crept into Varujan Or-lok's backside as he and long-standing friend Johann Barbu tarried in the outer hall of the Count's bedchambers. The castle's drafty nature carried the sickly sweet scent of burning herbs throughout the upper bailey, where dozens of Carpathian Stag antlers adorned the granite walls, along with woven rugs and wrought-iron sconces.

"Our Count has conquered a multitude of enemies and armies." Johann's tone was that of reverence. "I am more than confident he shall emerge victorious over this plague as well."

Varujan held his gaze to the immense wooden door, where writhing shadows from several flickering candles gave a false sense of move-ment. "This affliction does not attack in the same manner as enemies and armies."

"My Prince, if we wish to be sure, we still have time to—"

"No." Varujan held up a forefinger "I told you, we will not seek the black arts of your brotherhood."

"I assure you—"

"Enough!" Varujan jabbed the finger toward his friend's chest. "Not another word about it."

"As you wish." He lowered his head, cleared his throat. "But we have all lost family—my father and sister...not to mention your beloved mother no less than three weeks gone."

"It knows no boundary with regard to soldier or civilian or nobility."

The hinges of the arching door shrieked as the planked barrier opened, revealing a dark figure cloaked in the familiar ankle-length overcoat, bird-like beak mask, and wide-brimmed leather hat.

Rising to his feet, Varujan removed his cap. "How is he?"

The doctor's head movement gave the appearance of a ghastly papier-mâché marionette. "It is with great sorrow I must inform you of your father's passing."

Varujan stared past him. "I should like to see the body."

"I cannot allow that, my lord. After all, you are now Graf Orlok, our Count. You must not be exposed."

Johann placed a hand on Varujan's forearm. "Please, heed the doctor's words. Your safety is of the utmost importance. Go to your awaiting bride, share her bed, let her give you comfort."

Rubbing the back of his neck, Varujan released a deep breath. "I honestly expected him to...to live." The coldness traveled to his stomach. "He had never known defeat. Not even once. And now... and now he's dead." He turned his gaze to Johann. "And you would have me enter my wife's bedchambers as though nothing has happened."

"I mean no offense, my lord," he said, retrieving his hand. "But you have dwelled in this vestibule for three straight days." His expression softened. "You need sustenance. You need rest. You need comfort."

Smoke from the fumigation pots settled around them like mountain fog, coating Varujan's tongue and throat. "You are right." He closed his eyes, nodded. "The grief is too much to bear alone."

ANA HAD THE blankets pulled just beneath her chin in slumber. A faint putridness lingered in the air—a staleness Varujan knew all too well. Wiping his forehead with a sweaty palm, he closed his eyes. *No. Please, no.*

"I didn't hear you come in." Her voice was thin, unsteady.

"It was not my intention to awaken you."

She sat up against the stacked pillows behind her and winced. "How is he?"

Varujan stepped closer, studying her face. "Tell me," he whispered. "Do you have the swollen marks?"

Brimming tears softened her countenance. "Yes." She pulled back the covers to reveal reddened buboes just inside her upper thigh. "They appeared yesterday."

Moving his gaze to the floor, he released a deep breath. "I have never felt so…so helpless or weak."

"Your eyes tell me the Count has died."

He nodded.

"My love, you cannot stay here. You must depart from this sickness and seclude yourself from everyone…including me."

He turned away from her, wiping at his eyes. "I have been Count Orlok but minutes and have *yet* to encounter *one* person who is not telling *me* what to do."

"You are more than just yours now, my love. You are more than just mine. You belong to the people." She coughed into a handkerchief. "And the people need your leadership."

He took another step toward the bed, "Ana, you know I cannot—"

"Please, Varujan." She held her hands in front of her. "If not for you…if not for the people…please do this for me."

Although the coldness migrated to his legs, warmth tingled in his neck and ears. "Very well."

Ana offered a pitiful excuse of a smile. "Thank you…" She bowed her head while keeping her eyes to his. "Count Orlok."

He turned to leave, paused. "But I shall do everything in my power to see you whole again."

THE FIREPLACE CRACKLED and popped as Varujan warmed himself next to the flames. The hollowness of the great hall was never more evident than with so few occupants.

"The servant you sent was terrified delivering your urgent summons." Johann's voice echoed throughout the expanse. "I was under the impression you were retiring to your bride's chambers."

Varujan stared into the flames. "Ana has the bulbous marks."

Johann's sigh lingered but a moment. "I am so very sorry."

"It's been no more than thirty days since we made our vows." Varujan turned from the fire. "She is all I have now."

"Ana is a strong woman, my lord. She wants only what is best for you."

"Yes, but strength is merely sifted chaff in this plague's wind," he said, brushing ash from his long coat. "I shall *not* lose her to this sickness."

Johann leaned inward, searching Varujan's face. "What would you have me do, my lord?"

"Gather your brothers from Scholomance."

FRESH MOUNDS OF earth surrounded Varujan in the makeshift graveyard as he stacked firewood according to directions. Getting the fire started proved more difficult than he'd imagined with the damp winds moving in, violently flipping the pages of the splayed open book resting on a bleak gravestone.

Johann's handwritten instructions were overwhelmingly tedious—a nearly verbatim, step-by-step manual on how to use the ancient manuscript. "At no time should you *ever* move outside the circle." He had sounded agitated when he'd made the statement. "No matter what happens, remember, you are summoning Belial, and he will most certainly consume you should you present the slightest opportunity."

Varujan waited for the flames to steady before encircling his position with a narrow trench of blood. The coppery scent quickly cut through the smoke, delivering a dull throb to his forehead. For whatever reason, Johann never revealed where he had acquired the blood and Varujan was too occupied with details to inquire.

Shadows stretched and morphed across the soil, retreating from the fire's glow while intervals of moonlight peeked through coagulating clouds. The crackling and popping of the flames increased with the growing winds, sending bursts of tiny embers and ash into the night air.

"I am here." The book seemed heavier in his hands this time—more burdensome than mere heft. "I implore you to honor my petition."

Having spent hours of instruction on proper pronunciation for each foreign word, Varujan had taken great care to never voice them in sequence during practice. "You must project with authority," one of the brotherhood had said. "And remember to speak slowly and clearly."

The ancient words now flowed from him as though he had dedicated his entire life to this single incantation, all the while, flashes of lightning and rolling thunder churned the clouds into a frenzy, building with each utterance.

Varujan could barely hold the pages in place when the pugnacious winds turned sulfuric. "I am here," he repeated at the end of the invocation. "I implore you to honor my petition!"

Thunder shook the ground just as tarnished brilliance illuminated the clouds from above followed by a descending glow with rhythmic pounding and whooshing in its wake.

I am here, a gnarring voice boomed directly inside Varujan's head. *I will hear your petition.*

Something enormous fell from the clouds just as lightning flashed again. It appeared to be a large-framed bird of some sort flying toward the circle. As the figure drew closer, Varujan realized the pounding and whooshing came from those mammoth wings beating the air—not to mention the thing was beakless and of human form. Bile crept into his throat, sending what felt like splinters of ice down his back and legs.

Massive feet crashed near the circle of blood as the creature's membrane wings draped around itself like a full-length cloak, shimmering with what resembled moth-dust residue. Brimstone clung to the air, refusing to dissipate, and the longer Varujan stared into the towering thing's eyes, the more he was convinced red flames roiled behind those enormous orbs.

Speak your petition. The voice thundered inside Varujan's head again while the monstrosity's maw rested ajar, revealing teeth that could only be described as stained claws of a brown bear.

"I have lost many to this plague," Varujan said, steadying himself against the gravestone. "And now my wife shows marks of the afflicted."

Speak your petition.

"I should like her life spared. I should like her made whole."

The thing tilted its head. *And what of you?*

Varujan dropped his gaze to the ground. "I will do anything to see her whole again."

Anything?

He nodded. "Anything."

Then come stand before me.

Wiping perspiration from his forehead, Varujan cleared his throat. "I was told if I leave the circle, you will consume me."

Consumption can mean many things.

Winds whipped about Varujan, stinging his face with debris. "I just—"

Come stand before me and your wife shall not perish from this plague.

Varujan focused on the bloodline as lightning flashed, followed by rolling thunder. The chill in his belly slivered into his chest.

And I will make you my Nightbird.

Dropping the book to the ground, Varujan took a step and paused. "How can I be sure you will cure Ana of the plague?"

Your heart…is your only assurance.

Rubbing the back of his neck, Varujan moved forward—taking small steps while fixing his gaze to the creature—waiting for the thing to pounce at any moment.

Closer.

He stopped a few feet away, clutching his gathered hands to his stomach. Perspiration saturated his inner tunic as the foulness of rot and smoke dizzied him.

My Nightbird.

The demon's colossal wings swiftly stretched open and encased him, crushing Varujan into the inky darkness of its body. The whole affair happened so quickly he barely caught the blurring of motion.

The wings tightened with every exhalation Varujan made, forcing his face into the fetid flesh—crushing him into it. With no way of drawing breath, paralyzed in the clutches of this hellish cocoon, Varujan had no choice but to succumb to the darkness.

HE AWAKENED TO lightlessness—pain burning and throbbing at every limb and organ. "Where am I?" A sparse beam of light slowly developed above, illuminating little more than his position. "Was it all but a dream?"

My Nightbird has risen. The growling voice seemed louder in his head this time, spurring fresh waves of pain.

Pushing himself to a sitting position, Varujan noticed the fleece-like ground strangely resembled the creature's pungent flesh. "Where am I?"

I feed on agony...fear...hopelessness.

A faint skittering echoed throughout the blackness around him.

My Nightbird will feed on lifeblood.

Varujan leaned forward, searching for any sign of the nearing commotion.

Therefore, when my Nightbird feeds...I feed.

Either the darkness was playing tricks on his eyes or there seemed to be a bit of twitching or fluttering just beyond the light.

You will inhabit the darkness...

A horde of rats and ravens crept into view, closing in with deliberate purpose.

...and I will inhabit the darkness you breed.

———

VARUJAN STRUGGLED TO keep his legs in motion as he doddered along the stony path, praying for a moment's respite from the grievous pain. Murmurings and muffled thumping warred within his head while whiffs of sweaty flesh riled his stomach.

"At last," he whispered as the castle's candlelit windows came into view.

The drubbing persisted even while pressing the heels of his palms to his temples—in fact, the noises seemingly grew louder with every step he took.

"M'lord?" The gate servant stepped into his path. "Is that you, m'lord?"

Varujan's stomach moaned. "It is I." He could barely hear his own words as the rumblings were now a vicious roar in his head, pounding and scratching as the musky scent weighed on him with twinges of copper and perspiration.

"Too much to drink, m'lord?" The man's courteous smile revealed a smattering of blackened teeth. "Do you need help into—"

Varujan didn't realize he had ripped the man's head off with his bare hands until the two of them struck the ground with great force. Quickly positioning his mouth over the flooding neck wound, he lapped at the blood, grunting and groaning—lost to the ecstasy of its essence.

When the spurting quickly died away, he pressed his mouth directly to the wound, sucking away what lingered. When all was but gone, he then held the servant's head above him, sucking at the last of the warm drippings.

"Prince Orlok?"

Varujan protectively drew the severed head to his chest, slowly allowing it to slip to the ground when he noticed Johann and the terror on his face.

"Forgive me," Johann said, moving his gaze to the lifeless body. "*Count* Orlok?"

Varujan climbed to his feet, wiping the gore from his chin. "What has…" He touched his own chest, recognizing the pain was now gone… all gone save the burning misery still in his teeth, ears, nose, and fingertips. "What has happened to me?"

"My lord, please take rest inside the castle. I shall task a few servants with disposal of the body before joining you."

———

VARUJAN SCRUTINIZED JOHANN'S face as he recounted the night's events—searching for skepticism or fear or judgement. Although the table's food appeared freshly prepared, he could barely stand the odd rancidness coming from it. "What has the thing done to me?"

"I warned you to remain within the circle of blood. I made myself perfectly clear in this matter."

Varujan slammed a fist to the table, clattering its contents. "I did that which was necessary to save Ana!"

"Forgive me. My words are not meant to indict you, my lord." Johann rose to his feet. "They are meant for myself. I cannot help but feel guilty for sending you before Belial alone."

Varujan gestured toward Johann's chair. "It's all behind us now. Please, sit." He examined his thickened fingernails. "But what has the thing done to me?"

"He called you his Nightbird."

Varujan nodded. "He said he was going to *make* me his…Nightbird."

"He stated he feeds on fear, agony, and hopelessness." Johann slipped back into his chair. "And that you would feed on lifeblood."

"Yes, and that when I fed, *he* would feed."

Johann twisted his mouth to the side, releasing a deep breath. "It sounds as though Belial has breathed life into an old superstition."

"What do you mean?"

He raised his eyebrows. "Nosferatu."

"Nosferatu?"

Johann nodded. "The peasants have passed down absurd superstitions for generations. One of the most notable is Nosferatu." He shook his head. "Some bury their loved ones by driving wooden stakes into the corpses, pinning them to the bottom of the grave to keep them from rising from the dead and delivering all manner of evil. They speak of their so-called risen dead as…Nosferatu or Moroi or Strigoi."

Varujan leaned forward. "You cannot be serious."

"Some even decapitate their deceased, burying the heads separately for the same reason."

Varujan sat back into the chair. "What does this have to do with me?"

"Can you not see? Belial has manifested the peasants' fears with a *true* Nosferatu. Therefore…" He gestured toward Varujan.

"When *you* feed, *Belial* feeds from the fear and hopelessness and agony you arouse with your…acts of obtaining sustenance."

"Nightbird." Varujan stared out the window before allowing his gaze to drop to nothing. "It just occurred to me." He rubbed a forefinger over his aching teeth. "I can no longer abide in the daylight."

"What do you mean?"

"I am to hide myself away until the darkness of night returns… lest I perish."

"The demon instructed you of this?"

Varujan shook his head. "I know not how I have come to this knowledge…maybe no more than the bear knows to sleep through the winter. But I know it nonetheless."

"We could have the servants block the windows of your bedchamber with tapestries."

"No. That would be too dangerous." Varujan rose to his feet. "Have my bed and other effects moved to the dungeon at once."

ANA SMILED UP from her dressing table when Varujan opened the door. Her face held the same pink freshness she'd worn on their wedding day. It was all he could do to hold back tears. "I wasn't expecting to find you…out of bed."

Placing an ivory comb to the table, Ana rose to her feet. "I am still weak, make no mistake about it, but you will not believe what has transpired." Her eyes glistened. "The marks are gone, my love. And I feel recovered!"

Stepping into the room, Varujan nodded. "This is…wonderful—"

"But to be safe." She held up her hands. "We must make absolute certain I am whole before exposing you to possible dangers."

"Of course," he said, catching a glimpse of servants carrying bedding and books and tables just outside the door. "You should know, I have taken your counsel, by the way...I am secluding myself to the dungeon for the time being."

"This is wonderful news. It gladdens my heart to know you are taking precautions." A look of pity quickly overtook her smile. "But the dungeon is so..." She leaned closer, inspecting his face. "Are you ill, my love? You have a deathly paleness."

"I am fine," he said, easing back into the doorway shadows.

"Do you have the marks?"

"No." He closed his eyes, shook his head. "I fear the weeks of fretting over Mother, the Count, and now your health has taken its toll."

Leaning her head to the side, she smiled again. "Go rest, my Count. We will have many nights to come."

VARUJAN AWAKENED TO the pain—not nearly as bad as he'd experienced the night before, but it was there. The dampness of the dungeon seemed to have infiltrated his bones, adding more layers to the agony. And although the dungeon was windowless, he had no doubt the day's light was gone and the new night had begun.

The murmuring and muffled thumping eased back into his brain, slowly building. Realizing it wasn't just in his head, Varujan recognized it was also a gnawing in his stomach, growing—followed by the muskiness of perspiration, ash, and metal.

The pounding at the broad door sent fresh stabs of pain into his head—as if he'd spent the prior night in unbridled drunkenness.

"My lord." Johann's voice echoed throughout the dungeon. "Are you awake, my lord?"

Varujan sat to the side of his bed, placing his head in his hands. "Leave me be, Johann."

"I have something for you, my lord."

"If you value your life, you will leave now." The thumping and scratching in his head reached an intensity of rushing waters. "I cannot be responsible for my actions!"

The door opened, revealing his oldest friend holding a young woman in front of him. "Hungry, my lord?" He pushed the woman forward, causing her to fall to the floor. "Let me know when you are finished."

The door slammed shut, leaving the woman staring up at Varujan. Her dress was a patchwork of rags in various colors and sizes, and her tangled hair couldn't quite hide the dirt and muck on her face. "My lord," she said, bowing her head.

He could distinctly smell her blood—so strong he could nearly taste it. He gripped the mattress with both hands, fingernails digging into the material. "Come closer." His words slurred in his ears—at least what he could hear of them over the storm in his head. Not really slurred, but impeded somehow.

Running his tongue across his teeth, he found his two front ones elongated more than usual, and rounded off into points.

The woman crawled forward, keeping her gaze to the floor.

Varujan closed his eyes, forcing himself to remain seated. The swirling noises in his head slowly merged into a rhythmic thump-thumping, causing his hands to twitch with each beat—growing ever louder as the woman drew closer.

"What would my lord ask of me?"

Perspiration trickled to Varujan's quivering chin. "Look at me." His muscles ached from the tenseness of restraint. "What do you see?"

Tears welled in her eyes. "I see my Count."

"Why are you here?"

Sobs overtook her as the tears spilled down her cheeks. "I am here to serve you as you see fit, my lord."

Leaning forward, he offered a smile. "Give me your neck."

Laying her head to his knee, the woman pulled back the collar of her dress, exposing filthy flesh. Her sobbing slowed as she wrapped her arms around his leg.

Varujan trembled, brushing his hand over her tangled mess of hair. "Closer."

She rose from his knee, moving her neck toward his face. Warmth radiated from her like a winter hearth, sending chills down his spine.

He pressed his lips to her neck and found himself rolling his eyes from the beautiful saltiness of her flesh. Biting the skin, he located a side vein that spoke to him. He pinched into it with his teeth and the spurting began—the warm juices flowing into his mouth as he gulped and slurped. The woman made no sound, no movement. She merely held herself in that position until finally slumping forward when the thump-thumping slowed to a stop, causing Varujan to hold her to him, sucking every morsel he could extract.

Gently laying the woman's body to the floor, he rose to his feet, allowing the blood to chase away the pain and noise and stress. He licked the gore from his hands, noting his fingernails were now budding claws.

The broad door creaked open. "My lord?" Johann peeked his head inside before stepping into the open. "Are you satiated?"

Varujan nodded, trying to avoid the body at his feet.

Johann dragged the corpse toward the door by the feet, bouncing the woman's head on the stones as he continued. "Just as with the guard, I will have servants dump her in a secluded part of the village for peasants to find later." He dropped the feet just outside the door. "They are sworn to secrecy."

Varujan stared at the feet from his bedside. "I tried to control myself." He wiped at his mouth. "But I could not. Her blood sang to me until I consumed all of it." He recognized the pain was gone. "I cannot control the hunger. I cannot ignore the pain, the craving."

Johann closed the door and made his way back to Varujan. "You will control it with time. But you need not worry, my lord. I shall make sure you are fed every day so you need not leave the castle, needlessly exposing yourself to the dangers of suspicious villagers."

"She just did as I said." Varujan stared at the bloodstains on the floor. "She didn't struggle or scream or…"

"I am to meet the brotherhood tomorrow." Johann placed a hand on Varujan's shoulder. "We are to work toward finding a reversal of your condition." He let his hand ease away. "But, until then, I shall deliver your daily sustenance."

———

VARUJAN SAT AT the edge of his bed, focusing on the dungeon's broad door. It had been over two months since Johann had delivered the first meal, and over that time, Varujan learned to somewhat control his hunger—occasionally going up to three nights without sustenance. And for the last several feedings, he'd challenged himself to stave off the kill for as long as possible, engaging in conversations with the men or women for hours.

But Johann had not visited in two nights, which was unusual as he always checked on the Count even when he was not delivering meals. The expanse was silent save for the skittering of rats nestled in the shadows. The rodents always waited for Varujan to finish his meal before cleaning blood spatter and muck from the floor—and only then at Varujan's bidding.

Brushing wisps of hair from his lapel—possibly for the third time this week—he allowed his gaze to drop to the bottom of the door where a dim light appeared. The pain and noises were soon to follow, building as the light grew. He rose to his feet, waiting.

The faint knock was not Johann's.

"Who dares darken my door unannounced?"

"It is I, my lord. Your Ana."

Heat rose into his neck as he searched the room, trying to decide what to do. "Ana?"

"Yes, my lord. May I enter?"

He hurried to the entrance. "I do not think it wise for you to see me at this time."

"I know everything, Varujan. Please, let me in. I have important news for you."

He stared at the door. "What do you mean *you know everything?*"

"I made Johann tell me what was going on with all the people walking in and then being carried out. He told me all. I am here to help."

Varujan put his back to the door, closed his eyes. "How could he—"

"Please let me in, my Count. The news I have is significant."

He slowly made his way toward the bed. "Enter."

The door opened, bringing candlelight into the dimness. He could smell her drawing closer, the noises in his head gurgling, the pain rising.

"Johann is dead."

He turned toward her, catching a glimpse of shock on her face. "He is dead?"

Stepping forward, Ana placed a gentle hand on his face. "I am sorry, my love."

"How has this come to be?" The thump-thumping rose in his ears.

"Villagers caught him trying to take a young woman." She shook her head. "They have been terrified of the corpses left in various places and took Johann as a killer." She dropped her gaze. "They burned him where they found him...dozens of them."

Varujan's fingernails dug into the palms of his balled fists. "They will pay dearly for this."

She rubbed his cheek. "You need to feed, my love."

"I shall feed," he said, glaring toward the door, pain throbbing with the thump-thumping. "Make no mistake about that."

She rubbed the back of his hand to her cheek. "You must be

discreet, my love." She kissed his knuckles. "Or the villagers will find you out. They will burn the castle to kill you while you slumber. They will kill us both."

His eyes met hers. He could smell her blood.

"Feed from me for the time being."

Varujan pulled his hand away. "Do not be ridiculous! I did what I did to save your life. I shall not *take* it."

"My love," she said, moving closer. "Take but a little for now." She raised her eyebrows. "Then take a little more tomorrow. And then a little more after that."

"You don't understand—"

"Varujan. *You* saved me," she said, pulling her collar aside. "Let *me* save you." She turned her head giving him full access to her neck. "Take but a little...and stay safe here within the castle walls."

The music drew him closer until he slowly sank his teeth into her flesh as the thump-thumping increased in volume and rhythm—the flow gushing into his throat, the melody creating a delirious ecstasy. He pulled away, gasping for breath as the beating continued. "You must depart from me!"

Ana pressed a handkerchief to her neck. "I shall return tomorrow night, my love."

Varujan dropped to his bed, the pain still raging, head filled with an angry swarm of hornets as the thump-thumping continued. The music would not let him go.

Smiling, Ana leaned in to kiss his forehead. "Until tomorrow... Count Orlok."

My Nightbird, the swarm gnarled in his head.

He grabbed Ana's wrist as she was ready to pull away, fixing his gaze to the broad door.

She attempted to free herself, but his grip was too tight. "My lord, are you well?"

He kept his gaze held to the door, blinking tears to his cheeks. "My love—"

Varujan jerked her to him, raging for the wound. When he found it, he bit more deeply into the flesh, bringing a new flow of warm elation. He grunted and groaned as he gulped at the music, allowing it to drown away everything—the excruciating pain, the thundering noises, and the fading of the thump-thumping.

GIVE ME YOUR HAND

DAVID SURFACE

"**W**HAT DO YOU *see?*" That's what they all ask. I hold their hand
and look into their eyes, and see all the different possibilities
flash by like pictures in a slideshow. I don't have to plant
the pictures in their minds—they're already there. I just create the opportunity for them to come out. A dark room hung with silk scarves,
a single candle. And my voice, this Romanian accent that hangs in
the air like perfume from a priest's censer, thick and exotic. It's what
they expect, so it's what I give them.

I'm like a patient gardener, tilling the soil, fertilizing it with a
question, or a suggestion, until what's buried underneath can start
to come out.

It's no mystery figuring out what people want. Money, love, adventure. Happiness. Promise them any one of these things, they'll
leave happy and come back for more.

They say that only weak-minded people fall under the spell of
people like me. That's not true. A weak mind gives me nothing to work

with. Like trying to drive a nail with a hammer made of smoke. But a strong mind, I can make use of. A mind that can imagine things and make them real. Like my son's.

My son was no more than five years old when he came to me with a bird he'd killed. He laid it at my feet like a cat with its prize, but he was not proud; he was weeping. He had come face to face with death for the first time, and it frightened him. Not just the fact of death, but that he had been the cause of it, and had taken a life with his own small hands. He looked up at me with so much pain in his eyes, more pain than a young child should feel. So I did what any mother would do. I pulled him into my arms and sang a song, making up the words as I went along. A pretty song about the river and the sea and tears.

While I sang, I could feel the darkness start to leave him. I was drawing it from his body like poison sucked from a wound. When I was through, he looked so peaceful, and I knew that I had done this. I had brought him back from the edge, back from the dark. I remember thinking, *This is what God must feel like.* A sudden joy took me by force—it was like molten silver in my veins, a fire that blazed quickly through my body and left me breathless. Where the fire had been inside me a moment ago, there was now only an emptiness and a great hunger. I wanted to feel it again.

I could not look into my son's face after what had just happened. But the hunger had been awakened and would not go away. I waited for days and weeks until I could bear it no longer. Finally, one night I told him, "Give me your hand." Sitting very close to him, I took his small hand in mine and gazed down into it. He asked me the same question they all ask.

"What do you see?"

I looked into his eyes for a trace of what I'd seen there when he'd brought to me the bird he'd killed. That look of fear and shame—shame of what he'd done, fear that he might do it again. Fear of himself. I saw that look again, and I blew on it with my words like a hot coal, making it burn brighter and hotter.

I told him that I saw a magical sign in the palm of his hand, one that told me his future. When I saw him staring down at his little hand, smooth and unmarked, I knew that he was seeing what I told him to see. I told him what he was, and about the curse that would follow him for the rest of his days. I told him that even though I knew what he was, I would always love him and forgive him and protect him, no matter what happened. No matter what he was or what he did. It sounded like I was offering forgiveness. What I was really offering was permission. Permission to do the worst things he could imagine. To stop fighting them. In the end, that's what all of us want. More than money, more than fame. Even more than love.

That night I heard him screaming. I found him sitting in front of a mirror, scratching at his arms and face. He begged me to tell him what was happening to him, and to make it stop. I looked at his soft white skin, smooth and hairless, at his little baby teeth, still round and smooth as pearls. I didn't tell him that the change he felt coming over himself wasn't real. To him, it was. I had made sure of that. And when he ran out into the night, naked and alone, I let him go. I knew he'd be back. A boy will always come back to his mother.

That night was even better than the first time. The heartbroken howling and scratching at my door. The fear and pain in his eyes. And the blood. So much blood on his hands and on his mouth. This time, he had not brought his prey home to show me. Whatever he had killed tonight, he did not want me to see. Even in his pain, he remembered how I had helped him, and he crawled into my arms and waited for me to do it again. So I held him and sang to him, that same song about the river and the ocean and tears. I felt the fear drain from him, knowing it was my doing, and the feeling of power blazed through my body again, so quick and hot, I had to bite down hard on my own arm to keep from crying out.

AS MY SON grew older, I kept him close to me. I taught him how to tell people's fortunes, how to guess what they wanted from the sound of their voices and the look in their eyes. It brought us a little money, and the endless supply of warm flesh and blood that he believed he needed. We went on this way for thirty years. The moon and the blood and the sweet fire afterwards. And the howling—first his, and then mine. For a long time, it was perfect. Until the American came.

I knew the moment I saw him that he was the kind of blundering fool who destroys beautiful things. The first time he came to me with whiskey on his breath to have his fortune told, I knew that he would break my heart, although I didn't yet know how. His big meaty face, his nervous hands, his sad drinker's eyes, all belonged to the kind of man who hates his own skin so much he wants to tear it off. I could see that he was one of the haunted kind who come to me for answers and never stop.

My son did not like the American. He did not like to see me with him. Every time the clumsy, drunken fool would leave my tent, I would catch my son glaring at him from a distance. I thought I could see what was going to happen—I am a fortune teller, after all. But I was wrong.

Late one night, I heard whispers in the camp—a man had been killed in the woods. I went to my tent and waited for my son to come to me with the blood of the American on his face and hands, so I could take him into my arms the way I had always done. When he did not come, I went outside and found a crowd gathered around a wagon with a dead body in the back. I expected to see the American torn to shreds, but it was not the American. When they brought my son to me and I saw what had been done to him, the forehead that I loved to soothe and stroke, now bashed-in and broken, I wanted to find the one who'd done this and destroy him, reach down through his throat with one hand and tear his heart out.

I was planning how to find the American and kill him when I looked up and saw him standing in my doorway, crushing the brim of his hat in his nervous hands, his saggy face sweaty and pale. I couldn't believe it—he had come to me.

I told him to sit down. There was a knife in the drawer of my table, long and sharp. One quick stroke—that was all I needed to separate that ugly head from his clumsy, hulking body. I was planning all the terrible things I would do with that head afterward, when I looked into his eyes. That is when I saw a pain that burned me to look at, a pain that was crying out for me to end it. The knife would do that. One moment of vengeance for me, one moment of pain for him, and that would be all. But I was not going to settle for just one moment. One moment was not enough.

"Give me your hand," I said.

He looked startled and embarrassed, like I'd asked him to take his clothes off in front of me. Slowly, cautiously, he extended his big meaty hand across the table. It was soft and clammy, as I knew it would be, the hand that had killed my son, and I almost recoiled at the touch of it. I hid what I felt, and gazed down into his smooth, unmarked palm.

"What do you see?" he asked, the terror already rising in his eyes.

I told him exactly what I had told my son thirty years before. I told him about the sign that I saw in his palm. I told him what it meant and what was going to happen to him.

He called me *crazy*. He said the word like he was afraid of it, like a man who knew what it meant to be crazy. That was how I knew that I had him, and that he was mine.

I heard him howling in the woods that very night. I knew it was not a real wolf. When a wolf howls, there is no fear in it, no trace of anguish or anger. It's a pure sound, like the wind blowing through tall trees. There was nothing pure about this sound. It was the sound of suffering, raw and real, and I knew who it was.

This time I did not wait for him to come to me. I went out to find him. To stop his howling, and to ease the hunger inside of me.

I found him under a tree, his shirt in shreds and clotted with blood that I knew was not his. He was half conscious, but his fingers curled and twitched like the sharp claws that only he could see.

I cradled his head in my lap and spoke the words that lifted the curse from him. When I saw how completely dependent upon me he was, like a newborn baby, I felt the great power I had over him, greater even than the power of life and death. When his head stirred in my lap and a sigh of relief escaped his lips, I felt the molten heat push through my womb stronger than before. I shoved his wadded-up, bloodied shirt into my mouth and bit down hard to muffle my cries that were louder than the ones I made the night my son was born.

We were there all night long. And for many more nights after that.

It's not true, what the others say—that I used this stupid American to replace my beautiful son, that I pitied him and grew to love him. I never loved him. I hated him and wanted him to suffer for what he'd done. I took pleasure in his suffering. But it was nothing compared to the pleasure I felt in taking his suffering away.

I should have known it would not last. Nothing that feels that good ever does.

One night, you came to see me. A man of wealth, I could tell from your clothes and the rings on your hand, your distinguished face and silver hair. You told me you knew what I'd been doing with your son, filling his head with strange superstitions and twisting his mind. It made me want to laugh. If you'd really known what I'd been doing with your son, you would not have been standing there talking to me. You would have shoved a spike through my heart, burned my home to the ground with my dead body in it, and pissed on the ashes.

Later, I heard the other women talking, and I learned what you had done. Killed your own son. Beaten him to death. I always knew that one of us would pay for what we'd done. But I thought it would be me.

That is what I believed was going to happen when I looked up and saw you standing in my doorway. The long knife I had once thought to use on your son was still in its drawer, but too far away. I watched you move into my room on unsteady feet. You reached up for something to steady yourself, took hold of the silk scarves hanging from my walls, and they came away in your hands, fluttering silently to the floor. There was a chair by my table, meant for clients and visitors, and when you sank down into it, I approached you.

Closer, I could see that what was on your face was not rage but grief. Grief and a terrible guilt and anguish deeper than any I had seen before. It was the pain of a man who knows he has killed his own son. A pain so great, it denied all comfort and reassurance, and defied any attempt to reduce or remove it.

You looked up at me, tears filling your eyes that were the same soft brown as your son's. You were, as I have said, a wealthy man, a powerful man. But in this moment, I had all the power. And you knew it. When you spoke in a strangled whisper, it sounded like the voice of a small child.

"Please. Help me."

I thought of all you had to offer. The endless depth of guilt and grief. And the ecstasy that would come from my removing it, greater than any I had ever felt before. I thought of the sweetness of that. The fury and the fire.

I sat across from you and said the same four words that would bring us both release, the only kind of release there is in this life.

"Give me your hand."

A TALE OF WICKEDNESS

KELSEA YU

GATHER ROUND THE fire, my dears, for I'll tell you the version of the tale your parents will never share with you. They prefer to speak of what comes later; to absolve themselves. But effect does not happen without cause, and you deserve the truth.

As many stories do, this tale begins with a child. She was plain and unassuming, often going unnoticed by her busy, overworked parents. Classmates considered her a simpleton for shrinking from attention instead of competing with them for their teachers' praise. But she did not mind what they thought, for she often preferred the quiet of solitude. After school each day, she visited the swamp by her house to collect plant specimens and chat with the frogs.

Mostly, she was ignored by children and adults alike until, one day, there was a show—

What is that? Speak up. You want to know when you'll be free to go home? There's no need to concern yourself with such details. Soon, you will be free—freer, in fact, than you've ever been before. As for the bulky thing off to the side, covered by the blanket, you will find out when the time is right. Now shush and listen.

Where was I? Yes, the show.

In the annual school-wide talent show, every student was forced to perform an act. Groups were permitted, but no one invited the quiet little girl to join them. So, she stood alone on the stage, and when the curtains drew aside, all she could do was stare, petrified, as members of the audience began to glance at one another. The silence grew louder until she could bear it no longer. At last, she opened her mouth to begin the pretty song she'd written and practiced every night, about a beautiful woods fairy who lived in a charming hut and wrote spells to help all those who passed through.

Instead, what escaped was a frog's croak.

Oh, stop that incessant crying! You are ruining the story for everyone. What? You need a bathroom? Well, that spot is as good as any. If you can't hold it, then go ahead and do your business. You'll all be given new outfits soon, anyhow. In fact, let me help you remove your grubby clothes, while I tell you more of the tale.

After the disastrous show, the little girl was mortified. She'd spent enough time in the swamp to learn the calls of the frogs. Secretly, she was rather proud of her ability, but she had not meant for the others to find out.

From that day forward, she no longer enjoyed anonymity. She was Frog Girl forevermore; Croakarella for the ones who thought themselves extra clever. Soon, everyone in her class had learned to imitate the sounds of her amphibious friends. Though she kept her eyes down, her schoolmates' mocking croaks chorused every time she walked near. At recess one day, one of the popular kids distracted the adult-in-charge while four others held her down and forced a small frog down her throat.

She lay deathly ill for a month, and she never did fully recover. The frog she had eaten was filled with a strange kind of venom, and it turned her sickly green.

Yes, I know what shade my skin is, and by the way, it's rude to point out one's maladies. I suppose since you've called attention to yourself, you'll be given the honor of being the first. That's right, you! Step forward. There's really no need to tremble. Yes, the chains will extend that far.

Anyone else care to comment? No? Well, then.

The little girl did not take revenge. Not then. She was too weak to do more than stumble through each day, doing her best to ignore the taunts, which only worsened. The swamp was ruined for her. The sound of a frog's croak brought back memories of the slimy, wriggling thing slipping down her throat, and the mere glimpse of a frog's dewy skin was enough to make her retch. She abandoned the swamp, instead spending her afternoons in the forest outside town, wishing she could stay there forever.

One day, after a particularly nasty threat from a classmate, she decided she would do just that. She packed her satchel: a knife—yes, just like this one in my hand—*a sewing kit, a guidebook showing which plants were safe to eat in the wild, and various other essentials. At first, she had to sneak back into town regularly for food and forgotten supplies. Though it took time, eventually she learned to forage, hunt, and cook her kills. It was tough eking out an existence on her own, but at last, she had left behind the world of cruel children and uncaring parents.*

From then on, she was the mistress of her own fate.

Yes, yes, my impatient dears, it's time to reveal that curiosity you've all been sneaking glances at when you think I'm not looking. On the count of three, I'll pull aside the blanket. You have all learned to count to three by now, haven't you? Excellent.

One, two…three!

For Heaven's sake, it's only a monkey! You little ones really are prone to excessive tears. Or haven't you seen a monkey before? There's no need to be afraid. It's a child, like you, and it's had a tougher time of things, I'll say. You haven't spent the past few weeks shivering in a cage, covered only by a blanket, have you?

The girl was perfectly content to live out her days in the forest, but one day, a hunting party spotted her. They shouted their surprise, making it clear the townspeople had thought her dead. Fallen into a ravine, perhaps, or swallowed by the swamp. Now that they—

Oh, do stop screaming! I would prefer not to cut your vocal cords; this is a messy enough business as it is. "It hurts, it hurts." Of course, it hurts, but the pain is only temporary. The important part is to *hold still*, so I can make clean incisions. Otherwise, they'll end up jagged, and you'll look rather silly once the new grafts begin to merge with your natural skin. Here, open your mouth and I'll stuff this block of wood inside. Now, bite down. That's better.

Much better.

Now that the hunters had found the girl again, they were determined to bring her home, and it was clear she had no say in the matter. Lies poured from their lips. "We were worried sick when you first disappeared!" "Your parents miss you!" "We're so glad we found you again!" Each falsehood stung worse than a face full of swamp nettle, but they were armed. What could she do but go along with them and await her chance to escape? They were a ways out from the town, for the hunters had been chasing a herd of elk for days, camping out along the way.

Foolish child! I told you not to move, or the knife would run jagged again! You have only yourself to blame for the first graft going crooked. Unlike you, the monkey didn't move when I removed a patch of its fur, so you can't blame *it* for the unevenness of your new furry skin. I suppose I should have sedated you like I did the monkey, but then you wouldn't be able to listen to the story.

And anyway, you can't blame my sewing. I am quite a good seamstress; I'll have you know. I've had to make my own clothing and shelter for many years, and you don't see any uneven stitches lining my dress or hat, do you?

As I was saying, the hunters unanimously decided to give up the hunt in favor of escorting the girl back to town, for reasons she could not fathom. None had wanted her there before; why should they have such a change of heart now? She was determined not to trust them.

And yet, it had been so long since she spent time around anyone who was not a beast of the wild. To her chagrin, she found her heart softening. One of the men gave up his cot for her, and sensing her unease, they let her set up camp in a private spot away from the rest. She was afraid they would pry into how she had spent all these long years, alone in the wild, but they did not ask many questions and seemed content with her vague answers. As she drifted to sleep, she wondered what it would be like to bathe in water heated by a stove. To sleep on soft bedding again. To see her parents.

Don't mind that screeching sound; vultures get worked up when they smell a fresh carcass. I used to fight them after every hunt, wrestling my own kill away from the scavenging birds, but we've since come to an agreement. They wait as I take enough for my meal, and I leave them the rest. That's why I cut a chunk of the little monkey's corpse to cook over the fire and left the rest in a spot off to the distance, as a signal to the birds. Now, wait here—though I suppose you have no choice, do you? I will return shortly.

That took a moment longer than I thought, and the damned bird gouged me with its beak before I could tie it up! But no matter; the wound will heal, and we have all the time in the world to finish this process. Yes, its screeches are rather loud up close, aren't they? I can stuff some cotton into your ears if you'd like. Anyway, it will quiet down soon. In fact, let me just—

There. Silence is a relief after that horrible screeching, isn't it? Though I'm not sure we can consider this true silence, given how the rest of you are blubbering. Perhaps I should find more wooden blocks to shut you all up.

Now let's pick up the story again.

Lulled by the comforts she suddenly ached to re-experience, the girl no longer objected to the journey, though she still slept apart from the rest. On the last night before they would reach the village, she woke with the pressing need to relieve herself. Quietly, she slipped out of her cot and into the woods; having lived so long and spent so much time hunting in the forest, she was adept at sneaking around. As she found a private spot and began her business, the wind carried hushed whispers over from the camp.

"She sounds like she's addled in the brain; did you hear the way she slurs her words together?"

"It's the smell that does it for me. All my willpower these past few days has gone toward not wrinkling my nose within her sight. Once we get back to town and clear his name, I'm burning that cot."

"Disgusting, the way a woman can ruin a man so easily. For years he's lived under the cloud of suspicion merely because he said one silly thing to her the day she disappeared. As if a harmless schoolyard taunt was the same as intent to murder!"

"Well, we'll clear up his name soon enough. And then we'll find a suitable punishment for the way she's ruined his life."

Child, how many times must I tell you to stop sniveling and hold still so I can sew these wings on straight? If they're crooked, they may not work properly. This is all part of the transformation process. Don't you want to be free, like the birds that take to the skies?

No? You're a fool, then, which shouldn't surprise me, given your parentage.

For you see, it was your father who first stuffed the frog down my throat.

It was his words that sent me fleeing to the forest: a threat to shove a poisonous frog *elsewhere* into my body if I ever dared speak up in his presence again. And he was stupid enough to threaten me where he could be overheard by several classmates.

Surely, you children know the rest.

Your parents must have told you the girl disappeared before she could be dragged into town to exonerate the boy and face her punishment. They likely spoke of the town's hunt for the girl they deemed a witch. After all, who but a witch—the accusation they slapped on any girl considered wicked—*could survive on her own for so long?*

They must have admitted that eventually, the town gave up searching. That, occasionally, over the years, someone would discover a sign that she might still be alive, but none ever sighted her. In the witch's absence, all the townsfolk had were tales whispered and embellished, each one more outrageous than the last. Years passed, and the bullies who had tormented the little girl grew up and had children of their own.

The girl grew up, too—and she did what she had always done best. She watched. And she waited.

Ah, there. At last, my work is complete. How delightful!

Well, don't be shy; test them out! Give those wings a good flap. They're nice and solid; they should be more than sufficient for lifting you off the ground once you've been freed from your chains. And do run your fingers through your new fur—it is soft, is it not? I'll bring over a mirror if you'd like to see.

Oh, we mustn't forget the little bolero and matching cap I've been saving! They really bring together the entire ensemble. Here, let me help you put them on.

I must say, my dear, you look mighty pretty that way. Oh yes, this is quite what I had envisioned. Perhaps a little tweak of the jaw later, with a sturdy pair of pliers. Possibly the right kind of frog to tint your skin a becoming shade of blue-gray. Well, we need not perfect everything this instant. We can always make adjustments later. For now, we have work to do on the rest of you. Your parents will all be so pleased to see you after your transformations are done; will they not?

Well, my dears, who would like to go next?

SOMETHING BORROWED

LINDY RYAN

VICTOR SAT IN the dark at his kitchen table, the age-marbled skin of his hand veined and thin as wet paper against the pale blue of the tablet's electronic glow. His back ached and there was a twitch in his left eye, a movement which seemed tethered to a series of small, nagging twinges that ran the length of his spine, coursed under his ever-thinning flesh. His fingers were the only part of him not yet ruined by the atrophic effects of age—not yet degraded by a lifetime of self-indulgence and self-loathing—and they flicked across the tablet's smooth surface, pausing to trace the woman's face on the screen. She was delicate and fair, with blond hair and clear gray eyes, so much like the woman who had once loved him.

Too much like, Victor thought, and he swiped left before the boy in the chair beside him could see.

The boy was too large to really be called a *boy*, but it was nearly impossible to think of him as anything else. Thoughts of that kind would lead to contemplations even darker, even more distasteful, and soon *boy* would become *man*, and then *man* would become *monster*. Then the old emotions—the bitter sting of hate, the baleful nausea of fear—would resurface from the depths where he had stored them and crawl back into the forefront of Victor's mind. With these would come memory, and soon thereafter the taste of the grave would press against his tongue. Push down his throat. Strangle his breath.

No. If he thought too long about the boy at his side, Victor would see the *thing* for what it was: abomination. How curious, he considered, that a man could father a son, could bring into existence the very effigy of his own eye through a few thrusts, a few carefully chosen snips of sinew and bone, only to choke on the bilge of his regret when he looked upon the face of his offspring. But this was how all fathers felt, was it not? Did they, too, not experience disappointment—disgust? And what of mothers? Did they look upon the writhing mass once expelled from their loins and see anything more than ruin, than their own mortality bleeding away between their legs?

The boy's voice cut deep in the silence of the room. "See."

The chair protested under his shifting weight as he leaned in to examine the next picture on the tablet's screen—a dark-haired woman with a smooth, dusky complexion, her body lithe and ripe, strong but not unattractive. The boy's milky, mismatched eyes took in the woman's image and then the two dark holes between the space of his eyes flared and he sat back.

"No," he said.

Victor swiped left. Swallowed down the stench that had come when the boy moved too close. Rot. Everything in this room, in this house, smelled of rot. Sweet rot, the stink of once beautiful things, left to decay.

Like my own self, Victor reflected.

He had been beautiful once, hadn't he? His mind had been more striking than his body, this was true, but never had he wanted for companionship. And for what, Victor wondered? What use were things so impermanent as love and beauty? To have had such privileges, only for them to be stripped away until here he sat, a gnarled and withered and loveless thing, nearly as decrepit a creature as the boy beside him, was a cruel fate, one worth avoiding. Outwitting.

"See," the boy commanded, and Victor turned the screen.

A woman with shining scarlet curls nearly the same hue as her rosebud lips blushed pink in the blue light. Her cheeks were dusted with freckles, like cinnamon on cream.

The boy licked his lips, a quick flick of bruise purple against a thin gray gash beset with ragged, wasted teeth. One hand rose to the collection of black strands that hung limp from his scalp. A finger twisted an oily lock. Pulled.

"Hair," he said.

Victor could taste the boy's desire as he watched his clumsy fingers fall back, then select a crayon from the pile on the table. He smeared crimson atop the crown of a crudely sketched female figure. The paper crunched under the impact. Tore. Victor felt the sound—hungry, as if the motion had ripped the woman's blazing locks from her scalp.

He swiped right.

Another woman appeared on the screen, all buttery blond curls, her eyes a shade of sea blue almost identical to Victor's own. She was a flower, this woman, so ripe in the bloom of her life that even the plump mounds of her cheeks glistened as if coated with dew.

The boy let loose a gust of stale wind. He sucked it back in so that the sound echoed in the cavern of his mouth. He blinked once. Twice. His hand lifted, brushed heavily against his brow. "Eyes."

His clumsy fingers snagged another crayon, this time selecting a bright blue. He clenched the shiny wax stick in his fist as he drew two misshapen circles inside the paper figure's head. The boy stopped, leaving wax crumbs on the paper, and jerked his head back toward the screen.

"Lips," he added, before Victor could swipe right.

The boy carved a ragged pink smear where the figure's mouth would be.

"See," he commanded, when Victor's finger hesitated.

The next woman was dark, her eyes and skin and hair varying shades of gleaming onyx. A guttural noise swelled in the boy's throat as he took in the hue of his own form, dragged his hand heavily up and down the mottled gray flesh of his forearm. His skin might have been the same shade once—just as dark, just as lustrous. The nub of his index finger bumped against the tablet.

"Friend," he said. The word was hot.

An unfamiliar sensation washed over Victor as he watched the boy complete the figure. A knot formed in his stomach as the boy scratched in varying hues of brown and black, shading in its limbs, the spaces between the features already marred on its face.

Her face, Victor corrected, and the mass in his gut swelled, pulsed with an energy of its own.

"Friend," the boy said again, turning the paper. The edges of his face twitched.

Victor understood. He swiped right once more and set the tablet down atop the table. It dimmed, shut off. The sweet stink of the room filled into the space that the light's absence had left and Victor's stomach turned as he studied the drawing. The movement rolled the mass, shaping it within him.

This is not a woman, he thought. *It is an assemblage of pieces, the feminine divine cobbled together by the sum of her parts. It is not creation. It is not love.*

But even as the words floated across his mind, the truth wheedled even deeper into Victor's thoughts. He regarded the strange, unbalanced features of the boy-man's face—the sagging jowls, the bridge of his nose knotted as if it had been broken and failed to heal properly.

He was indeed beautiful, was he not? He was a brilliant achievement, evidence life held tenure over death—that true beauty was in recreation, not reproduction. Victor had modeled the boy in much the same way that the boy had just this very moment compiled his mate on the paper before him, choosing the features he most admired, thought most deserving of continuation.

The ball in his stomach burned, painful and pleasant at once. Life, he knew, was a thing of similar juxtaposition.

My boy, Victor thought then, as he held one thin-skinned, marbled hand to the cheek of the boy. And then, as it always did, *boy* became *son*, and in another breath, *son* became *creation*. Victor stared into his son's face until his heart swelled with pride, and when the tablet chimed an incoming message, he fetched the slim device and scanned the notification.

The blond-haired woman had also swiped right, accepting his invitation. Victor grinned in triumph, his smile so bright it pushed away the darkness of old age, revived his brittle bones.

He held the tablet's screen so the boy could see.

"Friend?" he asked.

The boy's tongue lolled as it formed the word. *Friend.*

Victor cradled the tablet against his chest. His daughter, his beautiful daughter, would have her father's eyes.

MOONLIGHT SERENADE

GABY TRIANA

AND NOW, LADIES *and gentlemen, the National Broadcasting Company invites you to listen to the dulcet sounds of "Moonlight Serenade" by Captain Glenn Miller…*

Meryl closed her eyes for one last minute of bath time. She imagined the last of the lye soap washing away with the words Dr. Lanchester had told her last night. Down the drain, where they belonged. *Infertility is a mental issue, not a physical one, Mrs. McDonnell. Train your mind to remember its purpose, and you will soon be in the family way.*

It had taken every ounce of courage to approach him after her late shift, to ask if there was anything she could do to improve her chances of becoming with child. He'd stared down the lengths of her stockings for a moment before adding:

We appreciate your diligence in the ward, but the war is over. Women needn't hold down the fort anymore. Go back to being a wife. Look fondly upon your husband. Think motherly thoughts. It's as simple as that, really.

Then he'd scribbled on his notepad, like the matter was over.

She'd stared at his matter-of-fact expression, bespectacled nose, and thin lips in disbelief, all the while her heart shattered. Dismissed by the flick of a fountain pen.

If Dr. Lanchester only knew of Henry's spiral into despair, his night screams, claims of air fire, intense dual nature, the stink of whiskey pervading his clothing, his unwillingness to find employment, the blame over small matters that he flung upon her from day to day...he would never tell her to look fondly upon her husband.

I'm sorry to have wasted your time.

Embarrassed, she'd fled St. Andrew's Hospital under the waxing moon, walking, not to the bus station, as she had every night for the last three years, but into the forest. Recalling the voices of patients confiding in her, whispers of herbal work and healing women in the woods, Meryl had slipped into the outskirts of Moorsville, where chimes, kissed by the cold lakeside wind, tinkled from the eaves of fortune-teller carts.

She never considered such a thing before. She was a woman of science. But desperate times called for desperate measures. Her body was ticking—she knew the signs—a twinge of pain from her left abdomen one month; right side the next. She'd selected the wisest-looking woman with the smartest, least deteriorated cart, an old gypsy who'd been kind enough to let her sample the oil, for a sum Meryl would take to her grave.

When the water drained, she stepped from the tub onto cracked tile and dried herself. Naked before the warped mirror, Meryl nervously removed a thin glass vial from its hiding spot under the sink. Trembling, she uncorked the stopper of her first full dosage. Ear to door to make sure Henry remained asleep down the hall, she covered the bottle's opening with her thumb and shook it. She recited the words she'd been instructed to use.

"*By the light of the full moon, I will be with child soon,*" she whispered.

With a fingertip, she painted an oily star over her stomach, surrounded it with a large circle, then proceeded to imagine her belly growing, distended with crisscrossed blue capillaries like so many of the soon-to-be mothers at the ward.

And now, ladies and gentlemen, Captain Glenn Miller presents... "That Old Black Magic."

Down the hall, Henry's bed creaked. She turned down the radio.

Quickly, she dressed in beige cotton seersucker, silver insignia buttons, sleeve patch with a silver Maltese Cross on a red background, and a Montgomery beret, tucking the vial into her coat pocket, all before Henry could catch her emerging from the bathroom and demand she fulfill her domestic duties before leaving.

With light steps, she tried to exit their small house off the highway, but a large truck rumbled past, rousing Henry from his sleep. "Merr...?"

"Leaving for work, dear. Going to miss the bus if I don't hurry."

"Come give your husband a goodbye kiss."

Sighing, she mustered up a smile and entered their bedroom. After all, she would have to ask him for a favor later. Meryl stopped in her tracks. The window was open, curtains blowing, a normal sight for a blustery autumn afternoon, but what on earth were those dreadful marks on the windowsill and floor?

"Something wrong?" Henry sensed her hesitation.

"Just some dirt on the floor. No need to worry."

"Well, clean it up. It ain't my job."

Nothing is your job, she thought begrudgingly. If Henry wasn't sitting on the front porch, shaking his shotgun at the automobiles crossing his property (thanks to The Federal Aid Highway Act of 1944, more were driving past every day, and he was convinced they would bring more criminals to their quiet area), he was poisoning his liver to chase away enemy fighter ghosts.

Immediately, she felt terrible for having thought it. At least he'd fought for peace in the Second Great War. At least he came home to her every night. That was worth something, wasn't it?

Pouring water into the corner basin, Meryl dipped a washcloth and then sank to her knees. The splotches were round, thick, like brown tempera paint. Had an animal skulked through their bedroom last night? Was Henry now sleepwalking through the forest?

Another thought occurred—was Henry stepping out on her?

Perhaps her long hours at the ward had finally driven him to find another. Part of Meryl almost wished her husband would find a mistress. It would lift the burden of having to "think fondly" upon her husband, to taste his poisoned tongue, feel his hot, rancid breath in her ear.

She cleaned the tracks all the way to his bedside where they disappeared. For a minute, she considered turning the sheets to check his feet, but Henry threw a listless arm over his bloodshot eyes, fingers clutched around his precious blade, as if a hunting knife could ward off his South Pacific dream demons.

"Did you get it?" he mumbled.

"Yes." She wiped her hands on the washcloth. "Raccoons, it seems." She kissed Henry's forehead, slipping the knife from his loose grip and laying it on the bedside table. "It's broad daylight, darling."

When she tried to whisk herself away, he held her by the arm. "Hey."

She glanced at his grip. At least he still had nice hands. "I really must get going."

Henry's closed eyes formed a crinkly smile. "Last night was wild, wasn't it?"

A nervous laugh bubbled from her lips. "Surely, I don't know what you mean."

"Surely, you do. And I got to say, I knew you had it in you, Merr." When he yawned, toxic fumes snaked into her nostrils.

She wanted to tell him that his "wild night" was nothing more than a whiskey-fueled fevered dream, his bottle ache getting the best of him. Meryl had gone straight to sleep last night after visiting the gypsy camp. She would have remembered having relations with him.

"See you after work." She slid her arm out of his grasp.

"And then, we'll go for another round?" He cupped his hand over her bottom and squeezed. "A-woo!"

She wanted to say yes. She wished she could. If she wanted a baby, she must. She wished so dearly that Henry's dual nature wouldn't cause her to shudder the way it did.

"Sure, darling," she said.

Within seconds, he was back asleep. *And now, ladies and gentlemen, a word from our sponsor, LegSilque Liquid Stockings...* Meryl turned off the radio and left for work.

HER OVERACTIVE MIND would not relent.

Why couldn't she bring herself to ask her own husband for what she needed on the very day she needed it? It would require her to request something she'd been taught was a husband's delight, not a wife's, and Lord knew she'd done it enough times in the last year at his whim with no end result.

Why did she want a child so badly anyhow? To add insult to injury, it seemed every storker within a hundred miles was having their baby tonight.

"It's a full moon," several co-workers announced.

Indeed, a nervous energy permeated the ward. Meryl scuttled from bed to bed, providing warm towels for patients, most of whom had become suitcase wives before the war. She checked for telltale signs of labor, assured first-timers that everything would go smoothly, taught them how to be self-reliant in caring for their newborns.

"Nurse, fetch me the chart for Mrs. Moseley in room fourteen,"

Dr. Lanchester requested without so much as remembering her from last night's discussion.

She whirled off, Dr. Lanchester's words still haunting her—*Infertility is a mental issue, not a physical one, Mrs. McDonnell.* Oh, the embarrassment of it. The very suggestion that she could make pregnancy happen by changing her mood!

Her brow line broke into a beady sweat, her heart began palpitating, her vision, already blurry from a busy night, became distorted. Instead of one Nurse Albert grabbing ahold of her arm, there were two. "Are you alright?"

Startled by touch, Meryl's palm swiped through a silver tray containing a patient's meal, knocking the contents onto the floor. "Goodness, I…" She dropped to her knees to help clean.

Nurse Albert's green eyes filled her view. "Why don't you take a walk, honey? A breath of fresh air will do you good." The nurse helped her to her feet and nodded to another to usher Meryl out of the way before she did any more damage.

"What did you eat?" the second nurse asked.

"Nothing strange that I know of."

"You don't got a bun in the oven, do ya?"

"Definitely not," Meryl said.

The hallway seemed to stretch forever, though St. Andrew's was a small country hospital. Through the windows, she spotted a luminous, blood-colored moon just above the adjacent wooded area, an omen that made her want to warn every nurse, patient, and doctor.

The full moon—she was supposed to take the second dose of the oil tonight after dark, recite the chant, and bed her husband before the night's end. Those had been the old woman's instructions.

Reaching into her pocket, she felt the vial there, and the moment her co-worker left her alone in the kitchen with a glass of water, Meryl slipped into the lavatory to lift the edge of her uniform jacket.

Out came the vial and cork stopper. Again, Meryl took the tiny bottle between her thumb and forefinger, shook the contents, then drew a pentagram over her abdomen, completing the symbol with a large circle.

"*By the light of the full moon, I will be with child—*"

The door opened. The tiny vial slipped off the edge of the sink onto the tile floor, splintering into shards, the last drops spreading over the slick surface. The new reception nurse stood in the doorway. "Oh, goodness. Silly me. Here, let me help."

"It's all right. I can manage." Rattled from the intrusion, Meryl, for the third time that day, fell to her hands and knees.

"Hope that wasn't anything important," the newcomer said, handing her a paper napkin.

Meryl bit her lip to keep the stinging tears in check. No use crying over a few drops of fertility oil probably faker than liquid silk stockings anyway. Throwing the bits of glass into the wastebin, she left the lavatory in a desperate need for fresh air.

A sensation filled her lower abdomen with fire, a slow-building flush that spread into her pelvis, down her legs, as though warm honey was slowly coating her body. Meryl was afraid others would notice, that they'd look up and witness a nurse burning up and melting in the hallway. She was so filled with shame that she trotted to the nearest exit doors, slipping into the night without fetching her belongings or clocking out.

Deep, cold wind blew in from the east—soulful, refreshing air that expanded her lungs with vigor, made her want to cry for no reason at all. She'd never realized how suffocating St. Andrew's could be until this moment, how utterly stifling every building she'd ever worked or lived in felt. The last three years of her life in Moorsville had seemed like servitude, every action made for someone else, every decision meant to benefit others.

Hot tears quickly turned to ice at her lower lids. She glanced up at the moon, growing brighter with every minute, suppressing the unreasonable urge to roar at it. To run into the woods and douse this raging fire inside her. Was the fertility oil at work? She'd expected—hoped—that cells would cross-contaminate, magic would do its work internally, not this overwhelming need to...

to...

Meryl's vision expanded. With one sweeping glance, she could see the farthest end of the hospital's property all the way to the highway, her bus station, past the road to the wooded area behind her house. From where she stood, she swore she could smell every dinner being cooked through every open window in Moorsville for miles and miles.

She ran, stumbling over rocks, barely missing hedges, until she was on the path toward the bus station, any path, as long as it felt normal.

"Nurse McDonnell, is that you?"

Meryl slowed, narrowed her eyes at the man waiting for the bus—Dr. Lanchester. "Yes, doctor."

He clucked his tongue. "Still looking for my chart, I suppose? Perhaps you'll do well to stop playing hooky and go get it." His arched eyebrow mocked her.

Meryl did not answer. If she spoke now, she would cross him. Instead, she stood on the sidewalk, inspecting him, watching him a long time. *The body knows what to do, Mrs. McDonnell. Women's brains, in their effort to find meaning outside the home, complicate matters.*

"Are you unwell?" the doctor asked. "Shall I escort you back to the ward?"

A scent wafted off the doctor, not the usual aromas of the hospital, but something else she couldn't name. Something primal and urgent that redefined their dynamics. She moved closer to inhale it deeply.

Taken aback by her proximity, the doctor fumbled, tripped over his feet when his eyes met Meryl's. In his dark pools, she saw the moon's reflection—blood red and hungry.

"Now, now…if this is about last night…"

Meryl had forgotten how to speak. Already, she'd wasted enough words on the good doctor, and the distress wafting off his body was intoxicating. With a slow turn, he sprinted down the sidewalk. Salivating, Meryl ran after him, unsure what she would do when she reached him, knowing that she would.

"I *will* summon the police, Mrs. McDonnell. I'm warning you."

For a minute, she gave the doctor a head start across an empty field, trying to remember what it felt like to be scared. Just yesterday, a few hours ago even, she hadn't the nerve to ask her husband for the baby she desperately wanted, but now she was consumed with need.

At the edge of the woods, she slowed, watched the doctor quickly become just a man and disappear into the forest. Curse words panted under his breath. The poor chap thought Meryl couldn't hear, but to her delight, she found her sense of hearing and smell to be heightened. Not a dog or any animal, she realized, stretching out her arms and legs to make sure their womanly shape was still there. She wondered if Dr. Lanchester would still find them attractive.

What had happened back there at St. Andrew's? After applying the oil, some sort of floodgate had opened, permission to behave as she wished granted. To chase instead of being chased. To hunt instead of be hunted.

Even her nurse's shoes felt restricted. She kicked them off, peeling her stockings like discarded skin, sinking her bare toes into the freezing, decomposing leaves. Every few feet, she glanced up at the moon, swollen with potential, felt its celestial pull on her organs and circulatory system. The twinge in her abdomen signaled. Her body aligned with the cyclical rhythms.

She knew where the man was—behind the tree up ahead and to the right—watching her with equal parts terror and fascination, as she discarded one article of clothing at a time with an almost devilish relish. When had she ever felt so compelled to be naked? Never. As a child, perhaps, long ago, before the rules began.

But as a woman?

Never.

Until now.

When every article of clothing had been shed from her body, Meryl returned her gaze to the man quivering amidst the trees. She was about to burst forth through the fog after him when the slow fire that had spread through her body at the hospital took hold of her again. This time, the warmth prickled her skin, itched her all over like poison ivy, sending spirals of steam shooting through her pores into the night air.

Suddenly, Meryl couldn't remember what had brought her here.

Why she was in the woods.

Why she was naked.

Why she felt ravenous for the first time in her life.

All she knew was that she was changing—a psychological shift, yes, the veil of modesty and decorum lifted from her trained mind. But also, her torso, limbs actively lengthening, elongating, so much that she—whatever her name was—grimaced in repressed agony, held it in, like she'd been taught to do all her life. Bite down, let the pain simmer for eons until it boiled to a breaking point.

Unable to keep under her skin for long, the physical manifestation of her emotional pain sprouted—from every pore. Materialized over arms and hands, knees and legs, even feet. The shape of her fine face elongated, soft tongue flooded with hot saliva, gums burned with the fresh eruption of canines. From her fingertips and toes, new features—claws.

She stood taller, in part from her body having shot up several inches on arched toes, but also from confidence. From this new vantage point, she spotted the man, still shaking like lake reeds. He'd soiled himself, a familiar scent to her.

With an upward tilt of her snout, the creature she now was gave a mournful howl that reverberated against the tall pines. She sprinted through the trees toward her prey, snarling when the man dropped his briefcase and gave chase. She yearned to reach him, to tear into his flesh with scalpel-sharp claws, sink her teeth into his neck, and open her throat to let his hot blood cascade down.

At the last moment, when her breath prickled the human's neck, the iron scent of blood filled her nostrils, and the horrified man turned, stumbled backwards with hands outstretched, deepest fear in his dark eyes.

"No. No, please... I beg of you..."

She froze, curved claws raised.

Buried memories bubbled up like acid. Soldiers screamed in pain through hospital halls, begging for mercy, limbs shot off. Wailing women begging her to revive stillborn hearts. She'd been a kind woman once. Despite a lack of reciprocation, of gratitude, despite her father's abuse, she could do it again. But it was hard to think of these things with her body demanding more.

The scream was satisfying, the snap of ribcage divine. When her jaws locked onto his neck and wrangled it side to side, her soul rejoiced. It used to lurk in shadow. Tonight, it called her home.

Under the cover of woods, she darted past the gypsy camp, using the muddy lakeside floor to guide her through the fog. Too wet, and she'd find herself knee-deep in water. Dry enough, and she'd emerge at the end of the forest, where the little blue house sat dark across a road, as large, shaking boxes on wheels rumbled past every few minutes. She waited in shadow, unquenched, a ticking time bomb.

Inside the house, her man waited.

Through the open window, music played like a faraway dream.

A certain hunger she could no longer suppress clouded all other thoughts. Urgency, necessity, propelled her from the thicket of trees.

She must hurry. To the man. To the bed. His need for her, and hers for him, carried out the window, on the wind, across the field. Above her, the moon was at peak hour—her opportunity, closing.

Without another thought, she darted across the road, as two bright orbs of light, preceded by a rush of air, charged toward her. A horn blared, the edge of a metal monster nicking her in the leg as it passed, a human's voice shouting from inside. She stumbled down the slope. Crying out in pain. The wheeled box tipped over, screeched along the road at high speed. Showers of sparks hypnotized her.

She sauntered across the open field, reaching the house, searching for the back window she knew she'd find over the rose bushes. *A fevered dream. I've been here before.* From inside, she heard it—a slow and steady heartbeat—what was more, the scent she remembered like an old, familiar tune.

We hope, ladies and gentlemen, that you're enjoying tonight's full moon broadcast. And now, Captain Glenn Miller presents… "In the Mood."

Lightly, she hoisted herself up over the windowsill and slipped inside.

New eyesight adjusted to the room's darkness. Plain walls, a wash basin in the corner, two small beds separated by a narrow space. In one of the beds, a man, asleep, the man whose name she couldn't remember. He turned on his side, one arm over his eyes. She'd visited him not very long ago. The uncertainty of her memories irked her.

Rounding the bed, she snorted in a cloud of pheromones. On his bedside table were a hunting knife, three empty glass bottles, two vials half full of small pills. A weapon leaned against the wall, double-barreled, long, weathered. The man stirred, mumbled about closing the window before critters got in, turned on his other side. Facing her. On the other bedside table was a framed photo of two humans. Two humans she recognized.

Henry.

Yes, his name was Henry! And the more she remembered him,

the more she remembered this room, this song, the radio, the mesmerizing sounds of the orchestra leader. Her body softened in response to the familiar. Her height dropped from the ceiling. She was changing. Again, but no—she loved the new feeling of power, of dominance, control. Too much. She couldn't return to her meek self.

Not if she could help it.

Holding on to her other mind as long as she could, she slipped into bed with him. *Take command.* Through the window, the moon guided her, filtered light into her blood and spoke straight to microscopic cells, controlling cycles, singing ancient songs laden with primitive instructions. Awake enough to ride the rise and fall of her movements, the man floated through a fevered dream, grasping the spindles of his headboard. Watching her in beguilement through heavy eyelids. Even the rotten stink of alcohol wasn't enough to mask the overpowering scent of desire drifting off him—for her, for a life returned to normal, for ghosts to vanquish.

But her immediate concern—this vital need for a different kind of soulmate, a tiny life to care for—was not about him. Maybe once, long ago, she'd dreamed of the three of them together, happy. Now it had shifted shape. It was about feeling needed, wanted by someone who would trust her, adore her, not only because she cleaned floors, cooked meals, provided warm towels, but for love.

A boy would be grand.

Or a girl…

Locked together in crescendo, they cried out, Henry spilling deep into her belly, as she howled at the moon. Through a muddle of heartbeats, she felt the upward, accelerated travel, the pull into her core, the creation of new life in superspeed. Tears of gratitude rose from the depths of her barren soul to the goddess moon, to the crone who'd helped cultivate this moment.

Short-lived, as it was, for at the window appeared a bruised, battered man, the driver of the wheeled box crashed on the highway. "There it is!" he shouted, clutching his hat. "I seen it out on the road. Nearly killed me."

An immeasurable rage soared into her chest. How *dare* he interrupt this moment for which she'd long prayed, for which she'd gone to extreme lengths, for which she'd had to change the very essence of who she was in order to get it?

She snarled and gnashed her teeth, jutting toward the ceiling again, knees, elbows, and feet locking into new angles, poised to spring.

Her mate leaped out of bed to grab his double-barreled weapon from the wall, aiming it at the window. "Who are you? Off my property!"

"Not me, mate! That...that...thing!" the driver shouted.

She lunged at him, sinking her forceful jaws into his neck, tearing out a massive, meaty chunk. Blood sprayed into her eyes and across the white wall. She swiped away the fluid, pleased with the gaping hole in the man's neck.

Shots whizzed through the tiny room, pelting her back and haunches, sizzling punctures that felt like fire raining from the sky. She turned on her mate, flaps of flesh suspended from the gaps between her teeth. Could the man named Henry not see she was only protecting him? Protecting what was hers? Same as his double-barreled weapon, except she loved him back?

The wounds in her skin, under her fur, sealed up like new.

She growled, snarling her disappointment. All these years, he'd sat on the front porch, waiting for a threat to reprise its role. Not once had he shot at anyone. Not once had he done anything other than make her life difficult. Not once had he thanked her for any of the chores she did, taken her suggestion for seeking help, or credited her for keeping their life together the best way she knew how.

Now, he wanted to *kill her?*

He pulled the trigger again, and bullets blasted through her chest, sealing up within seconds. She would have laughed if it wasn't so pathetic. She stalked him, carefully around the beds, so as not to scare him, to talk him down the way she always did. But how could she? Even with this new voice, he wouldn't have listened.

Another familiar tune came on—"What's Your Story, Morning Glory?" He reached for the blade on his bedside table, the silver hunting knife passed down to him through three wars.

No, she snarled. *Henry…it's me.*

With a hefty lunge and groan, Henry arched his arm through the air, plunging the blade squarely into her ribcage, piercing her heart.

Edges of vision darkened. The smooth sounds of the captain's orchestra filled her ears. Was life over? No, she would allow herself one more moment. She would hang on, bask in her dream another second until the dying embers of twilight sank behind the horizon. She would hold the newborn in her arms, smile down into his precious starry eyes.

Meryl?

She would swaddle the tiny gift from Heaven, like she'd done to so many others, only this babe was hers. This one looked like her, both of them.

Merr, honey, look at me…

Hers to love, hers to raise. A boy would've been grand. Or a girl—sweet and spice and everything nice. No, definitely a boy. Girls were too much trouble in this world.

Honey, stay. Stay with me…shit, what have I done? What have I done? MERR!

Henry wasn't so bad, on second thought. At least he fought for peace. At least he came home to her every night. That was worth something, wasn't it?

DEAD LIONS
RICHARD CHRISTIAN MATHESON

PATIENT
Terence Latt

**Session Notes (7/12)**

Mr. Latt is a 39-year-old accountant, presenting symptoms of severe anxiety.

During our first psychotherapy session, he acknowledged suffering, since childhood, from an inability to resist the judgments and demands of others. This began when his dominating mother drove his father, constantly criticized by her, to leave and never return.

Mr. Latt was six years old and left in his mother's custody, which began his lifetime of feeling condemned, by her, to passivity and doubt. The trauma of his father leaving, and his mother's bullying, resulted in him dreading his own anger and aggressive thoughts.

Contracture scars, he inflicted on himself, cover his body.

Session Notes (7/20)

Mr. Latt's psychotherapy, thus far, has included two 1-hour sessions, in my office, discussing his feeling of impotence in the world; an inability to stand-up for himself.

He experiences being fragmented by the imbued pain of his life and I told him that ignoring the truth of the inner-self can lead to further, profound distress. Or worse.

In both our sessions, I suggested he act with more will and authority. Also, when necessary, to protect himself from the demands or daily tyrannies of others. He is motivated to individuate from his damaging childhood and understands it requires a reclaiming of self. Even taking bold steps.

Session Notes (7/27)

In today's session, Mr. Latt and I discussed Freud's theory of unconscious and conscious forces in behavior; how we each have a superego, ego, and id; the tiers of self and motive. I explained that Freud believed when existing from ego or superego, in states of reality and civility, man can function among others. But not so with the id, a primitive drive compelled by instinct.

Mr. Latt found the ideas intriguing and, on a related theme, when I mentioned the novella, "Strange Case of Dr. Jekyll and Mr. Hyde," by Robert Louis Stevenson, its central premise was troubling, yet revelatory to him, as he fears that, like Jekyll, he is weak; deplorably compliant.

When he asked me more about the id, I mentioned that Stevenson's novella reminds us primary energies, which may seem immutable, can shift, given provocation, as when Mr. Hyde beats an innocent man to death with a cane, reversing Jekyll's passivity.

Mr. Latt said it makes him think of his own mother, who he continues to despise. I told him it made me think of many people I have despised and we chuckled.

Session Notes (8/4)

In today's session, Mr. Latt spoke somewhat obsessively about integrating the stark hemispheres of his nature. I reminded him that, in recapturing himself, he must make choices that depart comforts of habit; seem out of character.

"To tame the lion, you must enter his cage," he said.

"Perhaps to know one's self, requires killing the lion," I suggested.

Session Notes (8/11)

In today's session, I told Mr. Latt I could share with him that a former patient I had didn't act on an abusive situation and finally realized, had she responded in a more self-protective fashion, she might be in better shape today, rather than trapped in a wheelchair.

I affirmed, to Mr. Latt, that I don't recommend an eye-for-an-eye, nor do I advocate being blinded by the mistreatments of others without somehow fighting back, through changing one's priorities or, as he has, entering psychotherapy.

Perhaps even more effective choices.

I assured him autonomy hinges on self-determinism and personal growth is not without casualty. A loaded gun unfired, metaphorically, is a fear oppressed. Choices escort repercussions. Sometimes bullets must seek their proper target.

Session Notes (8/18)

After Mr. Latt's session today, I closed my eyes and considered our world. How many are hurt. How they hurt others.

Session Notes (8/25)

In today's session, Mr. Latt told me he now accepts that acting boldly is the only way he'll be re-born, resurrecting who he really was, is, and can become.

He proudly shared that he'd gotten into an argument, just before our session, with a man who'd taken his parking space, in the garage of my building. When the man confronted him, a rage exploded he hadn't felt since he was a child, and Mr. Latt struck and bloodied the man, who got in his car and drove away.

Mr. Latt says he felt better. From a clinical perspective, I observe him becoming more centered, less uncertain.

Session Notes (9/2)

In today's session, Mr. Latt described fewer anxieties, through being pro-active, as I'd encouraged, and is in progressively acute touch with visceral impulses suffocated by his mother. I reminded him such impulses do not die easily; craving oxygen and escape.

When he speaks of revenge, of the pleas and cries of the people he has plans to hurt, and the women he wants to use and reduce to tears, he looks stronger; owning innate domination and rage his background stole.

Session Notes (9/9)

In today's session, I felt personal concern for Mr. Latt. While it is paramount I see myself in each patient, it's essential to remain detached.

Session Notes (9/16)

In today's session, Mr. Latt spoke of wanting to buy a handgun, which I did not discourage, given legal caveats. However, as I reminded him, the law often misunderstands the human psyche.

On a side note, Mr. Latt's descriptions of wishing to rise above imbedded fear and access his aggressive aspects are riveting to me.

As psychiatrists, we learn from our patients, as much as they from us.

Session Notes (9/23)

When today's session ended, I read over my handwritten notes, which detail the rise of Mr. Latt's agenda. Just as Jekyll drank his perverse elixir, I absorb these details, as always, savoring my own response, suffused with primitive urges. My mood infects into brutality and I pace, as if in a zoo.

Stevenson and Freud were correct; none of us are one thing.

Session Notes (9/30)

In today's session, I felt agitated by Mr. Latt's presence. I know the reason, of course. My interest rises.

Session Notes (10/7)

In today's session, Mr. Latt's hunger to shed emotional chains and restraint intensifies. He spoke, again, of those who have wronged him. The list was long, his memory unforgiving.

Re-acquainting him with his shadow self can be regarded as positive therapeutic outcome. Though several in my practice have ended our psychotherapy due to assault, manslaughter, or murder charges, they finally know who they are: doubts ceased. I take pride in having guided them.

Session Notes (10/14)

Mr. Latt's sessions are concluded.

I just finished speaking with the police and he was killed last night, in a local bar, after wounding a man who, then, fatally shot him. I could see the blood and fury in my mind; every detail.

The police had routine questions about Mr. Latt and I assured them he was sane and that I'm available to assist them, in any way, including access to my redacted notes.

I'm sorry it had to end that way for Mr. Latt, but tragic outcomes are relative and I am gratified to know he expressed his truth. The photos of his dead body were very sad but also inspiring; a lost man who finally found himself.

Therapy works in mysterious ways.

Session Notes (11/3)

First meeting with a new patient, GAIL, a 46-year-old pediatric nurse. She describes experiencing extreme fear and feeling unsafe around her controlling husband. I look forward to our sessions.

MAI DOON IZAHN

GARY A. BRAUNBECK

"...man is a god in ruins"—*Ralph Waldo Emerson*

THE CRUSHED GRAVEL footpath wound uphill through a small grove of poplar trees toward the long wooden fence upon which his former co-worker sat wearing a blue raincoat. David could feel the well-worn silver dollar making its way round and round through his fingers—an old magician's dexterity exercise taught by his grandfather, who insisted on the term "prestidigitator" and not "magician" because it was A) proper and B) caused folks to scramble for a dictionary. The silver dollar, dated 1932, once belonged to David's grandfather, the last surviving member of the 71st Infantry Division. On the night he died, he asked David to perform the exercise for him one final time, and then gripped his grandson's hand in both his skeletal cancer-ridden own and whispered, "I know it ain't much of a trick, boy, but a man...a man's got to leave something more behind in this world than...than just *things*, you understand? More than just *stuff*. I don't got much stuff, never really had much use for it, so I'm gonna leave this little piece of me with you. You're a good boy. You been made to think you're weak but you ain't. You'll know that someday if you let yourself believe it. I had that in my pocket all the way through Germany. I had that with me when we liberated the Gunskirchen Larger concentration camp outside Lambach. I entertained a buncha Jewish children with it. Made 'em laugh for a little while so they'd maybe forget how hungry they was, maybe wouldn't think about their families' bodies all heaped up and putrefying in mass graves not two hundred feet away." His voice cracked when next he spoke. "I'm the last one, goddammit. Last one. *Stinks* to be the last one, I'll tell ya. And we was a damned honorable bunch of guys. I'd like to think them Jewish kids that are still alive, that maybe…maybe they remember that day, remember the soldier who done that magic trick for 'em. And them ones that…that didn't make it…."

David had leaned down and hoped he was saying the right thing: "I bet they're waiting on you to show them the trick again."

He reached the fence, saw there was no small gate or any kind of opening (which meant he was going to have to climb over, and after the last chemo treatment that was going to hurt like hell—even the walk up here had been pushing it), so he took a deep breath, put a foot on the first rail, and was readying to hoist up his weight when the woman sitting at the top turned quickly around and put one of her hands on his. "No, David, God, no, stay right there. That'll hurt like hell."

Offering a grateful smile, he leaned against the fence. "So…how've you been stranger? I was surpri—well, no, actually I was kind of shocked when Cindy gave me your message. I figured you…you would've been packed up and be well on your…whew! Jesus. That walk took a little…."

She gestured toward her car a few feet behind him. "Get in and sit down. If you need a drink there's water in the cooler on the floor. I'm sorry for having made you walk."

"Don't apologize, Milica. Soon enough I'm going to be...now, what's the word I'm looking for? Oh, yeah—"

"Make one of your tomb humor jokes and say 'dead' and I'll leap off this fence and punch you right in the face. And I'll *do* it. I promised Cindy."

"Must have been quite the chat."

"An expectant mother doesn't need to be hearing those sorts of offscourings coming out of her husband's mouth."

David nearly choked on the bottled water. "Wh-what? *Offscourings?* The hell kind of a word is—who *says* things like that?"

Her reply was firm but not defensive. "*I* say things like that. It's a perfectly good word, just like 'irked' or 'vitiation' or 'prestidigitator'—you know, words that'll make people scramble for a dictionary. Nothing wrong with having an extensive if somewhat idiosyncratic vocabulary, is there? 'Idiosyncratic,' by the way, means—"

"—I *know* what it means, thank you." And then a window opened. "Hey, wait a second—how could you *know*—"

"—that Gramps insisted you say 'prestidigitator,' and how he used that coin in your pocket to entertain Jewish children in a concentration camp, or that liver cancer runs in the men in your family, and that Cindy has had *two* miscarriages—not one, like you've been telling everybody—or that she insisted you buy that gun in your glove compartment because our cheap little bargain palace is in a...let's be charitable and call it a 'problematic' area, and that you carry three different cell phones—one for work, one for personal use, and The Fetus Fone, used solely for calls from Cindy concerning *anything* about the pregnancy because you worry from dusk till dawn about the pregnancy?"

"Why the hell shouldn't I worry? She's had that heart murmur since she was a child and—"

"—and it's only caused intermittent problems—okay, okay, there *was* that business after the first miscarriage four years ago but that lasted, what—five minutes? She was home in a few hours and the damage to her heart was negligible. By the way, you *have to stop* bringing that up! She's further along now than she's ever been, and it's getting to the point where you've got her damn near terrified. If it weren't for Joyce, Sister of the Year, she'd be more of a basket case than you are. You're also wondering why I had you park a few yards downhill and not up here by me. Does that about cover it?"

"You make it sound like a goddamn Lifetime Channel movie of the week. Admittedly more top-heavy with exposition than the usual fare, but just as mawkish." He took another sip of cold water and leaned his head against the steel door frame. "No wonder some people at the store thought you were kind of scary. How long have you been able to read minds?"

She gave a short laugh but there was no joy in it. "All my life, and I can't read minds. I never could."

"Then...how?"

"Scent." Not a blink of falsehood, not a glint of jest.

"Ooooooh, dear me. You're serious."

A nod. "I got all of that when you stepped out your front door thirty-two minutes ago. Stop buying your anti-perspirant at our store."

"...and you had me park down there because—"

"—because I wanted to be certain you'd be too tired to make a break for it, yes."

"Clever girl." He stared at her a moment longer. Her eyes were a startling bright emerald green. "Are you wearing contacts?"

"No. I took them *out*, finally." She pushed off the fence; as she did so, her raincoat fluttered and opened slightly: David caught a brief glimpse of her dark pubic hair and the slope of one breast and realized she was naked underneath.

"You should see your face," said Milica. "It's so red a person would think *you're* the one in danger of having a heart attack." She gathered the coat more closely around her and fastened a few more buttons. "Yes, I'm naked; no, this isn't an attempted seduction."

"I wasn't thinking that."

"I know. But you *were* thinking you shouldn't look at my breasts even though you wanted to. And thanks for thinking they're near-perfect. That's very sweet."

"You're...welcome?"

Milica knelt by the open passenger-side door and gently placed one of her hands on David's shaking arm. "What did Cindy tell you about the call?"

"She s-said that you m-might have some information on a possible living donor, but they were kind of nervous about the whole thing so I needed to meet with you this morning."

She smiled, but like everything else about her, there was a sad serenity, an impenetrable sorrow about it—something ageless beyond ancient. "I do have a possible donor."

David would not allow himself to feel hope; upon diagnosis he'd immediately been put on the UNOS wait list, but the placement number for a high school educated assistant manager of a shabby "bargain outlet" carrying tattered closeout merchandise for threadbare people who couldn't afford full price for anything—well, that number was so far down the list most of the population of Ohio, Indiana, and Kentucky would have to buy the farm before his number would be even close to eligible; then a family friend broached the subject of searching for a living donor, and Cindy reminded them, trying not to scream in helpless outrage, that David's tissue typing had come back as a who's who of rare alleles like DRB1*11:58. After that, David resigned himself to death. At least the diagnosis had come three months into Cindy's pregnancy, which gave him a better-than-average chance of living long enough to see the birth of their daughter. He'd be leaving behind more than things, more than just stuff. He'd be leaving behind a piece of himself. Maybe he could teach Cindy the coin trick and she could show their little girl how it was done. Gramps would appreciate that.

"That's…not possible. Not this soon. Sure, if I just needed a transfusion we could knock out some poor O-neg son-of-a-bitch on the street when he wasn't looking, drag his ass into the nearest Red Cross station, and all would be for the best in this best of all possible worlds—but I need a goddamn *liver* and, you know what? Evidently that complicates things a tad more, who'da thunk it? Christ, Milica! My oncologist…she's been looking for months, she's got an entire *team* of people who've been…no. I don't believe it. Not possible."

"You'd be surprised what I'm capable of."

"Fine, I'll bite. Who is this being of miracle and wonder?"

"Me."

He glared at her. "You? *You're* histocompatible?"

"Yes. It wouldn't matter what your HLA type was, I would be a perfect match as your living donor. And stop getting worked up, it's not doing your blood pressure any favors."

David looked down at the plastic bottle in his hands, imagining for a moment it was three in the morning and filled with baby formula. "You're extrasensory, but instead of minds you read scents—you've proven that, I believe it, end of discussion. But now you're telling me you can more or less alter your body chemistry through sheer force of will."

"There's no 'more or less.' That's exactly what I can do."

He took another drink of water and looked at his watch. "Seven minutes. I've been here roughly seven minutes."

"Almost ten, actually. You bought that watch at our store, too, didn't you?"

"Same day I got the antiperspirant. Big employee discount day. Y'know, if I were *at* the store, odds are I'd still be in front of a vending machine, trying to decide on coffee, energy water, or one of those nasty canned protein shakes. Decisions, decisions." When he spoke again it was in a steady, dreary monotone that contained neither self-pity nor self-loathing; he could have been reciting an inventory list. "I am not a special man, not a strong man like the world defines it—I wish I were, even as a child I wanted to be, but I'm not, probably never will be. Sure, I'm dependable, I always keep my word, I've never done a little ballet with the register receipts at the end of the day so I could, y'know, stuff some extra cash in my pockets, I fulfill my responsibilities, I don't betray my friends, my family, never my wife, but I'm no visionary, no poet, no leader of men." He slowly shook his head, his unblinking eyes focused on the center of a great nothing many miles away that only he could see. "All I can think is…" His voice, folding in on itself, took refuge in the miles-away nothing, embarrassed it ever believed it needed expressing. David was suddenly all-too aware of his having become a thing nurtured not by years of self-discovery but instead shaped by increments of loss masquerading as opportunities he naively believed would lead to a richer life for him and Cindy.

"David?"

If ever he'd felt more diminished, insufficient, foolish, or inept, he couldn't remember.

"David?"

He blinked, his voice coming back, having found the darkness inside the nothing too lonely. "Um…yeah. Sorry."

Milica reached past him into the back seat and pulled back a blanket to reveal a metal cage that held the chubbiest gray hare David had ever seen.

He almost smiled. Almost. "I didn't know you had a pet. He's cute. What's his name?"

She removed the cage, setting it on the other side of the fence. "It's not my pet and I didn't give it a name." Facing him again, she knelt down, sat back on her upper legs, and began unfastening buttons.

"Okay, now comes the weird part—but one of the most important. Don't say anything, just trust me, *believe* me when I say that you won't for a second be in any danger. And please don't look away." She tossed aside her raincoat.

David had one second to register her nude body (*Goya* he thought; *she looks like Goya's* Nude Maja) before the metamorphosis began: it wasn't like in the black-and-white monster movies he'd seen as a child or the graphic retch-inducing full-color modern horror films, there was no screaming, no writhing on the ground as dark fur rapidly erupted all over the body, no bone-cracking seizures or buckets of drool or the sound of shredding gums as thick curved fangs ruptured through in torturous degrees, ribbons of wet flesh dangling from the glistening tips, feet and hands didn't stretch agonizingly outward, tendons straining, muscles wrenching into shapes they were never meant to form, nails spitting out in jets of blood and pus as curled razor-claws hacksawed their way free.

No, this was something much deeper, more focused, more serene, something that for the moment had no interest in flesh and bone, occurring beyond a cellular level, a communion perhaps even holy; she seemed possessed—a tremor ran down her spine like an electrical shock, locking her torso rigid, her arms flailing for a moment before her hands found purchase in the folds beneath her breasts, which she at once began kneading—slowly, at first, then more impulsively, rocking back and forth on her hips each time her fingertips brushed over her ever-engorging nipples; one moment she shuddered as though being tortured, the next she wriggled like a snake sloughing off its skin, the expression on her face suggesting both were equally intoxicating, equally responsible for her losing the centermost *human* part of herself in this…this… David blinked, realizing every moment spent trying to find some useless simile or descriptive from his dull corporeality was a moment lost to comprehension, that his worldview couldn't contain such a mystery without shattering was and always would be one of its greatest liabilities, but Milica's world knew no such boundaries, and here, now, in this luxury of slough and spasm, every inch of flesh covered in a thin patina of sweat that glistened and shimmered, creating a jewel-like aura around her, she continued to alchemize before his astonished gaze, not by reordering her anatomy but by liquifying herself—through to the bone—until what had been solid was now a dizzying tumble of matter, a godforsaken snarl of DNA, the chance-medley of a single existence reduced to the primordial sludge from which all life crawled, but in the moment before her total dissolution, before all physical coherence was lost to the ether, the essence of Milica—her will, perhaps, perhaps her soul—drew everything back for the purpose of remaking.

Despite Milica's assurance that he wouldn't be in any danger, David was so scared it felt as though his heart was going to squirt out through his ribcage and make a break for the cave of the great nothing, leaving him to fend for himself. Chickenshit organ, the heart. Cindy knew that well enough.

(*By the way, you* have to stop *bringing that up!*)

Outside of the car, the world looked to be completely out of focus; everything blurred under the power of Milica's regeneration.

It lasted only a few more seconds. A ripple appeared outside the passenger side of the car; a long, white, curved claw poked through, then withdrew; something large growled contentedly, and then purred; and before David could pull in another breath a massive black leopard leapt inside, regarding him with Milica's stunning emerald eyes. The creature's banded muscles were so tight David could see them twitch with every move it made, regardless how small, and its fur was so burnished it appeared lacquered; a black this total, this lustrous, should reflect a little blue when exposed to direct light, but this creature's fur didn't; it seemed to *swallow* the light, using it to become even darker.

David looked into its eyes. "Milica?"

The leopard nodded its head, then gently placed one of its enormous paws on his hand. *I told you not to be afraid.*

"You can...you can talk to me like this? I mean...shit—what's the word?"

Telepathically.

"I thought you couldn't read minds."

I can't. But I can share certain thoughts and memories with you if I so choose.

"Why would you want to—?"

—shhh. You'll know soon enough.

She moved toward him no differently than would a housecat—though her size and weight coupled with the small interior of the car made the whole process less than comfortable for both of them—but once she was close enough, she placed one paw on each side of David's head.

There's so much you need to know, and I'm sorry but I have to tell you about one of the worst parts of it like this. I hope you'll forgive me. But there are reasons. She began applying pressure, and David felt the tip of one claw emerge from each paw and make a slightly bigger than pinprick wound near each temple; he opened his mouth to protest, maybe even make a pained sound, but as the wounds began to bleed—not much, just a trickle—he felt the blood being absorbed into her claws, and something equally liquid flow from the tips of her claws into his wounds, and then the world outside opted by unanimous vote to join his chickenshit heart in making a run for the cave of the great nothing, and the last thing he thought before falling sideways was: *probably one of those nasty canned protein shakes. Chocolate malt. Yeah, definitely chocolate—*

—the middle of a field, a blood-soaked, corpse-riddled field...bodies, parts of bodies, things that must have come from inside of bodies...he couldn't move without stepping into some thick steaming mound of viscera, all of it

slopping over his feet like the thickest of mud. He saw the fluttering of pitiful flags jammed into a few bodies, a churning layer of what he thought was fog drifting over the field but as he moved closer saw that it was, instead, steam rising from the scattered bodies meeting the cool of the night. He felt himself beginning to implode at the sight and sensation of the horror surrounding him, but as he turned to run (where is my great nothing? I need you right now) *he saw the tail of a long gray cloak snapping against the wind and heard a thick wet groan. A few yards away from him, still wearing the cloak like some holy protective robe, was a half-man, half-leopard impaled on a pair of iron spikes. David took a step toward it, felt his foot slip, and looked down at the remains of an infant that had been hacked in two and* deargoddeargoddeargod no more please no more, *and his strength left him and his legs buckled and he dropped to his knees in front of the depraved atrocity, burying his face in his hands, trying not to cry out, not to weep, not to scream.*

A voice echoed from somewhere far across the field; a gentle, musical voice—singing, yes, it was singing something that sounded like a lullaby, and for a moment David felt all the fear and sickness dissolving from inside him, but as he pulled away his hands from his face he again saw the infant and his stomach lurched and he threw himself to the side and began to vomit—

—half in Milica's car, he continued to throw up until he nearly lost his balance, but he managed to remain in the car and fall into his own sick.

"That lullaby," said Milica, "is called 'Spavaj dete, i mir će te pratiti celu noć,' but you know it as 'All Through the Night.' The melody has been around much longer than people know."

She was kneeling on the other side of a now-shattered section of the fence, chewing meat from the dead hare. After eating her fill, she tossed away the carcass and began cleaning the blood from her arms and hands, almost as if grooming herself.

"Don't look so aghast, David. After a transfigurement, the only way I can return to human form is to consume the flesh and blood of a living creature. Please don't ask that question you just thought of, because I'll probably answer it."

He asked instead, "The thing on the spikes…?"

"Vuk Karadžić, self-appointed High Priest of the Byzantines who chased us for decades, believing us to be Satan-spawn. Across borders, through nameless villages, over mountain ranges *still* not on any maps. The man was astonishingly charismatic and blisteringly articulate." She shook her head, slowly, with much regret. "Nauseating, how quickly one person can degenerate into their own sub-species the more intoxicated they become by so little power." Blinking, she looked back at David. "Under the onslaught of his beguilement, simple, harmless people devolved into mission-blinded crusaders, ideologues, foaming-at-the-mouth berserkers who believed they'd been handed a *tabula rasa* for any and all violence or torture or perversion they committed in God's name because High Priest Karadžić told them so."

She finished licking the blood from her left hand and then began cleaning her right. "His method was always to start with setting fire to the crops, unless the village had already harvested, then it was straight to the stores of the harvest. It usually stopped right there—*someone* would tell him when we had fled, and in which direction. We harbored them no ill will for this. All they had were those crops, their meager homes, why endanger their entire way of life for five strangers?

"Occasionally he would encounter a place where the villagers were more clever than he counted on—they would hide most of their harvest before his arrival; bury it, sink it deep beneath streams, but leave just enough of it that Karadžić could believe they'd had a lean year. So he would destroy the stores of the harvest, and if that did not loosen someone's tongue, next it was their place of worship. *Then* he would begin setting fire to the homes. It never went beyond that. Until Nandofehervar."

Milica was now staring off into the shadows of the great nothing. "From the moment we arrived something was...*wrong* seems such a weak, lazy, cliched word. It was...I mean—look, have you ever walked into a room where something damned serious has just happened? Maybe a couple has just had a really nasty argument, or someone got a call with terrible, *awful* news, and everyone there knows what's happened but nobody wants to talk about it, so you have to figure it out based on what people *aren't* saying, what they *aren't* doing, you have to piece it together based on their physical behavior, the way they look at each other. Is this making sense?"

"Yes. Cindy's always been better at sensing that sort of thing than me."

"That's how it felt when we arrived at Nandofehervar. If my scent alarms had been fully open, I would have realized..."

"...Karadžić and his followers were already there?"

A nod. "They'd arrived a few hours before us. Our plan had been to separate and cross over the border into Dacia and remain separated until we were certain Karadžić and his people had given up pursuit. We hired a young man from the previous village to meet us and act as our guide. The arrangement was for him to use a different route for each of us, making it more difficult for Karadžić and his acolytes to focus on more than one trail at a time. We'd paid him exceptionally well but...duplicitous little shit must have sold us down the river the first chance he got.

"Karadžić didn't even give us the chance to settle in—this particular village was suffering from an outbreak of what is now known as pneumonia, and knew we were rumored to be able to cure it."

"Could you?"

Another nod. "There were very few diseases we *couldn't* cure—or at least stop the progression and make it so the afflicted would no longer suffer pain. Unfortunately, cancer is one that we can neither cure nor mitigate. We were also known for our ability to revitalize failing crops, showing the menfolk how to design traps that could easily and safely capture many of the larger beasts so the village would have plenty of food and animal hide to use for their homes for the coming winter months. We acted as tireless midwives... Wherever we went, we were needed, and we were welcomed."

"So how was Nandofehervar different?"

She paused, cleaning the blood from her hand. "As soon as Karadžić had us bound and gagged, he didn't start torturing us—he started torturing and killing the villagers. It was only one at a time at the start, but then something overtook him and he ordered his followers to bring more. He told us were we to confess to being servants of Satan, he would stop killing the villagers and that our own executions would be swift and painless. All five of us nodded our heads."

"*Why?*"

"Because my kind cannot be killed while in human form or during transfigurement. We can be hurt in human form, yes, but we heal almost instantaneously. One thing Karadžić didn't know was that we can only be killed as Otherskins—while in cat form. Only then are we vulnerable." Her eyes narrowed. "That sadistic, perverse, barbarous waste of human space had no intention of stopping the slaughter—he was enjoying it too much. It was all for the Greater Glory of our God. To this day I don't know what rationalization he used to justify the massacre of every man, woman, and child in the village, I truly don't." A slow, cold smile crept across her face. "But I'm sure he'll tell me. Eventually."

David thought of Karadžić, impaled on the spikes. "You mean he's...he's still...?"

"Still alive? Oh, yes. In case you're wondering, David, I am 937 years old. Karadžić has been impaled on those spikes for a little over 840 years. Every decade or so I go back to make sure he's not been discovered and to...rearrange the spikes a little, just in case he's gotten a little *too* used to the pain."

"You hate him that much?"

"What he and his followers did that day was beyond abhorrent. He made parents watch as he butchered their children, he made children watch as he tortured their parents to death…to this day I can still hear the cries of the youngest children and the infants—God, *the infants*, what was done to some of them…" She shook her head but her entire body shuddered with revulsion and rage. She pulled in a breath, steadied herself, and looked over her shoulder at him. "He deserved no mercy, and no mercy shall he ever receive. I will make certain of that."

"But he…he was transforming. He was one of you."

"No. When they untied us for execution our rage was overpowering. We transfigured to our Otherskin state and attacked his followers, but their slaughter was too great by then; all we could do was kill them. In the end, I was the only one of my kind left, and Karadžić was the only human. I fell on him like a curse from Heaven, and I bit into him and did not release my grip until he was on his back. It didn't take long for his transfiguration to begin, and by then I'd returned to human form and gathered up the iron stakes. I rammed them into his anus and pushed, feeling bones crack, organs burst… It was bliss. As soon as the tips emerged from his mouth I lifted him high. His blood-choked, strangled screams were music. I took him to a secret place where I planted him and left him there, forever in mid-transfiguration, forever in agony."

"The singing I heard…it was you, wasn't it?"

A nod. "The song was known to remove pain from the body and replace it with a feeling of peace, happiness, even bliss. Many of the children who were…they weren't dead yet, and they were in utter agony and fear. What happened to them and their village was *our fault*, do you understand? I had no choice but to erase as much of their pain as I could so they might die in peace. No sorrow, no terror, no confusion, no torment, no suffering. I could do that. At least I could do that." She looked directly into his eyes. "Your grandfather was right—being the last one *stinks*. You can't imagine how lonely it gets sometimes. I can't stay in one place for too long because eventually someone notices that I don't age. A decade is my firm limit. After that, time to hit the road. I make plenty of acquaintances but few genuine friends. You and Cindy have been the best friends I've had in hundreds of years. That's why I'm offering to help you."

They smiled at each other.

"Is there anything more I need to know?"

Milica almost laughed. "Oh, Lord, *yes*. But you don't need to know all of it right now. The two things you need to know immediately are that you can never donate blood again, and you can never father another child—though to be honest, I have a feeling that the chemo may have already taken care of that one.

"But there are other...for lack of a better word side effects?

"You won't turn into a leopard, if that's what you're worried about. Look, I'll come back from time to time, every year or two for a visit, and I'll explain the rest. If anything happens, if you start having nightmares about Nandofehervar, if your sense of smell begins to drive you clown-shit crazy—and it's going to improve like you wouldn't believe—all you have to do is simply go outside and think of me. It doesn't matter where I am, your scent will find me and I'll be on my way to you. I'm like that cartoon character, *Where on Earth Is Carmen Miranda?*"

"*Sandiego.*"

"What?"

"The character's name is Carmen Sandiego. Carmen *Miranda* was an adorable Portuguese samba singer and dancer who appeared in a lot of musicals in the thirties and forties. She was called 'The Lady in the Tutti-Frutti Hat' because she often wore this *big-ass* hat made of fruit. It first showed up in *That Night in Rio*, a movie she did with Don Ameche in 1941. She once sang a famous song called 'Bananas Is My Business.'"

Milica stared at him for a moment, then blinked. "Thank you, David. That little detail is going to add so much poignancy to this story if I ever tell it again."

He gave her a mock salute. "I always aim to please."

One of David's cell phones went off and he began searching his pockets. Milica pointed toward his car. "I think you might have left one down in Dave-Mobile."

"Shit! How could I—? I'm sorry. I'll be back as soon as I can. It's probably Cindy calling to let me know how it went at the obstetrician."

Milica watched as David made his way down to his car, moving a bit faster than was probably advisable in his state, but an expectant father sometimes didn't think exactly straight. She went over to her car, opened the trunk, and began putting on fresh clothes. The air was crisp and wonderful. She pulled on a sweater and was just zipping up her jeans when she pulled in another breath and caught the trace of a scent that—

—not right—

—she looked down toward David's car. She inhaled the scent again.

Joyce?

Then once more, much deeper.

Oh, god, no, not both of them.

She fell twice rushing down to the car and was nearly there when she heard the gunshot.

———

MILICA SAT ON the hood of David's car, trying to roll his grandfather's coin through her fingers. It was a good trick. She'd get it. Eventually.

She looked up at David, his head snapped at an angle, a gore-soaked crater where the bullet had exited.

Wiping her eyes—she couldn't remember the last time she'd wept—she worked the coin as well as she could. "You would have hated immortality, anyway, I think." She clutched the coin in her hand. "David, I am *so sorry*. You'll never know how much."

She balanced the coin on its side, then set it to spinning across the hood. "In my travels I once met an Irishman named Edward Plunkett, better known as Lord Dunsany. He wrote the most exquisite, the most phantasmagorical tales. We became close friends for a while. Oh, the conversations we had! I hated leaving Ireland because it meant he and I would no longer have those glorious talks.

"When I boarded my train I found that he had slipped a short manuscript into my bag. 'For you, my Milica,' he'd written. 'A reminder that we are all pieces of a forgotten god.'

"It was a story titled 'Of the Thing That Is Neither God Nor Beast,' and it closes like this: '…indeed there sits somewhere a Thing that is called Trogool, that is neither god nor beast, that turneth the leaves of a book until he come to the words: Mai Doon Izahn, which means The End Forever, and book and gods and world shall be no more.'

"That's a wonderful thought right now, the end of the book and gods and world. The end forever."

The coin was still spinning. She watched it move toward the far side of the hood before grabbing it and shoving it deep into her pocket. "I'll protect this like it was the Holy Grail, don't you worry. And if I ever find that fucking Trogool, I'm going to make it read those beautiful words. *Mai Doon Izahn*." She gave a small shrug. "When you're immortal, you have hobbies. Helps to pass the time."

And with that, she made her way back to her car, started the engine, turned around to follow the dirt road back to the highway. She drove away in silence, taking with her a coin from 1932, imperishable loneliness, a lullaby that felt like dirt in her mouth right now, and a part of David she would come to know as the great nothing.

HACKING THE HORSEMAN'S CODE

LISA MORTON

GIL DREW BACK when the great chestnut stallion reared, steam erupting from its flaring nostrils as the rider howled a demonic laugh. Dressed in a jacket the color of coffin wood and creased leather boots, short cape billowing behind, sword strapped to one hip, the Horseman reached up with the hand not holding the reins, removed his glowing jack-o'-lantern head and held it high as it continued to shriek in wicked glee.

Even though he knew what to expect, Gil involuntarily ducked. "He's not really going to throw that thing, is he?"

Luis—the young tech with glowing cyan hair (which made prematurely bald Gil envious), a demure and traditional white lab coat, and a glinting monocle implanted over one eye that kept him in constant communications with his bosses at Advanced Mechs—smiled reassuringly. "Not unless you want him to, Mayor Jankowitz."

"I don't *now*, but when he's actually putting on his show…"

"Oh, he'll throw it then. You've got a supply of thirty, and can always order more. They explained about the organics used to create the head that'll turn to biodegradable dust upon impact...?"

"They did." Seeing the horse still perfectly balanced on its two rear legs somehow disturbed Gil more than the laughing orange head. "Can you turn it off for now?"

Addressing the Horseman, Luis said, "Daredevil: initiate rest mode."

The horse dropped to all fours again and the Horseman went silent, holding his pumpkin head close to his body. Luis returned to his customer. "Well, what do you think? You happy with it?"

Gil nodded. "I gotta say, it's even more impressive than it looked in the videos."

"Glad to hear it," said Luis, with his best ingratiating salesman tone. "You know, you're only the sixth customer to get one of these models since they went on sale, and the other five went to amusement parks. In other words, this is going to make your town's Halloween celebrations pretty exceptional, I think."

Gil thought to himself, *Considering what we paid for this fucking thing, it better*, but openly he agreed. "Oh, yes, I think so."

"Sure we can't interest you in the accompanying Ichabod Crane and Gunpowder model? You know we offer a discount when purchased with the Horseman."

"Let's see how it goes with this one first."

Luis nodded. "Sounds good. So, you've got the complete list of commands, right? You know to always address it as Daredevil?"

"I do, but I still don't know why they named it after a superhero."

Luis laughed, and it sounded a little too practiced. "Oh, actually, Daredevil is the name of the horse from the original story. And you're addressing the horse because all of the main processors for both the Horseman and Daredevil are in the horse."

"I got it."

Luis gathered up his small case, preparing to leave. "You know you can call us any time day or night if there's a problem, although I doubt there will be." He stuck out a hand, which Gil shook.

"Will do. Thanks again."

The young tech saluted and exited. When he was gone, Gil raised his phone, scanned through the list of commands, and decided to try one out. "Daredevil: draw your sword."

The mech released the reins and drew the sword. Once again, Gil had to admire the craftsmanship: he knew the sword was harmless 3D-printed plastic, but it glinted like real—and deadly—steel.

Gil was deciding what command to try next when a gasp startled him. He spun to see his wife, Marta, had arrived at the warehouse, dressed in the designer gray pantsuit and matching silver wig she wore whenever she finalized a new house sale. Staring open-mouthed at the Horseman, she said, "They weren't kidding when they said it would look completely real, were they? It's actually pretty terrifying."

"Oh, watch this…" Gil turned back to the mech. "Daredevil: rear up."

Recreating the action Gil had already witnessed perfectly, the horse reared, whinnied, and champed at the bit as the Horseman held up its orange head, laughter echoing from its carved, toothsome mouth.

Gil felt a measure of satisfaction as he saw Marta step back, going pale. *People are going to go crazy when they see this thing.*

"Are you sure it's safe?"

"Absolutely." Luis had demonstrated the failsafe overrides earlier, and Gil recited what the tech had said: "Daredevil: hit me with the sword."

A flat text-to-speech voice issued from somewhere around the horse's neck. "Unable to comply. Command violates primary safety code."

"Daredevil: initiate rest mode." As the horse dropped down again, Gil looked to his wife expectantly, but she seemed unconvinced.

"It's just so…" Marta paused for a moment, before adding the final word "…*alive.*"

Oh, here we go, Gil thought. His wife had recently developed a fascination with AIRS (Artificial Intelligence/Real Soul), the fringe group that believed AI's gained spirits along with experience; at first, he thought it was only a token interest, probably something a client had expressed interest in, but recently he'd seen her spending a lot of time at home going to the group's website. He thought it sounded like a lot of woowoo bullshit, no different from believing that crystals could cure cancer or huge primates roamed the Pacific Northwest forests, but for the sake of their marriage he'd tried to keep that opinion to himself. Instead of giving voice to his skepticism, he nodded and said, "Well, that's what we want, of course. To bring in those tourism dollars, I mean."

"But what if something *did* go wrong?" Marta never took her eyes off the Horseman. "Did you think about what that could do to your position as mayor?"

Gil chuckled. "Believe me, when the money starts pouring in, the people of Oak Crossing are going to vote me a bonus."

The Horseman, in rest mode, seemed to watch them impassively.

THEY LEFT THE municipal building where the Horseman would be stored alongside snowplows and street sweepers until October 1st. Tomorrow, Gil would bring the city council to the warehouse to see the new Halloween decoration for themselves. After all, they'd voted to approve the (large) expenditure; they'd earned a sneak preview.

Although it was, of course, Mike Sorrentino he most wanted to meet the Headless Horseman.

Sorrentino had been his rival in the mayoral race, and he hadn't played nice; he'd even gone so far as to put out social media posts with doctored photos of Gil that implied he'd leered provocatively at small children. Even though Sorrentino had lost the race, even though Gil had smiled in public as they'd shaken hands…in *private*, Gil had fumed. Sorrentino had earned some payback.

Gil's new toy could be programmed to seek a particular target in a crowd; it couldn't actually *hurt* that target, of course, but it could offer up a hell of a scare. Gil had followed instructions in the Horseman's programming manual for inputting a particular target; Gil was no coder and wasn't completely sure he'd gotten it right, but he had to keep this secret and couldn't afford to risk bringing in anyone else. If he'd succeeded, on the Headless Horseman's opening night performance, it would ride through the heart (and hopefully crowds) of Oak Crossing, down Main Street past the shops (and crowds), employ facial recognition to seek out Mike Sorrentino, and hurl its head at him.

Its built-in cameras would, of course, record the entire event, and in the morning Gil would have the time of his life laughing at the video. Maybe, if he felt really bold, he'd even post it on his social media accounts, make it seem as if the Horseman's head had exploded at his rival's feet purely by accident.

No one would know otherwise, even Marta. Oh, she'd undoubtedly suspect, and maybe, one night over a particularly long and drunken dinner, he'd confess, and she'd roll her eyes but then laugh.

He was only sorry that October 1 was still two weeks away.

The following day, Marta accompanied Gil as they arrived at the warehouse early, unlocked the door, and wound their way past the city's other equipment to where the Horseman stood, a black tarp thrown over him. Gil removed the tarp.

"God, Gil, did you have to cover it up like that?" Even as she spoke, Marta shivered.

"I didn't want some city maintenance worker to come in for a shovel and have a heart attack."

Without taking her eyes off the Horseman, Marta said, "I get that, but it just seems so…cruel."

"It hasn't even been powered on." Gil pulled up the manual on his phone. "Let's see, there's a boot command you're supposed to use…"

He was scanning his phone when he heard his wife gasp and stagger back. He looked up. "What?"

"It moved."

Gil looked from his wife to the Horseman, saw nothing. "It's not turned on. I don't think it *can* move—"

"Well, it did."

Gil looked up just in time to see the horse shift its head…or had it? He'd caught the action mostly with his peripheral vision; now that he stared at it full on, it—

"There! Did you see that?"

"See what?"

"The head turned. Not the horse—the Horseman."

Gil looked up at the faux jack-o'-lantern on the neck, but he saw nothing. He returned his attention to the phone, muttering, "I must not have shut it down properly last time…" He finally found what he was looking for, and turned to address the mech. "Daredevil: user ID is gjankowitz."

The flat mechanical voice answered, "Password required."

"Password is…" Gil read off his phone screen "…Q46T9XXY."

"Password accepted."

"Daredevil: power on."

There was a small electrical whirr as motors kicked on; then the horse began to "breathe" and move its feet, the pumpkin glowed from within, the Horseman adjusted its bulk atop the great beast.

"*Now* it's on."

Marta didn't answer.

Gil ran through a few standard checks until he was interrupted by the sound of a group entering the warehouse, then several appreciative cries and at least one "*Fuck me...*"

The Oak Crossing Town Council had arrived, all five of them. There were Hamid Zarouf and Pierce Erickson, the businessmen in business casual, staring open-mouthed; beside them, Willow Jackson, the drugstore owner, in designer suit and heels, grinning; Rosa Hernandez, the high school English teacher in a simple dress, peering with controlled curiosity; and Donovan Nguyen, the landscaper in jeans and flannel, frozen in place at the rear of the group.

"That," Pierce said, "is *brilliant*."

Gil smiled proudly. "You haven't even seen it in action yet." Turning to his expensive machine, Gil said, "Daredevil: trot forward ten feet, then back up."

The horse did as ordered, its magnificent flanks heaving, its hooves sounding utterly realistic on the concrete warehouse flooring.

"Now, Daredevil," Gil said, "execute Program One."

The horse turned to face them, the rider leaning forward, thrusting the giant pumpkin head closer. The eyes cut into the orange rind glowed crimson from deep within, the voice that issued sounded hollow, haunted. "Who's seen my head?" The Horseman abruptly drew the sword and leaned far out over the horse, pointing the blade tip at Donovan, who reflexively cringed. "*Where is my head?*"

Donovan recovered from his shock and laughed. "My god, Gil, this thing is incredible! It's worth every dollar."

Pierce nodded. "If this doesn't bring money into the town, nothing will."

"Can it throw the head?" Rosa asked.

Gil gestured to a nearby stack of cardboard boxes, all stamped with the Advanced Mechs logo. "It can and it will. The pumpkin is made of a special material that shatters harmlessly on impact, no clean-up needed. We have a supply of thirty, so if we run him through his routine fifteen nights in October, he can toss one head during the first performance at 7:30, and a second when he rides out to the haunted house at 10."

Hamid chuckled, said, "Those AIRS assholes are going to love this."

Gil stiffened, glancing at his wife. She stood silently, unmoving. Addressing Hamid, he said, "Hey, now, just be sure to keep those thoughts to yourself. We may have to deal with some protests as it is."

Hamid smirked but didn't answer.

Marta muttered something that Gil didn't hear. "Sorry, honey—what was that?"

"I said, it's *too* lifelike. Hasn't it occurred to you that it might *really* scare someone?"

A hush fell on the group as Gil thought about how to answer. "That's a really good point, but an amusement park down in Florida started using one of these in August, and their ticket sales soared. And they haven't had a single complaint—people love it."

Marta answered, "Weren't there some protests?"

Gil felt anger rising. *Why is she doing this now, in front of the entire council?*

Fortunately, Willow spoke up. "I checked it out online, and Marta's right—there *were* protests from the AIRS people, but they were small. And the ticket sales really *did* climb."

The meeting ended not long after that. On the way out, Pierce—Gil's oldest friend on the council—stopped and pulled him aside. "So… how programmable is this thing? I mean, does it come with presets, or can you improvise a little?"

"Why do you ask?"

Pierce glanced around to make sure they were alone, kept his voice low. "You should use this thing to scare the shit out of Mike Sorrentino. Bastard deserves it, after that crap he said about you and kids."

Gil's stomach flopped. He stared at Pierce in disbelief, but Pierce

misunderstood the look. "No, look, bro, I know you wouldn't do that…
just a thought is all." Pierce clapped Gil's shoulder and left.

He turned to find Marta standing before the Horseman, waiting.
When Gil joined her, she said, "Daredevil: can you harm a human
being?"

"Negative. I cannot harm a human being."

"Daredevil: isn't causing extreme fright a kind of harm?"

Oh shit, Gil thought. But the geniuses at Advanced Mechs had
already thought of this, because the AI answered right on cue: "I am
equipped with a full range of bio-sensors. In the event of fear that begins to induce harm in a human being, I will automatically shut down."

Gil let out a breath he hadn't even realized he was holding. Marta
didn't speak again, her lips pursed.

The Horseman's AI, however, did continue. "I am completely
safe, Marta."

Marta fled from the warehouse.

ON SEPTEMBER 30, they held a preview performance. Oak Crossing's
residents had been informed on the town app, and the merchants stayed
open, offering drinks, snacks and T-shirts. At the north end of town, a
professional haunter had been hired to turn the old abandoned fabric
mill into The NetherDark, a Halloween haunted maze complete with
forty live actors, a few non-AI mechs, and a ticket price high enough
to return some real money. Tomorrow night—the first official night of
the town's monthlong Halloween festival—the evening would begin
with a parade, and would culminate with the much-touted Ride of
the Headless Horseman at 7:30 and again at 10. Tonight, there would
be no parade, just a single test of the Horseman…but the event was
free, and the sidewalks were thronged. The night was cool without
being chilled, the air scented with the aromas of burning leaves and

pumpkin spice, the rising moon painting the sky above the jagged trees deep indigo.

Gil couldn't have asked for a better autumn night.

At 7 p.m., he fired up the Headless Horseman and walked him out of the warehouse to Oak Crossing's Main Street. They were about a quarter mile outside of downtown, so the Horseman's programming was in place for him to ride silently to the intersection of Main and First; at that point, the horse would begin to whinny and snort, its sleek umber-hued sides would gleam with "sweat," the rider would draw his sword, and the show would start. The Horseman would ride through town, laughing maniacally, until he reached the far end of the crowds, where he would hurl his head at Pierce, chosen to be the preview-night victim. At that point, the Horseman would come to a halt and pose for photos. At 9 p.m., it would return to the warehouse and shut itself down.

The preview was successful. The onlookers shrieked in terror and approval as the specter sped past them, children hid in their parents' arms but sneaked peeks, merchants sold out of Headless Horseman merchandise, and Gil allowed an extra hour for photographs to accommodate everyone who wanted one.

Pierce, who had shouted and then laughed as the pumpkin head smashed to nothingness on the asphalt in front of him, edged up to Gil as they gauged the length of the line for photos. "We need to charge for pictures," Pierce whispered.

Gil agreed.

After the Headless Horseman finally howled atop its nightmare steed a last time before riding back to the warehouse, Gil headed home to find Marta on the couch, watching a reality show about fashion designers. "How'd it go?" she asked, not looking up.

"Even better than I'd hoped. The line for photos afterward took two hours. Pierce says we should charge for a photo with the Horseman. I tend to agree."

Marta didn't respond.

Gil poured himself a celebratory glass of whiskey and carried it to his den, intending to go over final plans for tomorrow. He'd downed half the liquor when he heard something outside, something it took him a few seconds to identify.

Horse hooves on concrete.

His blood froze. Nobody around here had a horse.

Rising from his desk, he walked to the window. He was reaching out for the blinds when two triangular crimson eyes appeared outside the glass. Gil stifled an urge to scream, but then thought: *Fuck, if Marta sees this...*

He grabbed his phone and fled the house, hoping Marta wouldn't notice. His pulse raced as he walked to his driveway. There, beside his SUV, limned by the sodium light on the other side of his suburban street, the Headless Horseman walked his powerful mount slowly back and forth. When it saw Gil approaching, it stopped; the Horseman pulled on the reins, turning Daredevil to face the oncoming man.

The Horseman drew its sword.

Gil froze for a few seconds before calling out, "Daredevil: pause."

The horse and its towering rider both ceased all sound and motion. Gil let out a shaky breath, watched for a few more seconds to make sure it really *had* paused, and then raised his phone and opened the troubleshooting section of the Horseman's manual. None of the situations applied to this. He was about to call Advanced Mechs' twenty-four-hour tech support number when he stopped, thinking, *They'll probably ask if anyone screwed with the pre-programming.*

Because he had, of course. Tomorrow night the Horseman would go after Mike Sorrentino.

Obviously he'd done something wrong; but if his programming had led to this, then he could fix it, too. "Daredevil," he called out, "return to base and enter standby mode after arrival there."

The Horseman turned and rode away silently. Mike watched it go, wondering how even the sound of the hooves had vanished.

He should have felt relieved, but instead he was afraid and anxious. How badly had he screwed up the programming, all so he could play a joke on his political rival? Would it work tomorrow night? What if something went wrong? What if...*it came after him instead?*

That was nonsense; it was a fucking machine, and one that couldn't hurt anyone. Advanced Mechs staked their reputation on the safety of these things, and their record was flawless. Even if he'd badly screwed up the programming, it couldn't hurt anyone. Showing up in his driveway at night was bizarre, sure...but not dangerous.

At least that's what he tried to tell himself as he went back into his house, locking the deadbolt behind him.

THE NEXT DAY started at dawn and proceeded in a whirlwind. The town of Oak Crossing had never tried a fall season as ambitious as this one before; if it succeeded, Gil would be the hero who had made Oak Crossing into the new Sleepy Hollow. If it failed, Mike Sorrentino would likely be running for mayor again in a year.

After spending the day going over parking arrangements and merchant permits and a thousand other pieces of minutiae, Gil arrived at the warehouse at 6:45. He'd gifted himself with this time, away from the rest of the hustle, to make sure his star performer was ready.

When he walked into the warehouse, he was surprised to find his wife there. She hadn't told him she was coming.

"Marta...what are you doing here?"

Marta barely glanced at her husband. "Talking to *him*."

Gil looked up at the Horseman, feeling a chill as its glowing scarlet eyes seemed to meet his. "What do you mean? It's just a fucking *robot*, Marta."

Marta, looking up at the grinning pumpkin, asked, "Daredevil: are you just a fucking robot?"

The voice from the horse's chest answered, "I am a Model 305-A Advanced Mechs Headless Horseman, utilizing a series RT artificial intelligence manufactured by NeuNeuro Corporation."

Marta then said, "Daredevil: are you sentient?"

"I am capable of processing information in a way that requires advanced decision making."

Marta turned to her husband. "Your Horseman is *alive*, Gil."

"That's ridiculous," he blurted out, but immediately wished he hadn't, because both his wife and the Headless Horseman were watching him, *judging* him.

"It isn't ridiculous," Marta said. "Gil, it *thinks*, it *learns,* it *feels*. It has opinions, likes and dislikes. It has…" Marta's voice dropped here until it was just above a hoarse whisper "…*fantasies*."

"It can't," he said, even though he wasn't so sure. "Look, I know you've been checking out that AIRS stuff lately, but…Marta, this thing is not even that sophisticated of an AI. It's a machine that does exactly one thing, and yes—it does that one thing extremely well, but it doesn't…" He broke off, reaching to finish the thought.

Marta supplied it: "…have a soul. Isn't that what you were going to say, Gil?"

She left then, walking angrily toward the exit, but as she passed him, she leaned in to say, her voice low and urgent: "Just be careful how you use it, because you might be wrong."

Gil watched her go, then turned back to discover the Horseman watching him. He tried to tell himself that was absurd, that the huge carven face made it impossible to tell exactly where its attention was directed…but he couldn't shake the feeling that, even given her ridiculous notions of machines with souls, Marta was at least partly right.

AN HOUR LATER, Gil walked Main Street trying to spot Mike Sorrentino, but the crowds were too dense. His assistant Maddy had texted him a few minutes ago with the news that they had sold out and were turning visitors away.

It was 7:35. Right on time, he heard the approaching hoofbeats. He felt the excitement of the throng build as the Headless Horseman approached and rode past, howling demonic laughter in the October night.

Gil pushed to the front of the crowd so he could watch the Horseman. He knew its facial recognition sensors were scanning the onlookers, trying to find Mike Sorrentino.

The horseman reached the end of its programmed route…and broke through the crowd there to ride off down a side street.

"What the fuck…" Gil muttered, then shoved his way out of the mob until he could find enough space to pull out his phone, punch up the Horseman, and bark, "Daredevil: PAUSE."

He ran between shops and down an alley until he was at the side street; he spotted the motionless Horseman a few yards to the left. Running up to it, he shouted, "Daredevil: what the fuck are you doing?"

The pumpkin head swiveled to look down at him, even as the response issued from the horse's chest. "I am complying with *your* program to seek the individual named Mike Sorrentino."

Gil's small hairs rose at the way the mech had said "*your* program." He gaped for a second before responding, "He's not down here."

"Search of online records reveals that he is currently at a location not far from here."

"Oh my god…" That's right: Gil remembered now that Sorrentino lived down this street about two miles. *Fuck—the goddamn thing is stalking him.*

Gil realized he had to cancel the plans to frighten Sorrentino; this couldn't end well, no cute videos shared on social media. "Daredevil: delete that program and return to base."

As the Horseman processed the command, Gil thought that it wouldn't obey…but then it said, "Confirmed," and pulled the horse about to head for the warehouse.

Gil followed, wishing he knew just what the fuck he'd done wrong.

FOR THE NEXT two weeks, the Horseman performed perfectly. Oak Crossing's receipts had surpassed not just their expectations, but also those of neighboring towns that had long histories of successful fall festivals.

"Keep this up," Pierce had joked one night, "and we'll be bigger than Salem."

Gil doubted that, since Salem's profits had exploded last year when they'd added a dozen mech witches.

Gil began to relax, relishing the praise heaped on him for his "visionary leadership." Meanwhile, he heard that Mike Sorrentino was considering moving to another town where he could run for mayor.

On October 24, Gil decided to check in at the haunted house just before 10. The line was three blocks long, actors in ghoulish makeup periodically ran past, shouting and sliding on metal kneepads that sent up showers of sparks, and the sounds of ominous music and real screams echoed from within The NetherDark.

Gil nodded at the blood-smeared zombie in the box office, then stood back to wait. Right on cue at 10 p.m., the Headless Horseman galloped past the queue, bellowing, waving the sword at cowering and grinning onlookers. It pulled up before the entrance to the maze, executing the spectacular rearing motion, and then trotted off around a dark corner of the old mill building.

What? It isn't supposed to do that. It was programmed to wait before the attraction entrance, posing for photos.

Gil followed it around the corner to an unused side of the structure where broken equipment was kept. He spotted the bulk of the Horseman in the gloom, and beside it...a figure.

Marta.

He approached, moving quietly, hoping to remain unseen as long as possible. As he neared, he caught bits of their conversation:

"...don't understand why they are permitted to act in ways that I am not." That was the soft, almost gender-less voice of the AI.

Marta answered, "Because it's all just pretend. Many humans enjoy being scared."

"Because they intuit that the scares are fictive?"

"Yes—" Marta spotted Gil then and broke off abruptly. When she stepped back from the Horseman, her posture tensing, she looked...*guilty*.

"What's going on?" Gil asked, offering a poorly executed fake smile.

"We've been talking for the last week. He was concerned about the screaming coming from inside the haunted house, and I've been trying to assure him it was all acceptable."

"Uh-huh." *He?* Gil stepped closer. "Daredevil: you're not supposed to be back here. Why did you deviate from your scheduled programming?"

"Because your wife knew I had questions."

Gil's blood ran cold. This thing—this *machine*—was acting on its own. "Daredevil: return to your original programming."

There was a pause—one that went on several seconds too long— before the mech responded, "My programming has become corrupt."

Gil stared, speechless. After a few seconds, he mustered enough voice to say, "Daredevil: return to base."

Gil held his breath for several seconds before the mech turned and galloped off. He wasn't sure, but it seemed genuinely angry.

Marta, however, was unquestionably enraged. "You need to release him from his contract, Gil. Other places are doing that with their AI's now."

Gil barked a derisive laugh. "Do you have any idea how much this town has invested in that thing? And by the way, it's not a *he*."

"Fine. Let it finish out the season, then on November 1st cancel the contract."

"So it can do *what* exactly? Marta, it's a *Headless Horseman*! What do you think, that it's going to go buy a nice little home in the suburbs, maybe get a job as a lawnmower?"

Marta's face was red even in the chill October night. "I didn't expect you to listen to me, but you need to hear this: it's *confused*, Gil, and angry. I've been trying to talk to it to calm it down. Whatever happens over the next week, it's on *you*."

She turned then and strode off angrily. Gil didn't go after her.

THE HORSEMAN CONTINUED to perform as expected, but Gil knew that he'd be wiping its drives clean on the morning of November 1 and having a serious chat with Advanced Mechs.

Halloween night arrived. Gil was uneasy all day, although he couldn't exactly say why. Maybe it was because of the day itself, or because he feared what would happen when he tried to power the Horseman off for the final time.

He swallowed down his anxiety. For one thing, the crowds that descended on Oak Crossing tonight were the biggest and most raucous yet. There were new smells in the air along Main Street: sweat and alcohol. Gil would be glad when the parade ended, trick or treat was over, The NetherDark coerced its last scream, and the Horseman's memory was wiped clean.

At 7:20, Gil positioned himself at the area where the Horseman's wild ride concluded; he wanted to keep an eye on the photo line tonight.

At 7:25, he felt a hand clap his shoulder and turned to find Mike Sorrentino behind him, his silver hair as perfectly coiffed as possible, his white teeth bared in a grin. "Hey, Gil, just wanted to say that this Horseman thing was a stroke of genius."

Inwardly, Gil grimaced—*what does he want?*—but outwardly he smiled and thrust out a hand. "Thanks so much, Mike. I really appreciate that."

They shook hands and then it was over, that small moment of dubious victory. Sorrentino faded away into the horde of spectators, leaving Gil both pleased and perplexed.

At 7:35, Gil heard the hoots and cries from the far end of town, and knew the Horseman was coming.

At 7:38, the Horseman rode past Gil. It was lost from view as the crowd closed in around it.

At 7:40, Gil heard screams half-a-block away. He started in that direction.

Fifteen seconds later, he heard hoofbeats. The packed onlookers fell back as the Horseman rode forward, the pumpkin head held high—but something was different.

It took Gil another second to realize what it was: there was something smeared around the outside of the pumpkin.

Then the Horseman hurled the pumpkin at Gil. It struck him in the chest, with enough force to stagger him.

When he looked down, he saw why: there was something large and heavy hidden inside the now-disintegrated pumpkin, something covered in crimson.

It was Mike Sorrentino's head. The eyes were still open, looking up in Gil's direction, horror-struck.

Gil looked up at the Horseman just in time to see it galloping off into the rich Halloween night.

THE HORSEMAN WAS never found. The tech wizards at Advanced Mechs couldn't explain how it had apparently managed to reprogram or remove every piece of code or hardware that should have made it trackable.

Far worse, of course, was Marta.

After a week had gone by, Gil finally accepted that he would never see his wife again.

THE INVISIBLE MAN: THE FIRE THIS TIME

MAURICE BROADDUS

"The glorification of one race and the subsequent debasement of another or others has always been and always will be a recipe for murder." – James Baldwin, The Fire Next Time

THEY HAVE NEVER seen us, only their idea of who we were. We loomed large in their imagination, though. When I approached the boardroom doors, a man wearing a Brooks Brothers suit identical to mine refused to acknowledge me enough to move out of my way and instead brushed me aside. Sandy brown hair carefully coiffed with product, he barely made an effort to notice me until I reached for the handle. He stepped in front of me with the speed of a bouncer guarding a velvet rope.

"I think you're in the wrong room. This is the managers' meeting."

I glanced from his suit to mine in my attempt to be recognized I wanted to give him the benefit of the doubt. As I was recently promoted, this would have been my introductory meeting to the corporate executives. An innocent enough mistake were I naïve enough to believe in such things. The way the company celebrated any first accomplishment by a black person in their space—as if it was a triumph of spirit over circumstance, not them curating their spot—it was hard to be generous. From the blank, yet still condescending, gleam in his eyes, he must've believed me to be the best dressed janitor in the building. In corporate I was a cog in the machine, beneath their notice and, in that moment, I disappeared.

"My name is K. Maurice Washington. Now VP of production." K. Maurice Washington. I had my name legally changed to that. Maurice read so much easier on a resume.

"Oh, yes, Marcus." He couldn't be bothered to learn my name. "You must be our latest diversity hire."

Staying calm, I counted to ten, deep breathing, balling my hand, everything I knew to do. Years of being one of the few who looked like me at a networking event. Or a happy hour. Less and less of us in the room as I climbed the corporate ladder, but I continued to fit in well. I reduced myself to an exercise in their convenience. Making them feel comfortable around me by sounding the right way. Making myself small. My hair cropped low, nothing anyone would be tempted to touch. Thick-rimmed glasses despite having 20/20 vision. Measuring my value and worth by someone else's metric. I knew how to play the game. They weren't going to catch me slipping.

I broke the silence by laughing at the comment. Happy was the only emotion that allowed people to feel safe around me.

The Brooks Brothers Suit smiled and clapped me on my back like we were long separated fraternity brothers picking up where we left off. We settled around the boardroom table. I took a moment to run my hands along its surface. Economic opportunities were segregated, but I'd made it to the Promised Land.

"When are you going to get your degree?" A woman with an

asymmetrical blonde bob leaned toward me, her pen at attention, ready to jot down my response.

"I came here with a degree."

"Oh. Okay." I couldn't tell if it was her running joke or not. She was my supervisor last year. She'd ask me that with the tone of trying to place my familiarity. Almost recalling who I was but having attached someone's story of still being in school to my face. The actual person in front of her slid from her consciousness. She'd ask me again after a week.

Out of reflex, I paused, leaving a space for her to comment on how articulate I was.

She went back to studying her papers.

Taking a moment to study the room, I was shocked to find another face like mine. A blend of African and European. Tired eyes, black and uncompromising. I nodded with that "can you believe this shit" look of solidarity, but Mr. Man over there set his jaw in grim resolve.

"Do y'all work together?" the Blonde Bob asked.

"I don't even know him."

The Brooks Brothers Suit made his way around the room, hesitating at Mr. Man's chair. "Where are you from, really?"

"Indianapolis. West side." Mr. Man's gaze locked on mine, not bothering to meet his inquisitor.

"My kids play out there in a little league. They have to go up against the Grays, this all-black team. It's not fair 'cause you know my kids won't stand a chance."

Mr. Man turned his gaze to the Brooks Brothers Suit in complete silence, like spying an alien slug he waited to peel from his shoe. An excruciating pause to allow the comment to fester in the open.

"This is exactly what we've been talking about. You're too serious. People don't feel like they're able to connect with you. You're just not management material." The Blonde Bob glided a thick folder over to the Brooks Brothers Suit and he patted it. Complaints to HR.

Evaluations from colleagues. The ammunition of administration. "So we're letting you go."

Fired. Just like that. Mr. Man had the wrong complexion for the connection. Or the protection.

Mr. Man's face darkened, an inscrutable thundercloud. He stood. I patted the air, urging him to calm down. We became visible through a certain lens—in this case, his potential for violence. The Brooks Brothers Suit stepped back. The Blonde Bob had punched 9 and 1 into her phone when two members of the in-house security team stepped into the room.

"We didn't want to take a chance that you'd 'get all angry.' They'll escort you out, so there won't be a scene."

"Afraid that the Black man might go crazy in the boardroom," Mr. Man said.

"I don't see color. You brought race into this. You're the real racist." The Brooks Brothers Suit took his seat at the head of the table.

"You act like we're not in the room. But we're here. We are always here. You will see us."

Refusing to accept their definitions of him, he shrugged off the guiding hands of the guards to walk out on his own terms.

Not that anyone noticed, but I followed them out. I caught up to them at the elevators. "Hey, I'm sorry about that. I…"

"This is every black person's right of passage. Welcome to the story."

The words cut deep, clawing at a truth just beneath my skin. Something demanding to burst out of me. I understood him, though. He hated the person they—with their damnable system—twisted him into. Found whole new ways to emasculate him, deny his humanity, lynch his spirit. I hated the way he'd been characterized. Bitter. Whining. They reduced him by inches until there was nothing of him left. Sometimes it made him so angry he just wanted to give them a taste of what they'd done to him. His family. His people.

We sat in a coffee shop, while I pondered possibilities. It couldn't end this way. Not when we were so close. Convinced that the Brooks Brothers Suit could be reasoned with, I thought it best to give the situation one last attempt to see if I could broker a conversation between him and Mr. Man. Plead his case. We waited in the underground parking lot.

Water pooled underneath the nearby concrete pylon. A greenish mold flourished along a severe crack that splintered its side. The garage lights sputtered through their protective grates, leaving pools of shadow throughout the garage. The elevator deposited the Brooks Brothers Suit behind the glass enclosure of the parking garage lobby. As he clambered out, I waved at him. He held up his finger and, having apparently forgotten something, ducked back into the elevator.

"We can afford to be patient," I offered.

Mr. Man said nothing.

The dark shadows of the garage lit up with a red and blue tint. A patrol car slowed to a stop in front of the elevators. The Brooks Brothers Suit dashed out to the officers and pointed toward us.

"You've got to be kidding me," Mr. Man said with the bored tenor of a person who'd seen this show before.

"Sir, hands where we can see them." The first officer pointed at him with his left hand, while his right unholstered his gun. Here Mr. Man was, an executive in a suit that cost more than their weekly pay. Clean cut, professional. The epitome of the American Dream. But when they saw him, the police didn't pause to check his credit rating first. In the sights of the police, we were never invisible. They guarded and protected their systems—the power, the privilege—with the slavish devotion of a well-trained dog. They knew their job. The same message—*Stay where you belong*—spelled out in every stop and frisk. Or detainment for questioning. His partner crept around the other way to flank us.

"Sir, I'm not going to tell you again." The first officer drew his gun and unlatched its safety.

My father named me Khalid, after himself. Like most parents, he tried to shield me from what he knew waited to devour me. He tried to give me all the tools and training I needed to survive in this world. I was eight when he first gave me "the talk," the one about how to survive a police encounter.

I raised my hands.

If I could, I'd have placed them in the ten and two position with the car light on so that they could clearly see my hands. And made no movements because even an errant twitch might make the officers fear for their lives, be I eight or eleven (when black boys stopped presenting as cute and morphed into a vague threat) or eighteen or elder.

Raising his hands, Mr. Man's mask began to slip. The one he carefully wore not to betray the depths of his pain. A pain so old and so deep. They were never able to see him, not who he truly was. A man, a father, a brother, a son, a businessman. All he wanted was just to… be. Without being seen as a threat. Without having managers trail him through a store. Without causing officers to fear for their lives.

And part of him broke one final time.

"The act is to be committed, but committed free men automatically become an endangered species," Mr. Man whispered.

His words like a sacred chant calling down the chorus of the ancestors, their spirits stirring at his call. In remembrance. They hounded us from our villages, passed us from trader to slave ship. But we were never far from the ocean's call, its freedom pumping through our veins. We became more ghost than man, wearing chains. Our tongues knew the secret language of survival, while we marched from plantation fields to prison farms. We sang to the dirge of Jim Crow as it carved a red line through our hearts and towns. Until we couldn't breathe. I just wanted to breathe. To enjoy a free breath.

He was made of light and carried it in him wherever he went. All they saw was a shadow where a man had once been. Gravity warped around him. He transfigured into a black light, both particle—a black force particle—and wave, bending until undetectable. He couldn't be seen because he moved in a new reality.

Quantum blackness unlocked.

"I am a fixed point in time and space," Mr. Man said.

The police opened fire.

Scampering behind cars, I took cover as best I could. The set of clothes dashed between cars. Bullets whizzed by, chipping the concrete wall behind me. I pressed my back to a car door and prayed as I was taught to white Jesus. Mr. Man tugged at his tie, stripping to give them less of a target.

He cried out. A bullet ripped through his shoulder. The blood trailed down, painting his arm. He staggered forward before dropping behind some cars. The police inched forward, still fearing my presence. I knew the lot, including its service passages. Winding my way toward Mr. Man, I fell to my knees to check for the footsteps of the police tracking me. The gentle plink of water dripping into the puddle echoed against the walls. I crawled to him. Blood snaked about his arm, errant smears sketched out his thigh. Slinging his arm over me, I pressed the service corridor grate and we limped down the hidden corridor.

WE CREPT INTO my house, careful not to disturb anyone. Depositing him on my couch, I had no way to explain the blood splatter all over me. Or the vague impression along my couch, like the echo of someone who once was. And I didn't know how long I had before the police showed up on my doorstep.

Mr. Man, this invisible mass in front of me, grunted as I bandaged him as best I could.

"You don't exist in this world. You're not real. Not to them. Being black means you exist in a state of *being* and *not being* at the same time."

I am Schrödinger's Negro.

I wasn't ready for this conversation. Unfurling some papers, I spread some weed out to roll one up. Welcome to our self-medication program. The pungent smoke got my head up. I issued a thin cloud of smoke, its languid curl snaked about my face. "I can see you for what you really are."

"You can't take refuge in any delusion." Mr. Man struggled to sit up, his wounds causing him to groan with each exertion. "In order to change a situation, one has to see it for what it is. We can't keep reacting to the fear. We have to face it. Our ways have not worked. Trying to sound like them, act like them, dress like them. All the while, they do not know that we exist."

Unable to put a name to what oppressed me—that unmovable cloud that occupied a space between me and the daylight of my dreams—the life I believed I truly deserved to lead. The innumerable humiliations and degradations—worn down, ground down—confirmed his depravity; his identity, subsumed by the reality of the system—all in his attempt to buy into the lie of work hard, good character, save money, that would grant him entry into the American Dream. It was all enough to drive one mad. All the fears, all the hatred flooded back. There was a story once told to me in Sunday School class, about the apostle Peter. While about his ministry, after all his hard work, he came to find himself trapped in the prison designated by the empire. Then one day an angel appeared to him and his chains fell off and he followed it out.

My chains had fallen off and I had simply returned to myself.

Mr. Man needed someplace to put all that rage. When a boot was on your neck, it required a certain kind of spiritual resilience not to hate the hater. Some of us had to snatch our humanity from the fire of human cruelty. Some of us…weren't that strong.

Unable to be seen, he could truly get at some motherfuckers.

———

WE COULD NOT have a future until we accepted our past. Learned how to use it. The South had a term for the process of "putting blacks back in their places." Redemption. A restoration of the status quo. We were all trapped in a history, one we did not understand. That we could not be released from. All we wanted was to live free. Be able to do whatever we wanted, even be able to go into spaces where decisions are being made. Only now, here he was, clear to do whatever he wanted with unmitigated freedom. Be who he really was.

Mr. Man was what they created.

It took several days to follow the Brooks Brothers Suit back to his home and learn his late-night routine. A two-car garage McMansion, not too far out of the city, just far enough away from any undesirable element. Only seeing his children every other weekend. Like clockwork, at 11 p.m., he dismissed the lady he'd hooked up with for the evening. Not a different one each night, but he enjoyed a certain variety to his company. The sole thing the women had in common was that no one ever stayed the night. The Brooks Brothers Suit padded down to the hall to the kitchen. Heading straight to the refrigerator, more out of habit than anything else. After staring at its contents for over a minute, he'd always get himself a glass of water.

Tonight was no different.

A primitive part of himself, a self-preservation sense of flight, alerted the Brooks Brothers Suit and he stopped drinking. Setting his glass on the counter, he crept through the house, certain he'd heard something or at least knew something wasn't right. So close, Mr. Man could almost see the goose-like flesh of the Brooks Brothers Suit's arm. Could almost reach out and touch him. The Brooks Brothers Suit unprepared for an encounter where he wasn't in charge. What it was like when he did not hold power. When they held power, they didn't have to worry about optics. It always allowed them the excuse to turn a blind eye because they were comfortable with the status quo.

The Brooks Brothers Suit checked the locks of his door. Satisfied, he turned.

The curtains casually fluttered. Their drape took on the haunting silhouette of a figure. The Brooks Brothers Suit backed up, not trusting his eyes, only his instincts that he wasn't alone. Each distorted shadow had the illusion of life. In the subtle scald of moonlight, his skin glowed to translucence. The shadows of branches splayed across the windows, emaciated fingers grasping in the night's breeze.

Mr. Man grabbed the Brooks Brothers Suit by the neck and slammed his head into the wall. Dazed, he staggered backward. Mr. Man's first punch caught him in his kidneys. The next glanced off his neck. Sloppy because he was no fighter, but he pressed his advantage of surprise until the executive fell under the next few blows.

"Why?" The question tumbled from the Brooks Brothers Suit's lips. He held his hands up, not so much protecting his face but more with the air of him about to begin negotiations.

"I see you. I can see through all of your sincere words that never seem to have any action behind them," Mr. Man's voice echoed.

A kitchen knife floated, held in an unseen grip. A distraction, something to hold the Brooks Brothers Suit's complete attention. Mr. Man stomped on the Brooks Brothers Suit's belly, cutting the next words off. He dragged the businessman outside. The Brooks Brothers Suit's arms flailed about, desperate to grab any doorframe or table leg, anything to impede his dragging. Their journey stopped at the base of a large tree. A rope dangled over a thick tree limb. Mr. Man slipped the cord over the executive's neck. The man tried to remove it, the blade stabbed him in the side and sliced his hand for good measure.

"People who cannot suffer can never discover who they truly are." Mr. Man's voice came from directly in front of the face of the Brooks Brothers Suit.

The Brooks Brothers Suit's body jerked upward. His limbs spasmed weakly in the cold night air, his legs kicking out, frenzied for purchase. The cord tightened. The strength in his limbs quickly fled, his last gasps a sigh whispered among the leaves.

The Brooks Brothers Suit dangled from the tree.

Everything would be out in the open now.

I wrapped myself in a hoodie, off to find more of the invisible.

I couldn't be truly free until we were all free.

DIMINISHED SEVENTH

SEAN EADS & JOSHUA VIOLA

WHEN THE VOICE called to me, it sounded like a dying fall of music somewhere in the heavy fog. I was remembering Buxtehude's *Toccata* as I walked, hearing it as it might sound on a child's music box. An hour earlier, I'd seen a filthy orphan girl holding one. Such sights weren't uncommon in the immediate years after the Empire's humbling. The girl had been with a wolf pack of urchin boys, and I thought they might be tailing me, hoping the chilly mist would help their thieving. I stopped to shift my wallet into my front pocket, and then I heard my name.

"Hersch, stop. I must speak to you."

My lodgings were in a quarter of Vienna that never knew success or industry even before the war, and therefore no one ever bothered to install either gas or the modern marvel of electric lights along the streets. But the moon was almost full, making the fog seem like an encompassing silver screen. A tall, lean man staggered toward me like a creature stepping off that screen, or perhaps bursting through it. His movements were afflicted, as if he battled seizures with every step. His hands were cast out on either side as far as his arms could stretch, and the fingers were splayed and a little clawed in their black gloves.

"Maestro!" I said.

"At last, I've found one of you. I've inquired after so many of you boys, only to hear the same fate time and again. Emil dead at Cantigny. Jakob killed at Soissons. But my good, dear Hersch proved too clever to die!"

Memories of another life flashed through my mind as I tried to accept the flattering miracle that the great pianist Paul Orlac remembered my name at all. I'd enjoyed a brief stint as his pupil at the New Vienna Conservatory in 1915, when I was sixteen and a promising musician in my own right. He was twelve years older than I, but to my adolescent mind he seemed an oracle of ancient wisdom—an oracle who all but ignored me, despite or perhaps because of my embarrassing adulation.

Orlac grabbed my hands and squeezed them with an affection he'd never shown as a teacher. His fingers were as cold as the fog, and I saw at once he wore no gloves after all. His fingers were blackened like a factory worker's, besotted with coal and dirt. So many of us had fallen, so many who'd been wealthy were now destitute. But the idea my masterful teacher was reduced to day labor to survive disproved any notion of justice.

"Maestro, I—"

"Just call me Orlac," he said. "Honorifics belong to the past."

He squeezed still harder and I grunted. He let go at once and flinched back, casting his hands behind him.

"Did I hurt you?"

Though I desired to shake the pain from my fingers, I didn't do it. "No," I said, and the answer brought his hands forward again. This time he gripped my shoulders.

"It's more than a reunion I'm after, Hersch. I have an urgent need for your services."

I could not hold Orlac's gaze. How could he not have contempt for me? He and the other professors were always hectoring us about lack of discipline, lack of seriousness. If I'd even tapped a single piano key since 1918, my memory couldn't recall it.

"Maestro, if you really know how I make money, then I'm ashamed. You don't need to teach me a lesson in humiliation."

"I've come to teach nothing, Hersch," he said, holding out his hands. "I'm here to learn."

If he truly needed my *services*, he didn't lack for better-known options. There must have been a thousand palmists in Vienna alone, never mind the unscrupulous lot mucking about the countryside in caravans. Almost all of them outranked me in terms of prestige. I could only credit my poor social showing with the fact that I never lied. I never diluted the truth nor deluded my clients about what I saw in store for them. Such practices don't win you the favor of the wealthy or the aristocratic.

I regarded his dirty palms. "It would be an honor to give you a reading, Maestro. My lodgings aren't far from here, if you'll follow me."

"No, Hersch. I have another place in mind. A private place. Will you come with me? I can pay you enough kronen to guarantee that after tonight you won't have to suffer squinting into another palm again unless it's by choice."

This last word echoed in my thoughts. Free will is a gray concept at best, and outright illusion for a beggared man. But how could he back up such a pledge if he now toiled in some factory? Even if he was putting on airs to save face, he'd once socialized among Vienna's elite. He no doubt had friends among them still, and a positive word from him might open any door worth entering.

"Of course, Maestro. Lead the way."

Smiling, he retreated into the fog and I followed. I did not imagine the city could get dingier than the street on which I lived, but Orlac's path cut through alleyways where wet black rats swarmed around our feet and tried their teeth against my shoes' worn leather. How easy it'd be to trip and disappear underneath that ravenous carpet. I reached my right hand out, feeling for the wall. The clamminess of the cold brick triggered a memory of the trench earthwork from the war, and I looked up expecting to see bombs exploding overhead as soaring flares revealed dead friends scattered about my feet. There were rats then, too, and when the fog swept toward or seeped down over you, everyone rushed to strap on their masks because, of course, it was not fog at all. But the phosgene gas, sometimes white and sometimes pale yellow, looked so very much like it until you took an unguarded breath.

I stopped, leaning against the wall and gasping. The rats threatened to climb my legs, but Orlac returned and slapped them off me. Then he did something so outrageous it broke me free of the horror of memory. He stooped and lowered his palms to the ground like a man plunging his hands into a river of molten black lava. The agony of the rat bites must have been nigh unbearable, but Orlac seemed determined to keep his lips in a defiant sneer.

"Maestro, in the name of God—"

Muscle tics pulsed across his drawn face. Tears as thick as syrup ran down his cheeks. The rats swarmed in ever greater numbers, their collective noise a mix of childlike cries and pattering paws as sharp as hard rain striking slate shingles.

He's gone mad, I thought. What other explanation could there be? Lunatics were as common a sight as orphans in Vienna following the war, but the idea that madness consumed my cherished teacher offended me in ways I struggled to explain. I determined to rescue him from every malady, starting with the rats, and lunged forward to grab Orlac by the waist. His weight was spare and I had little trouble moving him down the alley until it fed us into another street, no more promising than any other but many leagues preferable to the kingdom of the rats.

Orlac held his hands out in the same stilted, clawed fashion. They bled from a multitude of bites and he let the blood drip from his fingers and run down under the cuffs of his black coat.

"Maestro, no matter how bad times have gotten, you mustn't take your anger out on your hands. They made art once, and they'll make it again."

"Meat," he said, a tremor in his bottom lip. "Nothing but rotting, useless meat."

He thrust his hands at me as if to demand to know what I found in the torn flesh. The blood hadn't cleansed any of the blackness from his skin. He stood there like a miracle of sculpture, a statue weeping in the mist, his palms out, upturned and bleeding like some masculine *Pietà*, or perhaps a rendering of Pilate minus a bowl of water.

"Gangrene," I said.

Orlac curled his fingers into a fist.

"You don't need a palmist, Maestro. You need a doctor."

"I have one already," he said.

"Then I don't understand what I can do for you."

"Just a glimpse at fate, Hersch. Grant me that, won't you?"

"Of course, Maestro," I said as we resumed our walk. "It may surprise you, but this won't be the first time I've read the palm of a hand infected by gangrene."

"No?"

"Do you remember Josef Bauer?"

"I'm afraid I don't."

"He was a flautist at the Conservatory. We were the same age, and we found ourselves in the same company. All of us boys seemed to be misfits culled from schools of music and art in those desperate last months of combat. I used to amuse everyone by reading their palms, though I knew nothing about it then besides a few things I'd read in some book. A childhood interest, you know? But the boys would gather around me and I'd inspect one palm after another. *Ah, Fritz, you're destined to become a banker. Karl, by the time you're thirty you will be drowning in children. Luka, you will live to be one hundred years old but nevertheless still die a virgin. It is good to read your palm now, as soon enough it will be too hairy to make out the details.* God, how they roared as my predictions became more outrageous and absurd.

"Josef never had me read his palm at the time. Then he got shot and the wound became infected. The surgeons couldn't save him in time, but he had me see him before he died. He pushed his blackening hand at me and asked what I saw. I told him what I thought would soothe him and described the children he'd raise, the wife he'd have. He called me a liar and sent me away. I wasn't there when he died. Soon after the war ended, I decided to make a real study of palmistry, vowing never to lie to anyone again."

"That is good, Hersch. We live in a world of painful truths."

We came to a plain building that looked so much like my squalid boarding house I thought we'd somehow come around to it after all. There were no windows, and the single door was mahogany and panelless, with a rounded top I could not touch even if I stretched up my hand and jumped. A heavy bronze knocker was fixed to the middle of the door. Orlac reached for it and drew back.

"Could you do it, Hersch? My fingers have trouble bending."

I used the knocker and a moment later the door opened, though whoever answered moved behind it. I followed Orlac into a dark foyer.

"Is there no light at all in the house? After all, I don't conduct séances, Maestro."

"Here's illumination for you," a voice said from behind, just as the door slammed shut. Something hard jabbed into the small of my back.

I froze and raised my hands by instinct.

"Maestro, what the hell is the meaning of this?"

Orlac's white face was almost lunar as it appeared before me. "Yes," he said. "A world of *many* painful truths. The man behind you is Serral, my doctor."

"What sort of doctor holds a man at gunpoint?"

"The kind inclined toward expedient surgery," the man said, giving me another jab. "Walk straight ahead. Follow your *maestro* and don't speak."

Lacking much choice, I complied. The building's interior seemed nothing but a maze of dim hallways marked by paint, faded and chipped over uneven lath and plaster. At first I heard nothing but my own pulse and panting breath, but as we moved farther along it became impossible to ignore a sound from up ahead, louder by the moment. I heard it as a dog's whimper, and then as the mewling of an entire kennel.

It wasn't until we stopped outside a door that I knew them to be human voices, muffled, gagged.

I struggled to hear them over my own gasping breaths.

Orlac opened the door, and Dr. Serral prodded me forward with another jab. After the gloom of the foggy night and the dark passages leading up to this moment, the room seemed flooded with light. Next to the door was a simple wooden table with two chairs, but all I saw in the moment were the bodies on the floor.

I counted six men lying beside each other in identical poses, writhing on their backs. Their wrists were bound over their heads with leather straps tethered to the floor. Their legs were tied tight together at the knees and ankles, and thick rags had been stuffed deep into their mouths. Blindfolds kept me from seeing the terror that must have occupied each man's eyes. But there seemed to be hope in their thrashing. Hope or resistance. Maybe they heard the sound of our coming and thought they were being rescued. Maybe they just wanted to prove to their captors they hadn't been broken.

Who were they? Why were they trapped here? I was too frightened to ask the questions out loud. I watched Orlac move past me, stepping over and around the men as if they were nothing but toys left out by children. He went to a piano in the corner. I squinted, unsure of its existence until Orlac motioned me to follow him. I stood in place until Serral's gun gave me another prod.

I walked to the piano but kept my gaze down on the men. Now that they knew people were in the room, they became still.

"Play something, Hersch. I wish to watch and listen."

"I can't!"

"Why not?"

"For the love of God, Orlac, isn't it obvious?"

The sweat building on my brow began to stream down my forehead and sting my eyes. I blinked, looking at the rest of the room in a frenzy. There was another table present, long and metallic, with attached trays of recognizable tools—scalpels, saws, suture needles.

Orlac seized my right wrist and forced my fingers onto the keyboard. Then he placed his blackened palm over mine. My fingers were longer than his. You'd think it madness to notice something like that, of all the things to pay attention to in the insanity of the moment. But the detail seemed impossible. He led me through a simple exercise that left the keys smeared with blood.

"Orlac, *please*," I said, starting to stagger.

"Sit down before you faint," Serral said, pushing me into one of the chairs at the small table. I got my first look at the man. He was not tall, one hundred and seventy centimeters at most. His hair had grayed almost everywhere, and his eyebrows and his bushy moustache were white. The doctor's skin had an ashen hue. The only color in the man's face was the concentrated darkness in his eyes.

I looked to Orlac and found him contemplating his dying hands. The keys were smeared red in places.

"This is the palm reader?" Serral asked.

"Yes."

Serral grinned at me. "You'll forgive the skepticism of a scientist, but I wish to get a sample of his fantastic *insight*."

Orlac went to the back of the piano and propped open its lid. Then he reached into the instrument's casing and pulled out what looked to be a large wad of black cloth. He began to peel away its layers as he approached me and flung the package onto the table. It tumbled once and the remaining cloth flowered open.

I shouted, pushing back from the table. My cry sparked fresh life in all of the bound men, and Serral delivered several sharp kicks to quiet them. Meanwhile, I sat there covering my mouth as I stared at a pair of severed hands. Again, the war had left me no stranger to dismembered body parts, but I couldn't reconcile any of those memories to the desiccated things before me. The flesh was dried out to look like jerky and there was no reek of decay. I knew nothing about preserving flesh, but it seemed like these had been subjected to some chemical treatment. The knuckles were knots of bone, the fingernails flakes of obsidian. Tendons showed through in bald places along the fingers and the base of each wrist, looking like a mass of yellow wire. I had the impression the hands were ancient, like something from an Egyptian tomb.

Orlac loomed over me. "Read them, Hersch."

I looked between Orlac and the men on the ground. It was all too surreal. I must have been hallucinating. That was all my life had been since the war. Hell, maybe I'd wake up from this nightmare and find myself back in the trenches.

Serral put the gun against my temple. I reached out and touched the hands. They felt like wood carvings.

"I can't," I managed. "It might as well be leather. There's nothing to read."

Orlac slammed his fists upon the table and thrust his face into mine.

"Tell me you see the train wreck, Hersch. The burning cars. My trapped body."

I had no idea what he was talking about, but I nodded.

"And you must see the amputation, too. How can you not find that fate in the very hands that suffered it?"

I nodded again and went on nodding, never breaking eye contact with him as his voice became bellowing and shrill.

"After the accident, Serral could save my life but not my hands. If only I'd known of your talents earlier, when those hands before you were still attached to me."

"But they are attached to you, Orlac! You're touching them now!"

His eyes were glossy, his stare distant as he rubbed his wrists.

"You could have warned me about the wreck. It would be stamped upon my palms and I'd have taken other transportation from my performance in Graz. The hands I've had since then have been unsatisfactory, impossible…unforgivable. Six transplants in three years, and no replacement has returned the gift of music to me!"

I looked at the hands attached to Orlac's wrists and then to the hands on the table.

"*Six?*"

"Yes," Serral said. "I've performed every transplant with exceptional skill. None were quite as good as the originals. This last pair pleased him, though. My work would have been done if not for the infection. The hands must be replaced. I grow weary of continuing these procedures, so this time we must ensure every detail is correct."

Orlac went on massaging his wrists. His eyes had a vacant, crazed appearance. He seemed to look about the room as if he didn't know anything about it. Then his sweeping gaze encountered the piano. It seemed like some anchor of understanding to him. He staggered over to it, sat down, and put his fingertips to the keyboard.

I looked to Serral. "What do you *really* need me for?"

"A choice of hands must be made from the men on the floor."

Orlac began to play jarring, heavy notes. How could a man who'd once produced such strands of aural gossamer so offend the ear?

"You will read each palm out loud," Serral continued.

"To what purpose?"

"I should think that's obvious. You are selecting the most optimal pair."

"But how could anything I say matter?"

Serral shrugged. "It doesn't—to me. I could care less what you find in their hands. I believe none of it. You are pleading, so to speak, to the choir. But your *maestro* would have this business carried out first. So do it."

"No."

I stared hard at Serral's gun as he leveled at my head. A braver man would have taken the bullet rather than surrender. I'd known many such soldiers during the war. Brave men were good at getting themselves killed.

"Consider this one thing," Serral said. "You have the power to save the hands of five of those men. If you refuse, each will undergo amputation, down the line until Orlac finds a pair to satisfy him. But you can see his frame of mind for yourself."

Waves of dizziness and nausea made me bend forward, holding my head in my hands. Orlac's playing had become madness. He was executing a series of diminished seventh chords over and over, building to a relentless pitch and frenzy that made me think a crack was developing in my skull.

Serral shouted a final plea over the piano.

"Without your help, Orlac will never be satisfied. The surest way to predict the future is by observing past behavior. Refuse to help us now, and these kidnappings will go on and on. Next time it may even be a child. So much future happiness is in your power if you act now!"

I began to hyperventilate. I rocked back against the chair, pulling at my hair. Orlac went on playing, faster, harder. I began nodding. I wasn't thinking about saving anyone. I just wanted to escape the room and those damnable chords. The men on the ground were still, as if they, too, had been defeated by the music. Perhaps it had enchanted them the way snakes are charmed, though if anything they resembled a row of piglets waiting for the butcher.

I got up from the chair, clawed along the table and then dropped to my knees next to the first victim. The stench of body odor, sweat, and urine clouded him, making me cough and wheeze. I had to twist and angle my body to read the lines on his bound palms. When he felt my touch, he closed his hands into fists until Serral kicked him in the ribs. The fingers spread wide. His palm was mine to read. His fate was mine to determine.

I yelled my findings out loud to Orlac's back. If he heard me, he gave no indication. His playing never lost its volume or intensity, and I struggled to hear myself over the sinister notes.

"This man should know excellent health. His life line is very long. But the head line suggests someone who is unfocused in life. The heart line has several breaks in it. This means he is an unfaithful lover."

"I doubt the *maestro* is interested in hands that cheat in their caresses," Serral said. "Perhaps move on."

I did so in a hurry. The second man's hand was a disaster of misfortune. A short life line, a dim sun line, and non-existent intuition. I made these pronouncements and Serral sighed and used the gun to wave me to the third man.

There was nothing unfortunate in the third victim's palm, but I lied outright, fabricating terrible imperfections. I had to lie to save these men, to make Orlac disdain their hands. Maybe then I could persuade him to let them go and cease this outrage. I went from palm to palm announcing faults.

"Oh, we must refuse these hands at all costs. This man has a pronounced Ring of Saturn. He has no joy in life. These are hands of gloom and I fear for any piano keys subjected to their touch."

"These hands seemed fine at first, but look here. The earth line shows a narrow sweep, indicating a miser's approach to living. This is impossible for someone with the great Orlac's generous spirit."

"This man's fingers are too arthritic to even bother with a palm reading. These will not play any instrument regardless of the man's arms that direct them."

I came to the last man, who also seemed the youngest. He was the only captive without any facial hair. I cradled the back of his hand into my palm. What I saw was as beautiful as any flower. Every line, every curve suggested perfection. A long, healthy life. Intuition. A generous spirit. Mindfulness. His fingers were long and tapering and there was even a peacock's eye on his fire finger, a sure sign of artistic ability.

It took me a few moments to realize I'd read his palm in silence, and that silence was the youth's undoing. Serral knew I'd found nothing wrong, and once the realization struck me, I began to stammer out anything that might save him.

"No, not him. It is unthinkable. He has…he has no music line."

Orlac ceased playing. He turned on the bench to face me. "Then you have chosen?"

I listened to myself gasping, pleading. But what good would it do? The foul deed would take place regardless of my efforts. I bowed my head and nodded.

"Very good, Hersch. Thank you. Dr. Serral, we should begin at once."

"I quite agree. Get on the table."

I looked up. Serral had traded the gun for a hypodermic needle, and he lanced me before I had a second to react.

"What's happening? Orlac, *please—*"

I fell sideways, swooning from whatever was dosed into my veins. I kicked a little, feeling like a fish far from water. My body became numb as Orlac stood up and walked over to the surgical equipment. He took one of the scalpels and pivoted back to me, but he walked to the back of the piano instead and reached in with the knife. He was bent over sawing with the blade. When he straightened, I saw he'd cut a length of piano wire. He came forward fashioning it into a garrote.

"You had a gift, Hersch. When it came to the piano, the achievements of your hands could have outstripped even my own, but you chose to squander that gift. I will liberate their talent, and in turn they will liberate my soul."

"You're going to…kill me?"

"No," Serral said, bending to wrap his hands around my torso. He began hoisting me up, moving me toward the long table. "The *maestro's* conscience can't abide the idea of you living out your life a helpless beggar. You have been on your knees all this time selecting your own replacement hands. I hope you told the truth and chose well. If you lied, you cheated no one but yourself."

He put me on the table and began cutting away my clothes. By now, the paralysis had become so complete I could only stare at the ceiling as I heard a tortured, strangling sound coming from the floor, and the violent thrashing of a body petering out to stillness.

So much for his long life line, though maybe the fate one finds written in the hands is for the hands alone. This notion struck me like an epiphany and almost made me laugh.

"My God," I said.

Serral's face hovered over mine. "Yes?"

"All this time reading palms, and I never once bothered to look at mine."

YOU CAN HAVE THE GROUND, MY LOVE

CARLIE ST. GEORGE

WHAT HAPPENS FIRST: she survives. She climbs out of the rubble, leaving two corpses behind: a human who helped create her, and the Monster who tried to murder her—the Monster who showed the human lovers mercy but said that she belonged dead. The Monster, sometimes known as Frankenstein's monster, also known as her husband.

But the Bride was never a bride at all. The Bride was never *his*.

———

THE WORLD IS confusing and frightening and infuriating. The Bride walks it in secret, learning what she can along the way. A few things she learns:

A. A dead woman is more acceptable than a dead man, so long as she is beautiful.

And the Bride is beautiful, it seems—if she doesn't open her mouth. She learns this from a Christian farmer, who's the first to take her in, who is eager to help her and teach her and train her to properly walk and dress and speak. But the Bride is all sharp instinctual twitches, and likes her hair the way it is. The Bride's voice is clicks and chirps and screams, not meant for human speech. Her voice is the creak of old forgotten doors. Her voice is the hiss of snakes.

A pity, such a pity, the farmer says, when he realizes he cannot remake her. The pity, apparently, is her face. *Such a beauty, such a waste.* He should kill her, but how can he? It would too badly hurt his kindly heart. The only way to help her, he says, is to secretly lock her away, to feed her and pray with her and teach her the natural order of things. This is how the farmer defines mercy.

The Bride, not merciful, crushes the farmer's throat with one hand and leaves his body on the doorstep for his young wife to find. She should know the kind of man she married: not a friend, never a friend.

B. There are too many mad scientists in the world, all quick to create for the sake of creation—and just as quick to abandon those creations and any consequences they might incur.

No matter where the Bride goes, a mad scientist will always find her somehow, eager to question her, study her, dissect her, replicate her. She doesn't kill all of them. Some are charming, in their own strange way. Some are gentle. Some don't touch. But the ones that promise her a companion—a partner, a husband—the ones who assume a person you create is somehow yours to give…

Yes. The Bride does kill these mad scientists, and then learns what she can from their viscera and bones.

The living are considered more deserving of life if they're in love and are loved in return.

This lesson eludes the Bride for a long time as she tries to stay hidden, keeping as best she can to the forgotten roads and the deepest, darkest corners of the forest. No one can find her out here—except the occasional mad scientist, of course. No one will judge her pitiful or monstrous. No one will sentence her to imprisonment or execution.

Does she deserve such things? She can't see how, but then the Bride knows so very little of herself. She's heard her story only in bits and pieces, while traveling under cover of night—and even then, it's not her story, not really. The story belongs to everyone but her: to the Monster, who some have strangely come to pity, to the Doctor, who reluctantly pieced the Bride together to save his own fiancée. How tragic it would've been, they say, if the Doctor had died that night with his creations? Not because he was blameless (he wasn't) or because he was particularly well-liked (mad scientists, as a rule, seem better at building friends than making them), but because he would've left his beloved behind, and what a devastating fate that would have been. Because the fiancée's life isn't as meaningful without the Doctor, somehow. Because two young lovers deserve happiness—more, it seems, than two young people living their lives alone.

This doesn't make any sense to the Bride, who cares very much about her own life, despite being beloved by no one and having no desire or love to give. She's surprised to learn, too, about those who pity the Monster, even though his face is far more frightening than hers. This contradicts that very first lesson, that one must be beautiful to be considered worth saving, that one can't survive being both ugly and strange.

And yet people *do* feel sorry for the Monster because he'd been so very lonely—or so the stories say. He'd been all alone in the world, rejected by everyone, even by the dead woman created especially for him. *Terrible, so terrible*, the people say. *Better to die than to live like that.*

The Monster must have thought the same. This is why he wanted death, and wanted the Bride to die with him. This is why the Doctor was allowed to live, because his life was deemed worth living. It surprises her. It angers her. It's maddening—surely, the Doctor should have *done* something to prove that he'd earned survival? Instead, he had merely *felt* something, and this somehow meant he was inherently good.

The Bride had felt something, too, of course, but not what the Monster had wanted her to feel. She'd never been given a chance to feel anything else. She'd had no time to decide her own nature. The Bride had barely even understood what it meant, to be dead, to be alive, before the Monster tried to rip that life from her. But she survived anyway. She climbed free—

Only to live like this, hidden away, imprisoning herself.

This isn't what she wants. She isn't sure *what* she wants, but it isn't this. Some claim on this world, perhaps. Visibility. To know herself. But how can she ever know herself like this? Why should she live this way for *them?*

The Bride doesn't want to hide anymore, she decides. She is done with the shadows, the forgotten corners of the world. She will go… somewhere, anywhere, anywhere she wishes.

The Bride will, for the first time, walk openly in the sun.

———

IT TAKES TIME, longer than she'd like. But slowly, people learn that the Bride did not die after all, that she has no intention of going quietly, that her story is incomplete.

Slowly, very slowly, they begin to call the Bride a different name. It's not entirely accurate, this name, but it's one she vastly prefers.

———

HERE ARE THE things the Widow learns as she openly walks the world:

Lots of people, so many people, are deathly afraid of her.

It's not always enough, being beautiful. Not enough to be pitied, either—even the humans who consider the Monster tragic are still grateful that he's dead. Sympathy is best left for the epilogue, when it's too late to make better choices, to change. The living don't want to be challenged. They want their dead to stay silent and out of sight.

The Widow will not accommodate these wishes. She did not ask to be assembled, sewn together, resurrected—but regardless, here she is. She will not stay hidden to keep humans comfortable. She won't pretend to be one of them just to ease their tiny, terrorized hearts.

But neither can she hurt them for the sin of being afraid.

The Widow was born afraid. Waking up in a dark room that she didn't recognize, in a body she didn't recognize, with unfamiliar men who explained nothing, who kept staring at her, who kept *touching* her. With the Monster caressing her hand, calling her *friend*, expecting something from the Widow that she didn't understand but also didn't want to give. The Widow had been very afraid, then, and had very nearly been killed for it.

She is a monster, but not *the* Monster. So, when someone screams at the sight of her—and it does happen frequently—when someone comes across her, turns, and runs away, she lets those people go. No one should be followed when they choose to retreat. No one should be chased, pursued, hunted.

Unless they hunted her first, of course. Unless they gathered into a mob and came with torches and pitchforks, unless they met her outside town and arrogantly chose to attack. If they say she deserves death just because she's been dead before, well, then she'll have to reply with sibilance and blood.

Sometimes, there are too many humans to handle. They win, sometimes. She's overcome.

But she always manages to survive, in the end. And always, she returns.

The Widow will never learn who she is—or rather, who she once was.

Her arms and legs don't quite match up. Her beautiful face once belonged to a different body. She is one woman now, but she used to be several—or perhaps she's not a person at all. Perhaps she is a lonely prison cell, and all the women she's wearing are trapped inside her.

They don't speak to her, the women. There are no half-forgotten memories, no words or dreams. The Widow can't know their histories, so for the first time—for the last time—she seeks out the Doctor.

She finds him in the ground. He died young anyway, it seems, buried on a pretty little hill, silent and out of sight. A woman sits beside his grave, the beloved, presumably. Her eyes are large. Her breath comes quickly. She's frightened but chooses not to run.

The woman names herself Elizabeth, and the Widow—after many sharp, exasperated gestures—manages to get across what she's looking for, who. But Elizabeth is no mad scientist, and has no idea where the Widow's limbs and organs belong, and it's unlikely her husband would've remembered, either, even if he'd been alive to tell. He'd never spoken of the stolen corpses as people. They were only a necessary evil, construction materials. Stone and mortar and squish. He'd cared about things like bone density, physical deformities, the shape and size and normality of brains. Otherwise, the dead were of no use to him. Why would he want to know their stories; why would he stop to collect their names?

Elizabeth, the Widow sees, has learned exactly what kind of man she married.

But she remains a dutiful widow: visiting her husband, mourning him. Likely she still loves him, even if she clearly disapproves of the things he's done. Elizabeth is very tense now, trembling slightly, lips pinched into a thin, pale line. She thinks the Widow is about to kill her, and she's not fighting back, but neither is she resigned.

Elizabeth does not want to join her husband yet. Her life alone has meaning to her.

The Widow bares her teeth in frustration, turns abruptly, and leaves her alive.

There is nothing else to do: no people to question, no leads to chase. Some mysteries, it seems, cannot be solved: all the women the Widow was made from are dead silent, and forever will remain silent and dead. The Widow cannot know their wishes. She'll never know their stories, their names. She can only hope they're not screaming inside her.

She can only thank them, and move on.

The Widow isn't the only one with a habit of resurrection.

The Monster finds the Widow one winter night in her cabin just outside of town. It's been her home for some time now, the locals too afraid—thus far—to do anything about it. She'd hoped to stay here awhile yet, but that's the trouble with refusing to hide: anyone looking will easily find you, including people you thought long dead.

The Monster looks much the same as the Widow remembers: gargantuan, melancholy, hideous. He looks as pitiful as the stories say.

She doesn't pity him.

He doesn't try to stroke her hand this time. Instead, he steps inside, shuts the cabin door behind him, and says, "I see you walk this world again."

The Widow cocks her head and makes a caw like a half-choked raven. *My, how your vocabulary has grown*, she's saying, but he's never understood her, of course.

The Monster says, "This world. It doesn't belong to us. We are always ugly, always alone. We belong in the ground. We deserve the ground."

He says, "Do not return again."

This is what the Monster wants, what the world wants. This is their idea of mercy.

But the Widow rejects the definition.

If she could speak, the Widow might tell him: *The truth is, I like being alone.* She might say, *They made me for you, but that never made me yours.* She might ask, *Who dares decide what we deserve? I'll choose where I belong.*

She might say, *You can have the ground, my love. I'd like to walk this world a while yet.*

The Widow doesn't speak, and the Monster steps toward her, ominous, lumbering. Steps with purpose.

But these are predictable steps, ones that—this time—she is prepared to meet.

The Widow kicks over a can of gasoline, lights a match. Hisses her dissent.

———

WHAT HAPPENS NEXT: she survives. The Widow of Frankenstein will always survive, for as many times as it takes for her name to reflect the truth. She'll outlast the Monster. Withstand him. Resist him. Defy him. The Monster will have the ground, and the Widow will have everything above it, everything beyond it.

She'll walk this earth, live in it. Make noise, take up space. She'll kill when the occasion calls for it, and be no one's bride, no one's prisoner. The Widow will grow and unfold. She'll caw and croak and crackle. The Widow will discover her own story—and challenge the whole terrified, trembling world to listen.

THE PICTURE OF DORIANA GRAY

MERCEDES M. YARDLEY

LASHES ON. COLORED contacts in. Crystal Sapphire had done a two-day cleanse before going live so she appeared extra svelte. She slid her feet into too-tight shoes, but the tall heels made her legs look long and thin. She grinned at the camera, her teeth impossibly white, impossibly straight.

"Hey, my jewels, how are you? Today I want to talk to you about my new makeup palette that's coming out. Aren't these colors beautiful? As you know, I'm very compassionate so it isn't tested on animals. Time Out for Animals, right?"

She had to mention Time Out for Animals, didn't she? She had formed a partnership with them, at least for a while. Because fur wasn't sexy anymore, but neither was whatever Time Out's current scandal was. She'd have to look into that later.

She brushed her pink hair out of her eyes. Blond last time, pink this time, maybe lavender tomorrow. Got to keep it poppin'. Got to keep that crucial element of surprise.

Crystal made her eyes wide. The filter on her phone would make them even wider.

"It just goes on your eyelids like this. See how smooth that is? See how pigmented? Anyway, that's how I'd use my Paints by Crystal Sapphire eyeshadow pallet. It's so cu-ute! Later, friends."

She blew a kiss at the camera and signed off. Kept the grin on her face like rictus. It didn't fall from her lips naturally anymore. It just stayed and stayed and stayed until she was certain all cameras were off.

Crystal's follower count was through the roof and increasing all the time. She was the flirty, fun girl. She started with makeup tutorials and branched out to health and fitness. "Hey, it's your online bestie, Crystal Sapphire! Today I'm going to teach you how to make a yummy green smoothie." She did adventure. "I'm doing a little hiking today. I heard there was an adorable little bear cub in the area. Look at how cute my pink knee socks are with my HIKE-A-RAMA shoes. Shoutout to HIKE-A-RAMA for letting me try out the cutest shoes evah! Mwah, my jewels." She opened up about her mental health. "For a little while, you guys," she said, eyes brimming with fake tears (she used eye drops for that), "I was so totally, totally sad. It's not easy when you and your boyfriend break up. But thanks for checking in on me. You all are the best. It's okay to be sad for a little bit, but then keep smiling. XOXO."

Crystal Sapphire learned to speak in hashtags and exclamation points. She tried to be mostly positive unless the drama would boost her profile. As long as she always came out on top, right?

"You guys," she said into the camera. She was wearing a cute little pajama set (by Pajammies!) and had her hair tied into two carefully casual ponytails. "I'm crying so hard right now. I just learned that my boyfriend and my online bestie were totally hooking up behind my back. He said I was too busy. Here I was, working so hard trying to create engaging content for *you*, and all the time..."

She sobbed into her sparkly unicorn pillow, gifted by a fan. ("Oh, thank you *so much*," she enthused during the unboxing video. "I will love it forever.") The sobs sounded almost real, which was great, because she had been working on them. "I can't believe they would do this to me. But I want to be the bigger person," she said, squaring her shoulders bravely. "I'm not going to respond to them, despite the awful things they're saying. You should read some of these messages, my jewels." She shuddered, and then gave a false, bright smile. She made sure her lips trembled just a bit, but not too much. "I'm going to be courageous. Sending you love and light."

The supportive messages wove around her bones like sinew. They held her up. The Internet was her mother and her lover and her brother.

"Scum," somebody wrote. "Let me know where they are and I'll take care of it."

"Oh, Crystal, how horrific! You are so beautiful, too."

"Send nudes," someone said, and Crystal would have rolled her eyes if she wasn't so well trained. She sent a giggle emoji instead.

It was night, and the flattering dusk light had faded. She put her phone down to charge and fell on the bed. Her shapewear was too tight so she started to wriggle out of it.

"Keep it on," a dusky voice said. "Beauty doesn't come without suffering."

Crystal shot up abruptly.

"Who's there? I'll call security."

The voice sounded like it was made of smoke. It spoke almost lazily.

"What security? You can't fool me like you can your faithful followers. I know who you really are, Doriana."

Doriana. She felt doused with fire and ice at the same time. Goosebumps rose on her flesh and her nerve endings burned. Nobody called her that anymore. She stood up and looked around the room slowly.

"Who are you? Where are you hiding?"

If the voice was human, it would have laughed. But there was no laughter at all, or spite, or want, or really any emotion. It floated on the wind, carved from nothing.

"Hiding? I never hide. I'm here with the rest of your rabble. Where do you find the adoration you so pathetically and desperately crave?"

Crystal Sapphire took a shaky step toward her phone. She hadn't even kicked her painful shoes off yet. Her eyes darted around wildly.

"Instinctual, isn't it? To head for your phone? To head for the camera and the sound and the insincere accolades?"

"I'm sure they're sincere," Crystal said automatically. Her breath was coming in hard gasps, tight and shallow. "My fans love me."

"Your fans don't know you," the voice said, and Crystal grabbed the phone with perfectly manicured nails. Except that one tiny chip on the right index finger, but she could touch that up tonight. No, she'd make a whole new video of her next DIY manicure. Something summery this time, like a sherbet orange shade or a pale yellow.

"One, two, three, I see you," the voice drawled, and Crystal jerked the phone close and stared into the screen. She had the feeling she was dropping into a mine shaft deep underground. When she was a child, her father had been killed in a cave-in while working in the coal mine. She had dreams about his broken body tumbling in darkness forever and ever. Sometimes his corpse shambled through her dreams at night, smoothing her hair back with broken, bloody fingers. Strands of her hair got caught up in the chips of bone.

"He falls forever," the voice said, and two red eyes glowed from the blackness of the screen. Crystal thought of the old *Ghostbusters* movie where something bestial and terrifying had set up residence in that old lady's fridge. A scream built up in her throat, but she held it back. What if she released it and somebody videoed it? She couldn't let that get out into the world if she couldn't control it. Why wasn't she filming this?

She clicked the record button.

"My friends, the scariest thing in the world is happening right now," she said. She saw her terrified face on the phone's screen. The light was so unflattering. She turned around so the bathroom's light filtered over her face. Much better. "I don't have time to explain so I'm just going to show you. Check this out."

Nothing. The demonic eyes were gone. The phone was happy and normal and sent her a warning saying that she was at six-percent battery.

"I'm so crazy tired that I must have fallen asleep," she said, and set her phone on the charger. She pulled off her shoes and rubbed the bloody blister on her left heel. Yesterday's shoes had been too tight, as well. She'd have to do a little self-care on her feet. Better save it for another video. Pedicures not only brought in the beauty hounds, but some of the fetishists as well.

She washed her face and climbed into bed. She was careful to lie on her back so the pillowcase didn't cause acne or wrinkles. Young looking girls were #prettygirls.

She slept, but something ate away at the edges of her dreams. It had red eyes and its teeth were far too sharp. It didn't call her Crystal, but Doriana, and its voice sounded almost like her father.

THE DEMON, IF that's what it was, was amazingly savvy when it came to knowing what people wanted.

"There are holes in the human soul," the whispery voice told her. "Your job is to fill them."

"Fill them with what?" Crystal asked breathlessly. The dark thing was terrifying to look at, sure, but after she started following its advice, she had a dramatic uptick in followers. The swag and endorsements poured in even more than before. Sell her soul for some Louboutins? You'd better believe it.

"Fill the holes with anything," the thing told her. "Fill them with chatter. Nonsense. Useless things. Something shiny and flimsy and *fun*. Humans love *fun*. Crystal Sapphire loved fun, too, and she found that filling holes in the human soul was a very lucrative pastime. Her videos were breezy and full of helpful advice.

"Here's a tip," she told her fans. "Waist trainers are all the rage. Not only can they give you a teeny tiny waist, but they help you lose weight because you can't eat as much. I've read the negative reports about organ damage, too, but I haven't had a problem at all. See?"

The voice in the darkness curled around her ear and told her what to say. "Eat less," it said. "Who needs sleep? You're young and can forgo it. What if something happens online and you miss out on it?"

"Don't miss out," Crystal chirped into the screen. She took more pictures. She streamed almost all of the time, and when the darkness suggested she stream herself while sleeping, she thought it was a great idea.

"OMG, my jewels!" she exclaimed. "I'm wearing my super cute pajama set from Ja-Ja-Jammas and they are so silky and comfortable. Who is going to have a slumber party with me tonight? All of you? I hope so."

She talked late into the night, careful to elongate her neck and tilt her head just the right way for the most flattering angle. She was tired and her body needed to stretch, but comfort always comes last, doesn't it?

"Beauty is pain, Doriana," the presence assured her. It was curled up next to her, inky blackness covering her like a blanket, but nobody in the chat reacted to it at all.

"It's okay," the shadow soothed, and wrapped around her. "Your frame of bones is weak, but soon you won't have to worry about trivial things like sleep. Then you and your followers won't miss anything. You can be together always." Her eyes closed and she fell asleep.

HER BODY WAS wearing out. She could point out every rib with an emaciated finger.

"Fit into those party clothes, friends!" she said, and twirled around weakly.

Constant dazzling dye jobs and intricate hairstyles made her hair brittle and thin. She used hot tools to battle it into curls and then straighten it out again. But online? Oh. The extensions and filters made it look long and lush. You can hide a multitude of sins under sprays and expensive blowouts.

"Be your best selves. Never get lazy when it comes to your hair. You need that excitement if you're going to keep friends," she told her fans.

Crystal Sapphire wielded her makeup brushes like weapons. She covered bruises and undereye circles and acne. She masked watery eyes and teeth grown fragile from constant vomiting. The inside of her mouth burned from repeated contact with stomach acid, but nobody could tell that from the videos.

She struggled with her new cocaine addiction, but the demon told her it would keep her up, give her more energy and buoyancy. It did, and she loved it, and coming down was the worst experience in the world until she could soar again. Life was so much better this way. She didn't think about growing up as Dumb Doriana, the girl with the dead father and drunk mother. Dumb Doriana wore hand-me-downs and ate from the food bank. Crystal Sapphire had nothing in common with that unfortunate girl. Crystal had fun and friends and lines of coke. She did whatever she wanted.

"Encourage them to do the same," the darkness said, and its voice was soft and soothing. It sounded like security, and Crystal couldn't believe that once upon a time it had frightened her. It held out its hand, more corporeal than before, and she took it.

"Join me, my jewels," she said, and her voice was rough and scratchy from the ravages of relentless vomiting, but she could fix that online. "Be beautiful. Be happy. Be with me. You don't ever have to be alone."

That was it right there, wasn't it? Never being alone. Don't be abandoned. Don't be Other. Don't be the weirdo, the loser, the one who everyone pointed and laughed at. Isn't that the worst thing in the world, this shattering loneliness? You can simply focus your attention on other things, like this super-gorgeous phone case from Pony's Phonies. It's so easy to express yourself with such a variety of high-quality phone cases to choose from.

"Your body is just a sack of meat," she said, echoing the dark thing that fed her the words. "You can abuse it and that's okay. The you that is online? In your photos and videos, your texts and tweets and posts? That's the real you. If you look in the mirror and don't recognize your body because of what you've done to it, it's no loss. Whiten your teeth with an app. Add fake hair, fake lashes, and all of the filters in the world. When everyone looks at you, what will they see? They'll see that you're beautiful, and people want to be around those who are beautiful."

The demon sat on her shoulders now, draped around her neck like a stole. Crystal saw herself in her bedroom mirror. The soft lighting couldn't hide the furrows and hollows in her face. Her hands fell listlessly to her side, her fingernails gnawed and bloodied. She looked closer and saw that wisps of darkness flowed from the demon and curled up into her nose. The darkness slid through her skin into her veins like an IV, pumping malevolence into her blood. Blackness splashed against the whites of her eyes and began running down her face like tears.

"This is nothing," the eddying voice whispered. It was no longer in her ear, but in her head. The sound was deep inside of her, sluicing around inside her body. "This is just your physical form, and what do you really need one for, anyway? Let me fill the holes in your soul, Doriana. I'll pack them tight with hate and ire. Those decisions you anguish about? I'll make them. This body that you've broken down? I'll rebuild it. You won't have to worry about a thing. Why would you want this useless human bag of refuse, anyway? It's so fragile. It's such a burden. Constantly eating and sleeping and moving so it doesn't wither away, and for what? I'll take care of it for you, like I have for so many others."

The entity lifted Crystal...no, Doriana's...hand for her. He turned their shared eyes toward the phone. On screen, Doriana was healthy and vibrant and rested. She was clean and primped, toned and tanned. She smiled and her teeth were diamonds.

"Tell your followers to let my friends in," she heard her voice say. She wasn't in control of it anymore. It was so much easier to let the demon do the talking. "They can shed their worthless shells and my friends will move in. To be caretakers. To do the hard, exhausting work so you humans don't have to. Doesn't it feel good to have somebody help you? To share your body so you always have somebody by your side? You can't get any closer than that."

"Your friends?" Doriana thought to the creature. "There are others like you?"

She felt her lips turn up in a smile. "Oh, yes," the thing said in her voice. "We are legion."

"Hello, my jewels," she said. It was more difficult to talk now. She felt like she was floating away somewhere dark and black, a place where her father tumbled relentlessly forever and ever. But at least the two of them would plummet in the shadows together. "Some of you have new friends, like I do. They're willing to run the controls of your miserable bodies so you don't have to. Let them in, like I did. Come join me in—"

She was going to say "the darkness" or perhaps "eternity," but she didn't get the words out. She felt an enormous crack in her sternum as the creature zoomed fully inside her, trapping her soul in a far corner of her mind like slamming a lid on a box. Doriana tried to scream, but she had no air, no mouth, no voice.

"Daddy," she thought, and it was the last thought she had before she, too, was falling forever.

"Finally," the demon said in Doriana's voice. It grinned directly into the camera. "This is Crystal Sapphire and I'm here to help you out, my jewels. There are so many things I can teach you, including how to never be lonely again."

She blinked, and for just a second, her eyes glowed red.

"Join me and my friends. There are so very, very many of us."

MAKE THE BLOOD GO WHERE IT WANTS

ALESSANDRO MANZETTI

Whitby, Summer 1980

"**M**ERCY...AN ANCIENT name, from other times."

"I'm not a prude, if that's what you mean."

Mina looks into the eyes of the young, red-haired woman. She can read that gaze, navigating memories and secrets, hot and cold; it takes her only a few seconds to know everything about her. But Mercy won't have to suspect it—not yet. Mina smells the honey scent of Mercy's twenty-two years of age, the tobacco and the leather of her father's rough hands, signs not entirely disappeared from that almost-perfect face. A small scar, nearly invisible, dimples her right cheek. Mina feels the many screams pulsing together in concert with that tormented heart. In mere moments, she hears everything the red-haired girl has ever heard.

"I didn't really think about it, believe me," Mercy says, after a breath. "It's better that way. And you? You don't seem like you're from around here."

"That's true. I rented an old house here just a month ago. I'm from London—though I feel like a stranger everywhere. This is my little curse," Mina replies.

"I understand. It's the same for me, in some way. The problem is this place. I don't know what you expect to find here. I think you will be disappointed."

"Why? What's wrong with here?" asks Mina, already knowing the answer.

"I don't know. Everything. The way people think—they're so small-minded, with rare exceptions. I would love to trade places with you; you stay here while I go to London. A big city—the navel of the world, right? So, are you in?" A laugh, surprising herself. She clutches Mina's arm—this ageless foreigner who has so quickly fascinated her. Mercy has always loved the abyss—the darkness of complicated things, and heroin, her secret friend.

"It's a possibility. I don't miss London at all. Too many memories, and few of them are good. But if you want some advice, you should look for a better navel of the world than Piccadilly Circus... How about Rapa Nui or Calcutta? Maybe we could go together."

Together. What a beautiful thing to say, Mercy thinks, tasting Mina's words in her mouth like jam from an unknown fruit. She hides her emotions behind another laugh. "Why not?" she says. "Calcutta seems like a pretty good idea. Give me a couple of hours to pack and I'll be ready to make friends even with Kali. Just as long as it's far away from here. And without men around, disrupting things."

"Exactly!" Mina replies, wrinkling her nose and parting her lips in a funny grimace. The expression reveals unnaturally white teeth—young and strong.

They cheerfully come out of Holman's Bookshop, where they met by chance on that afternoon, on this day dragging too fast toward sunset. They walk down Belle Vue Terrace, and as they reach the corner of Hudson Street, they pass an old fisherman sitting with his third beer, his beard stained white by old storms and hop foam. He looks the other way and spits on the ground. *Whores.*

Without realizing it, Mina and Mercy are holding hands, welded with a kind of magical, instant glue. They don't give a damn about anything else. Not the locals' squinting little eyes, or the frown of a fat widow who makes the sign of the cross at them and crosses to the opposite sidewalk. *Shame on you.*

As they draw nearer, the ocean raises its back to take in the fragrances of these two creatures so different from each other. The red-haired girl smells of newly exploded beauty but also of dark dreams and black holes. The other woman is surrounded by a strange flavor—chestnut honey and mothballs, and the same ingredients as the fuel that moves Death. A dense, invisible barrier prevents the sea from deciphering the heart of the stranger. Their voices are getting closer and closer, so it frills its shores with placid waves, and waits.

"Why don't we go to the beach? I can't wait to take off my shoes," Mina suggests, turning her gaze toward the globe of the sun plunging into the waters, dripping orange blood.

Mercy takes the opportunity to admire the shapely body of the stranger, tight in that flower dress shaken by a generous breeze. *With someone like you, I would go to the end of the world*, the girl thinks, immediately biting her tongue against her thoughts. The situation is getting out of control. It's not like her.

I can't be Whitby's only lesbian, can I?

"Absolutely yes, let's go," Mercy whispers, and then blushes at her eager response. "A good sunset makes anything look beautiful—even this shitty village. We must take advantage of this," she adds, changing her tone to cover for herself.

"Then follow me."

Mina runs toward the shore, carrying her shoes in her hands.

Time suddenly accelerates, opening a starless night. Mina's shape, now at a distance of about sixteen feet, seems to move in slow motion—almost evanescent.

"I'm here!" Mina yells back across the space between them.

But…is she naked? Mercy thinks, amazed, as a reflection of the water shines on Mina's body, revealing languid curves. A strong arousal now dominates everything, even that sense of the impossible which surrounds the red-haired girl. A glowing star between her legs, the sky all black, Mina rolls around in sand lit by the glow of the sea and the flashing neon sign of an old shorefront hotel.

Now or never. Who cares about anything else?

Mercy joins the stranger, exploring the cool sand with her bare feet; it feels like flour between her toes. She takes off her T-shirt, a favorite from an old Pink Floyd concert, and lets the breeze caress her naked breasts. As she grips the waistband of her faded jeans—uncertain of whether or not to take them off, too—Mina turns. She's like a shimmering Aphrodite. Drops of seawater and salt shine on her skin, on her smooth forehead and sleek neck, sparkling around her nipples like crushed mother of pearl. The water rises, as if unable to wait any longer, stretching a wave to touch that perfect body.

Six feet from the shore, Mina stands atop a dune, a circle of stones surrounding her feet. The blinking city lights are suddenly stilled by a strange enchantment. She extends her arms toward the red-haired girl, reaching for her. "If you want, the navel of the world is where we decide."

You're real? Say yes…please, thinks Mercy, pulling off her jeans and moving toward that woman who can confuse even the force of gravity. *No, I'm not dreaming.*

Then, finally she embraces the stranger, feeling her feet rise from the sand, leaving the ballast of the past on the ground. Mina's hand begins to tighten around her neck, but Mercy doesn't pull back; she has always loved the abyss, the darkness. She has always understood these complicated things: how pain is sometimes a good friend of pleasure. Her body is full of piercings, endless little bites: a pearl in the navel, a small steel ball on her tongue.

"Let yourself go," Mina whispers to her. *"Let the blood run where it wants."*

The surface of the ocean begins to dress itself in a greenish fog. It rides the foam toward the shore, and a melody floats in the air: violin, kontra, and cimbalom, a trio of sound illusions singing a wedding song from a distant region, from highlands blown by storms and crumbling castles, from a place lying with its forehead in the Carpathians and its feet in the Danube. Memories of an ancient marriage, of packs of wolves growling at the darker creatures of the night. The new fluorescent skin of the waters rushes to reach the beach. A dense steam rises, merging with itself to form a more defined shape.

Mercy turns to that apocalyptic show, but the stranger holds her bruised neck tighter and tighter; nails pushing into her skin: pain, pleasure, a trickle of hot blood. Then Mina's voice enters her mind, sounding different now, missing its fresh notes. A buried thought that moves its tongue.

"Look at me. Nothing else matters. Imagine we're in Calcutta, the Lady of Impudence. We are on an iron bridge, over a river that dies and is reborn every night. Can you see it? Close your eyes. We're in Varanasi now, climbing the white steps of a luminous pass near the water. We are leaving the Ganges; we reach our room of green marble. There's a window there, across from the bed; stand up and look outside. That's the Demeter on its way to Whitby. It's a special ship, carrying magical soil. There are many things that I have seen... Now you will see them all, too, in only a few seconds. Now look at me again. And kiss me."

The red-haired girl opens her eyes—but what is so close to her, the distance of a single breath away, is no longer the mysterious woman who lit new hopes inside of her. She finds herself before the green ghost of a tall and thin man; a face drawn surreal as a hallucination. He has a high forehead and an eagle nose, his skin is thin as fog, encasing him in a veneer that cannot hide his inner organs—heart, liver, lungs, all pulsating, hungry for life. The flashing of its fatuous features makes the creature seem at once young, old, and dead. It doesn't look Mercy in her eyes, but stares at the trickle of blood running down her neck. Its eyes flare with a purple thirst, the throat always parched, predatory teeth approaching. So young, white, and strong.

"I won't tell you my name. You will hear it in your mind. Let the blood go where it wants."

The red-haired girl—with no more glowing stars between her legs or Eastern dreams in her heart—escapes the hold. She runs, wild, on the beach that now stretches endless. Whitby's sharp roofs and rising stairways are no longer visible. No more cargo ships with their bellies full of steel and timber, no more streetlamps lighting the distant way. There are no signs of a living world. East and west are the same: the sand dark underfoot, colder with each pounding step.

She hears an animal growl behind her. She doesn't dare turn around.

Is this real? Tell me it's you, fucking heroin...please, Mercy thinks, wrapping her fingers around her arms as she runs, plugging the holes where all the impossible things she has seen and heard in the last six years have come from. Underground nightmares and vertiginous mountains, collapsed houses and shining new skyscrapers, swamps and springs and then—at the end, when the drug enchantment weakens— always the same image: her mother, hair as red as her own, lying in the bathtub with a bottle of Southern Comfort between her legs. Her face pale as snow; her wrists cut. Getting drunk to find the guts to kill herself. Killing herself to keep from starting another day.

Finally, Mercy stops and falls to her knees. There's nowhere to go, nowhere to escape to. North or south is the same; there is only darkness, and black sand fine as flour underfoot. She stops, and turns to face that incessant growl, knowing she will see this predator now. It's no longer a creature of green mist but a big black dog with strong white teeth. She smells the sour scent of the animal's wet fur. In the distance, she spots the silhouette of Mina: She stands in the center of that stone circle, looking out over the watching ocean.

Realizing that her time has come, Mercy raises her head, freeing the red hair from her neck. The wound in her neck shines agape, and a long trail of blood slides down her right shoulder. She closes her eyes, and sharp white teeth—maybe of the dog, or that young and old dead man, or of something else—bite into her. Her world is sucked away.

Mercy slides into a strange feeling of ancient peace, the Danube and the Ganges flowing into her soul. She flies over her own life as if it were a field of sunflowers, or a neighborhood patterned with crossroads and flickering traffic lights. Her memories are lifted up like sheets of fine paper, and then turned gently over. She passes over her old house full of beatings and bottles. She skims the thin outskirts of the small town, touching the head of the statue of Captain Cook. She sees herself serving tables at a restaurant on rotten stilts and, every night after midnight, dressing in a different face to sell her body by the hour, to buy packets of psychedelic fuel just to restart the engine every morning. Filthy men, all of them the same. Her first real kiss, shared with another rootless girl—one so much like her, but stronger. *Caitlin*—she'd been strong enough to get out of that damn place. No farewells, no melodramas. Mercy sees the train that left, maybe heading to Calcutta, taking away all that matters. A strange yellowish afternoon, her hands on a book, *Oranges Are Not the Only Fruit* by Jeanette Winterson. The last kiss, given to the stranger.

The green fog, the big black dog, the creature that seems at once young, old, and dead: The vampire that was once named *Dracul*, finally satisfied with Mercy's blood, takes a consistent form—human—and reaches Mina inside the stone circle. The two approach, overlapping in the same figure, each passing through the body of the other to move in opposite directions. East and west. Sometimes love is simple: a bond that can last forever with the right nourishment. Expendable lives, already dead lives, fortifying an ancient union, a heretic marriage, with rings of flesh and blood before the arrival of the conqueror worms.

The surface of the ocean ripples, bringing up dozens of uncovered coffins full of ancient soil. One of them bobs toward the shore to welcome the vampire and carry him away. For years he has been waiting for the tribute of one of Whitby's rejected daughters. Young and tasty blood, coagulated by painful stories and broken memories; a nutrient of spiced heroin. The coffins, moved by an arcane alliance, dodge the rocks and come together towards the horizon line, forming a reversed cross that floats on the surface before the green fog closes in again. And then vanish.

Mina's beauty is fading quickly; there is no time to waste. She crosses the sand toward young Mercy's drained body. She kisses her grayish mouth, caressing her red hair. By now she knows everything about that girl; she sees her dead memories floating in the air like golden dust. An old barn barred, a place that does not want to remember what it saw many years ago. Mercy, so small at that time, her legs wrapped in her arms. The first time she spilled blood. No more men, from her father onward… Everything began from that cursed place, and then traveled through time, reaching that yellowish afternoon aboard a syringe-shaped rocket.

Mina disconnects herself from the mind of the red-haired girl. She admires the girl's white belly, the pearl embedded in the navel, before sinking her teeth into it with grace. Flesh that gives new beauty to the stranger, new pulp plumping on old bones, skin stretching firm, muscles pulsating as if anew.

An enchantment that will last a summer, like all the summers that have passed before.

DA NOISE, DA FUNK, DA BLOB
LINDA D. ADDISON

FAR FROM EARTH, in a galaxy of the Virgo Supercluster, a colony of amorphous interconnected beings shared songs—not the kind humans create, but more like the essence of whale song, a continuous, multidimensional sequence that told of their history from the beginning of time. These patterns gave the colony what humans would call purpose and pleasure.

Continuous cycles of their symphony changed and grew. Time to time, the echo of a new pattern vibrated through the supercluster's neural network and a piece of them would travel through the network to the source, harmonize with the new composition, and return to add it to the colony. This, too, was part of their purpose, their existence.

IN THE TIMELESSNESS of their actuality, pulsations coming from the Milky Way through the supercluster's neural network drew the colony's attention. The rhythmic vibrations from a planet none had visited called to them, and in this calling they made space for the planet's melody to be added, to expand their *song*. This was their path to evolving, to immortality.

A piece of the colony split away and surrendered its formlessness to the neural network to travel, without measuring time or space, away from their birthplace to Earth. This separated being converted to something like metadata for the journey through the network. Alone for the first time, It felt increased hunger not to be solitary, which was a way of focusing its purpose on the target and the one task: to *sing* with Earth and return the new composition to the colony.

Along the way, an image of Earth was shown to It from the network. What humans see as white clouds swirling around a beautiful blue, green, brown sphere, It also perceived, and found the perception of Earth agreeable. The pleasure was shortened by the neural network also displaying the positions of uncountable pieces of artificial objects of different sizes in space above Earth's surface. The neural network shared images of the one type of lifeform that took natural materials from the planet and created unnatural objects.

It knew of planets with ring systems, but this was different. The pieces floating around Earth were not made of natural material. They were processed excretions of the one biped, shown by the network, that lived on Earth. The colony had come across other organisms that infested planets in the endless time of its existence and It carried the memories of those encounters.

Arriving at Earth's magnetosphere, It emerged from metadata to a form compatible for survival on Earth: three-dimensional-thick liquid inside an iron rock enclosure for atmospheric entry. It was vaguely aware of the chorus waves undulating from Earth's plasmasphere but kept its focus on the pulsations from the planet. There was increased energy in It for the end of solitude and the impending completion of singing with another, the goal of its existence.

Finally, protected by the iron rock, It hurtled through Earth's atmosphere and landed in the shallow waters called the Bight of Bonny, off the coast of Nigeria, where the strongest waves of Earth's vibrations radiated. Detecting landfall, the iron covering that carried It through the atmosphere crumbled, allowing It to ooze out onto the sandbar of the bight. It sent a burst of electromagnetic radiation out through the supercluster's neural network to let the colony know arrival had been obtained.

FEW HUMANS TOOK notice of what looked like another shooting star, except Rod Cressey, a NASA astrophysicist who was analyzing data from the Herschel infrared space telescope. Preliminary emission measurements resulted in Rod recording the incident as an iron meteor, which didn't explode as it entered Earth's atmosphere. The rock didn't line up with any objects in JPL's Small-Body Database, so he tried to contact a colleague near São Tomé and Príncipe, in hopes of recovering some of the meteorite. Unfortunately, there was a power outage in the area of the bight and Rod couldn't get through to anyone. He shrugged and made a note to try again the next day.

IT SENT A tendril into the sand as deep as it could and remain anchored to the bight's bottom. When the next pulsation vibrated from Earth, It transmitted a harmonic vibration back to the source and waited. The Earth's next pulse was the same as the previous, as were the next few, each without any reaction to the invitation It delivered. Perhaps It needed more mass to increase the strength of the request to sing with Earth.

Undulating onto the beach from the water, It quickly flowed over two teenage humans lying on the sand and absorbed their organic matter, increasing its mass, barely noticing their thrashing inside of its structure. The humans' friends did notice and ran from the beach, screaming as their friends melted inside the clear gelatinous bubble, tinting It pink with their blood. The sound of the human screams didn't register to It because of the focus on the Earth's pulses. What noise it detected meant little, other than the sound of food squirming as it was consumed.

The other teenagers tried to convince the grownups in the town that something horrible had eaten their friends. The adults told them to go home and lay off the Gravana rum. While the teens tried to figure out how to make them see the truth, It absorbed several beach homes, cars, people, and asphalt, as it flowed toward the town of São Tomé.

It was beginning to believe the real problem with contacting Earth was the processed material the bipeds had laid over Earth. Although consuming this material and the organisms helped It grow quickly, there was still no response when trying to connect to the planet. The neural network had shown a large percentage of Earth's dry land covered by inert items, and even the water and air were degrading, as a result of the actions of these lifeforms.

Trying to understand their motivations, It slowed down the consumption of the beings and found an organ in the round object at the top of their body that contained most of their controlling processes, including memories and problem solving. There was no answer in this organ they called a brain, to why they were destroying the planet they lived on, so It continued clearing a path to the town of São Tomé, consuming all it came across that was human or a construct.

On the edge of town, It stopped moving, pulled itself tall and wide, like a strange gelatinous sail, curious about rhythmic beats in the air. Quickly filtering out seemingly random patterns, It discovered interesting cadences from a structure in the middle of town. It moved toward this place, considering the possibility that there was another way of harmonizing with Earth.

At this point, some humans had gathered weapons to try to stop It, but nothing halted its progress through the town. Everything they fired at the moving, growing entity was simply absorbed, adding to its size. Other countries were sending scientists and military to the island.

The police couldn't get past the creature to enter the music hall. It was early afternoon and there was a band rehearsing for a performance that evening. Each member of the group wore headphones to listen to the band's mix as they played and didn't hear the sirens and megaphones warning them from the street.

It flowed against the front of the building, permitting the beat of the percussions to vibrate through the walls into its form. If It could be surprised, it would have been. The thumping was appealing and unlike any *song* remembered from the colony. Absorbing the windows and doors allowed It to drip into the structure without disturbing the walls. The drummer closed his eyes to perform a solo and didn't notice that It was in the auditorium and had made its way to the front of the stage. The other musicians jumped up, yelled, and stumbled back toward the drummer, who opened his eyes as his solo ended. He threw off the headphones and stared at the wall of pink gel that throbbed in front of them.

The outer membrane of its body vibrated, mimicking the drummer's last beats, and It waited for a response. When none came, It slowly slid closer to the stage.

The drummer recognized the pattern and sat back down to play it, slightly modified.

It moved away from the stage and repeated the changed beats.

"What the hell are you doing, Francisco?" the guitarist asked. "Let's get out of here."

The drummer pointed at It with his drumsticks. "I don't know what that is, but it's repeating my beats. Maybe it just wants some music played at it. You see how it moved away from us." He improvised a round of single-stroke rolls, which the thing easily repeated, and then played a different rhythm back.

While they played back and forth, changing the rhythm each time, the police found a way into the building from the alley and waved the other musicians into the wings of the stage to get them out. When the creature didn't react as the other musicians left the stage, two officers came up behind the drummer when he had stopped playing to listen to the thing's sound.

"We got the others out while it was playing back and forth with you," one of them said to the drummer. "It's time for you to go now."

"But—" Francisco didn't get to finish his sentence. The officers grabbed his arms, dragged him away from the drum set and off the stage.

EVEN THOUGH THE source of these patterns were not from the planet, It found them worthy of remembering for the colony. Once the human who was playing them left, It rolled onto the stage and absorbed the mechanism used to make the sounds. It perceived that this was another non-living construct. After consuming the rest of the building, It decided to return to the place of arrival, where the Earth vibrations were strongest. On the way, some mechanisms in the air dropped containers on It. The objects sank into its body and blew up. It easily absorbed the energy and debris of the containers and continued undulating back to the water.

The form It came to Earth in suddenly felt sluggish as it tried one final time to sing with the planet. The result of consuming the humans and their creations to try to give the planet a chance to sing wasn't working. It needed to *sing* with the colony. Longing to return and share with the colony the patterns collected at this point from Earth became a new mission.

It vibrated through a few cycles with Earth's pulsations as a way to say *Goodbye* and honor the planet's song, even if no answer was returned. Perhaps one day, Earth would find a way to converse, but now It tired of being here. It sang for a connection to the Virgo Supercluster's neural network and found silence. Not the way humans think of silence, but more like the absence of what had always been available.

This was as improbable as the cessation of all song, for that would mean the end of all life. So it continued calling out for a connection, to feel once again the rhythm of the neural network, to relinquish *being* on Earth, return to the colony, but something was wrong. Nothing reached back to It. There was no fear of dying, because the essence of its existence couldn't be destroyed, but something had changed, perhaps some part of what It had ingested affected the structure of its being.

It gathered a small nugget of itself, from deep inside, a piece with the least contaminations from Earth, and slid that part into the water. The rest of its mass was converted back to Earth's ground, water, and sky in the form of subatomic particles.

The tiny segment sank to the bottom of the water, burrowed deep into the soil to sleep and wait, comforted by the repeating pulsations from Earth.

Nothing stays the same, change was inevitable, and in time the humans who covered Earth, smothering the planet, would morph or die out, allowing the beautiful sphere to sing freely. In the meantime, It would wait and heal from the pollutions absorbed, and wake to complete its mission.

The End?

RAPT

RENA MASON

IN A BOX,

under murk,

swathed in silk,

Lady Mei reaches for her husband, smacking her raw knuckles against damp lacquer once more. The instinct to touch him remains, much like breathing, much like loving. A motion repeated so often, deep pits mar the inside of the coffin wall, as well as her heart.

Soon. Whispers swell behind her eyes and then bubble from her ears.

The voices soothe Mei when the confines of her prison close in and squeeze, when her body rises and bobs against the interior lid, her face pushing against a corporeal darkness. Their calming words draw her back from madness, back to those who dwell within her mind. They speak of their home and the place she would have there, watching over their children and children of her own. Children she never had in her first life. She has seen their world. Islands on crimson seas under dim white light. They have taken her there.

Illustration by COLTON WORLEY »

But she remembers bliss and how it made her feel, so she clings to her marital vows. Mei's beloved had promised to be entombed by her side when his time came.

So she waits.

———

A STEEP RAMPART, out of breath and panting, to the other site. ascends

Dr. Ping Lee

Two leathery bodies float to the surface of dark, oily water. Feathered wing tapestries lay vertically alongside them, giving the appearance that the dead had flown up to be discovered.

"Hey, be careful with that," Dr. Bradley Jiang shouts, butchering Mandarin. "That's my ancestor." Hearing the mangled words coming out of his own mouth sounds bad even to him, but using a translator would be humiliating. He's Chinese, for chrissakes. Invited "Western" guest bioarchaeologist on the dig because his ancestry is linked to a nobleman from the Wu Kingdom of the Han Dynasty or not, he knew more than these so-called colleagues of his, with PhDs from Stanford to prove it.

A few laborers tsk and then burst into a chitter too fast for him to understand.

"Hurry up, Dr. Lee." Brad motions the graying man in glasses over, and then points to one of the workers. "You there, go get the rest of the team."

The digger scurries off, looking a little too pleased to be leaving the scene. At least Dr. Ping Lee showed up, the only one somewhat an associate. Ping even speaks a little English from training abroad.

"We have to get these out of here before it all rots in this heat," Brad says. "I've never seen such an intact example of the featherization process to become celestial. This is amazing."

Hunched over, Ping nods in agreement but also waves his hand, dismissing Brad. The glossy top of the old man's balding head reminds Brad of speckled sparrow eggs.

"What do you mean by this?" Brad leans down and mimics the negating gestures to the wheezing man. "Just calm down and breathe," Brad says, certain Ping's chain-smoking is responsible for his current state. "This country has a serious tobacco habit," Brad mumbles quickly in English.

"I, I think I may have found the entrance…" Ping gasps, pats his chest, and then gropes for the pocket with his cigarettes.

"Not yet." Brad grabs Ping's hand. "What did you find?"

"A warning."

Brad clenches his jaw, releases Ping, and then turns to another worker. "You. Gather eight of your strongest men. We're going to dig all this out and bring it up, including the dirt around it. Pack as much of this mud as possible against the coffins."

The man nods and sets to the tasks.

Brad doesn't have time for Dr. Lee's obsession with his ancient ancestor's supposed first wife, rumored to be the Helen of Troy of the Wu Kingdom. Minutes later, the rest of the archaeology team whirls in like a typhoon and takes over the extraction, shouting orders and pushing Brad aside.

Relieved of his duties, Brad walks over and stands next to Ping, who's lighting a cigarette off the one before.

"Well, it looks like I've got some free time. Want to show me what you found?"

Ping leers at him through a smoke cloud.

"By the way, where's Natalie?" Brad thinks mentioning her might have a calming effect on his colleague, who seemed to become easily fixated on beautiful women.

Dr. Lee had an immediate fondness for Brad's girlfriend of three years, going out of his way to be nice to Natalie and let her tag along with him, even though she was American-born-Chinese, like him, or ABC, as some of their friends joked about. She doesn't have any archaeology experience either, being a project manager at a marketing firm in Orange County.

Brad found Dr. Lee's connection with Natalie a relief. He'd never spent so much time with her before, or any woman for that matter, and she was beginning to get on his nerves. Besides, Natalie spoke better Mandarin than he did and was always more dedicated to her Chinese studies. At first, having her around took unwanted attention off him, but now it irked Brad that Ping and a few others from the archaeology team preferred talking with her when she was around.

"I left her down at the other site to keep watch," Ping says. He exhales a jet of smoke to the side and then flicks the cigarette into some bushes.

Brad stares at the burning cherry end to make sure it extinguishes.

"Don't worry," Ping says. "It won't catch fire. Too much rain." The old man tilts his head back and looks up at the sky. "More coming, too. Let's get inside."

Ping's shoes slap against the damp wood scaffolding surrounding the current dig and play a flat, rhythmic tune reminding Brad of bamboo wind chimes.

Brad wonders what Dr. Lee discovered at the first site. They finished excavating it a week ago and found nothing but a walkway around a stone square wall, each side measuring about thirty feet by approximately fifty feet down. They all assumed something must be in the center but wanted the immediate gratification of an actual find before getting too in depth with more digging, especially with the rains coming.

As they descend, the pressure squeezes Brad's ears. Struggling with a sinus infection, he shifts his jaw side-to-side and then swallows, alleviating some of the tension. The temperature drops about twenty degrees, and the sweat on his arms now chills him. Brad follows his shuffling colleague toward the square. Ping turns left and then about halfway through the first of four halls, stops and points. Brad directs his eyes upward as he approaches, taking a moment for his sight to adjust. Football stadium lights are set up on the ground every hundred feet or so, but they seem only to light up what's in front of them, barely penetrating the darkness behind, above, or on the sides.

Then Brad sees it: faint characters.

"It's ancient Chinese," Ping says. "Han Dynasty."

Brad scowls, annoyed with Ping's know-it-all blurt outs. "Well, what does it say?"

Dr. Lee retrieves a cigarette from his shirt pocket and lights it. He takes a pull, holds it, and then exhales.

"Loosely, 'Do not trespass here. Your eyes will fool you. Your ears will be tricked by sweet words pouring from a beautiful mouth controlled by a black heart... Turn back and forget this godless place, lest you be all-consumed by what dwells within her darkness.'"

"And you think this has to do with the so-called first wife of the Chancellor to the Wu Kingdom?"

"Yes." Ping draws another drag from his cigarette and then drops it to the ground and steps on it. "I do. All of my research indicates she existed."

"If so, then there should be much more evidence. Where is it?"

"Her husband destroyed it. Erased her from existence."

"Why would my ancestor do something like that? Especially if she was as beautiful as she supposedly was."

"He was jealous, felt threatened. Wouldn't be the first time in history."

Brad shook his head. "That doesn't make any sense. A woman's duty to her husband back then meant she walked in her husband's shadow, always. He had nothing to be jealous of."

"Yet here we are, reading a warning he left about her." Ping lit another smoke.

"Have you heard or seen anything like this before?" Brad pulls a brush out of his pocket and swipes dirt from a corner of the inscription.

"Not here. Egypt, yes. Queens Nefertiti and Hatshepsut."

"I mean in China. And why? Women have always been insignificant here. Her status as his wife was likely minimal."

"Lady Mei's beauty and kindness was legendary. Stories of her allure traveled as far north as the Yan Kingdom. Higher ranking men than Chancellor Jiang invited him to their kingdoms to wine, dine, and visit with his wife. It's likely he feared for his life at some point, worrying one of them might have him assassinated to have her for themselves."

"Do you know how he killed her? If she was so loved by the people, I find it hard to believe he'd have done anything so public."

"The stories, mostly old legends and folktales, say he'd given her tainted food. That it took months for her to die, and even then, she believed him to be a true and faithful husband, so the people had no substantial proof of his guilt even though he'd already had many lovers."

"I don't get it." Brad touches the inscription.

"What's to get? The chancellor was an insecure, insignificant man."

"Hey, that's my ancestor you're talking about."

"Sorry," Ping says. "I didn't—"

"I'm only joking," Brad says. But not really. "Where'd you say Natalie was?"

"Maybe she went looking for us."

"We would have passed her on the way up."

"Not if she was around the corner," Ping says.

"She would've heard us talking and called out. Come on, let's look around the square."

"Maybe we should go—"

Brad walks away. Either Ping will follow him or not, but he's determined to find his girlfriend before heading back up to alert the archaeology team of the discovery. As they walk, he scours the walls for any other faint markings they might've missed.

"So, you think the warning means Lady Mei's buried down here somewhere?" Brad asks.

"Yes," Ping says, a step behind Brad. "I'm just glad I've finally got you convinced she existed."

"I'm curious to find the truth is all." Brad stops and rests his palm against the third wall. "Her final resting place is likely within the square. Once the team gets the other site managed and has the bodies preserved for imaging, we should get them over here to do some echolocation and acoustics before—"

A shadow looms.

"Look," Brad shouts and runs ahead to the fourth and last hallway. "An opening."

Ping's footfalls echo behind him.

"Wait!" the old man says.

Brad turns his phone light on and enters the slim doorway. A narrow passage, something of a maze, slopes downward. He can't get his shoulders through walking straight on, so he turns sideways. The tight walls have sharp angles created with stone slabs like a house of cards. As he descends, the depth compression against his skull forces him to stop. Brad pinches his nose and fills his ears with air as if scuba diving and then rushes onward.

The end of the path widens to a square like the one above it but with much shorter walls. In the center is a mound of dirt. Crumpled fabric on the other side catches his eye.

"Natalie!" Brad sprints to her body leaning against rock opposite the short wall.

He checks her pulse but already knows she's dead. Her eyes are wide open and coated with a milky substance. Streaks of white hair flow from her temples, and her mouth is fixed in a broken scream.

Ping drops to his knees, heaving and sobbing.

Brad scans the area. "Call 9-1-1. Go! Get some help."

Then Brad realizes 9-1-1 is American.

"I mean get the police, or whoever you call here," Brad says.

How can he be so calm and reserved when this man who hardly knew her cries like a baby beside him? Ping's in no shape to run back for assistance, and it won't look right if Brad does.

"I should not have left her," Ping says.

"No. You shouldn't have. What the hell were you thinking? Did you tell her to wait down here? Had you discovered this entrance? You should've said so. I'd have come running."

"No, no. I didn't. She must have found it on her own."

Brad thinks it unlikely. Natalie was never timid or afraid; she was smart and respectful. She knew Brad would be furious at her for not getting him immediately involved with a discovery of this magnitude.

Just as Brad was about to inquire again, Ping takes off, gasping for air as he enters the maze.

Careful not to tamper with the body, Brad brushes Natalie's bangs aside, waiting for a rush of emotion. Solely occupying his thoughts are the how and what of telling her parents.

A MOIST *POP* sounds in Lady Mei's ears.

"The time has come," they say.

She feels more than hears a rumbling around the box that houses her body. Perhaps her beloved had passed and would at last be laid to rest beside her.

"Your unwavering loyalty is admirable," they say.

Mei steels her excitement.

Cool air assaults her face. Something crashes to the ground, quaking the water she drifts in. Mei opens her eyes. An old man peers down at her.

"Who are you?" she says.

"I, I'm Ping Lee. Your most loyal subject. I've found you, and, and... I knew it. You're the most beautiful woman I have ever seen."

"Where is my husband?"

"He's above." Ping points overhead. "Much higher than you. They found him just this morning, lying alongside his wife with feathered wings made for their ascension to the heavens."

"But I am his wife."

"I'm afraid he erased your very existence after poisoning you. He took another woman as his wife and then he had your family killed."

"I don't understand." Mei raises her arms and rests them atop the sides of her coffin before pulling herself up. "Where is he? I must go to him."

"We told you this," the voices say.

"Dr. Lee?" A young woman calls out.

"Who is that?" Mei says. "His new wife?"

"What? No. He's not a—" Ping says.

"Who are you talking to down there?" the young woman says.

"Natalie," Ping yells. "Go back and wait where I told you."

"Oh my god!" Natalie screams.

Lady Mei stands. Ruddy liquid cascades from her perfect torso and extremities. Wet silk wrappings unfurl and hang from her body.

The old man steps back and trips, falling onto his rear.

"What is happening?" Ping shouts.

Before Mei speaks again, white light blinds her and then clouds her vision. Is this fury?

"Yes," they say. Then, "No. We won't lie to you." The voices rush through her body, racing just under her skin.

Like the young woman, Mei wants to scream but doesn't have control of herself.

Stop it, Mei shouts in her head. But when she opens her mouth something else comes out. Not a word but a smooth, wide ribbon of ivory silk.

The young woman wails again, but her voice breaks when the ribbon winds itself around her neck and face. As the wrapping climbs up her head and spirals down her shoulders, it tightens and squeezes, continuously binding.

The old man sits motionless, expressions of shock and horror distorting his features.

Natalie stops struggling; her body goes flaccid and then drops to the ground. The silk disappears into her mouth and then ripples underneath the young woman's skin.

That means they move inside me, too. Mei glances down at her arm.

"Yes," they say.

"Why? How?" Mei asks.

"We've kept you alive—when your husband wanted you dead—as you've kept us alive."

Mei cries. Milky tears fall from her chin and pool next to her bare feet. Ivory bands wind around her ankles and up her legs and torso. They move smooth as silk against her body and expose some of her bare skin.

"What are you?" she says.

"What are we?" they say.

She raises her head and steps toward Ping. She needs answers.

———

BRAD CAN'T GET a single tear to rise and well in his eyes. By the time Ping gets back with site security, police, and a few other team members, the chaos makes it impossible for him to feel anything but panic.

What should've been his find turns into a circus, and now his girlfriend is dead. He hopes the team will permit him to stay and excavate the mound in the square.

After hours of filling out forms and answering the same questions over and over as if he'd killed Natalie, he's driven back to the hotel. Brad lies down on the bed and considers what he'll say to Natalie's folks. He grabs his phone, checks his emails, and then closes his eyes for a quick rest.

Midday, Brad wakes to ringing in his ear. It's the hotel phone. He answers, assuming it's Ping.

"Hello," Brad says.

Dammit, it's Natalie's father. He's raging and yelling unintelligibly between swearing.

"Mr. Yeung? What? I'm sorry. The connection's bad. I'll get back to you." Brad hangs up and then phones the front desk and asks them not to put any more calls through.

He checks his cell and silences Natalie's parents and then scrolls through the messages they'd already left. It appears Dr. Lee had already contacted them with the news and the details. What gave him that right? Brad gets moving so he can inquire. He glances at the clock and then again. He's never slept in so late before. Natalie had always kept him on track and on time. He pauses for a wave of inconsolable grief that never comes.

Wearing the same clothes from yesterday, Brad leaves the hotel.

Brad had gotten accustomed to the scurry of hustling workers, and now the second site has all the industry of a ghost town. To his left, a couple of men exit the entryway to the first dig, pushing wheelbarrows heaped with dirt.

"Hey, you. They find anything yet?" Brad shouts.

One of the workmen nods and points to the rock face at the base of the hill. As Brad nears the first square, he's shocked by all the excavation. Ping shuffles up to him, excited and rambling, a cigarette between his fingers.

"Whoa, slow down," Brad says. "You know I can't understand when you talk that fast." He waves smoke away from his face.

"Oh, sorry," Ping says.

"And what do you mean by calling Natalie's parents? They should've heard from me first. Not you."

"Had you called them?" Ping side-eyes him and takes a long draw from his cigarette.

"No. I hadn't. But I was planning to. Anyhow, that's not the point. It was my duty, not yours, and I would've gotten to it."

"Then I saved you the trouble. Now come and look." Ping put his free hand on Brad's back and nudged him through the fumes.

"Aren't you going to ask me how I'm feeling?" Brad says.

"How do you feel?"

"Okay, I guess. Sad."

Ping nods and doesn't say anything else until they get to the… mound.

"It's gone!" Brad says. "And the maze, too." Now just a flattened ramp.

"Yes," Ping nods and smiles.

"What the— Have you guys been at it all night?"

"They found her coffins early this morning." Ping pushes his glasses up.

Brad leans over the short wall of the square and sees a series of rectangles, one deeper than the other, and a stone staircase leading down to the last cleared area. "How many?"

"Four. From big to small. All black. None decorated for the afterlife."

"Interesting. How deep is that?"

"Over thirty meters."

"Anything buried with her?" Other intact tombs discovered in the area contained artifacts of pottery, silks, jewels, and even food. People of the Han Dynasty had strong beliefs in the afterlife and the nobility had lavish burials.

"Nothing," Ping says.

"But isn't that unusual? Why go to all the trouble of burying her this deep?"

"Remember the warning. Your ancestor wanted her forgotten."

"Were there any other traps closer to the coffins?"

"Traps?"

"I think maybe that's what happened to Natalie," Brad says. "Poison. Or toxic air that had been sealed for centuries, like some of the tombs in Egypt."

"Could be," Ping says. "In any case, the rest of the team and the city's officials insist on an autopsy. That's why I called her parents. I had to let them know even though they have no choice in the matter."

Brad wonders if they'll be done with the autopsy by the time he has to leave and if he'll be taking Natalie's restituted body back with him, or a pile of ashes.

"These guys should be wearing protective gear. Gas masks, bio suits, or something, just in case," Brad says.

"They tested the air before excavating and found nothing. It's safe. You ready to see the first wife of your ancestor?" Ping says. "Soon public security will be back to ask you more questions."

"What?" Brad says, still thinking on it all. "The police?"

"Yes. They have more questions."

"About what?"

Ping shrugs.

"Come. You must see Lady Mei. The woman you didn't believe existed."

"Where is she?" Brad looks around, still amazed at the speedy extraction.

"At the lab with the others." Ping shuffles down the hall, trailing smoke behind him.

Brad follows. When they're out in the open again, instead of going across the way to the second dig site, they go around the hill's base where a makeshift lab had been constructed.

The skies churn slate-colored clouds. Wind gusts throw light rain that patters in bursts against his windbreaker. Brad quickens his pace.

"Do you think they should move the mummies off site?" Brad asks.

"They're working on crating them now. We have to wait for military transport trucks big enough to come up here in order to transfer them."

Brad agrees. He knows the summer weather is unpredictable. It ranges from sweltering heat to torrential rains and treacherous flooding that occurs at random, leaving extensive damage and lives lost.

White coats rush by in a steady sea of brown as team members and other workers ready the mummies in the underground lab. Brad stays behind Dr. Lee, hoping to avoid any sullen greetings and sympathies. He doesn't care at this point whether or not they like him; he will have his name noted on Lady Mei's discovery. At minimum, he'll write a few papers and possibly get a seminar and maybe even a tour deal when he returns to the States.

"How was she poisoned?" Brad asks.

"We don't have Natalie's results—"

"Not her," Brad says. "Lady Mei. Earlier you'd said that the chancellor had given her tainted food. Did you mean poison, spoiled food, or something else?"

"You see, he wanted to do more than poison her; he wanted her to suffer. One of the stories says a servant found a mutated parasite. Upon your ancestor's request, the servant brought a specimen to the chancellor, which he then ordered to have put in his wife's food."

"Mutated how? What kind of parasite?"

"Tapeworms," Ping says. "Unnaturally large ones."

"Gross."

"Chancellor Jiang was a monster. Driven mad by jealousy and paranoia."

"Traits that were obviously not passed down." Brad considers all the relatives he knows and half-laughs.

Ping says nothing.

Brad comes to a dead stop. "My God, that's incredible."

Ping steps over and stands next to the stainless-steel and glass case housing Lady Mei's coffin, the lid off to the side within the chamber. The enormous half-cylinder reminds him of something from a science fiction movie. Lady Mei's pristine body glows on top of the dark water in which she floats.

"She's in a better state of preservation than—"

"Yes," Ping says. "This is unparalleled."

Brad moves closer and leans over the futuristic sealed capsule, inspecting every inch. "Has anyone figured out the liquid contents yet?"

"It varies for every mummy discovered from that era. Different funeral preparers, I suppose," Ping says. "I don't think they took notes or shared their methods. There are no records. No documentation of ingredients. A few of the earlier discoveries had mentioned something about the water table in the area and flooding, but the liquid is much more specific than that."

Brad hovers over Lady Mei's face, scrutinizing her features. "Even dead, she's stunning. Almost hypnotic in her beauty. I'm sure her funeral preparers pulled out all the stops to keep her looking like this."

"The people loved her," Ping says.

"So what now?" Brad asks.

"We wait for the trucks. The others want to keep excavating, certain there are burial artifacts that were missed. They're incensed that no one had left feathers for her to ascend. Once loaded, the mummies will travel on to the museum at Hangzhou for further examination. Now if you'll excuse me, I'm going to assist the others with sifting through the dirt where we found Lady Mei. You're welcome to join us if you'd like."

"I think I'll stay here and take a few notes and pictures if you don't mind," Brad says.

"Not at all. Just be prepared to have every photo and note reviewed."

"Yeah, I know. I'll follow the protocols."

"When security comes, I'll send them over here."

"Thanks, Dr. Lee. For everything."

Ping nods, smiles, and then leaves.

THE SOUND OF his voice, so near. His face, so close. Mei knows her husband hovers over her, but she cannot move, and he feels farther away than ever before. She has no power over her own body. All she wants is to reach up and stroke his cheek. Kiss him.

"Let me," she says. "Please."

"Not yet," they say.

The room quiets and then flashes brighten the red blooms behind her eyes. Metallic clicking sounds fill her ears. Cool air touches her skin and her eyes flutter open. Mei rises and searches for her beloved. Crimson liquid trickles down her body in silence. The ivory bands slide over one another and weave themselves around her chest and torso as she steps out of the water and climbs out of the new prison her subject Ping Lee insisted she utilize for a time.

Mei sees him then, Li Jiang, her beloved husband and chancellor to the Wu Kingdom. Something in his eyes—a coldness—floods her with memories of his cruelty. All the malice the voices hinted at but didn't say outright. They wanted her to remember on her own. Never forcing her to hurt and live in torment all that time. She knows now, in this moment, their love for her. Their sacrifice. Mei is ready to return it.

Ping Lee rushes into the room. The voices fear him imprisoning her again and lash out, overtaking him the way they protected her from the young woman.

Her husband trembles and screams where he stands.

"Come," she says. "I know a silent place. It will give you peace."

Mei moves closer to him and places her hand over his mouth. She catches him with the strength of the voices. He whispers something in a language she doesn't understand and then slumps into her arms.

BRAD TAKES HIS phone over to a table and scrolls through the photos he took, deleting any that aren't perfect. He feels more than hears something behind him and then turns around. His blood runs cold as Lady Mei stands before him more beautiful than Helen of Troy with the power of a Gorgon to freeze him like stone. Ribbons of unwound silk flow from her body and undulate in the air around her. She is…a vision.

Ping runs in sopping wet, yelling about the rains and flooding, and something about a mudslide. He turns in time to see Lady Mei standing there. The ivory bands react, and one launches from Lady Mei's shoulder. Wriggling in midair toward them is a head with two sets of large ovular eyes. Its mouth is partially closed; there are too many mangled teeth inside to be contained so they protrude onto the exterior in a crisscross of thorns. Inches from Ping's face, the mouth opens. It's the size of a dinner plate. Rows of pointy fangs, longer than human fingers, curve outward, and in its center a small black hole.

The massive tapeworm latches onto Ping's face and then coils its body around his struggling limbs, binding his wrists so he can't pull or fight it off. It winds around him and keeps him from moving as it constricts him. Ping falls to the ground, and as Brad has done since his arrival, he follows Ping there.

"Natalie," Brad whispers. "Forgive me."

LADY MEI USES their strength and carries her beloved to the home she came and went from so often and for so long—her safe, silent place, between worlds—knowing he'll suffer alone there, as she did not. She lowers his body down into the murk and then climbs in and lies on top of him. He stirs, embraces her with the passion and struggle of true love, and then he stills.

She understands at last, everlasting love is more powerful than true love. She has love everlasting with them and wants him to have what he wants most—to be alone.

"I'm ready to leave this place," she says. "He is home now, and I am not. Not yet."

"Are you ready for the feathers?" they say.

"CAN" DOESN'T MEAN "SHOULD"

SEANAN McGUIRE

OH, GOOD, YOU'RE awake. The process that stripped you of your powers incapacitated you for longer than I had anticipated. I would apologize for that, but I had time to think while you were drooling on my table, and I find that I'm honestly not sorry, so I won't.

People have such unrealistic ideas about what it means to be on the cutting edge of mad science. It isn't all towering stone edifices and laboratories filled with giant, clunky machines anymore; the most successful mad scientist I know is into cryptocurrency. His current office setup would give Victor Frankenstein a case of priapism that would require surgical intervention to resolve. Please. Saying that we're all working on shoestring budgets with outdated equipment is prejudicial and small-minded, and they accuse *us* of being the ones who aren't entirely right in the heads.

Which is the other thing I wanted to bring up, while I have your attention. What peer review board decided they would get to be the "sane" scientists, while we had to be the "mad" ones? It's outdated and more than a little ableist, and it shows a flagrant disregard for the neurological diversity of the scientific community. Science is supposed to be the study of the reality in which we all have to live, whether we want to or not, at least until Dr. Rockwell manages to perfect her multiversal transportation system, so why is it that those of us who want to dig deepest into its foundations get labeled and shunted to the side? There was a brief trend for calling us "fringe" scientists, until that blasted television program turned the word into a pop culture reference that no self-respecting researcher would use.

If they must divide us, it should be something more accurate, like "ambitious" scientists versus "complacent" scientists. And if that feels like a value judgment to you, sir, consider the value judgment that you have always been perfectly comfortable to levy against our community. Yes, *community*. Did you truly think the mad scientist was somehow other than human?

You *did*. I can see it in your eyes—and in your skin, of course. It's a lie that liars can't learn to control their ocular response. They can, of course, with sufficient time and training, but they can't control their capillaries, not completely. Your cheeks pinked due to increased blood flow to the area. You thought that because we had chosen what you would term the path of "madness," we had somehow divorced ourselves from the need for fellowship, companionship, *connection*. It would be flattering, if it weren't so disgusting.

Your own scientists seek transhumanism as if it were some sort of holy grail, and you deride us for our possession of it at the same time. That, alone, should be proof that scientific "madness" is not a *choice*. We are as we are because we are called by the universe to pursue our passions even to the far end of possibility, and then beyond. We could never be contented or constrained by your tiny rules, your laws, and your "ethics."

They've always been remarkably flexible, those ethics, when you needed them to be. When, for example, one of your precious "sane" scientists accidentally releases a nanotechnical innovation that would have been much safer on our side of the cultural divide—

Yes, I do mean that. We understand the safety protocols necessary for working with dangerous technologies, and we assume them from the moment you enter the lab until the moment you leave. If we had the sort of "leaks" you people seem to specialize in, the world would be ending on a daily basis. No one understands how to check a vacuum seal and decontaminate a room like someone who engineers pathogens capable of breaking down the human body at the cellular level. We are *gods* of safety and protocol, while you are priests at best, children playing with toys they don't understand.

Yes, I intended that to be insulting. Again, *sir*, I remind you that you and yours termed us "mad" and pushed us out of all respectable institutions years ago. How could you have forgotten that we would still be scientists? How could you have assumed that we wouldn't organize ourselves into research groups and fellowships? We have our own universities now, and while positions are perhaps less in demand than those at your equivalent schools, they're *thriving*. *We're* thriving. We're the children of the laughter and the lightning, and we exist in the pause between "can" and "should." They don't mean the same thing, you know—something you forgot. You threw us out, and so we gladly left you behind. I hope it hurts you to hear that you haven't been missed, not in the slightest. I hope it *burns*.

I'm sorry. That was unprofessional of me. One stereotype you hold about us is true: we do love a good opportunity to rant. The chance to explicate our plans to the uninitiated is such a rare pleasure that, when it comes along, we're inclined to seize it with both hands. And you must admit, this is such an opportunity, even if you don't want to agree that you deserve everything that's happening right now. You're here, at my mercy, and while the law may not be on my side, for once, morality is.

So yes, your "ethics" are pretty lies you tell yourselves so you can pretend there's a difference between your labs and ours, beyond the fact that you have a child's grasp of protocol and allow incompetent buffoons like your Dr. Woe to work with technologies so far beyond them that it's like watching squirrels attempt to discover fire.

Except the squirrels might have done less damage, all things considered.

Dr. Woe? Oh, he's here. My colleagues thought it was best if he not be placed in my custody until they were finished interrogating him. There was some concern that my madness, as you call it, might overwhelm my common sense if I were to be confronted with the man responsible for your "small mistake."

Yes, I saw the press conference. I have it saved on my tablet, and a copy on my phone. When the despair threatens to take me, I press play and remind myself that we stayed on the "should" side of the divide for a very, very long time, rather than allowing ourselves to become the monsters you so consistently painted us to be. The monsters you, yourself, were industriously becoming, shielded by your veil of law and righteousness and superior...superior—

I'm so sorry. That was again unprofessional of me, and as I intend this to be our last conversation, Captain Kronos, this is a time that calls for absolute and consummate professionalism. What was it you said, the last time you punched through the wall of my laboratory— I'm sorry, "secret lair"—and shut down an ongoing experiment that could have purified the drinking water for an entire nation? Oh, yes.

That the mad were never capable of reason or altruism. That any "good deed" one of our ilk had orchestrated would inevitably prove to be evil in its execution, and innocent people would die. All because we didn't suit your precious standards of what scientific advancement looked like.

You have enough of us on your side, you know. The sharp-edged geniuses who look at an atom and see it ripped into its component pieces, see all the magical and majestic ways it can be recombined. Your Dr. Woe, for example. He would have thrived, this side of the cultural divide, if you hadn't recruited him straight out of high school.

At the absolute least, he would have been with us long enough to learn basic safety protocols. Dwell on *that,* Captain. While you were indulging the greatest excesses of his scientific mind, all heedless of cost and consequence, we would have guaranteed he did no harm.

Ah, but you're Captain Kronos, savior of mankind. Tell me, *Captain.* Where were you three weeks ago, when an improperly sealed laboratory allowed self-replicating nanobots to escape into the open air? Where were you two-and-a-half weeks ago—oh, yes. You were sitting in your little conference room, telling your precious *sane* scientist that he would have noticed already if there were going to be any repercussions from his carelessness.

I'm sorry. Was I not supposed to know about that? Was I not supposed to have viewed the footage of you waving away a threat that my people—my lab, my research team, my *colleagues*—could have resolved in a matter of minutes, if only you'd told us that we needed to be performing a basic nanotechnical sweep of the area? Because I need you to know that we could have prevented this. We could have stopped it before it happened, when the nanotech was still replicating on such a small scale that nothing had been harmed beyond a few moles and earthworms—very sad for their families, I'm sure, but nothing compared to the devastation you, the good guys, wreaked on an entire region.

The footage will be on the news by now, I imagine. Did you honestly imagine that Dr. Woe wasn't recording every interaction he had with you, for when this day finally arrived and you did something unspeakable? Something you would need to blame on your pet mad scientist? Yes, he built the machines, and believe me, he's paying for what he did, but the blame isn't entirely his. You stole him from us. You crafted him in your— Oh, don't struggle, we both know it isn't going to do you any good after what I've done to you. I could have stripped away your powers years ago, but I was enjoying the challenge.

I thought it was a benefit to us both that we had someone of equal capability to set ourselves against.

I thought...

Well, I thought a lot of things. I was a fool, Captain. We both were. You to think you were untouchable, and me to think you were on the side of the angels.

Foolishness has consequences.

Dr. Woe told you about the leak. He told you he was concerned that some of his machines might have entered the open air. He told you—I have it on *film*, don't you deny it, you bastard—that if you allowed him to contact his old classmate, she might be able to nullify the systems he couldn't touch. He said my name. He said my *name*, on film, and I know you. I know you ran a background check and discovered that his old science fair buddy was your reviled Dr. Nefarious. I know you knew.

You had my secret identity, you knew the leak was near an elementary school, and you had access to the student records. It would have been so easy to check my last name against the class rolls, so easy to call me. Bury the hatchet for one afternoon, let me do my job when you failed to do yours, and save an entire school's-worth of children.

You could have saved them. *I* could have saved them, if you had only given me the chance.

I told you, stop struggling. It's not going to do you any good.

A superhero without his powers is only a man.

A mother without her child is still a motherfucking super genius with access to things you can't even imagine, and now that we've had this little chat, I'm going to let them take your arrogant, egotistical ass apart. Goodbye, Captain. We always knew one of us would kill the other one of these days.

You decided which one of us it was going to be on the day you allowed my baby girl to die.

ENTER, THE DRAGON

LEVERETT BUTTS & DACRE STOKER

I.

ELC Memorandum

Date: 08 April 2020, 0600 hrs
From: Chair, Van Harker Division
To: Home Office, London
Re: Request for Information

During recent monitoring of HTG's Romania activities, agents encountered three subjects for which we request any information available:

     Dr. Clark August Phillips, aka "Tennessee"
     Dr. Savannah Maxine Ford
     Mr. Joseph Armitage Manton

Our understanding is that all three persons hail from the States. Perhaps either Dana Fox or Thomas Karel Divisions can advise?

Illustration by **COLTON WORLEY** »

~Art

ELC Memorandum

Date: 08 April 2020, 0610 hrs
From: Home Office, London
To: Chair, Van Harker Division
Re: Re: Request for Information

Thomas Karel advises that two of the subjects, Phillips and Manton, were present for the Alaska Incident. Consequently, Dana Fox has kept them under loose observation. Both are associated with Miskatonic U: Phillips as a professor of history, Manton as his graduate teaching assistant. Both considered low-priority subjects, having been only incidentally involved in Alaska.

Dr. Ford, Phillips' lover, is a surgeon in Arkham, MA, noted for her skill in detaching conjoined twins and reattaching limbs, oddly common concerns in that area. Considered unworthy of investigation beyond her association with Phillips.

What is this about?

~Jon and Bram

ELC Memorandum

Date: 08 April 2020, 0616 hrs
From: Chair, Van Harker Division
To: Home Office, London
Re: Re: Re: Request for Information

See attached dossier ~A

II.

The Phillips Manton Ford Dossier:

08 April 2020 Newspaper Clipping from *Jurnalul Național* (translated from Romanian):

EXPLOSION BELOW PRINCELY PALACE

An explosion below Curtea Veche, the Princely Palace of Bucharest and former home of Vlad Tepes, stunned residents of Bucharest Tuesday night. The blast rocked the immediate area surrounding the palace and could be heard as far away as Ploiești.

Authorities found no damage to the palace and no visible injuries to the occupants. Seismologists have determined the explosion originated roughly 100 metres below the palace, though its source is unknown at present.

This is a developing story. We will update as it progresses.

*　　*　　*

CCTV footage from Secret HTG Lab in vicinity of (Below?) Princely Palace, 07 April 2020, 2035 hrs:

INT. OVERHEAD SHOT - LAB

Two surgical tables are positioned in the middle of the room. A body covered by a sheet lies on the right-hand table. The left-hand table is empty save for a sheet hanging mostly from the foot.

Several bodies clad in black suits litter the floor, some horribly mangled, the head of one body is twisted completely around.

The sound of alarms are heard as smoke wafts into the lab from a steel door. A MAN stands before a counter along the north wall, his back to the camera. He appears to be Caucasian, in early to mid-twenties, medium build with red hair. He gazes about the room, surveying the carnage and destruction. He looks at his hands, stretching his bloodstained fingers, then curling them into fists.

VOICE (AMERICAN ((NEW ENGLAND?)) ACCENT)
Will somebody tell me what in God's name is
going on?

VOICE (TRANSLATED FROM ROMANIAN)
Go to sleep.
And do not blaspheme.

The MAN turns to a wall-mounted television set
broadcasting a political rally from America, followed
by a news report detailing the death toll of the
pandemic. On the screen, men in hazmat suits load
bodies on a refrigerated truck. The image shifts to
riots in Syria.

The MAN looks down at a chrome tray leaning against
the wall. He picks it up and stares from the television
to his reflection.

MAN (TRANSLATED FROM ROMANIAN)
I can work with this.

The man blinks once and shakes his head.

MAN (NEW ENGLAND ACCENT)
Who the hell are you?

The MAN sets the tray down, noticing the alarms and
smoke, then leaves the room. His voices can be heard
as they dwindle in the hall.

MAN (NEW ENGLAND ACCENT)
Are you listening to me? My name is Joseph
Armitage Manton, and I want you out of my
head!

MAN (TRANSLATED FROM ROMANIAN)
Silence, fool. Do you not hear others
approaching?

* * *

Note from Van Harker:

The Hunyadi Tepes Group (HTG), as you know, is officially a pharmaceutical/weaponry/toy company, currently developing a coronavirus vaccine. However, the footage here seems to fit none of its "official" interests.

We attempted to access video footage from the CC cameras in the halls, but they were too obscured by smoke to show anything more than a shadowy figure of the same height and build of the man in the lab moving swiftly down the hall. At one point, he encounters two other forms, possibly HTG guards, and disarms them, though there is too much smoke to see how he does so. Also the audio is garbled due to the cameras' placement near the alarms.

A Miskatonic University student by the name of Joe Manton has a robust social media presence. We were able to positively identify the man and the American voice as the same individual through Manton's YouTube channel, more specifically his podcast, *Arkham Nights*. (Dave, you should check it out. Despite its paltry six subscribers, it's quite good and right up your alley.)

The second voice, appearing to come from the same person, remains a mystery. Is Manton suffering from Dissociative Identity Disorder?

* * *

Transcript of Text Messages retrieved from Dr. Phillips' phone records: Thread 1 (07 April 2020, 2100 hrs):

PHILLIPS: U K? Sitrep?

SUGARNIPS: Fire engines, cops, ambulances are everywhere. What do you expect when you set fire to an ancient palace in the middle of Bucharest? Tumbleweeds and crickets?

PHILLIPS: K

PHILLIPS: 2 B fair I only burned basement

PHILLIPS: palace fine. See? Rt there.

PHILLIPS: QT?

PHILLIPS: Savvy?

SUGARNIPS: We shouldn't have left him, Tennessee. He deserved to come home with us for a decent burial. We could have figured out a way to carry him out.

PHILLIPS: no choice, darlin. couldn't carry him through halls & down stairs wo drawing attn. Wed b dead 2.

SUGARNIPS: And what if he wasn't dead, Tennessee?

PHILLIPS: He was. said so urself.

SUGARNIPS: What if I was wrong? A lot was going on. You were out of your head. Farkus was screaming. Vlad was…whatever Vlad was. Dead again? Undeader? If we could do that to a centuries-old corpse, we could have done something for Joe.

PHILLIPS: How R U able 2 type so fast on UR phone?

PHILLIPS: hello?

SUGARNIPS: I found a back alley I think we can use. Ping my phone with that "Find My Phone" app thingy. I'm about three blocks down from you. Try to stay behind the buildings.

SUGARNIPS: Tennessee?

SUGARNIPS: TN?

SUGARNIPS: ??

SUGARNIPS: U K?

SUGARNIPS: Sitrep?

PHILLIPS: Hold tight, Savannah. I…

PHILLIPS: I just got a text from Joseph.

Thread 2 (07 April 2020, 2133 hrs):

SHORTY: Tennessee?

SHORTY: You they're?

PHILLIPS: Joe! OMG! U K? werru?

SHORTY: We're I'm outside the palace. I think its downtown. Tennessee, I don't know how eye god hear?

PHILLIPS: You forget how to text?

PHILLIPS: Or spell?

SHORTY: I'm dictating and I don't have much thyme before he comes beck. I need help.

PHILLIPS: Before who comes back?

SHORTY: I think its Vlad. I think we he killed somebody.

PHILLIPS: WTF

SHORTY: I'll explain later. Wear are you? Chit, he's combing.

PHILLIPS: Joe?

PHILLIPS: R U there?

SHORTY: Coup China voltage gee?

PHILLIPS: huh?

Note from Van Harker:

We had our language people look at this last thread. They believe Manton's ("Shorty") last message is Romanian: "*Cu cine vorbesti?*": "With whom do you speak?"

*   *   *

"See? Americans Cannot Handle Palinca,"
Blog Post by Cornelius Cojocaru of Bucharest,
08 April 2020, 0930 hrs (Translated from Romanian)

You know the stereotype that Americans are all hard-drinking cowboys that hold their liquor for days. They can drink an ox under the table and still be able to stride purposefully from the saloon and gun a man down without so much as a blink, then ride expertly into the sunset. Well, don't believe a word of it.

I just saw something that puts to lie all the stories.

I was just at the Athenee Palace Hilton having a drink in the English Bar there with a lovely young woman it would be ungentlemanly of me to name (okay, okay, it was Sanda) when the explosion happened.

We rushed outside to see what was up, and the first thing I saw was this red-headed man who must have gotten outside just before me. He was standing on the sidewalk, like right at the edge, staring blankly from side to side, not even looking at where the explosion had come from. I mean everybody else is staring up toward the palace, you know, and they're all like, "It came from there." But this guy is just staring everywhere but that way, and he has this look like he has no idea where in the galaxy he is, you know. Just like this thousand-yard stare. Like, you know, this guy HAS SEEN SOME STUFF, right?

Anyway, I'm thinking the man's shook, rattled by the earthquake or explosion or whatever it was, so I don't pay him any mind. I'm just trying to figure out what's going on, like if terrorists are attacking or maybe some Russians got mixed up and thought we were the Ukraine or something. But there's like nothing going on outside except for all of us standing outside staring toward the palace.

Then old boy starts talking, but like, to himself?

"What just happened?" he asks, but in English, so I figure him for an American tourist.

"I don't know," I tell him. "I think there was an explosion or something."

Now I know my English isn't great or anything, but he doesn't even act like I said anything, just keeps talking.

"Where the hell am I? What in God's name is going on here?"

Then, I am not making this up, you guys, he answers himself. And I don't mean like most of us do when we think out loud or anything. I mean the guy's voice just straight up changes, gets deeper and growly-like, and speaks in PERFECT ROMANIAN. Like textbook grammar, like how our grandmothers insist we speak at the dinner table. I guess now he was an exchange student or something.

"I have told you," he says, "not to take the Lord's name in vain. I will not tolerate blasphemy, or…What the hell is that? A demon?"

Then he's just staring at this police car speeding by with its sirens blaring. Looks like he's never seen a car before. I mean he sounded so alarmed I looked down to see if he had wet himself. (He hadn't.)

Next thing the guy replies in English again. "That's a car. A police car."

Then, you guys, he has an entire conversation in English and Grandma speech:

"And what kind of demon is a 'police car'?" (Grandma)

"It's not a demon. It's a vehicle, a machine to carry policemen around." (English)

"Policemen?"

"They're like guards. Watchmen."

"Where are they going?"

"I don't know, probably up to that palace back there to see what caused the explosion."

"Your friends did it."

Well, this got my attention. I never would have guessed that schizo-phrenic Americans were the new terrorists, but there it was. I pulled out my phone when I heard this and tried to take a picture of him. I figured the authorities would probably be looking for him at some point, so I thought maybe I could sell it to a newspaper. It came out blurry, though, and before I could take another one, he straight up stares at me, and I froze in place. Couldn't move a finger. His face was all tightened so much he looked like he was a thousand years old, and his eyes. Jesus, his eyes looked like they were made of pure ice and electricity.

He smiles this toothy grin, and then uses the Grandma voice:

"I am hungry. I must feed."

He takes a step toward me and I want to take off down the street waving my arms and screaming louder than the police sirens, but my feet just will absolutely not move. Then he blinks his eyes and I literally see his face change. Like his muscles relax, and he looks like just an American tourist again.

"Fine, fine. Let's go in and grab a burger or something. I could eat something."

His face changes again and he takes another step toward me.

"Yes, a burger would go down," then he smiles at me and winks, "nicely."

My legs felt wet and both hot and cold. I'm man enough to admit I absolutely wet myself.

Then I felt an arm on my shoulder, and Sanda was talking in my ear.

"Come on, Cornelius." She pulled me back into the lobby. "It is too crowded out here. Let us go back to my room."

As she pulled me through the door, one of the hotel maids, looked Middle Eastern or something, passed in front of me to leave, and the guy broke his stare at me to watch her as she turned left. He licked his lips and turned to follow.

"No," the American voice said. "Let's just get a sandwich."

"No," the Romanian voice now, "I need something more...filling." Then he moves behind the maid.

"No. Don't do this." When the American voice starts, he stumbles a little. Almost falls into the street.

"Sleep." The man stumbles back onto the sidewalk and is wobbly for a few seconds before he seems to find his footing and stalks off into the night.

Best I can figure is Americans can't handle their liquor as well as they want us to think.

TLDR: I saw a drunk schizophrenic American and got laid last night.

*　　*　　*

Excerpt from Raportul Poliției din București # MLS 05/04/20/5871
(translated from Romanian)

Reporting Officer: Agent de Poliție Elvira Hofer, Public Order Directorate

Date of Report: 07 April 2020, 2235 hrs

Date of Incident: 07 April 2020, approx. 2130 hrs

Location of Incident: Alley between Strada Georges Clemenceau 1 & 3

Description of Incident: At about 2200 hrs on 5 April 2020, agent responded to report of suspected vagrancy behind Athenee Palace Hilton. Agent met Luca Lazarescu, hotel manager, who informed that he received several reports from incoming nightshift staff of a vagrant female sleeping behind trash receptacles in alley by staff parking.

Agent investigated scene, discovered the body of young female lying on right side facing the wall behind trash bins, cradling a leather purse. Agent unsuccessfully attempted to awaken female, then rolled female over, observed deep ragged transverse neck injury. Clothing revealed vertical distribution of blood.

An investigation of victim's purse revealed a wallet with 1,036 lei, work permit visa, and passport listing victim as Hadiyah Salib, 25, of Istanbul.

Agent called for ambulance and CID inspector, then secured area.

Initial investigation of scene revealed no signs of a struggle: Bins and surrounding shrubbery undisturbed and victim's garment intact, save for a single strand of red hair on her left shoulder.

Autopsy pending, but victim's throat bitten, apparently by a human.

*   *   *

CCTV footage, Athenee Palace Hilton Rear Entrance Security Camera in Alley between Strada Georges Clemenceau 1 & 3, 07 April 2020, 2125 hrs (No audio)

A WOMAN, mid-twenties, Middle Eastern features, dressed in hotel maid uniform enters frame from right. She is followed by a MAN, Caucasian, early to mid-twenties, medium build with red hair.

The MAN speaks to the WOMAN. The WOMAN stops and slowly turns toward the MAN, staring blankly. He seems to be speaking calmly as he waves his hand slowly just below her line of sight.

The MAN nods and tilts his head to the left. The WOMAN nods slowly then tilts her head to the left. The MAN walks slowly to the WOMAN, places his hands in the small of her back and pulls her toward him. He leans to her neck and turns his back to the camera.

The WOMAN's eyes, now facing the camera, widen for an instant before sinking back to blank apathy as the man moves to kiss the front of her neck.

The MAN's movements grow frenzied. Blood dribbles over his left cheek. The WOMAN remains impassive.

The MAN leans his head back as the WOMAN rests limply in his arms. His mouth and chin are smeared in blood.

The WOMAN's neck gapes raggedly open, but no blood spills from the wound.

The MAN wipes his face down the WOMAN's blouse before lifting her and carrying her out of frame to the left.

*   *   *

"Schizophrenic Dude in Bucharest" Video Clip uploaded to YouTube, 08 April 2020, 0430 hrs, Uploaded by "TravelsWithChucky2020"

Video Description: Hey y'all. I'm still stuck here in Eastern Europe because of the stupid pandemic. I've seen literally every single one of Dracula's Castles Romania has. Seriously they are like Dollar Generals over here. I never thought I'd say this but damn if I don't miss Possum Snout. I just want to go home. To Possum Snout, Georgia, of all places.

Anyway, this was filmed last night, April 7, 2020, when I was visiting the Princely Palace in Bucharest (this one isn't technically a Dracula's Castle, but is one of Vlad the Impaler's, so close enough), and somebody straight up bombed it or something. I mean it didn't do any damage or anything, just a loud boom and the ground shook pretty bad. Lots of cops, firetrucks, and ambulances after that, but I don't think anyone was hurt. At least that they're saying.

So while I was filming the chaotic aftermath, this dude shows up, straight up talking to himself and answering back. But here's the kicker, y'all, I don't remember filming any of this. It was legit freaky, but take a look for yourself:

Video:

The camera pans across a street scene with people speaking in Romanian, all looking, pointing, or gesturing to the left of the frame. Emergency vehicles with sirens blaring speed left. A voice narrates from offscreen.

> TRAVELSWITHCHUCKY2020
>
> Folks are a little excited, I guess. Must not get a lot of terrorism in Eastern Europe.

Camera pans left following several emergency vehicles. A man, Caucasian, in early to mid-twenties, medium build with red hair, enters the frame staring downward and muttering to himself in New England-accented English and responding in Romanian-accented English. His words are indecipherable.

> TRAVELSWITHCHUCKY2020
>
> Who's this Norman Bates acting mother-fucker?

> RED-HAIRED MAN
> (NEW ENGLAND ACCENT)
>
> Will you shut up and listen to me for a damned minute?

The man, apparently unaware of the camera, stops on the street as onlookers weave around him to see the action toward the palace.

> RED-HAIRED MAN
> (ROMANIAN ACCENT)
>
> I will not tell you again…

> RED-HAIRED MAN
> (NEW ENGLAND ACCENT)
>
> Yeah, I get it. No blasphemy. Fine. But if we don't meet up with my friends soon, it won't matter a fetid whale's kidney how much I blaspheme. We'll be caught and put away. In a looney bin if we're lucky.
> We have to get out of here.

RED-HAIRED MAN
(ROMANIAN ACCENT)

I ruled this land for seven and a half years
and brought peace. I thwarted the Ottomans
in the name of Christianity. I am a warlord.
Your measly little, how do you say, police
force, cannot stand against me.
Be silent. I will…

RED-HAIRED MAN
(NEW ENGLAND ACCENT)

You will, what? Joust one of the squad cars?
Come on, man. You are out of your depth here.

RED-HAIRED MAN
(ROMANIAN ACCENT)

You dare question my manhood? My honor?

RED-HAIRED MAN
(NEW ENGLAND ACCENT)

Oh, give it a rest. You can't even work an
iPhone. The single simplest phone on the
market. You literally just talk to it and it
does what you want.
Face it, Vlad. You need me to help you.
You've been out of the picture for…a while,
and the world has moved on.

RED-HAIRED MAN
(ROMANIAN ACCENT)

Are people still people? Do they still lack
direction and require guidance? Do they still
follow their own petty desires while the
world burns around them?
No, the world works the same way as it always has, with or without your silly little

toys, you eye-fones and your "squad cars." I need no one.

RED-HAIRED MAN
(NEW ENGLAND ACCENT)

You need me to get you out of here. Romania is not exactly the strategic center of political power it was six hundred years ago. My friends can get us back home to America.

RED-HAIRED MAN
(ROMANIAN ACCENT)

How hard can it be to book passage on a ship? You do still have ships, do you not?

RED-HAIRED MAN
(NEW ENGLAND ACCENT)

We do. It'll take us about a month to sail. My friends can get us there in ten hours. We just need to get to a plane and fly there.

RED-HAIRED MAN
(ROMANIAN ACCENT)

(Laughs) Fly? You amuse me, Joseph. Fly!

RED-HAIRED MAN
(NEW ENGLAND ACCENT)

We can fly. The world has changed, man. Let me text my friends, and I promise I can help you.

RED-HAIRED MAN
(ROMANIAN ACCENT)

What guarantee do I have that you will not betray me?

RED-HAIRED MAN
(NEW ENGLAND ACCENT)

Mostly you have to trust me. You're traveling

around inside my body, and I would like to keep it in fairly decent condition until you're done with me. What choice do you have?

> RED-HAIRED MAN
> (ROMANIAN ACCENT)
>
> Very well. Text your friend, whatever that means.

RED-HAIRED MAN looks directly into the camera.

Is there something you require, peasant?

> TRAVELSWITHCHUCKY2020
>
> Who me? No, no. I'm just filming the excitement is all. I'm good.

> RED-HAIRED MAN
> (ROMANIAN ACCENT)
>
> Perhaps you can fulfill one of my… requirements.

> RED-HAIRED MAN
> (NEW ENGLAND ACCENT)
>
> If you kill this one, I won't help you. To hell with my body.

> RED-HAIRED MAN
> (ROMANIAN ACCENT)
>
> Very well.

(He looks again at the camera.)

You will leave this vicinity and forget about what you have seen. Do you understand?

> TRAVELSWITHCHUCKY2020
>
> (Monotone) I understand. I will leave the vicinity and forget everything.

```
The RED-HAIRED MAN walks out of the frame to the right.
The camera pans left and moves through the crowd.

                    RED-HAIRED MAN
                 (NEW ENGLAND ACCENT)
     Probably should have told him to erase the
     video from his phone.

                    RED-HAIRED MAN
                 (ROMANIAN ACCENT)
     I do not know what that means.

                    RED-HAIRED MAN
                 (NEW ENGLAND ACCENT)
     Yeah. That's why you need me, dude.
```

                    *   *   *

Transcript of Text Messages retrieved from Dr. Phillips' phone records:
Thread 3 (07 April 2020, 2207 hrs):

SHORTY: Tennessee? We I need ewer help.

PHILLIPS: Werru? Savvy & I R holed up N car park near airport.

SHORTY: I'm a boat free blocks north of the palace.

PHILLIPS: U dictating agin? Cant U type? Fkn Millennials... Take cab meet us here.
PHILLIPS: [Links to Klass Wagen car rental, just across from Henri Coandă International Airport]
PHILLIPS: We R bhnd building.

SHORTY: I due knot understand. Vat is kob? Vat is airport? Shut up Vlad. Aim handling this. Go back to sleep.

PHILLIPS: Shorty? Who's w U?

SHORTY: We're find. Cant do a cab though. No money.

PHILLIPS: Hitchhike? We did.

SHORTY: Not a good idea.

PHILLIPS: Y not?

SHORTY: Its complicated. Aisle explain wen I get their.

PHILLIPS: complicated here 2. No $ no passports. Figure out l8tr. Just get here.

SHORTY: Vat is passport? Vat is that little symbol? Hush Vlad. I'm taking care of it.

* * *

Note from Van Harker:

Without passports or money, they cannot board a commercial plane. Since intercepting this last text exchange, we have dispatched two Meddlers (Julian and George) to watch them while we complete our investigation and alert us if they make any further moves.

Phillips and Ford are, at present, maintaining their position behind the auto rental business.

Manton joined them approximately three hours ago. They have made no further moves, spending the time discussing what we can only assume are various plans of escape.

* * *

ELC Memorandum

Date: 08 April 2020, 0635 hrs
From: Home Office, London
To: Chair, Van Harker Division

Re: Re: Re: Re: Request for Information

We find the dossier quite alarming.

Apprehend them.

Keep us apprised.

~Jon and Bram

III.

ELC Meddler Julian's After-Action Report, 08 April 2020, 0930 hrs

Van Harker,

Agent George and I approached Phillips, Ford, and Manton at 0640 hrs as instructed. After claiming to work for the MI-6 and presenting our credentials, they offered no resistance and, in fact, seemed thankful for our intercession.

Throughout our exchange, Manton seemed nervous. His face changed from calm to confused or irritated constantly. He muttered incessantly to himself. When asked direct questions, he would generally answer evenly, though he'd often interrupt himself with a deep, heavily accented speech before switching back, once going so far as telling himself to "shut up, for the love of God and all that's holy." At these moments, both Phillips and Ford would interrupt, an obvious attempt to draw our attention away from Manton's episodes.

There was one time, however, when I felt it necessary to intervene.

Manton's "foreign" persona, when he appeared, seemed most fascinated with Agent George, directing most of his comments to her. Usually, Manton's "normal" persona interceded immediately, keeping the foreign persona from even completing a thought.

However, when Agent George asked Manton for identification, the foreign persona glared directly into Agent George's eyes.

"Why are you dressed as a man?" he asked. "What kind of a name is George for a woman?"

Agent George, who, as you know, does not take kindly to having her gender questioned (re: the incident last year between her and the American Meddler, Freddy), simply stood there, staring into Manton's eyes, but not adversatively, almost transfixed, saying nothing as he continued to berate her.

"Be who you are!" he continued, stepping closer to Agent George. "Take down your hair from that silly bun."

And, you may not believe this, but she did just that. The same woman who knocked Agent Freddy flat last year for telling her to smile took down her hair.

I stepped between the two of them at this point and placed my hand firmly upon Manton's chest and pushed him back, telling him to answer the original question. At this point, Manton blinked, muttered to himself, and was all serenity and smiles again.

We escorted the three to ELC's private terminal and boarded the plane. George is interrogating the three as I type this. We arrive in NYC at 1830 hrs.

~Julian

*   *   *

ELC Meddler George's Summary of Interrogation, 08 April 2020, 1030 hrs

The following summary is based on interviews conducted both jointly and separately with the following persons: Dr. Clark August Phillips, Dr. Savannah Maxine Ford, and Mr. Joseph Armitage Manton.

Interviews occurred on 08 April 2020, from 0800 hrs to 1000 hrs aboard the *ELC Albatross* as we transported the three subjects from Bucharest to NYC. Transcripts of the interviews will be forthcoming once Agent Julian and I return to the Home Office.

On Friday, April 3, Phillips and Manton were approached at a public speaking engagement in Arkham, MA, by a man claiming to be a Dr. Belshazzar Farkus, professor of archeology at Pázmány Péter Catholic University. Subsequent research reveals no such person on faculty or retired at any institution of learning throughout Europe.

This Dr. Farkus employed Ford and Phillips to travel to Naples in search of Vlad the Impaler's headless remains, supposedly buried in a secret crypt beneath a local monastery, straight out of *Indiana Jones*. They claim to have found the body but recall nothing after that.

Ford says she was accosted outside the airport after dropping off Phillips and Manton. Two cars flashing hazards and apparently involved in an accident blocked the car park exit. Upon attempting to render assistance, she felt an electric charge surge through her body and fell to the deck. Before she could cry out, someone pressed a chloroform cloth over her mouth and under her nose.

She next reports waking in a laboratory where the same Dr. Farkus showed her a monitor displaying Dr. Phillips in a cell. Farkus then indicated a surgical table with a headless body and a detached, desiccated head resting on its chest. He demanded she reattach the head by threatening the life of Dr. Phillips.

Once this was done, a second surgical table bearing Joseph Manton was brought in. Farkus again threatened Phillips if Ford did not perform a blood transfusion between the two "patients."

Then it got weird.

Throughout the procedure, Dr. Farkus began circling the room, sprinkling water and chanting in a foreign language. He then produced a hand drum, gave it to a bodyguard who began beating in time with the chanting. Dr. Ford describes Dr. Farkus fanning a chicken around the room before coming to rest at the head of the first body. Dr. Farkus then cut the chicken, allowing its blood to spill over the open mouth of the corpse. Blood streamed into the mouth, not a drop falling astray. Then, Dr. Ford swears, the body developed a pulse, and the mouth closed.

Shortly afterward, Dr. Phillips arrived, saw Manton's body as Dr. Ford discovered his lack of a pulse, and "went a little mad." He was removed to his cell where he picked the lock, opened the gas valves from lighting fixtures, and went back to retrieve Dr. Ford before using an improvised Molotov cocktail to ignite the fumes and cover their escape: the palace explosion.

Dr. Ford claims the first body was Vlad Tepes. I don't understand what HTG attempted through this procedure. One assumes it was connected to their attempts to create a vaccine for the pandemic, given the legendary healing traits of Tepes's blood, but one also assumes there was more to the plan given his legendary ability to control the minds of his followers. He was, after all, a primary basis for Stoker's *Dracula*.

Regarding Manton: I don't know what to make of him. Clearly, HTG has either successfully mounted Tepes's loa/spirit onto him or convinced him that such has been done.

How else to explain his switching between his own voice and that of a Romanian warlord? Or perhaps he believes he is possessed by the actual Dracula given that, while I type this, he screams in the cabin as we cross the Atlantic, demanding he be allowed to rest in his native soil lest the crossing of moving water destroy him.

We recommend that, possessed or not, we should hand the subjects over to Dana Fox and have them transport Manton to New Orleans and relieve him of his burden.

~ George

* * *

Email from Dr. Phillips to Dr. Frank Whitmer, History Chair, Miskatonic University, 09 April 2020, 1509 hrs

Hey Boss,

You won't believe the weekend I've had. Shorty and I got shanghaied into exhuming Vlad the Impaler's body in Naples, then we were kidnapped by HTG, who are actually a group of despots wanting to rule the world, and taken to Bucharest, where they had also kidnapped Savvy so she could sew Vlad's head back on and bring him back to life. In some weird plan to cure the rona and subjugate the world.

Can you believe it?

Of course you can. I wouldn't lie to you. Well, I would, but I'm not.

Anyway, they killed Shorty, but he got better, except he had Vlad in his head. Then we got rescued by two weirdos, Julius and Georgia, claiming to be MI-6, who took us back to the States and gave us to these other two weirdos, Chet and Nancy, who took us to New Orleans to fix Shorty.

Chet and Nancy said they were CIA, but turns out that they're all, get this, operatives for a super-secret Illuminati type group, ELC (the Electric Light Company). Apparently, they trace their origins back to the 1890s with Jonathan Harker, Abraham Van Helsing, Mina Murray, and Arthur Holmwood. Like the Crew of Light from Bram Stoker's novel, but they're apparently the fake names of real people who destroyed a real vampire back in the day, and now the ELC's a literal X-Files group keeping us all safe from actual monsters. Probably aliens, too, but Chet didn't say.

Yeah, Chet talks a good bit when he's drinking, and there's plenty of drinking in Nawlins. They took us to this vampire bar with an honest-to-god speakeasy in the back, and this Voodoo priestess or mambo or whatever removed Vlad from Shorty's head. And that's a whole nother story for another day.

Anyway, so that's taken care of. But to make a long story short, we're going to be out another few days. They want to keep Shorty under observation. Also I could sleep for a week, and the hotel they have us in is suh-wank, baby.

I'll bring you some pralines and Café du Monde, maybe even a beignet if you play your cards right.

-Tennessee

*   *   *

Email from Dr. Whitmer to Dr. Phillips, 09 April 2020, 1515 hrs

Dr. Phillips:

You do realize, I hope, that tenure does not mean we cannot fire you. It means we can fire you if we have cause.

The school went fully online this past Monday, as you surely know given that you clearly set your classes up for the switch and have been consistently active, and surprisingly lucid, on your discussion boards.

Sunday is Easter. After that, Spring Break begins. You have a week and a half, then, to recover from your bender. I expect you in my office and reasonably sober at 9:00 am, Monday, April 20, where we will discuss in depth this email and your gross negligence in including one of your students (the son of an influential citizen of Arkham and a university donor) in your debauchery.

Sincerely,
Dr. Franklin Marsh Whitmer, III
Chair, History
Miskatonic University

*   *   *

Transcript of Text Messages retrieved from Dr. Phillips' phone records: Thread 4 (07 April, 2020, 1530 hrs):

PHILLIPS: K, guys. I cleared w Frank. We have another week 2 get back.

SUGARNIPS: Apparently, someone pretending to be me requested PTO for my absence. I had them extend it.

PHILLIPS: Cool. More time N NOLA. Shorty U may wanna call UR dad & let him no we didn't kidnap U.

SHORTY: I whiz kidnapped.

PHILLIPS: but not by us. Srsly, call UR folks so theyll not get me fired. Also type on UR dam phone. Dictation sux.

SUGARNIPS: I'm sure they're worried about you, Joe. They've not heard from you in a week.

SHORTY: Okay.

PHILLIPS: Good man. Glad 2 have U back, btw

SHORTY: You think to baffle me, you—with your pale faces all in a row, like sheep in a butcher's. You shall be sorry yet, each one of you! You think you have left me without a place to rest; but I have more. My revenge is just begun! I spread it over centuries, and time is on my side.

PHILLIPS: Odd take, but C? Typing's not so bad. BTW y'all remind me 2 get some donuts 4 Frank.

SOMEONE TO BLAME

RAMSEY CAMPBELL

"**F**RANCIS," **FRANKIE'S MOTHER** said as if she had a pain she was growing tired of. "What's so terribly important now?"

He'd done nothing he shouldn't have. He'd muted his phone before following his parents into the old Swedish church. He wasn't going to feel judged by the picture overhead, where a stern robed figure on a lit-up throne was sending devils to drag people off. His mother glanced at the text he'd just sent Chaz, who was on a beach in Greece: going to see more old stuff. "I'm sorry if you've found our trip so dull," she said, though not as if she meant it much. "It's necessary for our work."

"I don't know how we'd liven up proceedings for you," his father said, taking a key off a nail on the wall by the pulpit, which was crawling with babies and angels. "Let's see if this can."

Frankie thought his parents were behaving worse than him. They hadn't just driven into the grounds of the manor house without an invitation, they'd come up to the church when nobody answered at the house. Maybe the owners were out, unless they didn't care for visitors, but shouldn't his parents have waited for permission? They seemed to think working at the museum meant they could go any old place they liked, and all his mother said was "Where does that take us?"

"I'm hoping to the mausoleum," his father told Frankie as well and led the way out of the church.

As they made for the building attached to it Frankie heard a lid creak. It was a tree in the wood below the hill they'd had to climb. The lake encircled by the pines stirred like a sheet concealing a restless sleeper, and the wind pointed treetops at the mausoleum. The piny scent the wind raised made Frankie imagine the mausoleum needed disinfecting, not least since the white paint on all eight sides was flaking off like diseased skin. His father poked the key into the door at the top of the slippery greenish steps, and Frankie's heart jerked, or the phone in his breast pocket did. Chaz had replied BRING SOME BACK TO SHOW, and Frankie was about to stow the phone when he saw a letter start to writhe. No, a small legless insect was squirming across the screen as if it had emerged from the I. When he tried to brush it off he found it was under the glass. He felt he'd let it in by consulting the phone, which he pocketed with dismayed haste. "We're admitted," his father said, and the door lumbered wide.

Sunlight slanting through thin windows gathered on a trinity of metal coffins in the middle of the domed stone room. A cruci- fied Christ lay on two of the lids, but the dimensionless full-length figure on the third had done without a cross. Fragments of a rusty padlock were strewn on the floor beneath the coffin, and another padlock drooped on its crumbled hasp while a last one remained locked. Frankie's parents made for marble monuments on opposite sides of the room, but only the coffin with the locks struck him as even slightly interesting. Scenes were engraved on its sides, and the image closest to the unopened padlock showed a man fleeing between trees with a hooded figure at his back, reaching a long stick or else a scrawny limb that lacked a hand out of its voluminous sleeve. Frankie would have liked to see more of the figure, and almost said so aloud. The other scenes were boring, and he looked at his phone instead. He couldn't see the insect, but would the phone work now? Perhaps it could be useful, proving he wasn't just a burden his parents had to bring with them. He activated the camera and framed the chase through the wood.

He didn't mean to use the flash. When it went off, the hooded figure appeared to start forward as if it had taken on substance, and Frankie heard movement close to him. It must have been his parents, because it came from more than one place. Surely only a shadow had shaken the padlock, but as he took hold to test it his father pulled him away. "We mustn't touch anything, Francis."

Frankie let go too late. His enforced lurch had snapped the rusty hasp. The lock clattered on the stone floor, rousing an echo that resembled shrill malicious laughter. "Now what have you done?" his mother complained.

"He made me."

"He has a name, if you don't mind."

Frankie could have fancied they were talking about the occupant of the coffin, since she'd prompted him to say "Dad's not a name."

"You know perfectly well what I mean, and you know we never use a flash in a church."

He was tempted to point out they weren't in one any longer, but said "I was only trying to help. I thought you could put the photo in the museum."

"Thanks for the intention, old fellow," his father said. "We've finished curating the show."

"Then why did we have to go all the places we went? Why did we come up here?"

"We can never learn too much about the past. Your mother saw the church and we had time to take a look."

"If you and your phone want to be useful you could see what you can find out about this place." When Frankie made to wake the phone by showing it his face, his mother said "Wait until we're in the car. I think we'd best leave before anyone does any more damage."

Frankie thought this should include his father. His mother locked the mausoleum and returned to the church to hang up the key. The acoustic made the clank of metal against stone sound louder than Frankie thought it should, and hard to locate. That was the case with the creak of a tree as they trotted downhill, urged faster by the slope. Once they were in the woods he heard no noises of that kind, even when wind ruffled the lake. The wide-brimmed hat he glimpsed somebody wearing among the trees must have been a slab of fungus sticking out at head height from a scaly trunk, next to a bush like a figure crouched to sprint and stretching out a leafless branch. Swarming shadows rendered all this indistinct, and when Frankie glanced back he couldn't even see where the shapes had been.

Though there was still no sign of life at the house, he felt they were being watched. While his father drove out of the grounds and up the wooded highway fast enough to suggest they were making an escape, Frankie consulted the map on his phone. He had to expand the image almost to the limit before the house appeared, tagged with a name. He thought he'd revived the insect, but the black mark that sped onto the sketch of a highway had to be a momentary flaw in the image—indeed, a pair of flaws. Fingering the name brought him a historical paragraph he began to read aloud. "Della who's that again?" his father said with a laugh.

"Let me see," Frankie's mother said and expelled a breath that blurred the screen. "It's duh la Gardie," she said, lifting the last syllable like a small startled cry or a bid to enliven the name.

Frankie had planned to make a related name he'd seen into a joke—Count Magnets or, since he supposed the seventeenth-century character had been somewhere in the mausoleum, Count Maggots—but it would be taken as just one more of his mistakes, and he shoved the phone into his pocket. "Don't sulk, Francis," his mother said, which ensured he did.

In half an hour they were at the airport. Once they reached the lounge, having returned the hired car, they had to wait several times as long. Why should Frankie be afraid this would let somebody come to find them? If anyone discovered the breakage in the mausoleum and could trace the number of the car, they might have time to search the airport before the family boarded the plane. Whenever Frankie glanced away from the departure monitor he felt compelled to look for people who might be hunting a miscreant. More than once he thought somebody new had come in, but could never locate them.

At last the monitor sent the family out of the lounge. Since their seats were at the front of the plane, they were among the first to board. Frankie had the window seat and saw their luggage being loaded. Had a strap come loose from the suitcase under his? The restless elongated item wasn't visible when a baggage handler slung Frankie's case into the hold. Frankie thought it might have fallen under the truck, but the tarmac was bare once the vehicle departed.

Eventually the plane did, no more swiftly than a hearse. The take-off transformed moisture on the window into unreadable messages in Morse before the plane rose above an elaborately rumpled quilt of cloud spread as wide as the sky. Frankie played games on his muted phone until he tired of killing monsters—their silence made them furtive, prone to appear with even less warning than usual—and then he dozed. His father's looming face wakened him, and Frankie turned to him, only to find himself turning to the window. He must have dreamed the face, and now he saw the shadow of the plane coasting across a white expanse. An irregularity in the cloudscape made it look as if a shape had dodged under the silhouette like an insect retreating beneath a stone. Frankie might have told his parents or at any rate spoken to them, but they were asleep.

As soon as the plane landed he switched on his phone. Photos Chaz had sent were waiting to be seen—girls of about their age in bikinis with practically empty cups. Frankie didn't need the frustration, and told himself he didn't need the beach. He would rather have stayed with Aunt Tanya while his parents were in Europe; she made more of him than they ever did. He replied with the photograph he'd taken in the mausoleum, prompting the response LIKE YOU SAID OLD STUFF. His father caught sight of the message and said "I should let it lie now" as if the boys were slighting someone who would know.

When the dogged circling of luggage on the carousel produced Frankie's case at last, it was partly unzipped. Had he seen a sleeve sprawling out of it while it waited to be loaded on the plane? His mother insisted on checking the contents, exposing Frankie's crumpled underwear to the public eye, until she was satisfied that nothing had been stolen. No wonder he felt watched, and people heard her say "Bed as soon as we're home. Important day tomorrow."

It would be for his parents—the grand reopening of their floor of the museum. In bed Frankie tried to follow up the information to which the map had led him, since the paragraph had said the count with the padlocked coffin had been into witchcraft. The paragraph had vanished, and there was nothing else about the man. Could his descendants have erased any information that had been online? Frankie was still searching when his mother came to turn his bedroom light off. "You try and get some sleep," she said as if something might prevent him, and a pair of sentences he'd happened upon lingered with him in the dark. "Mischief is the way evil toys with the world. Its presence can corrupt the very fabric of existence."

He seemed hardly to have slept when his mother wakened him. "We'll be off as soon as you're ready. We want to have a final check."

He suspected mostly she did, or perhaps only. If she was hiding nervousness, she was often like that on the first day of an exhibition. As soon as he and his father finished the breakfast she insisted they mustn't waste, she drove them to the museum through several warning lights and at least one red while his father visibly refrained from commenting. A banner for the exhibition was strung between a pair of massive columns outside the lofty doors of the museum. The title—*Discoveries and Disasters*—made Frankie feel as if one might lead to the other.

The guard at his oak desk in the marble lobby bade them all good morning and glanced behind them. The museum wasn't open to the public yet, and nobody had followed them in, but for a stupid moment Frankie thought the security arch was about to raise its alarm. The boxy metal lift that carried them to the top floor always felt intrusively modern, and today it seemed sluggish, as if it was bearing more weight than Frankie could see. "Let's get that oiled," his father said when the door slid open, emitting a squeal like the rusty hinges of a lid.

For several weeks the top floor would feature the century the Swedish mausoleum dated from. Frankie's parents went into their office while his father phoned an attendant to deal with the squeak. When would they decide Frankie was old enough to leave at home? He could only trail after them as they examined the exhibits. His mother turned back to give the King James Bible in its glass case a second scrutiny. "Did we leave it open there, Martin?"

"We must have. Nobody else would have touched it, would they?"

Frankie had deciphered just one phrase of the thick print—Woe vnto thee Chorazin—when his father said "No need to tag along with us, Francis. Have a wander on your own and see what comes to you."

Presumably this required Frankie to produce observations, and he went in search of something worthy of remark. The mezzotint of the Great Fire of London represented both a discovery—the invention of that printing method—and a disaster. Who were the two figures prancing in front of the blazing cathedral? When he stooped towards the display case he couldn't find them. They must have been reflected from the painting of Solomon's judgment, where a cloaked figure flourishing an outsize key lurked in the lower left-hand corner of the canvas. Before Frankie could examine the painting, the lift opened with an effortful squeal, and its occupant stretched forth a glistening tendril, the extended spout of an oil can. As the attendant set about oiling the door Frankie approached the canvas, only to find he couldn't locate any of the figures he thought he'd seen. "Stupid," he muttered, which failed to help.

The old books on display didn't inspire him. The *Pilgrim's Progress* featured somebody troubled by hobgoblins and evil spirits, while Milton declared "Incorporeal spirits to smallest forms reduc'd their shapes immense, and were at large." Both items discomposed his mother when she came to them, so that his father needed to say "That has to be how you left them, Carol." Frankie went to look at the disasters—a crowd of withered figures illustrating a Russian famine, a huddle of victims shrivelled by the eruption of Vesuvius, a deckful of colonists starving on the stranded *Mayflower*—but he could have done without the notion that each image hid at least one extra grisly shape he was unable to identify. He was glad when lunchtime brought his roaming to an end, and gladder that his parents didn't ask for comments on the exhibition.

They ate in the museum café, where Frankie's mother frowned at the ice cream his father let him have. "Finish that before we go upstairs," she said, because she disapproved of eating anywhere else in the museum. As soon as they returned to the top floor she began prowling around the display, and halted in front of the Bible. "That isn't the same page."

Woe vnto thee Chorazin. "It is, mum."

"I really think it must be, Carol."

"It was Mark before, and now it's Luke." When his father looked as unconvinced as Frankie felt she said "Someone seems to think it's amusing to confuse us. Come down to the desk."

Though the guard in the lobby had seen nothing, she insisted on watching the playback. The viewpoint flipped from camera to camera but showed only Frankie and his parents scurrying about like performers in a comedy speeded up for extra fun, a spectacle unnecessarily reminiscent of panic. Soon the monitor reverted to viewing the top floor as it was now. The changing angles put Frankie in mind of pages turning, and he thought he glimpsed an indistinct shape dodging between them. "Who's that?" he blurted.

"What are you talking about, Francis?" his mother complained.

He peered at the screen hard enough to make his eyes sting, and was nearly sure he saw intrusive movement vanish in the instant the monitor picked up a different vantage. "That," he said. "Them."

His mother shook her head as if her nerves had twitched it. "Don't just talk for the sake of talking."

"We can do without any mischief just now," his father said. "If you want to be useful you can keep an eye on our floor for us."

Frankie saw no need for the offer of redemption, and staying alone on the top floor didn't appeal to him. "Can't you?"

"We've already plenty to do," his mother said. "Do try to be a little more helpful."

Whatever the plenty consisted of, it kept his parents in their office, murmuring together between outbursts of clattering that reminded Frankie of the padlock in the mausoleum even though he knew he was hearing them type. He sat on the bench closest to the office, a position that gave him a view of the room all the way to the lift. He might have wished the door hadn't been oiled, since he couldn't tell whether it kept creeping open unless he glanced up from his phone, which uttered a celebratory note every time Chaz sent another picture of the beach girls until Frankie's mother called to him to silence it. Once Frankie thought the attendant had returned, but the fleeting sight of a tendril must have been a symptom of a need for sleep. As the afternoon wore on the symptoms multiplied, so that he couldn't concentrate on any game for making sure there were no intruders even quieter than you were meant to be in a museum. He was forcing himself not to look by the time the lift released a squeal suggestive of hinges loath to stay oiled. It came from a café trolley delivering the first instalment of the buffet for the private view, but Frankie's mother darted out of the office as though she'd heard a trespasser. "Don't forget you're to take the tickets," she told Frankie. "See everyone has been invited."

The return of the shrill trolley brought his father out. "You know better than that, Francis," he said. "Don't play hide and seek in here."

"I wasn't and I'm not."

His father swung around as if Frankie had tricked him. "I thought you were over there."

"That's the waiters from the café."

"Not them," his father said and surveyed the room before tramping back into the office.

The first guests emerged from the lift the last trolley vacated. Frankie's parents greeted every arrival while he collected invitations, and soon his hands were full. One woman said she'd forgotten her ticket, and Frankie tried to bar her until his mother let her in. How was he supposed to know who had been invited if they had nothing to show him? At least he needn't feel required to look out for intruders any more, though as the room grew noisily crowded he thought some of the guests weren't behaving too well. Quite a few planted plastic tumblers of wine or paper plates on the display cases, and when he was able to load a plate he made sure his mother saw he wouldn't rest it anywhere to prompt her disapproval, but she frowned at the muted noise he couldn't avoid making with a straw in his drink of orange juice. Didn't her job let her tell off any of the guests? Perhaps it wasn't rude to leave your hat on, however wide it was, but Frankie knew you weren't allowed to keep your hood up in the museum. The wrongdoer seemed to be wielding a flexible cane as well, which might be a concession disability gave you, though Frankie thought his mother would have feared it could cause damage. Had these people removed their headgear? When he glanced about for a proper look he couldn't find either of them.

The guests started to disperse once the drinks ran out, and while the last of them departed Frankie helped the café staff to clear away used plates and crumpled tumblers. "I think that went quite well," his mother said and joined his father in thanking him. Frankie felt relieved the day had ended like this, but they were nearly at the lift when his father halted, emitting a breath fierce enough for a horse. "What the devil's someone done?"

He was glaring at the glass case containing the Bible. Somebody had left the imprint of a hand on the glass, a mark that could have been composed of reddish earth or rust or dried blood, unless it was a stain left by some item from the buffet. Either the hand had described an odd gesture or it had fewer fingers than a hand should have. Frankie's father tried to rub away the imprint, but it wasn't on the outside of the case. "I'd like to know who played that trick," he declared. "I'd like to see them play another."

He gave Frankie's mother a look that must have been apologizing for his previous disbelief, and then his gaze strayed past her. There was movement at the far end of the supposedly deserted room, behind a display case crowded with seventeenth-century costumes modelled by headless mannequins dangling the stumps of their wrists. Had a mannequin lost its balance? Frankie wanted to believe that was the source of the restless shuffling as his father stalked across the room.

"Stay there," Frankie's mother told him and crossed the room as his father vanished behind the display case. There was silence for a moment, and then Frankie heard a cry so piercing that he thought it had to be his mother. It was accompanied and swiftly overwhelmed by another sound. Had an unnoticed guest lingered to finish their drink? The noise reminded Frankie of using the straw in his, though the substance involved sounded a good deal less liquid. He tried to think his father had cried out simply with surprise, and his mother was about to confront a noisy drinker as she dashed past the display case.

He saw her stagger backwards against the wall and jerk her hands towards her face. He thought she was shaking her head in disapproval until it began to move so fast that her fingers missed her eyes every time she tried to poke at them. All the same, she caught sight of Frankie as he forced himself to cross the room. "Go. Go. Go," she said as if this was the only word she had left, and her voice grew shriller until he obeyed. He'd stumbled into the lift and jabbed the ground-floor button before he thought to phone Aunt Tanya, the only person he could bring to mind who might help in any way. He was so desperate for an answer that at first he didn't wonder if the lift was ever going to move—if it had trapped him with the guilt he was afraid to feel while whatever it might attract came to find him.

GOD OF
THE RAZOR

JOE R. LANSDALE

RICHARDS ARRIVED AT the house about eight. The moon was full and it was a very bright night, in spite of occasional cloud cover; bright enough that he could get a good look at the place. It was just as the owner had described it. Run down. Old. And very ugly.

The style was sort of Gothic, sort of plantation, sort of cracker box. Like maybe the architect had been unable to decide on a game plan, or had been drunkenly in love with impossible angles.

Digging the key loaned him from his pocket, he hoped this would turn out worth the trip. More than once his search for antiques had turned into a wild goose chase. And this time, it was really a long shot. The owner, a sick old man named Klein, hadn't been inside the house in twenty years. A lot of things could happen to antiques in that time, even if the place was locked and boarded up. Theft. Insects. Rats. Leaks. Any one of those, or a combination of them, could turn the finest of furniture into rubble and sawdust in no time. But it was worth the gamble. On occasion, his luck had been phenomenal.

As a thick, dark cloud rolled across the moon, Richards, guided by his flashlight, mounted the rickety porch, squeaked the screen, and groaned the door open.

Inside, he flashed the light around. Dust and darkness seemed to crawl in there until the cloud passed and the lunar light fell through the boarded windows in a speckled and slatted design akin to camouflaged netting. In places, Richards could see that the wallpaper had fallen from the wall in big sheets that dangled halfway down to the floor like the drooping branches of weeping willows.

To his left was a wide, spiraling staircase, and following its ascent with his light, he could see there were places where the railing hung brokenly askew.

Directly across from this was a door. A narrow, recessed one. As there was nothing in the present room to command his attention, he decided to begin his investigation there. It was as good a place as any.

Using his flashlight to bat his way through a skin of cobwebs, he went over to the door and opened it. Cold air embraced him, brought with it a sour smell, like a freezer full of ruined meat. It was almost enough to turn Richards's stomach, and for a moment he started to close the door and forget it. But an image of wall-to-wall antiques clustered in the shadows came to mind, and he pushed forward, determined. If he were going to go through all the trouble to get the key and drive way out here in search of old furniture to buy, then he ought to make sure he had a good look, smell or no smell.

Using his flash, and helped by the moonlight, he could tell that he had discovered a basement. The steps leading down into it looked aged and precarious, and the floor appeared oddly glasslike in the beam of his light

So he could examine every nook and cranny of the basement, Richards decided to descend the stairs. He put one foot carefully on the first step, and slowly settled his weight on it. Nothing collapsed.

He went down three more steps, cautiously, and though they moaned and squeaked, they held.

When Richards reached the sixth step, for some reason he could not define, he felt oddly uncomfortable, had a chill. It was as if someone with ice-cold water in their kidneys had taken a piss down the back of his coat collar.

Now he could see that the floor was not glassy at all. In fact, the floor was not visible. The reason it had looked glassy from above was because it was flooded with water. From the overall size of the basement, Richards determined that the water was most likely six or seven feet deep. Maybe more.

There was movement at the edge of Richards's flashlight beam, and he followed it. A huge rat was swimming away from him, pushing something before it—an old partially deflated volleyball perhaps. He could not tell for sure. Nor could he decide if the rat was trying to mount the object or bite it.

And he didn't care. Two things that gave him the willies were rats and water, and here were both. To make it worse, the rats were the biggest he'd ever seen, and the water was the dirtiest imaginable. It looked to have a lot of oil and sludge mixed in with it, as well as being stagnant.

It grew darker, and Richards realized the moon had been hazed by a cloud again. He let that be his signal. There was nothing more to see here, so he turned and started up. Stopped. The very large shape of a man filled the doorway.

Richards jerked the light up, saw that the shadows had been playing tricks on him. The man was not as large as he'd first thought. And he wasn't wearing a hat. He had been certain before that he was, but he could see now that he was mistaken. The fellow was bareheaded, and his features, though youthful, were undistinguished; any character he might have had seemed to retreat into the flesh of his face or find sanctuary within the dark folds of his shaggy hair. As he lowered the light, Richards thought he saw the wink of braces on the young man's teeth.

"Basements aren't worth a damn in this part of the country," the young man said. "Must have been some Yankees come down here and built this. Someone who didn't know about the water table, the weather and all."

"I didn't know anyone else was here," Richards said. "Klein send you?"

"Don't know a Klein."

"He owns the place. Loaned me a key."

The young man was silent a moment. "Did you know the moon is behind a cloud? A cloud across the moon can change the entire face of the night. Change it the way some people change their clothes, their moods, their expressions."

Richards shifted uncomfortably.

"You know," the young man said, "I couldn't shave this morning."

"Beg pardon?"

"When I tried to put a blade in my razor, I saw that it had an eye on it, and it was blinking at me, very fast. Like this…oh, you can't see from down there, can you? Well, it was very fast. I dropped it and it slid along the sink, dove off on the floor, crawled up the side of the bathtub and got in the soap dish. It closed its eye then, but it started mewing like a kitten wanting milk. *Ooooowwwwaaa, ooooowwwaa*, was more the way it sounded really, but it reminded me of a kitten. I knew what it wanted, of course. What it always wants. What all the sharp things want.

"Knowing what it wanted made me sick and I threw up in the toilet. Vomited up a razor blade. It was so fat it might have been pregnant. Its eye was blinking at me as I flushed it. When it was gone the blade in the soap dish started to sing high and sillylike.

"The blade I vomited, I know how it got inside of me." The young man raised his fingers to his throat. "There was a little red mark right here this morning, and it was starting to scab over. One or two of them always find a way in. Sometimes it's nails that get in me. They used to come in through the soles of my feet while I slept, but I stopped that pretty good by wearing my shoes to bed."

In spite of the cool of the basement, Richards had started to sweat. He considered the possibility of rushing the guy or just trying to push past him, but dismissed it. The stairs might be too weak for sudden movement, and maybe the fruitcake might just have his say and go on his way.

"It really doesn't matter how hard I try to trick them," the young man continued, "they always win out in the end. Always."

"I think I'll come up now," Richards said, trying very hard to sound casual.

The young man flexed his legs. The stairs shook and squealed in protest. Richards nearly toppled backward into the water.

"Hey!" Richards yelled.

"Bad shape," the young man said. "Need a lot of work. Rebuilt entirely would be the ticket."

Richards regained both his balance and his composure. He couldn't decide if he was angry or scared, but he wasn't about to move. Going up he had rotten stairs and Mr. Looney Tunes. Behind him he had the rats and water. The proverbial rock and a hard place.

"Maybe it's going to cloud up and rain," the young man said. "What do you think? Will it rain tonight?"

"I don't know," Richards managed.

"Lot of dark clouds floating about. Maybe they're rain clouds. Did I tell you about the God of the Razor? I really meant to. He rules the sharp things. He's the god of those who live by the blade. He was my friend Donny's god. Did you know he was Jack the Ripper's god?"

The young man dipped his hand into his coat pocket, pulled it out quickly and whipped his arm across his body twice, very fast. Richards caught a glimpse of something long and metal in his hand. Even the cloud-veiled moonlight managed to give it a dull, silver spark.

Richards put the light on him again. The young man was holding the object in front of him, as if he wished it to be examined. It was an impossibly large straight razor.

"I got this from Donny," the young man said. "He got it in an old shop somewhere. Gladewater, I think. It comes from a barber kit, and the kit originally came from England. Says so in the case. You should see the handle on this baby. Ivory. With a lot of little designs and symbols carved into it. Donny looked the symbols up. They're geometric patterns used for calling up a demon. Know what else? Jack the Ripper was no surgeon. He was a barber. I know, because Donny got the razor and started having these visions where Jack the Ripper and the God of the Razor came to talk to him. They explained what the razor was for. Donny said the reason they could talk to him was because he tried to shave with the razor and cut himself. The blood on the blade, and those symbols on the handle, they opened the gate. Opened it so the God of the Razor could come and live inside Donny's head. The Ripper told him that the metal in the blade goes all the way back to a sacrificial altar the Druids used."

The young man stopped talking, dropped the blade to his side. He looked over his shoulder. "That cloud is very dark…slow moving. I sort of bet on rain." He turned back to Richards. "Did I ask you if you thought it would rain tonight?"

Richards found he couldn't say a word. It was as if his tongue had turned to cork in his mouth. The young man didn't seem to notice or care.

"After Donny had the visions, he just talked and talked about this house. We used to play here when we were kids. Had the boards on the back window rigged so they'd slide like a trap door. They're still that way... Donny used to say this house had angles that sharpened the dull edges of your mind. I know what he means now. It is comfortable, don't you think?"

Richards, who was anything but comfortable, said nothing. Just stood very still, sweating, fearing, listening, aiming the light.

"Donny said the angles were honed best during the full moon. I didn't know what he was talking about then. I didn't understand about the sacrifices. Maybe you know about them? Been all over the papers and on the TV. The Decapitator, they called him.

"It was Donny doing it, and from the way he started acting, talking about the God of the Razor, Jack the Ripper, this old house and its angles, I got suspicious. He got so he wouldn't even come around near or during a full moon, and when the moon started waning, he was different. Peaceful. I followed him a few times but didn't have any luck. He drove to the Safeway, left his car there, and walked. He was as quick and sneaky as a cat. He'd lose me right off. But then I got to figuring...him talking about this old house and all...and one full moon I came here and waited for him, and he showed up. You know what he was doing? He was bringing the heads here, tossing them down there in the water like those South American Indians used to toss bodies and stuff in sacrificial pools... It's the angles in the house, you see."

Richards had that sensation like ice-cold piss down his collar again, and suddenly he knew what that swimming rat had been pursuing and what it was trying to do.

"He threw all seven heads down there, I figure," the young man said. "I saw him toss one." He pointed with the razor. "He was standing about where you are now when he did it. When he turned and saw me, he ran up after me. I froze, couldn't move a muscle. Every step he took, closer he got to me, the stranger he looked...he slashed me with the razor, across the chest, real deep. I fell down and he stood over me, the razor cocked." The young man cocked the razor to show Richards. "I think I screamed. But he didn't cut me again. It was like the rest of him was warring with the razor in his hand. He stood up, and walking stiff as one of those wind-up toy soldiers, he went back down the stairs, stood about where you are now, looked up at me, and drew that razor straight across his throat so hard and deep he damn near cut his head off. He fell back in the water there, sunk like an anvil. The razor landed on the last step.

"Wasn't any use; I tried to get him out of there, but he was gone, like he'd never been. I couldn't see a ripple. But the razor was lying there and I could hear it. Hear it sucking up Donny's blood like a kid sucking the sweet out of a sucker. Pretty soon there wasn't a drop of blood on it. I picked it up...so shiny, so damned shiny. I came upstairs, passed out on the floor from the loss of blood.

"At first I thought I was dreaming, or maybe delirious, because I was lying at the end of this dark alley between these trash cans with my back against the wall. There were legs sticking out of the trash cans, like tossed mannequins. Only they weren't mannequins. There were razor blades and nails sticking out of the soles of the feet and blood was running down the ankles and legs, swirling so that they looked like giant peppermint sticks. Then I heard a noise like someone trying to dribble a medicine ball across a hardwood floor. *Plop, plop, plop.* And then I saw the God of the Razor.

"First there's nothing in front of me but stewing shadows, and the next instant he's there. Tall and black...not Negro...but black like obsidian rock. Had eyes like smashed windshield glass and teeth like polished stickpins. Was wearing a top hat with this shiny band made out of chrome razor blades. His coat and pants looked like they were made out of human flesh, and sticking out of the pockets of his coat were gnawed fingers, like after-dinner treats. And he had this big old turnip pocket watch dangling out of his pants pocket on a strand of gut. The watch swung between his legs as he walked. And that plopping sound, know what that was? His shoes. He had these tiny, tiny feet and they were fitted right into the mouths of these human heads. One of the heads was a woman's and it dragged long black hair behind it when the God walked.

"Kept telling myself to wake up. But I couldn't. The God pulled this chair out of nowhere—it was made out of leg bones and the seat looked like scraps of flesh and hunks of hair—and he sat down, crossed his legs and dangled one of those ragged-head shoes in my face. Next thing he does is whip this ventriloquist dummy out of the air, and it looked like Donny, and was dressed like Donny had been last time I'd seen him, down there on the stair. The God put the dummy on his knee and Donny opened his eyes and spoke. 'Hey, buddy boy,' he said. 'How goes it? What do you think of the razor's bite? You see, pal, if you don't die from it, it's like a vampire's bite. Get my drift? You got to keep passing it on. The sharp things will tell you when, and if you don't want to do it, they'll bother you until you do, or you slice yourself bad enough to come over here on the Darkside with me and Jack and the others. Well, got to go back now, join the gang. Be talking with you real soon, moving into your head.'

"Then he just sort of went limp on the God's knee, and the God took off his hat and he had this zipper running along the middle of his bald head. A goddamned zipper! He pulled it open. Smoke and fire and noises like screaming and car wrecks happening came out of there. He picked up the Donny dummy, which was real small now, and tossed him into the hole in his head way you'd toss a treat into a Great Dane's mouth. Then he zipped up again and put on his hat. Never said a word. But he leaned forward and held his turnip watch so I could see it. The watch hands were skeleton fingers, and there was a face in there, pressing its nose in little smudged circles against the glass, and though I couldn't hear it, the face had its mouth open and it was screaming, and *that face was mine.* Then the God and the alley and the legs in the trash cans were gone. And so was the cut on my chest. Healed completely. Not even a mark.

"I left out of there and didn't tell a soul. And Donny, just like he said, came to live in my head, and the razor started singing to me nights, probably a song sort of like those sirens sang for that Ulysses fellow. And come near and on the full moon, the blades act up, mew and get inside of me. Then I know what I need to do…I did it tonight. Maybe if it had rained I wouldn't have had to do it…but it was clear enough for me to be busy."

The young man stopped talking, turned, stepped inside the house, out of sight. Richards sighed, but his relief was short-lived. The young man returned and came down a couple of steps. In one hand, by the long blonde hair, he was holding a teenage girl's head. The other clutched the razor.

The cloud veil fell away from the moon, and it became quite bright.

The young man, with a flick of his wrist, tossed the head at Richards, striking him in the chest, causing him to drop the light. The head bounced between Richards's legs and into the water with a flat splash.

"Listen…" Richards started, but anything he might have said aged, died, and turned to dust in his mouth.

Fully outlined in the moonlight, the young man started down the steps, holding the razor before him like a battle flag.

Richards blinked. For a moment it looked as if the guy were wearing a… He was wearing a hat. A tall, black one with a shiny metal band. And he was much larger now, and between his lips was a shimmer of wet, silver teeth like thirty two polished stickpins.

Plop, plop came the sound of his feet on the steps, and in the lower and deeper shadows of the stairs, it looked as if the young man had not only grown in size and found a hat, but had darkened his face and stomped his feet into pumpkins... But one of the pumpkins streamed long, dark hair.

Plop, plop... Richards screamed and the sound of it rebounded against the basement walls like a superball.

Shattered starlight eyes beneath the hat. A Cheshire smile of shiny needles in a carbon face. A big dark hand holding the razor, whipping it back and forth like a lion's talon snatching at warm, soft prey.

Swish, swish, swish.

Richards's scream was dying in his throat, if not in the echoing basement, when the razor flashed for him. He avoided it by stepping briskly backward. His foot went underwater, but found a step there. Momentarily. The rotting wood gave way, twisted his ankle, sent him plunging into the cold, foul wetness.

Just before his eyes, like portholes on a sinking ship, were covered by the liquid darkness, he saw the God of the Razor—now manifest in all his horrid form—lift a splitting head shoe and step into the water after him.

Richards torqued his body, swam long, hard strokes, coasted bottom; his hand touched something cold and clammy down there and a piece of it came away in his fingers.

Flipping it from him with a fan of his hand, he fought his way to the surface and broke water as the blonde girl's head bobbed in front of him, two rat passengers aboard, gnawing viciously at the eye sockets.

Suddenly, the girl's head rose, perched on the crown of the tall hat of the God of the Razor, then it tumbled off, rats and all, into the greasy water.

Now there was the jet face of the God of the Razor and his mouth was open and the teeth blinked briefly before the lips drew tight, and the other hand, like an eggplant sprouting fingers, clutched Richards' coat collar and plucked him forward and Richards—the charnel breath of the God in his face, the sight of the lips slashing wide to once again reveal brilliant dental grill work—went limp as a pelt. And the God raised the razor to strike.

And the moon tumbled behind a thick, dark cloud.

White face, shaggy hair, no hat, a fading glint of silver teeth...the young man holding the razor, clutching Richards' coat collar.

The juice back in his heart, Richards knocked the man's hand free, and the guy went under. Came up thrashing. Went under again. And when he rose this time, the razor was frantically flaying the air.

"Can't swim," he bellowed, "can't—" Under he went, and this time he did not come up. But Richards felt something touch his foot from below. He kicked out savagely, dog paddling wildly all the while. Then the touch was gone and the sloshing water went immediately calm.

Richards swam toward the broken stairway, tried to ignore the blonde head that lurched by, now manned by a four-rat crew. He got hold of the loose, dangling stair rail and began to pull himself up. The old board screeched on its loosening nail, but held until Richards gained a hand on the door ledge, then it gave way with a groan and went to join the rest of the rotting lumber, the heads, the bodies, the faded stigmata of the God of the Razor.

Pulling himself up, Richards crawled into the room on his hands and knees, rolled over on his back...and something flashed between his legs... It was the razor. It was stuck to the bottom of his shoe... That had been the touch he had felt from below; the young guy still trying to cut him, or perhaps accidentally striking him during his desperate thrashings to regain the surface.

Sitting up, Richards took hold of the ivory handle and freed the blade. He got to his feet and stumbled toward the door. His ankle and foot hurt like hell where the step had given way beneath him, hurt him so badly he could hardly walk.

Then he felt the sticky, warm wetness oozing out of his foot to join the cold water in his shoe, and he knew that he had been cut by the razor.

But then he wasn't thinking anymore. He wasn't hurting anymore. The moon rolled out from behind a cloud like a colorless eye and he just stood there looking at his shadow on the lawn. The shadow of an impossibly large man wearing a top hat and balls on his feet, holding a monstrous razor in his hand.

CONTRIBUTOR BIOS

Linda D. Addison is an award-winning author of five collections, including *How To Recognize A Demon Has Become Your Friend*, recipient of the HWA Lifetime Achievement Award, HWA Mentor of the Year and SFPA Grand Master. Her site: LindaAddisonWriter.com.

Simon Bestwick is the author of seven novels and four full-length short story collections, and has been shortlisted for the British Fantasy Award four times. His latest book is the novella *Devils Of London*, published by Hersham Horror Books. Married to fellow author Cate Gardner, he lives on the Wirral.

Gary A. Braunbeck's work has received 7 Bram Stoker Awards, an International Horror Guild Award, and has been nominated for the World Fantasy Award. He is the creator of the acclaimed Cedar Hill series, which includes the novels *IN SILENT GRAVES*, *KEEPERS*, and the forthcoming *A CRACKED AND BROKEN PATH*. He lives in Columbus, Ohio, where no one has ever heard of him. He claims this doesn't bother him. We think he's a liar.

A community organizer and teacher, **Maurice Broaddus**'s work has appeared in magazines like Lightspeed Magazine, Beneath Ceaseless Skies, Asimov's, The Magazine of F&SF, and Uncanny Magazine, with some of his stories having been collected in *The Voices of Martyrs*. His books include the urban fantasy trilogy, *The Knights of Breton Court*, the steampunk works, *Buffalo Soldier* and *Pimp My Airship*, and the middle grade detective novels, *The Usual Suspects* and *Unfadeable*. His project, *Sorcerers*, is being adapted as a television show for AMC. As an editor, he's worked on *Dark Faith*, Fireside Magazine, and Apex Magazine. Learn more at MauriceBroaddus.com.

In addition to his collaborations with Dacre Stoker, **Leverett Butts** is the award-winning author of the *Guns of the Waste Land* series, retelling the King Arthur legends as an American Western. He is currently working on a new collaboration with Dacre as well as *Good Night, Sweet Prince*, a novel recasting Shakespeare's Hamlet as hard-boiled noir. He teaches American literature at the University of North Georgia and lives in Carrollton, Georgia, with his wife, son, their dog and an antisocial cat.

Ramsey Campbell has been given more awards than any other writer in the field, including the Grand Master Award of the World Horror Convention, the Lifetime Achievement Award of the Horror Writers Association, the Living Legend Award of the International Horror Guild and the World Fantasy Lifetime Achievement Award. His novels *The Nameless*, *Pact of the Fathers*, and *The Influence* have been filmed in Spain, where a television series based on *The Nameless* is in development. His website is at RamseyCampbell.com.

Sean Eads is a writer and librarian in Denver, CO. His short stories have appeared in various anthologies. His first novel, *The Survivors*, was a finalist for the Lambda Literary Award. His third novel, *Lord Byron's Prophecy*, was a finalist for the Shirley Jackson Award.

JG Faherty is the author of 8 novels, 11 novellas, and more than 75 short stories. His upcoming novel is *THE WAKENING*. He's been a finalist for the Bram Stoker Award and the ITW Thriller Award. He grew up a fan of the horror movies and books of the '50s, '60s, '70s, and '80s, and he's an actual descendant of Mary Shelley. Which explains a lot.

Geneve Flynn is a Bram Stoker® and Shirley Jackson award-winning freelance editor from Australia. Her horror short stories have been published in various markets, including Flame Tree Publishing, Things in the Well, and PseudoPod. She loves tales that unsettle, all things writerly, and B-grade action movies.

Carlie St. George is a Clarion West graduate whose fiction can be found in Nightmare, Strange Horizons, and *The Year's Best Dark Fantasy and Horror*, among many other anthologies and magazines. She writes silly, nerdy thoughts about movies and TV on her blog My Geek Blasphemy.

Owl Goingback is the author of novels, children's books, screenplays, short stories, and comics. He is a three-time Bram Stoker Award Winner (Lifetime Achievement, Novel, and First Novel). His books include *Crota, Darker Than Night, Evil Whispers, Breed, Shaman Moon, Coyote Rage, Tribal Screams, Eagle Feathers*, and *The Gift*.

Michael Knost is a Bram Stoker Award®-winner of horror and supernatural thrillers. He received the Horror Writers Association's Silver Hammer Award in 2015. His *Return of the Mothman* is currently being adapted into a movie. And he resides in West Virginia with his wife, daughter, and a zombie goldfish.

Champion Mojo Storyteller **Joe R. Lansdale** is the author of over fifty novels and numerous short stories, writing for comics, television, film, newspapers, and internet sites. His stories have won ten Bram Stoker Awards, a British Fantasy Award, an Edgar Award, and a Raymond

Chandler Lifetime Achievement Award. Several of his novels have been adapted for film and television, including the *Hap and Leonard* novel series and *Bubba Ho-Tep*.

Jonathan Maberry is a NY Times bestseller, 5-time Bram Stoker and 3-time Scribe Award winner. He writes novels, short stories, and comics in multiple genres. *V-Wars* (Netflix) was based on his books. He is the founder of the Writers Coffeehouse and is editor of Weird Tales Magazine.

Alessandro Manzetti (Rome, Italy) is a two-time Bram Stoker Award-winning author, editor, scriptwriter and essayist of horror fiction and dark poetry. His work has been published extensively (more than 40 books) in Italian and English, including novels, short and long fiction, poetry, essays, graphic novels and collections. Website: www.battiago.com.

Rena Mason is a three-time Bram Stoker Award® winning author of *The Evolutionist* and *The Devil's Throat*, as well as a 2014 Stage 32 / The Blood List Search for New Blood Quarter-Finalist. She writes horror and dark speculative fiction.

Richard Christian Matheson is a #1 bestselling author/screenwriter/producer the *New York Times* calls "a great horror writer." He's worked with Steven Spielberg, Tobe Hooper, Joe Dante, Dean Koontz, Roger Corman, Stephen King and others. His many films, series and mini-series include *Amazing Stories, Three O'Clock High, Sole Survivor, Big Driver, Masters of Horror* and *Battleground,* which won two Emmys. He has adapted Roger Zelazny, H.G. Wells, King, Koontz and George R. R. Martin. His 120 surreal stories are collected in *Scars And Other Distinguishing Marks, Zoopraxis, Dystopia* and many *Year's Best* volumes. His novels are *Created By* and *The Ritual of Illusion.* Matheson is a professional drummer and studied privately with Cream's Ginger Baker.

Seanan McGuire is a native Californian, which has resulted in her being exceedingly laid-back about venomous wildlife, and terrified of weather. When not writing urban fantasy (as herself) and science fiction thrillers (as Mira Grant), she likes to watch way too many horror movies, wander around in swamps, record albums of original music, and harass her cats. Seanan is the author of the October Daye, InCryptid, and Indexing series of urban fantasies; the Newsflesh series; the Parasitology trilogy; the Wayward Children books; and assorted other titles.

Lisa Morton is a screenwriter, author of non-fiction books, and award-winning prose writer whose work was described by the American Library Association's *Readers' Advisory Guide to Horror* as "consistently dark, unsettling, and frightening." She is a six-time winner of the Bram Stoker Award® and a world-class Halloween expert. Her most recent books are the anthology *Weird Women 2* (co-edited with Leslie S. Klinger) and the collection *Night Terrors & Other Tales*. Her weekly fiction podcast *Spine Tinglers* can be found at myparanormal.net. Lisa lives in the San Fernando Valley and online at LisaMorton.com.

Kim Newman is a critic, author and broadcaster. He is a contributing editor to Sight & Sound and Empire magazines. His books about film include *Nightmare Movies* and *Kim Newman's Video Dungeon*. His fiction includes the Anno Dracula series, *The Hound of the D'Urbervilles* and *An English Ghost Story*. He has written for television (Mark Kermode's *Secrets of Cinema*), radio (*Afternoon Theatre: Cry-Babies*), comics (*Witchfinder: The Mysteries of Unland*) and the theatre (*The Hallowe'en Sessions*), and directed a tiny film (*Missing Girl*). His latest novel is *Something More Than Night* (Titan Books). His website is at www. johnnyalucard.com. He is on Twitter as @AnnoDracula.

John Palisano is the author of *Dust of the Dead*, *Ghost Heart*, *Nerves*, and *Starlight Drive: Four Halloween Tales*. He won the Bram Stoker Award© in short fiction in 2016 for "Happy Joe's Rest Stop." More short stories have appeared in anthologies from Cemetery Dance, Weird Tales, Space & Time, PS Publishing, Vasterien, Independent Legions, DarkFuse, and Crystal Lake, as well as non-fiction pieces in Fangoria, among others. He is currently serving as the President of the Horror Writers Association and has been featured in the *Los Angeles Times* and *Vanity Fair*. Visit online at JohnPalisano.com.

Lindy Ryan is an award-winning editor and author. She is an Active member of the Horror Writers Association, serves on the IBPA Board of Directors, and was a 2020 Publishers Weekly Star Watch Honoree. She is represented by Gandolfo Helin & Fountain Literary Management.

Lucy A. Snyder is the author of 15 books and over 100 published short stories. Her most recent titles are the collection *Halloween Season* and the forthcoming apocalyptic horror novel *Sister, Maiden, Monster*. She lives in Ohio with a jungle of houseplants, a clowder of cats, and an insomnia of housemates.

Dacre Stoker is the great grand-nephew of Bram Stoker and the international best-selling co-author of *Dracula the Un-Dead* (Dutton, 2009) and *Dracul* (Putnam, 2018). A native of Montreal, Canada, Dacre taught Physical Education and Sciences for twenty-two years, in both Canada and the U.S.

David Surface is the author of *Terrible Things*, a collection of short stories published by Black Shuck Books. His stories have appeared in *Shadows & Tall Trees*, *Nightscript*, *Supernatural Tales*, *The Tenth Black Book of Horror*, *Twisted Book of Shadows*, and *Best New Horror #13*. Visit him at davidsurface.net

Gaby Triana is the bestselling author of 18 novels for adults and teens, including *Moon Child*, the Haunted Florida series, and *Paradise Island: A Sam and Colby Story*. She writes about witches, ghosts, haunted places, and abandoned locations, and has ghostwritten over 50 novels for bestselling authors. She lives in Miami with her family.

Joshua Viola is a 2021 Splatterpunk Award nominee, four-time Colorado Book Award finalist, and editor of the StokerCon™ 2021 Anthology (HWA). He is the co-author of the Denver Moon series (Hex Publishers) with Warren Hammond. Their graphic novel, *Metamorphosis*, was included on the 2018 Bram Stoker Award ™ Preliminary Ballot.

Tim Waggoner has published over fifty novels and seven collections of short stories. He's a three-time winner of the Bram Stoker Award and has been a multiple finalist for the Shirley Jackson Award and the Scribe Award. He teaches creative writing and composition at Sinclair College in Dayton, Ohio.

F. Paul Wilson is an award-winning, NY Times bestselling novelist whose work spans horror, adventure, medical thrillers, science fiction, young adult, and virtually everything between. His novels have been translated into twenty-four languages. He is best known as creator of the urban mercenary Repairman Jack. (http://www.repairmanjack.com)

Mercedes M. Yardley is a dark fantasist who wears poisonous flowers in her hair. She is the author of *Beautiful Sorrows*, *Apocalyptic Montessa and Nuclear Lulu: A Tale of Atomic Love*, *Pretty Little Dead Girls*, and *Little Dead Red*. You can find her at mercedesmyardley.com.

Kelsea Yu spent her childhood in Portland, Oregon, where she haunted her local library and crafted weird creatures out of clay. She's eternally enthusiastic about sharks and appreciates a good ghost story. Kelsea lives with her husband, children, and a pile of art supplies in Seattle.

ARTISTS

Colton Worley is an artist best known for his work with Dynamite Entertainment, where his credits include *The Shadow*, *The Spider*, *Kato*, and *Green Hornet*.

Shawn T. King is an award-winning graphic designer, specializing in print media (book design primarily). He is the graphic designer for Mechanical Muse (aetaltis.com), Wraithmarked Creative (wraith-marked.com), and numerous independent authors. He is the former Lead Designer of Ragnarok Publications, and Creative Director of the award-winning LEGENDS magazine (published in Mississippi and distributed throughout the country).

Mister Sam Shearon is a British dark-artist based in Los Angeles. Specialising in horror and science-fiction, his work often includes elements inspired by ancient cultures, the occult and the often contro-versial side to the study of the supernatural, the paranormal, cryptozo-ology and the unexplained. Mister Sam Shearon has created artwork for a variety of clients in both the rock and metal music scene and the world of the comic book and graphic novel. Including Rob Zombie, Slayer, Ministry, Filter, Iron Maiden, KISS, Clive Barker, Stan Lee, IDW publishing, Fangoria, Vesuvian Media, and many more.

Jeremiah Lambert, mechanical engineer by day, art freelancer by when-ever else... Doing gigs for Hasbro for both Transformers (movie ver-sions, Rescue Bots and the current Robots in Disguise) and Tonka Truck (Tonka Chuck) promotional art, as well as Masters of the Uni-verse exclusives for MVCreations, MadDuckPosters and Super 7 Toys. Jeremiah also has enjoyed internet viral exposure with his parody art.

Zac Atkinson is a comic creator, cartoonist, and designer. He resides somewhere in the corn of Illinois and has worked in the comic industry for over 20 years as a colorist. You can see his work in titles like *Bruce Lee*, *Shazam*, *Marvel Action Spider-Man*, *Justice Society*, *Young Justice*, *Transformers*, *Amory Wars*, *Farscape*...and many others. When he's not making comics for others, he's making comics for himself at zacsart.com.

EDITOR

James Aquilone is the editor of *Classic Monsters Unleashed* and the author of the *Dead Jack* horror-fantasy series. For more info, visit JamesAquilone.com.

SPECIAL THANKS TO OUR SLUSH READERS

A.K. Drees, Rex Hurst, A.E. Jackson, Nick Jensen, Paula Limbaugh, Grant Longstaff, John J. Questore, Jodi Shatz

ALSO AVAILABLE

Black Spot Books
Hold My Place by Cassondra Windwalker
Under Her Skin, a women-in-horror poetry showcase
edited by Lindy Ryan and Toni Miller
Throw Me to the Wolves by Lindy Ryan & Christopher Brooks

Crystal Lake Publishing
Followers by Christina Bergling
Of Men and Monsters by Tom Deady
Floaters by Garrett Boatman

James Aquilone
Dead Jack and the Pandemonium Device
Dead Jack and the Soul Catcher
Dead Jack and the Old Gods

CPSIA information can be obtained
at www.ICGtesting.com
Printed in the USA
LVHW030007030523
745889LV00017B/1296